TITLES IN
DR RIBERO'S AGENCY OF THE SUPERNATURAL

DR RIBERO'S AGENCY OF THE SUPERNATURAL:

THE CASE OF THE DEADLY DOPPELGÄNGER

Lucy Banks

Amberjack Publishing
New York | Idaho

Amberjack
PUBLISHING

Amberjack Publishing
1472 E. Iron Eagle Drive
Eagle, Idaho 83616
http://amberjackpublishing.com

Publisher's Cataloging-in-Publication data
Names: Banks, Lucy, author.
Title: Dr. Ribero's agency of the supernatural : the case of the deadly doppleganger / by Lucy Banks.
Series: Dr Ribero's Agency of the Supernatural
Description: New York, NY: Amberjack Publishing, 2018.
Identifiers: ISBN 978-1-944995-47-8 (pbk.) | 978-1-944995-48-5 (ebook) | LCCN 2017943709
Subjects: LCSH Ghosts--Fiction. | Lyme Regis (England)--Fiction. | Great Britain--History--To 1066--Fiction. | Mystery and detective stories. | Paranormal fiction. | Fantasy fiction. | BISAC FICTION / Fantasy / Paranormal. | FICTION / Mystery.
Classification: LCC PS3602 .A641 D63 2018 | DDC 813.6--dc23

Cover Design: Emma Graves

Printed in the United States of America

To Al, Danny, and Dylan—who are always my inspiration. And the ghosts in the cupboard under the stairs, of course.

CHAPTER 1: THE DEMISE OF DEIRDRE

Still partly pillowed in the comforting dregs of a dream, Deirdre Baxter opened her eyes. She looked up, and, to her surprise, found herself staring straight into a mirror, barely inches from her nose. She blinked in confusion. Her reflection blinked back, bemused, wrinkled around the edges and owlish with sleep.

This was strange enough. What was more peculiar was that the mirror hadn't been there before. Even odder, the mirror seemed to be hovering in the air and glistened with a moist, shimmering light.

Deirdre winced. Her reflection winced in response. She held out a wondering finger, thought better of it, then burrowed her hand under the duvet.

"Errol?" she hissed. The reassuring hump of her husband grumbled in response, rolling like a minor earthquake. "Errol dear, are you awake?"

No, but I am.

Deirdre jumped. The voice was soft as a whisper in her head, though, simultaneously, it clanged as discordantly as a broken bell. She sat up as fast as her arthritis would permit, heart racing. *Why didn't I hit my head on the mirror when I sat up?* she wondered, eyes scanning the darkness. *Where has it gone?*

I'm here.

"Jesus Christ, Errol, wake up!" Deirdre squawked and prodded her husband as hard as possible on the rump. He drew a deep breath. She waited for him to speak. Instead, he passed wind, a low, reverberating whine under the bed-covers, before exhaling in satisfaction. Deirdre pursed her lips, wishing, not for the first time, that she had divorced him back in the nineties when she'd had the chance.

"Whadd'ya want?" he murmured, still full of sleep.

"I can see myself!" she exclaimed, unable to tear her eyes away. "Right there, in front of me!"

The mirror now quivered at the base of the bed. Except it wasn't a mirror. She could see that now. There was no frame around the reflection, no shine of glass in the milky moonlight, no flatness to the figure that floated in front of her.

My god, it really is me, she realised, momentarily fascinated into silence. *There I am, standing, looking at myself, by the foot of my bed.*

"Go back to sleep, you daft woman," Errol mumbled, then tugged the duvet over his head. His snoring resumed with impressive ease. Deirdre fought the temptation to clobber him with the nearest heavy item.

The other-Deirdre smiled, raising a hand. Her fingers were laced with a grey-blue aura, as spectral as wisps of spider web in the air. Deirdre didn't quite know what to do, so she raised her own hand in response.

I'm sure this is a dream, she thought, forcing herself to calm down. *After all, things like this don't happen in real life, so it must be.* She studied her mirror image and felt somewhat depressed at the size of her bosom, which was so much larger and nearer to her waist than she'd realised. The other-Deirdre smiled again before obligingly folding her arms under her chest to hoist it a little higher.

That was kind of me, Deirdre thought with a dreamy rub of the eyes. *Almost like she can read my mind.*

Maybe I can, the ghost-twin whispered inside her head.

What am I thinking then? she thought back as she chuckled at the sight of her own self, grinning in the half-light. It was too absurd a dream to take seriously, so she may as well enjoy it while it lasted, until the morning light brought her back to consciousness.

You're wondering when you'll wake up.

I suppose so, Deirdre acknowledged, warming to the strange experience, now she knew she was safe. *Now what am I thinking?*

You're wondering when this will all be over.

She frowned. That hadn't been what she'd been thinking at all. In fact, she'd been wondering what to make for breakfast, and whether there were any eggs left in the fridge or not.

Do you want to know the answer?

What, whether there are any eggs? Deirdre thought back.

No. When you'll wake up.

Deirdre glanced at the alarm clock. 5:30 a.m. It'd be at least another two hours before she got out of bed, providing Errol didn't get up to go to the toilet. These days, you could guarantee he'd rise at least once before eight to urinate noisily in the bathroom next door. She thought these thoughts as clearly as she could, then waited for her other self's response. To her surprise, other-Deirdre began to snigger.

Why are you laughing at me? Deirdre thought. A vague tinge of panic crept over her, though she wasn't sure why. After all, it wasn't real. *Or is it?* she wondered, feeling the first cold fingers of doubt take a grip deep within her stomach.

The strange creature laughed harder, until it started to shake.

To Deirdre's alarm, the shaking didn't stop but became more urgent, until her ghost-twin was quivering uncontrollably in the shadows like a wet dog. It was a curious movement, rather unnatural, especially when it failed to stop. Deirdre stared.

"Are you alright?" she whispered aloud, quite forgetting she was dreaming.

The thing continued to convulse. In fact, the movements were speeding up, until it was vibrating as fiercely as a pneumatic drill. Deirdre felt the bed shudder with the force of it and blinked in astonishment. *This may well be a dream,* she thought, feeling sweat prickle her forehead, *but it feels very real.*

"Errol?" she whispered again and hastily patted his side of the bed. "Errol, can you wake me up? I'm having a bad dream."

It's no dream, Deirdre.

The voice rattling in her head didn't sound like her own voice anymore. It was colder, grainier, and reminded her of a rusted engine, hoarse and hostile. Her heart began to thump against her ribs.

Stop shaking like that! she thought, fear suddenly choking her. The sight was unbearable; the blur in front of her was out of control, like a boiler about to explode. *I don't like this anymore. Please, someone wake me up!*

NO.

"Errol, help me!" Deirdre tried to shake him awake, but her fingers were useless sticks, poking him as ineffectually as twigs in a breeze.

NO. NO HELP FOR YOU, DEIRDRE.

"What are you?" Deirdre gasped. Her words faded into the early morning darkness like dissolving mist. The thing—she could see quite clearly that it was a *thing* now, not a Deirdre at all—was *changing.* Changing horribly, shifting and warping into something unspeakable, something from her worst childhood nightmares. Her heart throbbed and pulsed, and she fumbled for her angina pills on her bedside table.

I WANTED TO GO HOME.

"What? I don't understand!" Deirdre clutched at the lid of the medicine bottle, but her hands were shaking so much, she dropped it on the floor.

SHE WAS MEANT TO TAKE ME BACK. I'LL HAVE TO FETCH YOU INSTEAD.

Deirdre started to cry. She felt as though cement had been poured down her throat, hardening around her heart and stopping her lungs. *God help me,* she thought without any real hope.

The thing changed. Its mouth stretched, wider than any human mouth reasonably should, and *something* crawled out. Something rank. Something vile and made of mist, which seeped into the air like a stain. Something so dreadful that her heart ceased to beat entirely. And Deirdre fell backwards, into complete darkness, a final sigh escaping her lips.

Errol rolled out of bed at eight. True to form, he stumbled to the bathroom, scooped up the toilet seat with a cough, and wondered for the thousandth time why men were expected to put the seat down for their wives but never the other way around. Sighing with satisfaction as his bladder emptied, he whistled a jaunty little tune from his favourite television programme. *That'll wake her up,* he thought with a nasty grin as he hauled his underpants back up. *She won't thank me for that.*

Task completed, Errol peered back into the bedroom. He could make out Deirdre's sizeable silhouette in the weak morning light, the twin turrets of her bosom looming large under the duvet. Her mouth hung open in a rather unflattering position, he noted with a touch of bitterness. *A bit like a dog panting.* He rolled his eyes before trudging down to the kitchen.

"No bloody eggs again," he muttered as he peered into the fridge, which let out its usual cheerful hum, vibrating against the aged washing machine. "Not even a scrap of bacon. What's a man supposed to have for his breakfast, eh?"

He made do with a slice of toast, and, spreading butter thickly over the surface, ate it in exactly four large mouthfuls. Errol prided himself on his manly eating habits. No silly nibbling for him. That was for women, children, and effeminate men, in his opinion. No, he liked to do what he called "man-bites." It reflected his nature.

No-nonsense Errol, that's what they call me, he thought with vague pride, even though no one had ever called him that in his life.

It was only after he'd made himself a cup of tea and settled on the chair by the window that he realised the house was particularly quiet. Deirdre usually woke up when he did. *Normally moaning about something,* he added silently with a vague curl of his lip. *Having a good whine about something or other that I've done, or forgotten to do, or should be doing now but am not.*

But this morning, the house was completely silent apart from the insistent throng of the fridge. Normally he hardly noticed the sound, but today, everything else was so quiet that it stood out, as pronounced as a distant bee-hive.

Without knowing why, Errol swallowed. His mouth had gone dry. Something felt *wrong.* He couldn't say what exactly, but there was a *wrongness* to the air. In fact, the whole house felt completely incorrect. It wasn't a comfortable sensation.

"You up yet, Deirdre?" he called. His voice hung briefly in the air, solid as wood, before disintegrating into the unnerving quiet.

He waited. Something made him hold his breath. He wasn't sure what. It was the oddest sensation, as though time itself had been paused, but had forgotten to pause him with it. Standing up, he felt that every movement was steeped in syrup. Everything was too slow, too unnatural. And again, that feeling of serious *wrongness* now filled the house, making his heart beat a little faster.

"Deirdre, it's nearly half eight, time to be up," he called again, then lumbered reluctantly back up the stairs. *Silly woman, she probably stayed up too late reading her sodding Mills & Boons,* he thought, forcing himself to be rational. *Probably had too much sherry last night too. She thinks I don't know that she steals into the kitchen to pour herself a sneaky glass every evening, but I do.*

The bedroom was still dark, the curtains drawn. Deirdre's mouth was still open. Too wide. Much too wide for his liking. It looked like a cave—dark, empty, fathomless. He edged nearer. A line of drool was hanging from her lower lip, glittering in the muted morning light.

"Deirdre?" he hissed. "Deirdre, you alright, love?"

He leaned over, then reared back just as quickly. Her eyes were open, staring upwards. They were the blank, empty eyes of a corpse. No doubt about it.

Errol stumbled backwards, tripping over his wife's discarded book. He looked at her face again, unable to believe what he was seeing.

The line of Deirdre's saliva, disturbed by his footfall, stretched out before falling to the floor. Errol slumped beside her, clutching his stomach, and looking at her hand hanging lifelessly over the edge of the bed.

She saw herself in the night. I'm sure that's what she said. She said she could see herself, right in front of her. With a single finger, he reached out and touched her, more gently than he ever would have bothered to had she been alive.

She's been fetched, he thought senselessly.

My wife has been fetched.

Chapter 2: The Lyme Regis Job

Kester eyed the wastepaper bin over the top of his glasses. It was the moment of truth, and he knew it. The pressure was on. Tightening his jaw, he flicked the scrunched-up paper ball, watching it spin into the air before landing a few centimetres away from the bin with a sombre plop.

"You really are rubbish at this, aren't you, mate?" Mike smirked, following the path of the ball as it rolled to a disconsolate finish by the base of Pamela's desk. "That's 24-0, to me." He leaned back, then folded his arms across his expansive, flannel-shirted chest with obvious satisfaction.

"I think it's the angle I'm sitting at," Kester muttered as he scooped up the ball. "Or there's a breeze coming in through the window that keeps knocking it off course. There's something not quite right, anyway."

"Nah, you're just not very good," Mike concluded with a pragmatic nod. "Call it a day?"

"Yes, call it a bloody day!" Serena snapped from behind her

computer. "Haven't you got work to do?" Her narrow eyes glittered, eyebrows knotted beneath her razor-sharp fringe. Most things in life irritated her to some degree, but idleness was particularly high on her list of loathing. Mike himself was also close to the top spot.

"Lunch break," Mike and Kester chimed automatically.

Serena looked at the wall clock then rolled her eyes. "It's half-past two."

"Late lunch."

"That's absolute crap, and you know it. You ate your sandwiches about an hour and a half ago."

Miss Wellbeloved, ruler-straight in her seat, nodded—a narrow totem of grey hair and steely eyes. "I quite agree," she added, looking disapprovingly at the pair of them. "You've been messing around for two hours now. Get on with your work please."

"It was his fault," Kester protested, pointing at Mike. "He set the challenge."

"Wasn't much of a challenge, to be honest," Mike replied. "Your performance was horrendous. I reckon a toddler could've done better."

Miss Wellbeloved clicked her tongue and waggled her biro in their direction. "It's worse than running a crèche in here," she complained. "Now Mike, get back to your desk, and both of you get on with something useful, rather than wasting your time. When Dr Ribero returns, he'll want to see everyone working."

Kester sighed, tugging his laptop open. He doubted that Ribero would be too cross at him, but he didn't want to risk it. Although he'd known his father for close to four months now, he still wasn't quite sure where the boundaries lay, both as a parental figure and as his boss.

He leant on his desk, which, unfortunately, happened to be a makeshift camping table. True to form, the legs instantly buckled under the weight. Kester screeched, grabbing at his laptop as it subsided rapidly into the folding middle. *When will they finally buy me a proper desk?* he wondered, not for the first time. It collapsed at least twice a day, and it was amazing his laptop hadn't completely broken yet, not to mention his feet, which had been crushed under the table-top on numerous occasions.

"Try not to break the office, Kester," Miss Wellbeloved ordered, not taking her eyes off her notepad.

"Doing my best," Kester wheezed as he strained to pop the table legs back into place.

Just as he'd managed to balance the laptop back on the table-top, the office door flew open and hit the wall behind it with a thud. Kester nearly fell against the table again with shock, but managed to stop himself by pinning his elbows firmly to his sides.

"Well, that was a waste of time, right?" Dr Ribero thundered into the room, threw his overcoat at the sofa and missed completely. Pamela followed, gliding across the floor like a cumulous cloud. She caught Miss Wellbeloved's eye and shook her head.

"Oh dear," Miss Wellbeloved muttered. Reaching over, she snatched up the coat and placed it neatly on the hooks on the back of the door. "Not a success then?"

Ribero spluttered. Raising an elegant finger, he clicked at the store-cupboard. "Coffee please," he demanded of no one in particular. "I need it."

"I'll do the honours, shall I?" Pamela offered, bustling off as though blown by the wind.

"Tea and two sugars, love!" Mike called after her.

Miss Wellbeloved guided Ribero to the threadbare sofa, then eased him gently down. "What happened?" she asked as she perched on the desk next to him. "I thought this job was an easy one?"

"Ah!" Ribero exclaimed, throwing his hands theatrically

upwards as though waging war against the ceiling itself. "This woman, she was a crazy old bat, yes?"

"If you say so."

"Yes, I do. A crazy bat. Turns out this spirit she kept seeing was her dressing gown."

Mike snorted, then hastily transformed it into a cough.

"How on earth can someone think their dressing gown is a spirit?" Miss Wellbeloved asked, frowning. "I mean, the two are rather different."

"Yes, one floats around a lot and makes a nuisance of itself, the other . . . er . . . doesn't?" Kester added. Serena tittered loudly.

"You would think so, yes?" Ribero continued as he swept his hands through his perfectly waxed hair. "But no, this silly woman, she thinks that her dressing gown is a ghost, so she goes to the effort of hiring a supernatural agency to get rid of it. What am I meant to do, eh?"

"Take the dressing gown to the charity shop?" Mike suggested. "That should solve the problem."

"I suppose that means she won't pay us?" Miss Wellbeloved said, rubbing her forehead.

Ribero nodded. "Another afternoon wasted. I am sick of these false call-outs. They are driving me mad."

Pamela trundled out, a tray full of steaming mugs wobbling precariously in her hands. "Thought you'd all like a brew," she said, presenting each mug like a trophy. "Nothing like a cup of tea or coffee to make you feel better."

Ribero grunted, then slurped morosely at his drink, glaring into space.

Kester frowned. He could see how irritated his father was. Pent-up frustration oozed out of his pores like oil, marring his smooth, suave demeanour. Despite his age, Dr Ribero still remained a handsome man and retained much of his youthful Argentinian charm. But at present, he was starting to show his age, his frown creating deep furrows in his forehead and around his eyes.

"That's the third time-waster this month, isn't it?" Kester commented as he sipped at his tea. He was disappointed to note that Pamela had only put one or two sugars in it, despite the fact that he himself had asked everyone to help him cut back a bit. *Three or four sugars are so much more satisfying,* he thought with a tinge of gloom. So far, his efforts to diet had failed to reduce his gut by any noticeable margin, though at times, his trousers did feel a little looser. *Probably just hopeless optimism,* he thought with a sigh.

"Yes!" Ribero agreed. "You are right, three time-wasters! And here we are, an award-winning agency, dealing with this silliness! It is not right, no?"

"We were only nominated for the award, we didn't actually win," Miss Wellbeloved corrected. "However," she added hastily as she caught his stormy expression, "you're absolutely right. Being nominated for a GhostCon award is no small thing, and we shouldn't be expected to deal with mad women who think that their nightwear is supernatural."

"Right," Ribero concluded with a mutinous nod. He looked around the office and eyed each of them in turn. "And what have you been doing while we have been working hard, eh?"

"I've been working on our bid for the Dorchester job," Serena said, clambering out of her seat. "Quite frankly, I don't see how the government could resist. It's open-bid, and I saw what Larry Higgins was charging. Extortionate as ever. Nearly as much as Infinite Enterprises, in fact."

"Bloody Larry Higgins," Ribero muttered darkly. "I do not want to hear about the Higgins. You submit that bid and make sure we get the job, okay?"

Serena nodded. "Consider it done," she purred, crossing one leather-clad leg over the other as she folded herself back into the chair.

"So, what have the rest of you been doing, eh?" Ribero enquired as he drained the dregs of his coffee with a loud smack of the lips. "Working hard? Winning new projects?"

Miss Wellbeloved looked over at Mike and Kester, who both squirmed under her iron gaze.

"Just doing a bit of research," Kester squeaked, pointing at his laptop as though its mere presence would verify his claim.

"No, you haven't!" Serena squealed. "Unless 'research' constitutes seeing how many times you can get a scrunched-up bit of paper into the bin."

"That was only for a few minutes!" Kester snapped.

"If by 'a few minutes' you mean twenty-seven minutes, then yes, I suppose you're right."

"My goodness, you were actually timing us?" Kester stared at her in disbelief. Serena made no reply, only nodded again with infuriating self-satisfaction. *She really is a rotten git at times,* he thought.

"Hmm, that does not sound like research to me," Dr Ribero commented, glancing at his son. "It sounds like you were doing the pillock thing, yes?"

Kester paused, then hung his head in defeat. "Yes, I was doing the pillock thing," he agreed before adding, "but Mike was too!"

"Oh, cheers mate!"

"Too much pillocking around and not enough work," Ribero muttered, then rose to a standing position. Placing his hands on his hips, he awarded both of the young men with the full force of his thunderous South American glare. Kester and Mike quailed, shifting in their seats.

"Well, I'm sure another job will come up soon," Miss Wellbeloved said. She leaned over and patted Ribero on the arm. "There's no point everyone getting cross, is there?"

"Actually, here's a new job that sounds quite interesting," Serena announced, popping her head over the monitor. "And it's quite local—over in Lyme Regis."

"Oh, I do like Lyme Regis," Pamela chimed as she waved her mug in the air. "Lovely antiques centre. I always find a good bargain there."

"When did the job come in?" Mike asked, leaning over Serena and peering at the screen.

"Only an hour ago, by the looks of it," she replied. "It's on the national list too, so it's a good one."

"Good, I am done with the regional list for now," Ribero said, giving his thigh a resounding slap to emphasise the point. "Too many ladies with dressing gowns, not enough real work. What is this job, Serena? Read the brief, please."

Serena cleared her throat, evidently pleased with the attention. They gathered around her like pigs at a trough, all eyes fixed on the screen.

"It's close to Marine Parade," she began. "That's right next to the beach, isn't it?"

"Oh wonderful, that's close to the antiques centre," Pamela said, clapping her hands. "Very convenient."

"Yes, yes, enough with the antiques!" Ribero snapped. "What is the case?"

Serena narrowed her eyes. "Sounds rather vague," she said. "Woman dead, husband claims that she saw herself before she died. Don't know what that's all about."

"Saw herself?" Miss Wellbeloved echoed. "What does that mean?"

"That's all it says. The husband was woken in the night, heard his wife saying she could see herself, then in the morning, he found her dead. Apparently, it's the fourth time this has happened in the town—all four cases were within the last six months."

"What, did she spot herself in the mirror or something?" Mike said, giving his beard a thoughtful scratch.

"I think if she'd merely seen herself in the mirror it wouldn't be regarded as a supernatural case," Miss Wellbeloved retorted. "It sounds like some sort of doppelgänger spirit to me."

"I am not so sure of that," Ribero replied. "Doppelgängers don't kill people."

Miss Wellbeloved nodded. "That's true. They're normally passive spirits."

"Hang on," Kester interrupted, putting his empty mug down. "Can someone please tell me what a doppelgänger is?"

Miss Wellbeloved sighed. "Have you read the spirit encyclopaedia we gave you?" she asked.

"Yes," Kester said defensively. "I'm a complete expert on poltergeists, banshees, nixies, and Grey Ladies now. I've just haven't read the doppelgänger bit yet. I've heard the word before, but what is it?"

"It is a German word. Your mother did not mention it, no?" Ribero asked.

"No," Kester said. "Just because mum was German, doesn't mean she told me about spirits that happened to have German names, funnily enough."

"Oh, for goodness' sake!" Serena interrupted and slapped the desk hard. "Look, doppelgänger translates into two German words. 'Doppel' means double. 'Gänger' means goer or walker. So it's a double-walker. A double of yourself. Get it?"

"Like a spirit twin?"

"Yes, that is right!" Ribero twinkled. He pounded Kester on the back and knocked his glasses askew. "A spirit twin. Just so."

Kester prodded his glasses up his nose before gazing at the screen. "So, there's some evil twin spirit lurking around Lyme Regis, causing people to snuff it?"

"Sounds like it," Mike concluded. "Only thing is, have we got the capacity to cope with a killer spirit? That's a bit above our level, isn't it?"

Dr Ribero swung his head around and fixed Mike with a tiger-like glare. "I do not see why not," he barked. "We handled the Bloody Mary spirit, didn't we? The case that we won an award for?"

"Nominated, not won," Miss Wellbeloved corrected.

"I'd hardly say we handled it," Mike retorted, massaging his shoulders. "Serena ended up in hospital and the rest of us were thrown around the room like beach-balls. I've still got problems with my neck after that."

Kester shuddered. He remembered the occasion well. The Bloody Mary had been his first real case: a vicious, ancient creature hidden in a Victorian portrait of a green-dressed lady, painted by a local artist named Robert Ransome. It had been a hair-raising experience, and he'd only just managed to get her through the spirit door in time. Rather more alarmingly, it was the first and only time that he'd managed to successfully use his talent as a door-opener to the spirit realm—and he was starting to think that he'd lost the ability to do it.

"Let's not forget Mike nearly burnt the house down," Serena added.

"Not this again," Mike groaned. "Seriously woman, you love the fact that I accidentally singed their wallpaper a bit, don't you?"

"You didn't just singe the wallpaper, their sofa ended up a pile of ashes after you'd finished with it. Not to mention their expensive Persian rug."

"Well, I had to get rid of the portrait somehow, didn't I, smart-arse? While you were unconscious, some of us had work to do."

"That's quite enough," Miss Wellbeloved interrupted. She turned to Ribero, pursing her thin lips together so tightly that they formed a singular line. "Do you really think we can cope with a murderous spirit?" she asked. "Obviously, we haven't read the full file yet, but the brief suggests this is a complex case."

"Ah, we will be fine," Ribero breezed, grasping her by the shoulders. He smiled. "We will bid on it, bid nice and low, and hopefully we will win it, yes, Jennifer?"

Miss Wellbeloved frowned. "If you say so," she said with a watery smile of her own. "We should think strategically, though. I don't want us getting into hot water again, we must keep building our reputation. And don't bid too low," she added hastily. "We need the money."

"You can guarantee whatever we bid, Larry Higgins will bid far higher," Mike said.

"Yes, but he's still getting a lot of work," Miss Wellbeloved said. "They've invested in an additional office; they're doing very well indeed."

Ribero growled like a rabid dog. "Do not mention the Higgins in here!" he said, jabbing a finger in the air. "I am about to go for my afternoon siesta, and I do not want to dream of Higgins." He turned, spinning on a polished heel, before looking over his shoulder at them all. "And when I wake up, I want to hear that you all have been working hard. None of this throwing the paper into the bin silliness, okay?"

"He's a bit late for his nap today, isn't he?" Mike muttered as the door to Ribero's private office clicked shut.

Miss Wellbeloved gave a wry smile, then ushered them all back to their desks. "He needs his sleep," she said. "He's very tired at the moment. Serena, Pamela, can you prepare a bid for that doppelgänger job?"

"Are you sure it's a good idea?" Pamela asked. "Much as I love Lyme Regis, I'm not so happy about trying to control a murdering spirit. It's a bit out of my comfort zone."

Miss Wellbeloved sighed, then shrugged. "It's what we've been told to do," she said. "And Dr Ribero is right. We need the money. The more jobs the other supernatural agencies keep winning, the less we win. We need more regular work." Walking to her desk, she paused and gave Kester a significant nod. "Besides," she added, "we've got our very own spirit door-opener here. And that's a big thing."

Kester slunk behind his camping table, trying to hide his concern. He knew that the others had high expectations of him. Since he'd managed to force the Bloody Mary back into the spirit world, the others looked upon his ability as the key to the agency's survival.

The dreadful thing is, he thought as he switched on his laptop to start researching doppelgängers, *I don't have any control over it. I've only seen the spirit door a handful of times, and I've only used it to get rid of a spirit once. I'm not even sure I can do it anymore.*

Ignoring the niggling worry, he buried himself in his research. If there was one thing guaranteed to soothe his nettled nerves, it was discovering facts. Kester loved nothing more than to root around in old texts or snoop around online to discover little-known websites.

Browsing through a few sites, he swiftly found plenty of information on doppelgängers. Most of it was contradictory, as was often the way with the supernatural. Some sites seemed to suggest that the spirits were completely harmless. Others stated that they were harbingers of bad luck. They had a rich, fascinating history dating back to ancient Egyptian times, when they'd been referred to as *ka,* or spirit-doubles.

In fact, Kester became so absorbed in his reading that he hardly noticed his father emerging from the office an hour and a half later, his traditional post-siesta cigarette simmering between his fingers.

"Have you written up a bid for that job?" he barked at Serena, forgoing any niceties.

"Certainly have," Serena replied efficiently. She swung around on her chair and flexed her stilettoes. "Pamela and I got it sent over half an hour ago. Hopefully they'll review all offers fairly quickly; it sounds like an urgent job."

"Good," Ribero said with satisfaction. He smoothed down his moustache, which had puffed up into two alarming bushy brushes during his nap, then glanced at the clock. "We may as well close early today. Nothing else to do but wait, right?"

"Excellent! Time for a pint!" Mike chimed, rubbing his hands together. "Who's joining me?"

"Are you buying?" Pamela said playfully as she squeezed herself out of her chair.

"Certainly not."

"Oh, go on then. Where are you headed? The Fat Pig?" She eased herself into her brightly coloured coat, which was vaguely reminiscent of a garish circus tent.

"Count me out, I've got work to carry on with this evening," Serena said primly.

"Not a problem, you weren't counted in anyway," Mike replied.

"You might find you do better in your career if you worked more and drank less."

Mike scoffed loudly, then folded his arms across his chest—a pose that made him look exactly like a Canadian lumberjack. "I'm writing a book on the best draught ales in the southwest. This is research."

"Getting so paralytic that you fall off a bar stool is not research, Mike."

Kester swung his satchel over his shoulder, nearly knocking over his precarious camping table in the process. His father sidled over to him, smoothly as a cheetah prowling the savannah.

"We should get you a new desk, yes?"

Kester gave the camping table a tentative prod. It gave a weak shudder in response. "That would be rather useful," he replied with a grin.

"I will walk back with you today," Ribero continued. He reached over and plucked a piece of fluff off Kester's collar. "We can chat, okay?"

"Er . . . yes, of course," Kester replied, wondering what his father wanted. Normally, Ribero avoided his house like the plague. Kester had moved into rented accommodation ten weeks ago, and now shared a home with two other people—a slightly mad woman with bright red hair called Daisy and a man with a penchant for tie-dyed shirts who referred to himself as "Pineapple". Kester didn't blame Ribero for not wanting to get on speaking terms with either of them. He wasn't overly fond of talking with them himself, to be honest.

"I'll walk with you to the bus stop at the end of your road. I will not come in, though. I don't like the cups of tea that you make. They taste of soap."

"That's because Daisy always forgets to rinse the mugs properly," Kester said apologetically as he trotted after his father. "I wouldn't mind so much, but she also likes using that organic eucalyptus washing-up liquid, which tastes particularly vile."

Ribero snorted loudly to demonstrate his contempt for anyone who would choose to use organic eucalyptus washing-up liquid, then ushered Kester down the stairs and out into the brisk autumn air.

"So, I want to talk to you about something serious," Ribero began without any preamble.

"Gosh." Kester suddenly felt rather anxious. *What have I done this time?* he wondered irrationally. *Did I accidentally mess up on a job without even realising it? It wouldn't be the first time.*

"Hey, don't look so concerned," his father said and gave him a slap on the back. "It's nothing for you to worry about. I want to talk with you about the agency, nothing else."

"Oh, okay." Kester neatly side-stepped an enormous puddle. "What in particular?"

Ribero looked at him severely, then up at the sky. Dishwater-coloured clouds slid uneasily over their heads, hurried along by the wind. It was a grey, sombre day, and it was already getting dark.

"We are in trouble," he said finally. "But you knew that already, right?"

"I know the agency is struggling financially," Kester

acknowledged. He followed his father as he turned down the narrow alleyway that led out on to the high street. "But we'll get through it, right? I mean, you've always managed in the past."

Dr Ribero smiled grimly. "Yes, we have scraped by, that is true. But it is tiring to keep scraping, right?"

Kester nodded. He could see how the lack of work was affecting the rest of the team. After the success of the Bloody Mary case, morale had been high, but in recent weeks, the mood had steadily slipped, leaving them in a state of disappointment and worry.

"However," Ribero continued, "the other agencies, they are offering things that we cannot. Infinite Enterprises have all the sophisticated equipment, right?" He spat out the word *sophisticated*, making it sound like the most despicable thing equipment could possibly be.

"Yes, I know," Kester said. "And Larry Higgins has got another office opening up."

"Ah, do not mention the Higgins!" Ribero exclaimed, pressing his hands theatrically to his ears. A few seconds later, his shoulders dropped. "Of course, you are right," he admitted. "Extra offices. All this money, all these companies doing very well. But not us."

"Why not us?" Kester asked, picking up his pace to avoid the large gang of youths approaching the other way. Although only twenty-two himself, young people made him nervous, and he always felt sure they were about to mock his portly figure and spectacles. Mainly because that had happened several times in the past. To his relief, they passed without giving him a second glance.

"Good question!" Ribero said energetically, oblivious to Kester's concerns. "Why not us? There is plenty of work, plenty of projects to bid on. But not so many coming to us. And this does not make sense to me, because people know that we have *you*."

Kester gulped at the distinct emphasis placed on the last word. *Oh no, not me again*, he thought. *I hate being the thing they're relying on.* "Yes," he stuttered, stumbling to keep pace with his father, who was now striding purposefully along the pavement, heedless of other people walking the opposite way. "But I'm not sure my ability to open a door to the spirit world works very well."

"You have said this before," his father said impatiently and waved his protests away. "But I have seen you, Kester, my boy. I have watched you in action. You have the talent, just like your mother. Dear Gretchen would have been so proud of you."

Why does it always have to come back to my mother? Kester thought irritably. It was exhausting always being compared to Gretchen Lanner who, from what Kester could surmise, had been something of a legend in the supernatural world, until she'd accidentally got pregnant with him. *I'm not as good as her*, he thought despondently. *I don't think I ever will be.*

Ribero coughed, reading his expression. "We must keep the agency going," he said, wisely moving on, "for Jennifer's sake, if not for everyone else. It's her family's agency. It means everything to her."

Kester nodded. He knew that it had been Miss Wellbeloved's ancestors who had first set up the agency, back in the Victorian era. In those days, her well-connected relations had turned it into a great success, but as the years went on, and the more people became cynical about the supernatural, the more the agency had been pushed into the shadows.

"I made a promise to Jennifer's father," Ribero continued. "I promised I'd keep this agency going. And I must keep my word, yes?"

Well, you didn't seem to have a problem breaking the other promise—the one about marrying his daughter, Kester thought, his mouth twitching just a little. *Still, I suppose the little matter of having an affair with my mother didn't help much.*

Ribero flinched, correctly interpreting Kester's thoughts. There was an uncomfortable silence. "Anyway," he carried on eventually, "I want to talk to you about your role in the agency."

"What bit of my role?"

"All of it."

"Ah, I see." Kester chewed his lip. He knew full well that his father wanted him to be more active, to come out on more jobs and develop his skills, rather than staying behind to do research on the computer. But the truth was, he *hated* being around spirits. Even after nearly four months of being immersed in the supernatural, he still struggled to cope with it all. The very existence of spirits, much less an entire world of spirits, was more than his rational brain was prepared to deal with.

"I want you to start working on your practical skills."

"You mean you want me to deal with spirits more often."

Ribero roared with laughter. A huddle of old ladies standing by a nearby shop window jumped and tutted at him, brows furrowed over their spectacles. He bowed, delivering them one of his most charming South American smiles, and they all melted in unison. Kester felt somewhat irritated, not to mention jealous, despite the fact they were at least fifty years older than him. *Why didn't I inherit some of his success with the ladies?* he wondered, stuffing his hands into his pockets. *Doesn't seem fair to me.*

"Yes, I do want you to deal with the spirits!" Ribero continued energetically. "I want you to embrace it all, Kester. It is nothing to be afraid of, right?"

Are you kidding? Kester thought. He mentally reviewed the list of spirits he'd seen so far. Even the not-so-scary ones had been bad enough, and the worst ones had been the stuff of nightmares. *The last thing I want to do is get up-close and personal with any of them,* he thought, tugging his coat collar up to keep the cold out.

"We have to win those new jobs first," he said finally. "Not much point in me saying I'll come with you to sort out the spirits when there aren't any spirits for us to work with, is there?"

Ribero winked with the caddish confidence of a silent movie star. "Ah, but there will be some jobs soon," he whispered conspiratorially. "I feel it in my bones, you see. You will have a chance to shine."

Oh good, thought Kester glumly. *Looking forward to it.*

He glanced upwards. It had just started to rain, a mild patter of moisture that looked set to work its way into a fairly violent drenching.

He hoped it wasn't a sign of things to come.

CHAPTER 3: GETTING THE JOB

It was Saturday. A fact which Kester felt especially pleased about, given that it was nine o'clock, which meant that he could wallow in bed for at least another three hours. However, something wasn't quite as it should be. There was a *something* keeping him from dozing off again into a wonderful morning nap. Something loudly, rudely intruding on the peace and quiet. *What exactly was it?*

Then he realised. Someone was shouting his name. Over and over again. Kester sat up blearily and rubbed his eyes. He hadn't appreciated, until this very moment, how annoying his name was when repeated in the same monotonous shout twenty times in a row.

"Yes, alright!" he shouted back grumpily, getting his legs tangled in his duvet. "Coming!"

Throwing open his bedroom door, he gazed back wistfully at his bed, which looked deliciously inviting in the morning light: toasty, snug, and completely the opposite of the chill air that was currently whisking around his pyjama-clad body. They still hadn't managed to fix the heating, and now winter was fast approaching, which made Kester really wish they had.

"What is it?" he shouted over the peeling bannister. Pineapple grinned back at him, hair scooped up into an exorbitant topknot that teetered to one side like a drunken hedgehog.

"Phone for you, bruv," he said as he waved the receiver impatiently in Kester's general direction. "It be your old man, like."

"My old man?" Kester blinked in confusion. "What old man?"

Pineapple raised his lurid neon-pink vest to scratch his enviably flat stomach. "You know," he said stoically. "Your old man. Your dad, innit?"

"Oh, is it?" Kester echoed flatly. "What does he want?"

Pineapple shrugged, then flung the handset into Kester's face. "He sounds all excited, like. Dunno what's going on there, man."

"Yeah, he always sounds like that," Kester said as he grasped the phone. "That's his default voice."

"Dee-falt, yeah man, tight." With these incomprehensible words, Kester's housemate sashayed into the kitchen where he set about rummaging for something in the fridge. Kester sighed, wiping the sleep out of his eyes.

"Hello?" he asked reluctantly. It was bad enough having to see his father every day at work, and he wasn't overjoyed at the prospect of his weekend being interrupted by him too, even though, admittedly, Kester had no plans apart from eating an entire tube of Pringles and sleeping a lot.

"Aha, you are finally up! What a lazy boy you are, yes?" Ribero's voice trilled through the phone, strident as ever.

Kester grimaced. "I was just in the bathroom," he lied.

"No you weren't, you were lolloping around in bed. Your friend told me. The fruit man."

"Pineapple," Kester corrected automatically. "Anyway, what do you want?"

"You need to come to our meeting."

Kester groaned. "What meeting?" he asked, not wanting to hear the answer.

"Very important meeting. Serena just called me. We must all meet in town."

Oh, for goodness' sake, Kester thought with a sigh. If Serena had arranged the meeting, it was bound to be about something tedious and or problematic.

"What time?" he asked, resisting the urge to simply hang up and retreat to the warmth of his bed.

"Half an hour. At the Glorious Art House café."

"Why not just the office?" Kester said. "Isn't that easier?"

"No, the Glorious is just over the road from Serena's flat. And they do very good chocolate cake, you know."

Kester brightened, then peered down at his stomach, which was currently bulging from beneath his flannel nightshirt like a naughty child peeping over a bedsheet.

"I'll never be there in half an hour," he said finally, self-consciously pulling his shirt down. "I'm not even dressed."

"Catch the bus, silly boy!" Ribero barked. "It leaves in twenty minutes, right? Hurry up, go get your clothes on. I will see you there."

The phone went dead. Kester stared disbelievingly at the handset before placing it slowly back in its cradle.

Well, he thought irritably as he trudged back up the stairs. *There goes my lie-in.*

After tugging on the nearest clothes he could find, Kester scampered urgently down the street, just managing to clamber onto the bus before it pulled away. It was only then that he noticed he had odd socks on. *How could I have failed to see that one was green and the other was yellow with navy spots?* he wondered. Still, at least he'd noticed his trousers were on back-to-front before leaving the house, which was something.

The bus chuffed to a halt at the end of the high street, depositing Kester and a cluster of other early-morning shoppers outside a dated department store. Without further ado, he trotted down the road. Vintage stores, charity shops, and tiny bars lined the streets, but Kester marched purposefully on, halting only when he reached the colourful façade of the café in question. Mike waved cheerfully at him from the sofa in the window.

"What's going on, then?" Kester said curtly, sinking into the only available seat, which happened to be a squidgy armchair. "I had plans for today."

"So did I, love," Pamela said, snuggled into the corner of the other sofa like a large, fluffy cat. "I was going to sort through the dead plants in my greenhouse and take Hemingway for a walk. But it'll have to wait."

Miss Wellbeloved neatly poured herself another cup of herbal tea. "We're just waiting for Serena herself, ironically," she said as she peered out the window to the art deco buildings opposite. "You'd think, given she only lives across the road, she might have been the first here."

"My dad's not here yet either," Kester commented, then attempted to catch the eye of the lady behind the counter. He badly needed a cup of tea to wake him up.

"Yes, but he doesn't count. He's never anywhere on time," Pamela said.

Shortly after Kester ordered his tea, plus a slice of caramel shortbread, which he was sure wasn't nearly as calorific as a piece of chocolate cake, Ribero and Serena both walked through the door. Ribero looked excited. Serena, rather surprisingly, looked a little like a dog who had managed to sneak a sausage from the barbeque, only to realise it was a spicy chilli sausage and rather painful to eat. Her expression conveyed a mixture of emotions, and Kester couldn't work out what she was thinking at all.

She eyed Kester's cake. "Thought you were cutting back?" she declared, nodding significantly at his stomach.

"Yes, I was until I got dragged out of bed on a Saturday," Kester retorted, then defiantly took a large bite. It crumbled down his jumper, something that bothered him, but he refused to give her the satisfaction of seeing him dust himself down.

To his surprise, Serena reached over, grasped the shortbread between two manicured fingers, and inserted it into her own mouth. He watched her, aghast, until she started laughing, spraying crumbs out onto the floor.

"Look, my need is greater than yours," she spluttered as she perched on the side of the sofa. "Trust me. It's been quite a morning."

"Nice to see you actually eating for once," Mike commented, happily tucking into the chocolate cake. "Thought you only ate little children, like all the other nasty witches."

"Hilarious," she growled. "Anyway, shall I get straight to it?"

"Yes, what's going on?" Miss Wellbeloved asked. "I'm dying to know what's so important that we had to meet up at the weekend."

"Me too," muttered Kester darkly before dumping another spoon of sugar into his tea. Once again, images of his temptingly warm bed came to mind, and he felt himself getting cross all over again. He watched the last of his caramel shortbread disappear between Serena's lips and sighed. *This is a rubbish start to the weekend,* he thought.

"Well," Serena began dramatically, oblivious to Kester's glare. "I've got some very, very good news. And," she continued before anyone could interrupt her, "I've also got some slightly not-so-good news. In fact, I'll be honest, it's pretty bad news actually."

Ribero nodded impatiently, then prodded her with his metal-tipped umbrella, which he was still clasping in one hand, despite there being no rain outside. "Go on then, tell us the good news! That is what we need at the moment, yes? Forget the bad news. That's not so important."

Serena grinned. "Okay then, good news it is. I was checking the system this morning, to see if we'd got any messages about any of the jobs we'd bid on."

"And we got something?" Miss Wellbeloved interrupted, colour rising in her cheeks.

Serena nodded. "We certainly did!" she confirmed. "Do you remember the Lyme Regis job, the one we think might be a doppelgänger?"

"You mean the satanic spirit-twin, out to murder every old biddy in town?" Mike asked.

"That's the one," Serena replied. "We've got the job; our bid was successful. So, that's the good news."

"That's marvellous, yes?" Dr Ribero exclaimed, thwacking his umbrella even more enthusiastically into Serena's leg. "Now we have some money coming in, at last! What did I say to you only a few days ago, Kester?"

"What's the bad news, then?" Kester said pointedly, determined not to be cheered by anything today. He was still too tired, and he had been denied his sugar-hit, which made him even grumpier yet.

Serena shifted about awkwardly on the sofa, then made a show of rearranging the giant tasselled cushion behind her. "Well, I only said it was 'not-so-good news'," she muttered, "not outright bad news."

"No, you said it was pretty bad. I remember you saying it," Kester said.

Serena tutted. "Whatever. The main thing is that we've got a job. Everything else pales by comparison, right?"

"Yes!" Dr Ribero agreed enthusiastically. "That is exactly right. I knew this would be a good day."

"Perhaps it pales by comparison, perhaps not?" Miss Wellbeloved added with a note of apprehension.

"Probably not, if your face is anything to go by," Mike said, belching out cake crumbs all over the table. "Serena, just spit it out. What's the bad news?"

Serena turned pink and mumbled something under her breath, a sentence which sounded suspiciously like it might have the words 'Larry Higgins' in it.

"What was that?" Mike said loudly. "Speak up, woman."

"We've got to share the job with Larry Higgins."

Mike guffawed deafeningly, then stopped abruptly. The others simply stared, mouths open. Even the few other customers in the café went quiet, turning their heads to see what was going on.

"Are you . . . you're not actually *serious*, are you?" Mike said incredulously. He looked at the others. "I mean, come on."

"No, I'm afraid I am actually serious," Serena said quietly. "Both bids were accepted. It's a joint offer. His agency and ours. We've already had an email come through, which said we need to liaise directly with Larry Higgins to arrange a time when we can all be briefed on the case."

"Oh, no," said Ribero, rising to his feet with the severity of a seismic tectonic plate. "Oh no, no, no. *No*. Absolutely not. This is a joke, right, Serena? You are trying to be witty, yes?"

"Er, no. I'm telling the truth. We've got to work with Larry Higgins."

Dr Ribero let out a noise that was the perfect hybrid of exploding steam train and hysterical hyena. He clasped his hair, then shook his head wildly. "Absolutely not!" he shouted suddenly, waving his umbrella into the air and nearly knocking down the ceiling light in the process. "There is no way on earth that I am working with the Higgins! Never!"

He started to storm out of the shop, but he was bounced back like an elastic band by Miss Wellbeloved, who had nimbly grabbed him by the back of his coat.

"Don't be so silly," she said crossly before pushing him firmly back down on the sofa. "You really do fly off the handle sometimes, don't you?" She turned back to Serena, who was looking more nervous by the second. "What else did the email say?"

Serena gulped. "Not much, really. Just that both tenders had been accepted, and that we were advised to speak directly to Larry Higgins to sort out a day we can meet and find out the details. Apparently, the case is quite a complex one—it was originally a regional, but it has been upgraded to a national, due to its severity."

"Hang on, if it was a regional, why didn't we automatically get it?" Pamela asked. "Dorset is normally our area, isn't it?"

Miss Wellbeloved shrugged. "Who knows anymore?" she said with a mournful look. "Unless the case is actually here in Exeter, nothing seems guaranteed."

"Anyway, ladies, you are all missing the point, I think," Ribero interrupted. "We will not be taking this job. There is no way I will ever work with Larry Higgins, and that is the end to it, okay?"

"Oh, for goodness' sake!" Miss Wellbeloved snapped. "I would say it's about time you got over this silly squabble you have with Larry. He's a perfectly pleasant man."

"He has the personality of . . . how do you say it? A *slug*. That is it. A slug. He is a worm of a man."

"He looks a bit like a massive slug too, doesn't he?" Mike added. "A bit like Jabba the Hutt. About as self-important too."

Miss Wellbeloved sighed. "Yes, thank you for that, Mike. There's no denying Larry Higgins can be a little full of himself at times, but he's really not a bad person. And this silly fight needs to come to an end. Honestly, you've been at war with him for decades, Julio!"

Dr Ribero folded his arms furiously, looking rather like a tantrumming toddler, despite his greying hair and wrinkles.

"Why do you hate him so much?" Kester asked. "Apart from him being like a slug and a worm, I mean."

Ribero snorted. Miss Wellbeloved sighed. "We were all at

university together," she explained. "Julio and Larry studied the same course. Dr Ribero is convinced that Larry Higgins stole his thesis idea; he hasn't forgiven him since."

"He did steal my idea!" Ribero exploded as he slammed his fist against the sofa. "And he won the prize for most innovative student! That is why he has done so well, yes? On my idea! Mine! All his success, everything he has today, it was because he stole my idea, yes?"

"Was it definitely yours?" Pamela asked doubtfully.

Ribero fixed her with a glare so filled with righteous rage that she shrank visibly back into the sofa.

"Well, don't you think it's finally time to let that go?" Miss Wellbeloved pressed on, ignoring his thunderous expression. "Given that it was decades ago?"

"Never," Ribero swore, placing his hand ardently to his heart. "I will *never* forgive that man."

"Sounds like you might have to," Mike said chirpily as he leant over and poured himself another cup of tea. "If we actually want to get paid this month."

"It's because of his second office in Southampton, I suspect," Serena said seriously. "I did rather wonder if this would happen."

"If what would happen?" Ribero asked stormily.

"If he'd start winning southwest business," she replied simply.

Ribero's face darkened even further. Kester wagered that even if a thunder-god himself had descended from the skies at that very moment, they would have been intimidated by his father's expression and chosen to give it a miss and head back instead.

"Have you replied to the email yet?" Miss Wellbeloved asked.

Serena shook her head. "I thought I'd better wait and see what you said first."

"Let's reply to them saying we'll get in touch with Larry

Higgins first thing Monday."

"No!" wailed Dr Ribero, grabbing at Miss Wellbeloved's arm so hard that she nearly wobbled off the sofa. "No, you would not be so cruel! Serena, tell me, have none of our other bids been accepted?"

"Nope, just this one."

Ribero shook his fists at the ceiling, eyes rolling dramatically. "Madre de dios! Qué desastre!"

"Oh dear, he's slipped into Spanish," Mike whispered to Kester over the noise. "That's never a good sign."

"Shall I go and reply now?" Serena said loudly, struggling to make herself heard above the Spanish cursing.

Miss Wellbeloved patted her encouragingly. "Yes, you go and do that. Thank you very much for being on the ball. This is good news. Really, it is." She shot a disapproving look at Ribero before nodding at the others. "You can all head off if you like. We don't want to take up any more of your precious weekend."

"Ah, I didn't have anything on anyway," Mike said. "Apart from watching films all day."

Kester eyed his father nervously—Ribero was now balling a velvet cushion between his hands like a wrestler squeezing the life out of his opponent.

"Yeah, perhaps I'd better stick around for a bit, check he's alright," he said reluctantly.

Miss Wellbeloved tutted. "Oh, he gets like this every so often, Kester. Don't worry, he'll run out of steam soon."

"Higgins! Que feo Ingles!"

Mike chortled. "Doesn't look like he's running out any time soon." He leaned over and patted Ribero's arm comfortingly. "Don't sweat it, mate. It might be nice meeting your old university chum anyway."

The howl of anguish that emanated from Ribero's lips was only upstaged by the mugs falling over as he walloped the table's surface.

"Thanks for that, Mike," Miss Wellbeloved said tightly. "Why don't you boys head off? We'll discuss this more on Monday morning."

"Bye Dad," Kester said nervously with a little wiggle of his hand. His father whimpered in response, flopping back against the sofa like a man on a death sentence. Miss Wellbeloved nodded firmly towards the door, settling herself beside Ribero and trying to ignore the curious stares of the other people inside the café.

"Well, that was a good bit of drama for a Saturday morning, wasn't it?" Mike commented breezily as they stepped out on to the pavement. "Who would have thought it? Ribero and Higgins. On the same job. What a nightmare."

"Will it really be that bad?" Kester said doubtfully as he pulled his jacket tightly around him. A stiff wind blew against them as they made their way back up the steep hill.

Mike glanced over, eyes twinkling dangerously. "Oh, yes," he said with a bit more enthusiasm than the situation called for. "It'll be bedlam. Just you wait 'til you meet that fat sod Higgins. See if he annoys you as much as he does the rest of us."

"I won't have to meet him, will I?" Kester said nervously. "I mean, you'll be the ones on the job, not me."

Mike chortled, then whacked him on the back, hard enough to make him wince. "Yeah right," he sniggered. "Your dad has plans for you, and they don't involve hiding in the office anymore. You've got to practice your skills somewhere, haven't you?"

"But my skills are hiding in offices! That's what I'm good at!"

Mike leant over and nudged him playfully. "Not anymore, Kester. Not anymore."

Kester thought despondently about the tube of Pringles waiting for him at home. But even that didn't help.

It's a worrying day when the thought of a nice salty snack can't even make me feel better, he thought as he angrily kicked the nearest puddle. *Could things get any worse?*

The water splashed over his other foot, soaking into his yellow sock and instantly filling his shoe with horrible cold dampness. Kester groaned.

Chapter 4: The Murder of Meredith

The front door was stuck again, no doubt because of the cold weather and sudden wet spell. Not to mention the stiff sea breeze, which carried with it the weighty stench of salt and seaweed. Meredith Saunders pressed a tweed-coated shoulder against the wood, sighed with exasperation before, finally, it gave in at the meagre pressure of her weight.

"Frank?" she called as she threw her handbag over the bannister. "That door's being difficult again. You'll need to phone Charles, see if he can come over and have a look."

From the kitchen, she could make out her husband grunting something in response. A tinkle of metal against ceramic indicated that he'd just made himself a cup of tea.

It would be ever so nice if he actually spoke from time to time, she thought grumpily, peeling off her coat and scarf. Since his hip operation, her husband, who'd been fairly quiet to begin with, had become positively taciturn. Surly even. Still, she couldn't grumble. Despite her age, she was in good shape, and the brisk walk down to the seafront, despite being cold, had done her no end of good.

"Saw David at the bakery," she said while she wandered through to the kitchen. "He said to tell you that the next meeting is on Tuesday. Apparently, he's got a guest speaker. Some ammonite expert or something."

Frank grunted again, sipping his tea. Meredith rolled her eyes.

"Sally's back at work," she continued, trying hard not to be irritated by her husband, who was now tapping erratically at the countertop. "I told her it was far too soon after her treatment, but she said she couldn't be away for long. What a trooper, eh?"

The tapping paused for a second or two before continuing. She sighed, then reached to the fridge for the orange juice, though in truth, a gin and tonic would have gone down far better. However, it was only five in the afternoon, which really was a bit too early to start drinking.

"Well," she concluded finally as she poured herself a large glass. "I may go and have a bath. Warm up a little. You don't want to eat yet, do you?"

Frank shook his head, then gave her a little smile. She smiled in return, feeling a little less hostile towards him.

"Fish and chips?" he suggested quietly.

Meredith chuckled, patting her stomach. "Goodness me, any more batter and I'll start to look like a deep-fried haddock, I think. We really should eat a few more vegetables." Noticing Frank's face falling, she quickly nodded. "But yes, fish and chips would be good, wouldn't it? And let's get the fire going too, it's ever so cold in here."

"Peter Hopper called earlier," her husband muttered as she went out into the hallway.

"Oh, did he? I haven't heard from him in a while," she replied. *In fact,* she thought, suddenly feeling rather depressed, *I haven't heard from any of my friends in a while, since all the deaths*. Peter had taken it all particularly badly; she missed his dry, northern sense of humour, not to mention the fortnightly meetings in the town hall. "Did he want me to call him back?"

Her husband shrugged in response before returning to the kitchen.

Meredith took her orange juice upstairs and started to run the bath. Stripping off her sweater and skirt, she tried hard to avoid looking at her unclothed figure in the mirror. *I don't need any more reason to feel glum about my old age,* she thought wryly, dipping a toe tentatively in the water. *At least if I don't look, I can still pretend I have the taut figure of a twenty-year-old.*

Easing herself into the lavender-soaked water, she exhaled with pleasure. There was something so deeply *satisfying* about having a bath. She'd always been a water-lover, even from a young age, when her parents used to take her swimming at the local outdoor pool. It was hardly surprising she'd ended up living somewhere like Lyme Regis, surrounded by the sea. Closing her eyes, she leant back, relishing the moist steam against her face and the warmth as it penetrated her muscles.

What a nice way to unwind after a walk, she thought dreamily, allowing her thoughts to drift. She'd been finding it increasingly difficult to remain cheery recently, especially after the deaths of her friends. Earnest Sunningdale. Edna Berry. Jürgen Kleinmann. And now Deirdre Baxter. All within six months. *It's almost as if they were all cursed,* she thought with a shudder, then tutted at her own superstitious thoughts. *Come on now, Meredith,* she scolded herself. *They were accidental, or health-related. Don't start getting silly about it all. It's just a dreadful coincidence that they all happened so soon after one another.*

She hadn't been quite such good friends with Deirdre, though they'd known each other well enough as members of the same history club. Meredith had always found her rather *flighty,* not to mention a bit fanciful at times, with her strange ideas. Their neighbours, Mr and Mrs Biggins, had been great friends with Deirdre and Errol though and been terribly shaken up by her death. Mrs Biggins had even suggested, with a rather alarming gleam in her eye, that the recent spate of deaths had been *supernatural,* which had made Meredith chuckle a little. It was quite remarkable how often people liked to believe in such things, despite having no evidence whatsoever to support their beliefs. Still, it was a sad affair. Deirdre's husband Errol hadn't been out much, but on the rare occasion she'd spotted him, he'd looked very thin and tired.

A breeze ran through the room. Meredith opened an eye, checking the window. The panes were original, and it wasn't uncommon for the wind to creep through from time to time. She sighed, closed her eyes again, and sunk back into the water.

Strange, she thought. *The bath suddenly seems colder.* Hastily, she turned on the tap again, allowing more hot water to fill the bath, and rested back against the cool ceramic surface, determined to relax. The water drifted warm tendrils around her thighs, then cooled again just as quickly.

Good heavens, whatever is going on? Meredith opened her eyes again, suddenly alert. Someone was watching her. She was sure of it. She had that disconcerting sense of being observed and of something being undeniably, unaccountably *wrong.* Awkwardly, she swivelled in the bath, then cursed as her neck cracked uncomfortably.

"Frank, is that you?" she called. Was her husband lurking outside the door? Why would he do such a thing? Only silence answered her, which seemed as deep and hostile as a tomb.

Meredith frowned. *It's because I was thinking about what that silly Mrs Biggins said about the deaths,* she thought, laughing out loud. *Oh dear, don't tell me I've become superstitious in my old age!*

She eased herself back down in the water, refusing to think on it anymore.

Hello.

Meredith's eyes popped open, then widened. A scream rose in her throat, lodging itself like a stuck lozenge. There, perched at the other end of the roll-top bath, was *herself*. Or rather, a mirror image of herself, sitting in exactly the same position, completely nude, facing her.

I said I didn't want to see myself naked, Meredith thought irrationally with a hysterical snort of laughter. She squeezed her eyes shut, then opened them again, expecting to see nothing but an empty bath.

I'm still here.

"Oh, my goodness," Meredith squeaked, rigid with fear. "Oh, my dear lord."

She looked at her other self with horror, examining every wrinkle, every damp wisp of grey hair, the same wry grin that she gave herself in the mirror every morning. *This isn't real*, she thought, desperately trying to get a grasp of reality. *Come on, Meredith, old girl. Pull yourself together. This is not real.*

It is.

Meredith screamed—a pitiful, dry wail that sounded like a drowning kitten. "What are you?" she croaked as she scrambled to climb from the bath. She slipped and fell painfully back into the water.

I am you. Hello, Meredith.

"You're not me . . . it's . . . not possible," Meredith wheezed, pressing herself against the porcelain in terror. "I must be going mad."

Maybe you are. Or maybe not.

"What's that supposed to mean?" Meredith babbled, as she finally managed to get a good grasp on the side of the bath. "Frank! Frank, help me!"

IT'S TOO LATE FOR THAT.

"Frank!" she shrieked. Fighting to control her shaking limbs, she began to drag herself out of the bath. "Frank, please! There's something in here; it's pretending to be me!"

To her relief, she heard vague footsteps, which padded quickly along the hallway downstairs before echoing flatly on the stairs. *Thank goodness, he heard me,* she thought, shaking and dripping wetness onto the black and white tiles.

Turning, although every instinct told her not to, she faced her other self again. It grinned, an obscene gesture that contorted her mirror-features, making her twin look suddenly completely unlike her. Then, it began to shake. Initially, Meredith thought it was mimicking her own frightened quivering, and she edged slowly away from the bath, like a mouse trying to sneak unnoticed from a cat. Then, her other self began to shake harder, until it was positively vibrating.

What the heck is it doing? she thought as she watched with horrified fascination. By now, it was shaking harder than her old washing machine on full spin, a dreadful blur that made her eyes ache to see it.

"Stop it! Stop it now!" she shouted, biting her lip to hold back the tears.

"Meredith?"

Thank goodness, it's Frank, she realised, and let out a pitiful sob. *Oh, thank the lord, he's come. I'm going to be okay.* She didn't think she'd ever loved the sound of her husband's voice more than she did at that moment.

"Frank, help me," she choked whilst the creature whirred on: a shimmering, uncontrollable whirl of form. "Oh please, you've got to help me. There's something terrible in here with me."

The door-handle rattled urgently.

"I can't get in. You've locked the door. What's in there with you? What is it?"

"It's me," Meredith said weakly, momentarily hypnotised into quiet. "My god, it really is me."

The creature had stopped whirring. Instead, its mouth began to gape, impossibly wide, and *something* began to crawl out. Something dark. Something oily and smoky. Something from an unimaginable, frightening place. It advanced towards her like a spider scuttling across the floor.

I NEED TO GO BACK HOME.

"I don't know where your home is!" she whispered, frozen in horror. The thing pulsed towards her, then enveloped the bathroom in darkness.

She scrambled backwards, heedless of Frank's increasingly panicked shouting. The handle rattled harder, and she dimly heard the crunching sound of her husband's slipper-clad foot, desperately kicking at the door.

YOU'RE MINE.

"No," she whispered. "You can't have me."

The last thing Meredith remembered was her foot as it slid wildly on the slippery tiles. The bathroom pitched upside down, a crazed montage of floral wallpaper, art nouveau prints, and finally, the vast ceramic underside of the toilet. Her skull cracked against the floor, as weak and vulnerable as a free-range egg.

The glass of orange juice fell from the side of the bath, spilling over her body. Shards of glass mingled with the dark blood and the juice, creating a mosaic of red and amber. The room dimmed.

And Meredith knew no more. *Was* no more.

Finally, the bathroom door flew open, hitting the wooden towel rack with the force of a steam train. Frank stood motionless in the doorway, kitchen knife suspended quivering above his head, and surveyed the scene. Water, juice, blood, and glass over the floor. A picture, flung at a wonky angle. And finally, his wife, naked on the floor, eyes open, staring into nothingness.

He glanced around, waiting for his conscious mind to catch up with the sensory evidence.

There was no one else in the room, just his wife.

His *dead* wife.

Frank began to scream.

Chapter 5: The Higgins

"So, just to clarify, you absolutely need me to come to this meeting?" Kester asked for the third time since they'd set off from Exeter to Southampton.

"For goodness' sake, Kester. Yes, we do!" Miss Wellbeloved snapped as she checked herself in the mirror and patted down her hair. "Your father wanted you to be there so you could gain better understanding of the case. Now will you please stop asking?"

He sighed, fiddling with his tie. It was pink. He'd thought a bright colour might be a wise choice, to establish himself as a young, energetic member of the team, but now, he just felt slightly silly wearing it. In fact, the more he reviewed it, the more he realised that it was the sort of hideous item of clothing that someone like Pineapple would wear, not a sensible person such as himself. He glanced over at Mike, who was wearing an open-necked denim shirt and looked irritatingly, effortlessly comfortable.

"What are we going to say about Ribero, then?" Mike asked, as they pulled into the car park.

"Oh, I don't know. We'll just say he's ill or something. It will all be absolutely fine," Miss Wellbeloved said tightly. "Now let's stop fussing and get on with this briefing. We're already fifteen minutes late."

Kester clambered awkwardly out of the van and surveyed the drab concrete offices in front of them.

"Doesn't look like a supernatural agency," he said, smoothing down his suit. "Looks more like an insurance company or something."

"And what exactly is a supernatural agency supposed to look like?" Miss Wellbeloved asked pertly as she joined Kester and Mike on the tarmac.

"I think Kester still believes we should be working in a haunted house," Mike answered before locking the van. "It'd be a lot more exciting, wouldn't it?"

Miss Wellbeloved gave them a look that was reminiscent of a teacher surveying two particularly badly behaved children. "Come on, you two," she said firmly. "Let's hurry up and get this over with."

Kester dutifully followed her as she strode through the entrance, her heels clipping against the pock-marked linoleum floor. Why he'd been chosen to be the third person attending the meeting, he didn't know. Serena would have been far more qualified and, indeed, had been livid to discover that Ribero had chosen Kester instead. Even Pamela had offered to go in his place, but his father had been adamant that it had to be him, much to his dismay.

The corridor was strangely quiet with an uncomfortable airless atmosphere that made Kester feel instantly breathless. He tweaked his tie, wondering if he had time to whisk it off and stuff it into his pocket.

"Shall we?" Miss Wellbeloved said, gesturing to the door at

the end of the corridor. A simple sign outside declared it was the Larry Higgins Agency, complete with copperplate writing and rather pompous gold edging. It was an ominous indication of what to expect inside.

They stepped into an office that looked even more remarkably like an insurance company than the exterior. Wooden desks and partitions lined both sides of the room in a showy display of productivity. The gentle hum of computer screens and central heating added to the general atmosphere of efficiency.

"Aha, glad you could finally join us. Took your time, but got here eventually, I see."

The owner of the nasal, sarcastic voice stepped over to greet them, a rotund hippopotamus of a man, complete with wild tufts of balding white hair and a patronising expression. Kester bit back a chuckle. *Mike was right, he really does look like Jabba the Hutt,* he thought.

"Larry," Miss Wellbeloved said smoothly, stepping forward to shake his hand. "It's been a long time. I trust you are well?"

Larry Higgins smirked, then gestured around him. "Very well, as you can see," he said. "The man from the government has already started briefing us, as you were so late. Shall we go and join the rest of the team?"

"Steady on, we're only fifteen minutes late," Mike said indignantly. "I drove as fast as I could."

Higgins checked his watch, then nodded sanctimoniously. "Nearly nineteen minutes late, actually. But if you're still driving that dreadful old van, it's not surprising."

"Well, let's go and get started," Miss Wellbeloved said hastily when she caught sight of Mike's thunderous expression. "Lead the way, Larry."

"Just one second," Larry said, holding up an imperious hand. "Would you mind removing your shoes? We've just had the new carpets put down and they're real sheep's wool."

"But your shoes are still on," Mike pointed out.

"Yes, but mine have been thoroughly cleaned before entering the space," Larry replied. "Whereas yours might have all sorts of unpleasant things stuck to the bottom, like dog mess or something."

"I've not stepped in any bloody dog sh—"

"That will be fine," Miss Wellbeloved interrupted as she removed her shoe in one deft flick. She nodded meaningfully at Kester's shoes and gave him a subtle wink as she did so.

After they'd lined their shoes neatly by the wall, Higgins led them to the far end of the office, nudging them through a door. Inside, the blinds were drawn. Kester noted the other people in the room: a brooding man with shining, dark hair and a black woman with a fierce buzz-cut sat around an oversized circular table. An older man, with spindly limbs that reminded him of a daddy-long-legs, stood by a glowing PowerPoint display.

"Ah, excellent!" the spindly man announced as they stepped into the room. "Marvellous that you could make it."

"Mr Philpot," Miss Wellbeloved said, then reached across to shake his hand. "It's a pleasure to see you again after all this time. These are my colleagues, Kester and Mike."

"Quite so, quite so. Kester, Mike; I'm Curtis Philpot. I work for the government—the Ministry of the Supernatural. I've heard an awful lot about you, Kester. I saw the video footage of you forcing the Bloody Mary through the spirit door. Very impressive."

Kester blushed, aware of Larry Higgins's contemptuous glare burrowing holes into his back. "Yes, well, it was only an accident really, I didn't—" He stopped as Mike elbowed him in the ribcage.

"Of course." The man nudged his glasses up his nose, then gestured to the empty seats. "Well, good to meet you. Shall we begin?"

"We'd actually begun fifteen minutes ago, but I suppose we'd better begin again, hadn't we?" Higgins said with a sarcastic laugh before placing himself on the nearest chair, which wheezed under his weight. "Before we start, allow me to introduce my team here. They'll be working with us on the case. This is Lara Littleton, my spirit extinguisher. Highly qualified. One of the best in the field."

The woman with the close-cropped hair and the most spectacularly high cheekbones Kester had ever seen gave them a dazzling smile. Kester noticed that her sharp collar was trimmed with metal, like a cowboy's shirt. *Nice touch,* he thought as he smiled in return. Indeed, it was impossible not to. Her huge grin insisted upon a response.

"Howdy," she said, tapping her forehead. "Nice to meet you folks."

"Nice to meet you too," Mike replied, rather over-enthusiastically.

"And this," Higgins continued, "is Dimitri Strang. He's our resident psychic. Also highly adept at accountancy work."

"Always a valuable skill when getting rid of spirits," Mike muttered.

Dimitri folded his long fingers and bowed his head in greeting. He looked ever so slightly like a B-movie vampire: dark, ominous, and menacing. *What has he got on his hair?* Kester wondered as he eyed him with fascination. *My father always uses way too much hair wax, but this guy looks like he's dumped a whole pot of oil over his head.* However, he conceded that the man was handsome, in a heavy-browed, humourless kind of way.

"Well, niceties over, shall we commence?" Curtis Philpot said after he tapped at his watch. "I've only got another half hour to spare, and this is a complex case."

"Yes, let's crack on, shall we?" said Higgins, leaning back in his seat like a languid walrus. "We've got plenty of work to be getting on with too. I presume time isn't quite so pressing for you, is it Jennifer? Heard you were struggling to pick up any work at present."

Miss Wellbeloved smiled tightly and shot Mike a warning look. "Indeed," she said quietly. "Let's get started."

"Well, as I was just saying," Philpot continued, "there have been some rather alarming developments."

"Another old bird has been bumped off," Higgins interrupted with a satisfied nod. "Her husband said he heard her saying she'd seen herself before she died, so it's obviously the same spirit."

Curtis Philpot coughed. "Yes, thank you, Larry. That's absolutely correct. Mrs Meredith Saunders, to be precise. Lyme Regis again. She slipped and fell in the bathroom, and suffered fatal head injuries. As Larry just said, the husband reported hearing her saying that she could see herself. It correlates perfectly with the other cases."

"How many victims so far?" Miss Wellbeloved asked, leaning forward.

"This one brings the total to five," Philpot replied smoothly. "First incident was a Mr Earnest Sunningdale. We weren't initially sure it was supernatural, especially given that his wife runs a business as a professional tarot-card reader down by the beach. She wasn't exactly the most reliable eyewitness, if you take my meaning. Those charlatans are all the same."

"What was in his wife's report?" Dimitri Strang asked in a velvety Russian accent. He flashed a look at the others with dark, tunnel-like eyes, as though daring them to object to his question.

"She claimed that she heard her husband shouting that he was being haunted by himself shortly before he died."

"And how did he die, exactly?" Miss Wellbeloved asked.

Curtis Philpot looked uncomfortable. "Nasty business, really," he said, then glanced at the females in the room. "Hardly makes for pleasant conversation."

"Oh, I reckon we can take it," Lara Littleton said brightly. She had a deep, rich Texan accent, which explained the ranch-er-inspired clothing. "Hit us with the facts. After all, how are we going to get this son-of-a-bitch if we don't know what it's doing, eh?"

Mike chortled, clearly impressed.

Curtis Philpot pursed his lips. "Very well. The poor gentleman appeared to have tripped in his shed. Perhaps frightened into tripping over, we don't know for sure. But anyway, he managed to fall upon his shears, which impaled him through the chest."

"Ouch, that's got to sting," Mike declared.

"Quite," Philpot concluded drolly. "Second victim, Mrs Edna Berry. Vicar's wife. This was when we realised the case was supernatural. Again, her spouse reported hearing her say she was being haunted by a 'devil pretending to be her'."

"How did she snuff it?" Mike asked.

"She managed to hang herself when she was practicing bell-ringing in the church."

"Is that even possible?" Miss Wellbeloved said sceptically, rapping her biro against the desk.

"Apparently, Mrs Berry used to practice the bell-ringing every evening. This time, something scared her enough to cause her to tangle herself in the ropes. She was hoisted up into the belfry, and by the time her husband reached her, she had already asphyxiated."

"Jeez, what a way to go, eh?" Lara declared, then delivered a warm smile around the room as though discussing the weather. "Quite a dramatic exit for a vicar's wife."

"Third victim," Philpot continued, ignoring their comments, "Dr Jürgen Kleinmann. Retired doctor, his wife heard him shouting in German, claiming his doppelgänger was pursuing him. He fell down the stairs and twisted his neck. And our fourth was a Mrs Deirdre Baxter. Found dead in her bed. Heart attack. Her husband said he'd heard her talking about seeing herself in the night."

"So, it seems pretty clear-cut then," Larry Higgins interrupted and pummelled his fist against the table. "We've got a dangerous doppelgänger on our hands."

"Something like that," Philpot concluded. "However, this case has been raised to high priority, given how frequently the spirit is striking. It needs to be dealt with speedily, efficiently, and effectively. There's no room for errors."

Higgins shot a look at Miss Wellbeloved. "Think you lot can manage that, Jennifer?"

Miss Wellbeloved straightened in her seat. "I see absolutely no reason why not," she replied sharply. "The question is, can you, Larry? After all, this isn't your region. You don't know the area as well as we do."

"Ah, come now, Jennifer," Higgins said patronisingly, eyes gleaming. "A spirit is a spirit, whichever part of the world it chooses to haunt. The question is, are you still using water bottles to trap them?"

Dimitri and Lara both raised an eyebrow.

"We are using an effective form of spirit storage," Mike interrupted, folding his arms across his chest. "I don't see why you felt the need to raise that, to be honest."

"Well, I personally prefer using my bottle of water to drink from, not to contain potentially murderous spirits," Higgins replied, clearly enjoying every minute of the conversation. "But each to their own. Hopefully one day you'll be able to afford some proper equipment. For this job, you're welcome to borrow ours. It's state-of-the-art, of course. Designed by the top developers at Infinite Enterprises."

Mike muttered something under his breath which contained a rather audible expletive. Miss Wellbeloved shook her head, silently warning him to keep his cool.

Curtis Philpot tapped at his laptop, and at once, the PowerPoint display changed to an image of a map.

"These red crosses," he said, pointing earnestly, "are the locations of the deaths. As you can see, they're all contained within a two-mile radius. This might be worth keeping in mind when you're investigating."

"That is curious," Kester said as he studied the map. "I wonder why that area in particular? And why only old people? Why does this spirit strike in Lyme Regis and nowhere else? It's a bit odd."

"Does it matter?" Higgins scoffed. "At the end of the day, it's a problem, and we need to get rid of it. It's not going to benefit us much to start digging too deeply."

"Sometimes it's worthwhile trying to understand why a spirit is acting in a certain way," Miss Wellbeloved said dryly. "If we can work out why the spirit is behaving in this manner, it may help us to address the problem."

"Is that the way you normally go about solving your cases?" Larry Higgins mocked. "No wonder you take so long. We prefer to get the job done, with minimal time wasted."

"We prefer to understand each case, rather than blundering in blindly like a stampeding elephant," Mike retorted. Lara tittered, then stopped at the sight of Larry Higgins's expression.

Curtis Philpot coughed loudly. "I do hope there's no animosity between the agencies?"

"Goodness me, no," Miss Wellbeloved exclaimed with just a fraction too much sincerity. Higgins snorted disdainfully and made no comment.

"Very well." Philpot rummaged in his briefcase before pulling out two enormous folders and slamming them on the table. "Here's the case notes. I suggest you all acquaint yourselves thoroughly with them before commencing." He straightened his tie, then scanned the room severely. "Now, we've set a provisional deadline for the case as the fifteenth of January. This gives you precisely two months. Does that sound about right?"

Miss Wellbeloved choked slightly. Larry Higgins nodded, rolling his fingers smugly across his large stomach.

"No problem at all," he said grandly and delivered a significant wink to his team. "In fact, probably too much time, if we're honest."

Mike muttered something under his breath that definitely included a vulgar word or two.

"Righty-ho," Philpot concluded as he shut his briefcase with a dry snap. "Any questions then? Or shall I leave you to discuss the details?"

"Er, may I ask a question about payment?" Miss Wellbeloved asked tentatively, hand quivering in mid-air.

Philpot frowned. "Yes," he said slowly. "What about it?"

"Is there any advance payment for this contract, to cover expenses and so forth?"

"We pay expenses one month after you've filed them," Philpot announced curtly. "Standard procedure for national cases, unless it's a priority project. I trust this isn't a problem?"

"Oh dear," Higgins said, voice dripping with barely concealed glee. "Are we a bit short on cash, Jennifer?"

Miss Wellbeloved ignored him. Despite her glacial composure, Kester could see that she was getting irritated. Her left eye was twitching ever so slightly, which was a sure sign that a severe, headmistressy outburst would shortly follow.

"Don't worry," Higgins continued, then he waved a flabby hand in the air. "If you need to borrow any, we'd be more than happy to lend it. Anything to get the case completed. We're dedicated to the job."

"What a load of cobblers," Mike muttered.

"I shall bid you all farewell then," Philpot said as he shut down his laptop and folded it under his arm. "If you require any further information, you can contact me via email."

After the door had closed, Larry Higgins leaned back in his chair and sighed with obvious satisfaction.

"So," he began, eyes twinkling with unbridled hostility. "Old Ribero didn't want to face me today, did he?"

Miss Wellbeloved clucked irritably under her breath. "He's not very well," she muttered. "Though of course, he asked me to send his warmest affections."

Higgins snorted, sounding uncannily like a piston firing on a steam engine. "Like hell he did. Is he cowering back in Exeter, sending you to do his dirty work for him?"

"That's my father you're talking about," Kester piped up suddenly, quite forgetting himself. "I'd rather you didn't refer to him like that."

Larry's gaze slowly shifted to his direction, then narrowed. "Ah, so you're the prodigal son, are you?" he spluttered and eyed Kester with open scepticism. Kester reddened, noticing that the gazing seemed to focus rather disproportionately on his pink tie. He wished he'd taken it off before he'd entered the building.

"I'm his son, if that's what you mean."

"And the famous spirit door-opener," Lara Littleton interrupted, then leant across the table. "I've never met anyone who could do that; it's damned amazing, my friend. How does it work?"

"Well," Kester began, feeling rather pleased with the response, yet somewhat embarrassed at the same time. He never had been very good at talking to women, especially when they were very good looking and dressed like cowboys. "Um, I'm not sure really. It just kind of happens."

Higgins snorted again, even more loudly than he had done before. "Well," he wheezed, crossing his arms across his chest. "If you're that talented, why don't you join a decent agency? I'm sure the whole country would be willing to hire you. Your talents are something of a rarity."

"I'm happy where I am, thank you," Kester snapped. "I like working with my dad."

"Hang on," Higgins replied as he took a deep breath. Kester realised with foreboding that the man was clearly just starting to get into his stride, like a sumo wrestler limbering up before a big fight. "You're telling me that you feel loyal towards the man who never bothered with you? Why?"

"I don't see how that's any of your business," Miss Wellbeloved said crisply. "And exactly what it has to do with the case, I have no idea. You always were a stirrer, Larry."

Larry Higgins held his hands up in protest and cast a wink at his team. "Ah, come now Jennifer, I'm just asking," he said, batting his hand against his thigh. "No need to get hostile. Though I did always wonder why you stuck around with Ribero too. Given that he was giving Gretchen a good seeing-to behind your back . . ."

"Mr Higgins!" Miss Wellbeloved snapped, composure finally broken. "That is Kester's mother you're talking about!"

"Not to mention the fact that you're being bloody rude to Miss Wellbeloved here," Mike growled, then rolled his sleeves up threateningly. The atmosphere darkened considerably as the two agencies glared at one another furiously across the table.

"This Doctor Ribero. He sounds interesting," Dimitri commented. He scooped up one of the case note files, completely oblivious to the hostile looks around him. "I want to meet this man."

"Well, you'll be seeing lots of him soon," Mike said sarcastically. "Given we'll all be working together like a big happy family."

"I'm really looking forward to it!" Lara proclaimed. "I think this case sounds so interesting. I literally cannot *wait* to get started." She leant across the table, patting Kester on the arm. "And I wanna hear all about your talents. I ain't never met someone who could see spirit doors before. Your gift is like gold dust. It'll be great to see you in action."

Mike sniggered and gave Kester a wink. "You're in there, mate," he mouthed in a manner that was horribly obvious. Kester blushed furiously.

"Well, moving forward," Miss Wellbeloved snipped, trying

her hardest to regain her composure. "Where do you propose we start on this case, Larry?"

"We need to visit the houses where the murders took place," he answered as he settled himself to business. "Interview the spouses. See if we can get any clues about where the spirit is likely to strike next strike next."

"Perhaps we should collect a list of old people living in this Lyme Rebus place?" Dimitri suggested in a voice so clipped it was verging on robotic.

"Lyme Regis," Miss Wellbeloved corrected automatically. "That's not a bad idea though. Especially if this spirit is targeting people within a two-mile radius. Mind you, the town is known for being a popular retirement location. There might be rather a few OAPs there."

"OAPs?" Lara asked, raising an eyebrow.

"Old aged pensioners," Miss Wellbeloved explained. "People in their sixties or above."

"Much like Larry here," Mike added with a snigger.

"No need for that, thank you very much." Higgins fixed Mike with a glare of magnificent proportions. "Let's start with arranging interviews, then go from there. I'll get things coordinated, then get back to you with times."

"I suspect Dr Ribero will want to take a more active role with the organisational side of things," Miss Wellbeloved reminded him.

"If that's the case, he should have bothered coming to the bloody briefing then, shouldn't he have?"

"Yes . . . but he's not very well at the moment."

"Not very well, my arse. But let's not waste any more time discussing that idiot. No offence intended, Kester."

Lara gave Kester a sympathetic look, which made him feel a little better. He stared at the floor and resisted the urge to give Larry Higgins a piece of his mind. *After all,* he thought morosely, *we're stuck working with him for the next few months*

*at least. I suppose I have to be polite or risk jeopardising the entire
project.*

"Let's be off then," Mike announced as he shoved his chair
back with considerable enthusiasm. "I don't know about the rest
of you, but I'm finding it a bit stuffy in this room."

"Stuffy?" Higgins retorted, standing up to show them out.
"I'll have you know I've got full air conditioning in here." He
jabbed a finger in the direction of the ceiling, pointing out the
large, shiny unit mounted to the wall.

Mike shrugged. "Perhaps it's the smell that's doing it,"
he said casually as he pulled open the door. Miss Wellbeloved
smiled, then hastily covered her mouth.

"Smell?" Higgins grunted, eyes narrowing to suspicious slits.
"What on earth are you talking about?"

"Not sure really. There's just a very unpleasant whiff circu-
lating around this office area."

"I doubt that very much," Higgins spat, scuttling behind
them as they marched out into the main office. "We've got
expensive air fresheners all over the place."

Mike paused and frowned, then clasped his chin for added
dramatic effect. Kester fought the urge to laugh. He had learnt
to recognise when Mike was winding someone up, and it was
always enjoyable to watch, particularly if the recipient was a
colossal prat like Larry Higgins.

"I've got it!" he announced abruptly, then clicked his fingers.
"I knew I recognised that smell from somewhere."

"For goodness' sake, there *is* no smell!" Higgins barked,
turning a dangerous shade of plum. "I should know, my nose is
particularly well-tuned to odours."

"It's dog poo."

Lara guffawed, then slunk back to her desk when Higgins
fixed his furious gaze upon her.

"I'll have you know that it is NOT . . ."

"Yep, definitely dog poo," Mike repeated as he sniffed the

air and wrinkled his nose. He scooped up his shoes and pointed at the door. "If you don't mind, I'm going to put my shoes on outside. Don't want to get them dirty in here."

"I don't know who you think you are, young man, but I won't have you saying that my carpet is riddled with dog faeces. This is finest woven Scottish sheep's wool, for your information."

"Hmm," Mike mused, then opened the door slowly. "Perhaps it's sheep poo then." He grinned, slipping on his shoes and skipping down the corridor before Larry Higgins could think of a response. "Toodle-pip, Mr Higgins!" he called gamely over his shoulder. Kester laughed out loud. He couldn't help himself. The sight of Mike's burly shoulders merrily waltzing down the miserable concrete-clad corridor was just too funny.

Miss Wellbeloved cleared her throat and patted Larry Higgins on the arm, whose purple face looked alarmingly like someone had inflated it with a bicycle pump. "We'll be in touch regarding the interviews in Lyme Regis," she suggested in a valiant attempt to divert his attention. "If you'd rather we conducted them, just let us know. We're much nearer than you are."

"No, I don't think that will be necessary," Higgins muttered darkly, still glaring down the corridor in fury. "I think it's best if we handle the interviews, actually. We don't want any mistakes made."

"Perhaps we could take half each and divide the work?"

"Fine. Whatever." Larry Higgins folded his arms crossly, his smug composure clearly shaken. "I'll be in touch."

Miss Wellbeloved nodded graciously. Kester gave a little wave, felt instantly silly, then quickly lowered his hand again. To his pleasure, he noticed Lara Littleton raise her hand in response. Even Dimitri managed a small, sharp wave before slinking back to his desk.

They walked to the van in silence.

"Well," Mike said cheerfully as he switched on the ignition

and ground the van into reverse. "I thought that went very well."

Miss Wellbeloved said nothing, only buried her head in her hands and groaned.

Chapter 6: Bacon, Anya, and Supernatural Schools

Kester wearily pushed his front door open. It was one of those particularly unpleasant floral frosted glass and metal doors, which frequently got stuck in the frame, only to be released by a forceful shove. It was dark, cold, and the day had been an especially awful one.

The door did nothing to improve his bleak mood, and the strange ohmming noise coming from the lounge further darkened it. *Another of Daisy's yoga sessions,* Kester realised, wondering if it would be a better idea to simply walk straight out again, phone Mike, and see if he wanted to go to the pub.

"Hey, mate, had a good day, like?"

Kester looked up to see Pineapple's topknotted head poking from behind the kitchen door. He shook his head grimly.

"No, it's emphatically not been a good day," he replied, images of Larry Higgins still looming large in his mind. "In fact, it's been bloody awful."

"You're home late, innit?"

Aren't you, not innit, Kester thought instinctively but said nothing. Experience had taught him that correcting Pineapple only resulted in more confusion and yet more incomprehensible words. "Yes, I certainly am," he said instead, creeping past the lounge to ensure he wasn't spotted. The ohmming grew louder, and he caught a brief glimpse of Daisy and her friends sitting cross-legged in front of a yoga DVD. He scurried past, nimble as a mouse.

"What happened then, bruv?" Pineappple asked as he leapt up and sat cross-legged on the kitchen table. "Working long hours or something?"

"No, Mike's sodding van broke down again," Kester replied, putting the kettle on. "We had to wait just outside Poole for about two hours until someone came to help us out."

Pineapple nodded, then pulled a couple of mugs from the cupboard behind him. "That's tough, man, real brutal," he said, throwing an herbal teabag into one mug and a builder's teabag into the other. "Like, vans . . . they just do that, don't they? I mean, it's technology, innit?"

Kester didn't have a clue what he was talking about but nodded nonetheless, welcoming the warm smell of the tea being made.

"Kester-pops, I thought you'd come in!"

Kester resisted the urge to groan. He turned towards the lounge, smiling weakly. "Hello, Daisy," he said; he tried not to grimace at the sight of his housemate, who was wearing a flowery bandana and a matching leotard, and dripping with sweat.

"Sounds like you're stressed," she said, her voice oozing syrup. "Bad day, hon?"

"Er, yes," Kester replied uncertainly. "It was, rather."

"Why don't you join us for some Bikram yoga? Help unlock

your chakras?"

Kester had no idea what a chakra was, but he didn't particularly relish the prospect of unlocking one. Actually, all he really fancied was a large bacon sandwich, preferably followed up by at least five chocolate digestives.

"That's kind, but I think I'll just make myself a spot of dinner," he said politely and reached for the fridge.

"Why don't you let me cook for all of us?" Daisy offered with a breezy wave of the hand. "Me and the girls are nearly finished in here, I can rustle up a nice quinoa salad."

"I'm alright babes, I'm heading out, like," Pineapple said, tugging at his tie-dyed top. "I'm seeing this girl from Brixton. She's proper tranquil. We're off to a rave."

"Sounds exciting," Kester said flatly. Actually, he thought it sounded horrendous, but he didn't like to say so aloud.

"Oh, that's mega!" Daisy said enthusiastically. A lock of cherry-red hair fell into her eyes, and she glued it back against her wet forehead. "I'd be so up for coming too. Where is it?"

"It's down in Plymouth, right? You fancy it too, Kester? Fudgella has some sweet, sweet mates, you'd be swimming in lady-lust."

"No, I think I'll pass on the whole swimming in lady-lust thing tonight, thank you anyway." Kester pulled open the fridge, then let out a groan. "Hang on, where's my bacon gone?"

Pineapple emitted a guilty cough and hastily tipped the rest of his herbal tea down the sink. "That was yours, was it?"

Daisy rolled her eyes and laughed. "Oh dear," she said dramatically. "I think I'll leave you boys to it."

Kester crossly swivelled around as soon as the lounge door was closed. "Did you eat my bacon?"

"Um, I can't remember, mate. I think I might have had some today, right?"

"No, not right! Not right at all!" Kester spluttered. He felt a sudden urge to cry. He'd been looking forward to that bacon.

It had been a long day, he was tired, and he felt he deserved some compensation for having sat by the side of a road next to a broken-down van for two hours.

"Ah, but I didn't know it was yours, bruv. I didn't realise."

"You didn't realise?" Kester repeated incredulously. "Who else would it have belonged to? Daisy's a vegetarian!" He paused. "Hang on, aren't you a vegetarian too?"

Pineapple nodded, then shook his head. Then nodded again. "I'm a porkatarian," he said, clearly pleased with himself. "I only eat pig-based meat. Not any other sort. You feel me?"

"No. Not at all," Kester muttered. He lurched towards the front door, feeling utterly furious with the world in general.

"Hey, where you going?" Pineapple called after him. "You only just come in, man."

"I'm going to the shop to buy some more bacon," Kester shouted angrily as he swung the door open.

"Oh sweet, could you pick me up some chocolate when you're there? I really got the munchies."

Kester growled and slammed the door behind him.

He trudged furiously down the pavement, tried to thrust his hands angrily in his jacket pockets, then realised he'd forgotten to put his jacket on. The autumnal evening air hit him with unpleasant coldness, making his dire mood even more lemon-curdlingly sour than before.

A car soared casually past, showering him in freezing puddle water. Kester wasn't normally one to swear, but he felt the occasion called for it. His best work trousers were now plastered damply against his legs, and the positioning of the splash made it look uncomfortably like he'd wet himself.

Grumbling under his breath, he stormed into the local store. *Woe betide them if they don't have bacon,* he thought vengefully and glowered in the direction of the chilled cabinet. *I may just strangle someone if they don't have bacon.*

He peered at the selection of meats, trying not to meet

the eye of the person standing close by, who, judging by the ominous parka hood draped over their face, was clearly some sort of petty criminal.

"My goodness, you look like you are about to kill someone!"

Kester looked up. He recognised the voice, though he wasn't sure where from. A slender hand emerged from the thick parka sleeve, pulling the hood back and releasing a smooth fountain of dirty-blonde hair.

She smiled. "Remember me?"

Kester reddened, then grinned sheepishly. "Yes, of course," he replied, trying not to notice how pretty she was, despite the geeky black-rimmed glasses sitting on her nose. "You're Anya from the library," he said, remembering their last encounter a few months before. They'd met when he had been researching the Bloody Mary case, and, even more importantly, she hadn't seemed to notice either his bespectacled gawkishness or sizeable belly. "Are you still working there?"

She nodded, then waved a bottle of cheap gin in his direction. "Yes, that's right, I cannot believe you remember my name! That is so nice!"

He felt his face turn from pink to a humiliating shade of puce. "Yes, I do remember, you were very helpful," he said. He also remembered, with deep embarrassment, bumping into her by the river and thinking that her pet ferret had been a rat.

"So, who are you going to kill?" she asked, gesturing at the chilled cabinet. "The cocktail sausages? The ham?"

"My housemate actually," Kester replied with a wry chuckle. "He ate the last of my bacon."

"Oh, that is not fair," she replied seriously. "Where I come from, if someone takes your bacon, you're free to . . . how do you say? Castrate them. That's right."

Kester laughed nervously. "I take it that's not true."

Anya laughed loudly. "No, don't worry, it's not true. Denmark is very civilised, we don't go around cutting off private parts. But bacon is a big deal." She reached inside the cabinet, pulled out a packet and presented it to him. "Here you go. Danish bacon. Only the best!"

Kester took it from her, laughing. "Yes, you're probably right. Always nice to meet a fellow connoisseur of fine cured meats."

Her eyes twinkled in the artificial light, bright as miniature stars. "Yes. We should meet up for a bacon sandwich sometime, don't you think?"

Oh, my goodness, has she actually just asked me out on a date? Kester thought with an alarming blend of excitement and heart-stopping panic. *Surely not. She's probably doing another strange Scandinavian joke.* He looked down at the floor awkwardly, caught sight of his damp trousers, which looked more horrifically like he'd wet himself than he'd imagined, and quickly twisted his legs together.

"Well, what do you think?" Anya said, giving him the full wattage of her dazzling smile, complete with endearingly gappy front teeth. "I know a place in town that does a great fried breakfast."

"Well . . . yes. I mean, yes, that would be lovely."

"We can talk about books more," she said enthusiastically. "You're like me, I can tell, you love books, right?"

"I certainly do," Kester replied, daring to smile. "Okay then. Er . . . when did you want to meet?"

Anya delved into her pocket and pulled out a battered mobile phone. "Tell me your number, I'll give you a call? That's easiest."

"Oh yes, quite so," Kester replied, trying to look as casual as possible even though his heart was thumping uncomfortably against his ribs. *Is this really happening?* he wondered and glanced down at his bacon in disbelief. *Or am I hallucinating because I've had such an awful day that I've passed out somewhere? Am I actually lying on the pavement outside, getting soggy, and dreaming all of this?*

"So?"

"So what?" he spluttered, snapped out of his reverie.

"What's your number?"

Oh Christ, what is my number? Kester thought with panic. In the anxiety and excitement of the moment, he couldn't remember any of it. And he'd left his phone at home, stuffed into the pocket of his suit jacket.

She waited patiently. "Does it begin with 07?" she suggested with a giggle.

Come on, you cursed brain, remember it! Kester reprimanded himself. Trust his memory to let him down at a moment like this. He'd always suspected that his mind was plotting against him, ensuring that he'd never ever get a girlfriend, and now he had conclusive proof.

Finally, he managed to remember it and choked it out in a rush, in case he forgot it again. Anya grinned, then popped her phone back into her coat. She shook her bottle of gin in his direction.

"I'd better go and pay for this," she said, winking. "I need it, after the day I had today."

"Oh yes, and er . . . I need my bacon." He jiggled the packet enthusiastically in the air, then promptly lowered it, feeling idiotic.

He returned home feeling distinctly happier than he had been when he left it. Even the thought of his irritating house-mates couldn't dampen his spirits. *After all,* he thought, not even noticing the cold, *I've just been asked out on a date. Or at least, I've been asked to go to a café with a member of the opposite sex, which is closer to a date than any other incident in my life thus far.*

To his relief, the house was quiet, suggesting that the others had already left for their rave. He sighed with satisfaction, relishing the prospect of a night in front of the television. Just him, the bacon sandwich, a glass of wine, and a good documentary. Perfect.

A dull buzzing pulled his attention to his suit jacket, which was still hanging on the bannister. It took him a while to realise that it was his phone, still left on silent after the meeting at Larry Higgins's agency.

Gosh, she's keen! he thought with a gleefulness that verged on self-satisfaction. Hastily, he fished his phone out just before the vibrating stopped.

"Oh." The screen indicated that it was his father, not Anya. Kester tried not to feel disappointed and quickly hit redial. "Hello Dad, what's up? Bit late for you to be calling, isn't it?"

A strange sputtering noise wafted eerily through the phone like a pitiful ancient bullfrog croaking out a final chorus.

"Dad?" Kester repeated uncertainly.

"You must . . . you must . . ."

Kester's eyes widened. "God, Dad, are you alright?"

An abrupt stampede of dry coughs echoed through the receiver. Kester waited, bacon temporarily forgotten.

"Kester?"

"Yes, I'm still here. What's the matter? You sound awful."

"I need you. Need you here, my boy. Please, come now."

Kester scratched his head. "How can I get there? I don't drive, do I?"

"Taxi, silly boy!"

Kester felt himself brighten a little. If his father could still summon up the energy to insult him, he couldn't be that ill.

"I haven't got any money, apart from two pound fifty in my pocket."

His father tutted indignantly. "I will pay, then! Just come soon. Come now. Please."

The line went dead. Kester gawped aimlessly at the hallway mirror, caught sight of his reflection, and wondered, not for the first time, whether or not his father was actually, *really* his father after all. There wasn't much of a resemblance, either in appearance or temperament. Dr Ribero was all fire and energy, with leonine sleekness and ageing elegance. Kester was rather more like a slightly overstuffed rag doll with affable features, wispy hair, and a perpetual look of worry on his face.

"Marvellous," he muttered sarcastically, then phoned for a taxi cab. *So much for the bacon,* he thought, rolling his eyes at the kitchen. *Looks like I'll be going hungry tonight.*

It took twenty minutes for the cab to arrive and a further twenty minutes to get across to the other side of the city. By the time they pulled up at his father's ranch, Kester was more than ready to get out, especially given the driver's tendency to grumble about every aspect of the journey.

"What a bloody awful track to drive down. Nearly bleedin' sent me off into the ditch, it did." The taxi driver rapped at the meter, which indicated £9.60 was owing. "I should charge extra for havin' to clean muck off me vehicle. You didn't say it was in the middle of nowhere."

"Yes, I'm sorry about that," Kester said as he scrambled out of the car. "Blame my father for living out here."

The taxi driver shook his head belligerently. "Hurry up and get the cash then," he muttered, peering up at the property. "Strange gaff your dad's got, ain't he? Like a ranch or something. Looks like it should be in the Wild West."

"Yes, he's Argentinian," Kester explained, then he exited the car and ran up to the front door. He didn't think he could endure much more of the driver's moaning, especially after the day he'd had.

He rapped as forcefully as he could.

"Ah, what took you so long?" Ribero threw open the door, resplendent in his red velvet smoking jacket and stripy pyjama bottoms. He looked over at the taxi. "That's a very dirty car. We should pay him less, right?"

"No, we shouldn't," Kester said firmly and clicked his fingers impatiently at the leather wallet in his father's fist. "He needs

£9.60."

"How much?" Ribero squawked, eyeing the taxi with suspicion. "That is daytime robbery, yes?"

"Not really, it's about the going rate," Kester retorted, a wave of tiredness suddenly coming over him. He really didn't have time for any of this, and he was feeling even more put out now he could see that his father wasn't actually ill at all. *What exactly has he dragged me up here for?* he wondered. Was he just wanting someone to offload to? Did he want details about the Larry Higgins meeting? Either way, Kester wasn't terribly enthused by the prospect.

Still muttering, his father marched down the drive like a knight about to do battle. He swooped down to the window of the taxi, then exchanged terse words with the driver, which Kester couldn't quite hear. With a screech of tyres on gravel, the car suddenly reversed, leaving Ribero shouting angrily in Spanish and shaking his fist.

"What happened?" Kester asked reluctantly, massaging his temples.

"That man, he told me that he has no change for ten-pound note. I told him that is a criminal offence. So, he starts to swear at me, then drives off like a little Cockney coward."

"Oh well," Kester rationalised, as he pulled his father gently by the sleeve. "Let's not get too upset about forty pence. Shall we go inside?"

Dr Ribero nodded crossly and padded down the hallway, slippers swooshing across the polished wooden floorboards. The wall lamps cast an inviting amber glow, almost like sunlight, and, despite himself, Kester suddenly felt rather glad he'd come. *I wish my house was a little bit more like this,* he thought as he followed his father into the kitchen. *And less like a horrible bedsit with no heating.*

"Well?" he began, as he leant against the fridge. "Why did you want me to come over tonight?"

His father gave a dramatic sigh, then sank down by the breakfast bar and poured himself a large glass of Merlot.

"It is too awful," he said finally and waved his glass ominously in the air to emphasise the point.

"What is?"

"Everything."

With this existentialist declaration, Ribero sank down against the wall, clutching his head with the desperation of a man trying to stop his brains falling out of his skull.

"Everything, as in working with Larry Higgins?" Kester guessed as he helped himself to a glass.

"As in the Higgins. As in the Agency. As in *everything*."

"And how can I help with that?" Kester didn't mean to sound curt, but he failed to see the point of being dragged over here, only to hear his father spout forth about the injustice of the world.

Ribero pursed his lips together, then clicked his fingers at his cigarette case, which Kester dutifully slid across to him. With expert speed, Ribero pushed a cigarette into his silver holder, lit it with a single flick of his lighter, and inhaled deeply. He pointed its glowing tip directly at his son.

"You can help," he said seriously. "In fact, Kester, it is only you who can help. You, and you alone. You see?"

"No, not really."

"You are the next generation, yes?"

Kester wasn't quite sure where the conversation was going, and furthermore, he wasn't convinced he wanted to go along with it.

"Ye-es," he said slowly, raising his glass to his lips and taking a fortifying gulp. As ever, it was excellent wine, though Kester now knew not to expect anything less than good quality Argentinian booze at his father's house.

"So, it is up to you to step to the mark, right?"

"I thought I had been stepping to the mark," Kester replied

testily. "I thought that was why I went to the meeting today, to represent you in front of Larry Higgins?"

Ribero winced and drew heavily on his cigarette. The smoke tendrilled gently out of his nostrils like two sinewy trails of evening mist. "Ah, yes," he acknowledged. "But I mean more than that."

"Like what?"

"Like, who will take my place when I am done?"

"Done doing what?"

"Done with the job, silly boy!" Ribero snapped, pressing his index finger against the wooden surface of the breakfast bar. "Done with life. I am an old man now. Who will take on the agency after me, eh?"

Kester frowned. "Not me, I hope."

"Yes, you, I hope!" Ribero barked, pummelling the table for emphasis. "Why not you?"

"I'm only twenty-two; I don't think I'd be a terribly good candidate for managing an agency. Not to mention the fact that your entire business is based around the supernatural, and I'm scared of ghosts."

"Ah," Ribero shushed, waving his hand dismissively. "You are not scared of them anymore. And you should be more scared of me getting angry because you won't take your place in the family business."

"Actually," Kester replied, choosing his words carefully, "it's Miss Wellbeloved's family business really, isn't it? I mean, her father owned it, and her grandfather and . . ." He faltered to a stop, quailing under his father's indignant glare.

"But it is the Ribero business now. And you are a Ribero, yes?"

"I'm not though, am I? I've got Mum's surname. Always have had."

Ribero snorted with the skulking ferocity of a bull, then poured himself another sizeable glass of wine, which he quaffed with alarming speed. He wiped his lips, slammed the glass on the table, then directed an accusing finger in his son's direction.

"You may be called Kester Lanner, but you are a Ribero by birth."

"Nope, it definitely says Lanner on my birth certificate."

"That is paper!" Ribero exclaimed, cheeks reddening. "I am talking blood. Thick, rich Argentinian blood that runs through your body, yes?"

Kester looked down at the puny blue veins of his wrists. It didn't look terribly Argentinian to him. "I suppose so," he said hesitantly. "But what does that matter? I'd make a useless manager of the agency. I don't really know the first thing about running a business, much less dealing with spirits."

Ribero grinned suddenly and held a triumphant finger in the air. Kester felt his stomach sink. With a mouth full of gleaming teeth, his father looked uncomfortably like a great white shark about to chow down on a little fish. He watched with growing alarm as Dr Ribero rummaged in the drawer next to him until he found what he was looking for.

"So, if you don't know how to run a supernatural business, you learn, right?"

Oh no, Kester thought, following the huge brochure in his father's hands as it was slapped loudly in front of him. *You cannot be serious.*

He looked down at the front cover.

"The SSFE?" he read aloud, frowning. Then his eyes travelled to the line below. "Ah. I see. The School of Supernatural Further Education. Hmm."

"That is where I got my qualification," his father declared, then prodded it several times, just in case Kester hadn't noticed the front cover. "It is the highest ranking school in the world for supernatural education. I have already picked the right course for you, okay?"

No, not really, Kester thought, opening the brochure and

skimming through the contents. Apart from the obvious ghostly slant to the prospectus, it looked much like any other university brochure, full of smiling, smug-looking students reading various books and pointing at attractive buildings.

"I can't go here," Kester said finally as he closed the brochure. "Firstly, why would they let me in, given I've only been doing this supernatural lark for five minutes? And secondly, it's in London. I don't want to go to London."

Dr Ribero rolled his eyes extravagantly, stubbing out his cigarette with a hiss. "This is not the Middle Ages, Kester. This is the twenty-first century! The age of the internet. You learn online, like everyone else does."

"Oh," Kester said. He took a breath, then opened the brochure again. "Well, I suppose that's a bit different."

"And you like doing the academic stuff, right?"

"Yes, I do like doing the academic stuff."

"See?" his father concluded, leaping on the vague sign of enthusiasm. "You would love it. And then you will be ready to take over the agency. And everyone is a winner."

Kester scrunched his nose and looked thoughtfully into the distance. "None of these courses sound terribly useful though," he said, flicking through the index. "I mean, an MA in Poltergeist Studies? A BSc in Spirit Communication and Negotiation? How's that going to help with the agency?"

Ribero leaned over and rolled his thumb down the page until he found what he was looking for. "There," he said with a significant nod. "This one."

Kester read on. "A BA in Spirit Intervention and Business Studies? Well, I suppose that does sound plausible."

"It is very plausible!" his father barked, jabbing at the brochure. "So, you will enrol, yes?"

Kester glanced out of the window. The pines brushed against the panes, reminding him suddenly of his old home in Cambridge: how the branches of the beech trees used to scratch at the windows and keep him awake. *Except back then, I thought monsters and ghosts were all make-believe,* he thought with a dry smile. *Rather ironic that I was completely wrong about that. Still, it's a good thing I didn't know at the time, I suppose.* "Can I take the brochure away with me and have a think about it?" he said finally.

His father's eyes narrowed. "Well, don't think too long. I know what you are like. All thinking and no doing."

Kester smiled. He glanced down at the page again. *A BA in Spirit Intervention and Business Studies,* he mused as he tapped at the smooth surface of the page. *I suppose that might be interesting.*

"The teacher of the course has a strange name," he said, looking over his glasses. "Dr Ark'han Barqa-Abu. He sounds fascinating."

"She," Dr Ribero corrected. "Dr Barqa-Abu is a very respected supernatural expert. I went to many of her lectures when I was studying there."

"Blimey, how old is she?"

"I think about three thousand, give or take?"

Kester choked on the remnants of his wine and sprayed his father with red droplets.

"Excuse me?" he spluttered, pounding his chest to dislodge the wine. "I presume you didn't mean three thousand years old, did you?"

Ribero reached into his breast pocket and pulled out a silk handkerchief. He dabbled his face deliberately, tutting his disapproval.

"I mean exactly what I say," he replied with a stony glare. "Dr Barqa-Abu is a Jiniri."

"What the heck is one of those?"

"Ah, my goodness!" Ribero exclaimed as he shook his fist towards the ceiling. "A Jiniri! You know, one of the Djinn. You know what I mean."

"Nope, haven't got a clue."

"A genie!" Ribero stormed. "Have you learnt nothing since you have been with us, eh? How can you not know this?"

"A genie?" Kester repeated, blinking furiously. "You mean, like an Aladdin-style genie that lives in a lamp?"

"I pray you never say that in front of Dr Barqa-Abu, for your sake," Ribero said with a dark look. "The Djinn are ancient spirits. Very respectable. Not nasty gimmicky things that live in lamps. They get very upset if people say that. Understood?"

Kester scratched his head. "But I don't get it," he said, struggling to get his head around the concept. "I thought you were trying to get rid of spirits, now you tell me that some of them are teachers?"

"Not many," Ribero clarified. "Only few spirits are able to live alongside humans. Mainly the very old ones, like daemons and the Djinn, who are also very sensible. Well, most of them are."

"I'm not sure how I feel about being taught by a genie," Kester replied. He thought back to all the spirits he'd encountered so far and shuddered.

"Oh, don't you let Jennifer hear you say that," Ribero cackled. He eased off the bar stool and paced elegantly towards the lounge, glass in hand. "She would say you were being a spiritist."

"What the heck is a spiritist?"

"Someone with the prejudice towards spirits," his father explained before settling into the largest of the leather sofas. Kester ambled to the other, which was pleasingly close to the crackling open fire.

"What, like a racist? But I thought everyone didn't like spirits? This is all very confusing."

The sofa squeaked as Ribero leaned slowly back, draping his arm across the leather like a contented king. "This is why you must go to college," he continued as he twirled the corner of his moustache. "Then these things will not be confusing to you anymore, and you will be a very successful supernatural agency owner, like me. Yes?"

The fire popped suddenly and spat a glowing ember onto the wooden floorboards. Ribero paid it no attention. Indeed, judging by the sheer volume of black marks dotting the floor, it was obviously something that happened on a fairly regular basis. Given that the whole house was built of timber, it was remarkable it hadn't been burnt to the ground.

"So," Kester began slowly, momentarily hypnotised by the dancing flames, "was that why you dragged me over here? Just to tell me to go back to college?"

"I did not do any dragging," Ribero corrected irritably. He glanced down at his hands. Kester glanced too and noted, with surprise, that they were trembling slightly. *I suppose I sometimes forget how old he is,* he realised, feeling a little sad. *It's a shame we didn't know each other when he was younger.*

"Why did you want me to come over tonight, then?" Kester asked. "You could have easily given me this brochure at work tomorrow."

"Well," Ribero began slowly, "it is more than just that. I want to share something with you. Something that I cannot tell the others. Not yet."

Oh god, Kester thought as he scanned the old man's face. *He's going to tell me something awful.* "Go on," he said aloud, trying to keep his voice as neutral as possible.

"There is a reason why you need to be ready to take over the business, okay?"

"What's that then?"

His father sighed, then leant his head against his hand like a weary, woebegone lion. "I've been seeing the doctor recently. And they have finally told me what is wrong with me."

"What?" Kester asked. His father's expression was worrying. He gulped. *Don't tell me the old man's dying,* he thought with sudden panic. *I've only just lost one parent, I don't much fancy losing another.*

"I have got the Parkinson."

Kester bit his lip. "You mean Parkinson's?"

"That is what I said!" his father snapped indignantly. "The Parkinson, yes."

"Parkinson is a talk-show host on television."

"Ah, this is no time to get technical, is it?"

"No, I suppose not," Kester agreed quietly. He thought about it, letting the words sink in. "Gosh," he said finally.

"Yes. Gosh," his father echoed bitterly. "Big lots of gosh." He grasped his wine glass. Too firmly, Kester now noticed. *Firmly so his fingers don't tremble,* he realised. *Poor old man, I wonder how long he's been keeping it from us all?*

"But you can carry on running the agency for now, can't you?" Kester asked. "I mean, it's not a death sentence, is it?"

Ribero shrugged, watching the flickering fire. "It's impossible to say, yes? Some people, they get worse quickly. Some people it takes longer." He leaned forward, then surprised Kester by taking him by the hand. "Look," he began, fixing his dark eyes on Kester's own. "I know I was not there when you were a boy. I know you feel like you don't know me. But this agency, it is my life. I have given myself to it completely. And I could not bear shutting it down. It needs to go on. You see?"

"I do," Kester replied, then gently slid his hand away. "But I'm not convinced I'm the man for the job."

"Well, if you aren't," Ribero replied bitterly, returning his hand to his lap, "then I do not know who is."

Chapter 7: On the Case

The following week in the office was a flurry of activity, quite unlike the ponderous calm that Kester had become accustomed to. Although it was never said aloud, it was quite obvious that everyone was keen to swot up on the doppelgänger case as much as possible, to ensure they gave Larry Higgins absolutely no reason to ridicule them when they met up in Lyme Regis.

Dr Ribero, ruffled by the continual ringing of the phone and the uncharacteristic bustle of his team, retreated to the smoky sanctum of his office, only emerging at small intervals to demand a cup of coffee or a cream cake from the local bakery. Miss Wellbeloved was more severe than usual, and Serena more sarcastic. Even Mike was focused on his work, busying himself with the development of his latest piece of equipment, which, as far as Kester could tell, consisted of some sort of dented tin box with a few red wires popping out the sides. He was relieved when the week was finally over, even though it meant having to face the odious Higgins once again.

The day of the Lyme Regis meeting was portentously stormy. As they drove along the dreary main road into Dorset, weighty clouds rolled restlessly overhead, hanging over the surrounding trees like steel-wire pillows.

"Ah, here we go," groaned Mike as the first raindrops patted against the windscreen. He flicked the wipers on, which squealed in protest on every downward stroke. "Told you it was going to pour down."

"Yes, and it's bloody freezing in here," Serena said as she cranked the heating up. She folded her arms tightly, shivering. "I hate this van," she muttered, mutinously glaring at the others as though it was somehow their fault. "It's more like a bin lorry than a professional vehicle."

"Oh, do stop moaning, Serena," Miss Wellbeloved said from the back seat. She pulled a Tupperware pot from her handbag and opened it up. "Would anyone like a hemp-seed and vegan cream cheese slice?"

"No, but I'll have that Mars bar in the glove compartment," Mike said and clicked his fingers at Pamela, who was squeezed directly in front of it. "Go on love, fish it out for me."

Kester tried hard not to feel jealous as Mike noisily chomped into the chocolate and, instead, peered at the homemade bars on Miss Wellbeloved's lap. They looked disturbingly like slices of baked mud, smeared with curdled foam.

"Would you like one?" she asked hopefully. "I made them only last night."

"That's okay," Kester replied. He patted his stomach. "I'm on a diet."

Serena chuckled. "Doesn't seem to be working out too well for you, whatever diet you're doing."

"I'll have you know that I've lost three pounds!" Kester hastily sucked his stomach in as hard as he could and tried to look dignified. The rain began to fall in earnest, hitting the flimsy roof of the van like nails on a rusty drum.

"The only time you've lost three pounds is when you spent it buying a huge chocolate cake," Serena scoffed. Kester bristled. The comment was unfair, he felt. He *had* lost three pounds. Admittedly, it wasn't much, but he still felt rather pleased with himself, especially given that he was due to go on a date with Anya next week, who had texted him to confirm. *Some people obviously don't think I'm too fat,* he thought, comforting himself. *In fact, maybe she thinks I'm quite dashing, in a nerdy kind of way.*

"So," Miss Wellbeloved said with a stern look, "do we actually know where this café is that we're meeting in?"

"Yep, I typed it into the sat nav," Mike announced, then swerved, narrowly missing a yellow-ponchoed old man pedalling wildly uphill on a rickety bicycle. "I know exactly where we're going."

"You do realise that looking it up on your computer at home, then printing out the directions, isn't the same as sat nav, don't you?" Serena said archly. She scooped up the print-outs and waved them in the air. "In fact, this is just a list of directions. Not sat nav at all."

"Same difference."

"No, it isn't," Serena replied in a sing-song voice. "Sat nav would be a piece of technological equipment, mounted on a smart, modern dashboard, in a car that actually worked. What we've got here is a scrap of paper that's been printed at home on a knackered old printer, in a clapped-out van that should have been written off years ago."

"Will you stop going on about the bloody van?" Mike exclaimed.

"Bet Larry Higgins doesn't drive around in a van like this."

"No," Pamela interrupted, "he probably swans around like an idiot in a convertible, I should imagine."

Mike laughed. "Quite," he agreed. Serena shrugged, conceding the point.

Eventually, they arrived in Lyme Regis. It was hard to see the harbour ahead, thanks to the thick mist rolling off the sea. As far as Kester could tell, it was a typical Victorian seaside town, with narrow streets, quaint houses, and a variety of tempting pubs lining the high street. After a brief argument about directions, they finally located the café down a tiny cobbled street close to the seafront.

Kester braced himself as he climbed out of the van into the soaking rain. He immediately spotted Larry Higgins sitting on a high-backed chair in the window and glowering at them suspiciously through the fogged-up glass.

"Looks like they're here already," Kester shouted over the noise of the downpour. The others didn't react, only filed through the narrow door in grim silence. A large cowbell tinkled invitingly overhead as they crowded into the small, cosy space.

"Took your time," Larry Higgins greeted them without preamble. "What happened? Van break down on the way? And Ribero still hasn't bothered to turn up, I see."

"Good morning to you too, Larry," Miss Wellbeloved said and shook the moisture from her hair. She looked over at the blackboard above the counter, squinting at the menu. "Are we going to be here long, or are we just debriefing before heading over to Errol Baxter's house?"

"Well," Larry said, peering over his half-rimmed spectacles in a horribly sanctimonious manner. "I wouldn't order a full English breakfast and pull out your copy of *War and Peace*, if I were you. I was rather hoping to crack on with things. Keep to the deadline and all."

Kester smiled at Lara Littleton and Dimitri Strang, who were sitting on either side of their boss. Lara gave a cheery wave, before raising her mug of steaming coffee in salute. Dimitri grunted, then looked away, rubbing his trimmed goatee as though pondering on a deep, philosophical matter.

"Have I got time to have a sandwich?" Mike asked as he looked longingly at the list of paninis.

"It's not even ten o'clock yet," Serena snapped. She turned to Larry Higgins and his team, eyed them with open hostility, then elegantly placed herself on the bench by the wall, swinging one stilettoed leg over the other.

"So," she commenced as she patted the table. "Shall we get started?"

Larry Higgins chortled. "You must be Serena Flyte," he said as he studied her with scathing interest. "I've heard about you."

"You've actually met me too," Serena replied, narrowing her eyes. "Back at the London networking event a few years back."

"Did I really?" Higgins retorted. He polished off the last of his hot chocolate, then licked the cream off his lips in a manner that resembled a cow slobbering at a fence post. "Can't say I remember. Anyway, Serena, you'll be pleased to know you're not the only spirit extinguisher on this job. Lara Littleton here is also an expert extinguisher. She graduated with honours last year."

"Oh, so you're new to the job?" Serena said, giving the other woman a hard stare. "I presume you've not had much experience, then."

Lara rubbed her cropped hair. "Nah, I guess I'm the newbie," she drawled with a grin. "I'll just have to watch you, to make sure I learn the ropes."

Serena smiled apprehensively, looking flustered. Kester sat down next to her.

"Right," Larry Higgins began, leaning forward and taking up most of the table. "As promised in the email, Dmitri here has compiled a list of interview questions for the deceased's husband, Mr Errol Baxter. I propose that I conduct the interview, and Lara will sit in with me."

"And Dimitri will be working with me, I presume?" Pamela said, squeezing beside Kester and wedging him uncomfortably close to Serena's bony thigh. "As we're both the psychics?"

Dimitri studied Pamela, his expression twisted into something that might have been a smile, or possibly a panicked grimace. Kester couldn't tell which. *Gosh, he's positively sinister,* he thought with fascination. *He's ideal for this sort of work!*

"Yes, you'll conduct the appraisal of the property," Higgins continued. "See what you can pick up, if there's any residual energy there." He nodded in Mike's direction. "And I take it you've brought along this frequency projector you were talking about on the phone?"

Mike squirmed in his seat. "Well, I thought I'd use my old thermo-projector instead for today."

"What he means," Serena added, "is that he managed to blow the frequency projector up yesterday and hasn't got a clue how to fix it yet."

Mike threw her a murderous look. She winked in response.

"Oh no, that really is a nuisance," Larry Higgins tutted and poked his glasses further up his nose. "I don't see how a thermo-projector will help us in this instance, given that the house has experienced no spectral activity since Deirdre Baxter's death."

"Yes, it's a real cock-up, isn't it?" Serena agreed with far too much enthusiasm. "Mike basically connected the battery to the wrong wire by mistake. We're still finding bits of the frequency projector all over the office carpet now."

"It was malfunctioning!" Mike snarled. "Anyway, the thermo-projector may still pick something up. Sometimes residual cold spots linger for a while."

"Not three bloody weeks!" Higgins spluttered. Mike fell silent and glowered at Serena, who gleefully pretended not to notice.

"So, I presume that leaves myself and Kester to undertake a visual investigation of the property then?" Miss Wellbeloved continued crisply. "Do we know if we have full access to the house?"

Larry Higgins nodded. "Yes. Spoke to Baxter on the phone yesterday, he's happy for us to go nosing through his entire home if we need to. You never know what we might uncover." He looked at his watch, making sure to flash it deliberately in the direction of the others, presumably to emphasise that it was an expensive Rolex.

"It's getting on for quarter past," he concluded. "I suggest we start heading over there now."

In a clutter of screeching wooden chairs, they manoeuvred awkwardly out of the small café into the rain.

"No point getting back in the van," Higgins shouted over the wind as he tugged his anorak hood over his balding head. "It's only five minutes away."

"But it's horrible weather!" Kester squeaked as he squinted down the narrow road. He could scarcely see ten metres in front of them. The mist had created a solid wall of white, only interrupted by the violent darts of rain.

Higgins reached over, slapping him unnecessarily hard on the back. "You're only a youngster," he bellowed as he strode forward into the cold. "You need to stop moaning so much, young man!"

And you need to stop being such an irritating old pillock, Kester thought, giving him a grim look, but followed nonetheless.

As they emerged onto the promenade, the wind hit them with the force of a battering ram—a horrible wall of wet icy-coldness. They struggled along, following Higgins blindly as he marched ahead. After a few minutes, he disappeared down another narrow alleyway, and they sloped after him, desperate to get inside again.

At last, they arrived at a small house with a dishevelled-looking front garden filled with over-stuffed wheelie bins, broken garden tools, and a few weathered garden gnomes. The modern façade, with its metal-poled porch, looked rather out of place amongst the surrounding fisherman's cottages—like a mongrel at a pedigree dog show.

"This'll be the place then, right, boss?" Lara said as she peered sceptically upwards. Dimitri wrinkled his nose and shoved his hands deeper into his leather jacket pockets. Kester thought he looked rather like an angry eagle with his sharp features and overhanging brow; he could tell the Russian didn't approve of this house or, indeed, the entire town.

"Absolutely, this is the place," Higgins confirmed and shook the rain off his hood. "Shall we?"

"Anything to get out of this horrible weather," Pamela said, prodding Larry Higgins in an over-familiar manner. Without waiting for a response, she pushed through the crooked garden gate and pressed the doorbell.

A cheap mechanical doorbell chimed from somewhere within the house, and a few seconds later, the door inched open. Through the crack, a dark eye and wiry grey beard appeared.

"I take it you're the agency then?" Errol Baxter rumbled, arthritic fingers curling around the doorframe.

"Yes sir, Larry Higgins's Supernatural Services, that's correct," Higgins announced and patted himself on the chest.

"Dr Ribero's Agency of the Supernatural is here as well," Miss Wellbeloved hastily added.

The door opened fully, releasing a potent gust of scrambled eggs and burnt toast into the air.

"You'd best come in then," Mr Baxter muttered and gestured into the dingy hallway. "I've not tidied, so you've been warned."

I should say not, Kester thought. He surveyed the threadbare floral carpet, the nicotine-stained wallpaper, and the thick dust lacing the dado rails. It was a house that had given up and lost hope, eerily still and grimy, just waiting until the day its owner moved out and consigned it to demolition. He shivered. If he'd have been the more superstitious type, he would have said that the house had a bad atmosphere. Judging by the frowns on Pamela and Dimitri's faces, their psychic powers were telling them the exact same thing. There was something that just felt very *off* about the place, a lingering millieu of airlessness and hostility that made him instantly want to turn around and go back to the van without looking back.

"How does this work then?" Errol Baxter asked wearily. He crossed his arms over his shirt, which had faded in the wash to an unpleasantly dreary grey.

"Well, for starters, a cup of tea wouldn't go amiss," Mike suggested.

"Excuse me, I don't believe Mr Baxter has offered you one!" Higgins hissed, cheeks reddening. "I do apologise, Mr Baxter— Mike has momentarily forgotten his manners."

Errol Baxter waved the comment away. "It's not a problem," he said, then without another word, lumbered towards the kitchen.

"What?" Mike said defensively as he caught sight of Higgins's glare. "I only asked for a cuppa."

"We're here to work, not for a tea party!"

"Jeez, calm down. It's not as though I asked him for a three-course sit-down dinner, is it?"

Miss Wellbeloved scowled, then pointed a warning finger at both of them. "No fights!" she hissed. "Let's try to show some decorum in front of our clients, shall we?" Kester noticed with satisfaction that even Larry Higgins had the decency to look abashed.

With a final warning glare, she strode down the hallway towards the kitchen, and the others followed, obedient as a line of lambs following their mother.

The kitchen was no better than the front of the house. Kester couldn't tell if the cupboards were meant to be beige or whether years of dirt had simply attached themselves to the formica surfaces. He noticed that several dead flies lay on the windowsill—their legs sticking plaintively into the air like minute twigs. *Poor sods,* he thought, looking around. *It's like a little graveyard for bugs.*

The kettle finished boiling, and Mr Baxter poured out some tea into several chipped mugs. Kester was handed one that said

"World's Best Grandad" on the side, and he sipped it tentatively, trying not to notice the slightly sour flavour.

"So," Mr Baxter began as he leant next to the sink and looked at them warily. "What exactly do you need to know then? I don't understand how all of this works, you see. Before a few months ago, I didn't even believe in any of this supernatural stuff."

"That's only to be expected," Miss Wellbeloved reassured him. "We can only imagine how hard the last few months have been for you, and we'd like to offer our condolences."

Mr Baxter sighed and gazed out of the window. "She was a good girl. A bit of a mouth on her at times. She'd let herself go a bit too. But she had a good heart. She didn't deserve what happened to her."

Larry Higgins coughed pointedly. "Well, it's all very straight-forward," he began, getting back to business. "Myself and Miss Littleton here would like to ask you a few questions, and if you're happy for my colleagues to look around the house, that would be most appreciated."

Mr Baxter frowned. "I don't mind, but I can't imagine what you hope to find. Nothing's changed since she was alive."

"We will be examining the residual energy," Dimitri drawled and eyed the kitchen with obvious distaste.

"The residual what? What the blazes does that mean?"

Pamela bustled over to the sink. "Psychic energy, love," she explained patiently. "Every creature, whether they're a spirit or human, produces energy. This often stays in the atmosphere long after the creature in question has gone."

"Especially if it is bad," Dimitri added severely.

Pamela nodded. "That's right. And Mr Baxter, I'm already picking up energy in this house, and plenty of it. That'll give us an idea of what sort of spirit we're dealing with."

"I looked it up online," Mr Baxter said suddenly. "It was difficult, I'm none too good with this whole internet thing.

Normally I ask my daughter to help, but obviously you've all told me I'm not allowed to tell anyone about this."

"What did you find online?" Kester asked, suddenly more interested. Research was definitely his thing, and he loved nothing more than nosing around on websites and in books, ferreting out useful information.

"About doppelgängers. That's what this ghost is, ain't it? A doppelgänger?"

"I can see you've done your homework well, Mr Baxter," Miss Wellbeloved said approvingly. "We believe that you may be right. We believe your wife has been the victim of a doppelgänger, much like the other murdered people of Lyme Regis, and we're going to do our best to stop it."

Mr Baxter spluttered on his tea. "Sounds a bit like a Sherlock Holmes story, doesn't it?"

Larry Higgins puffed out his chest. "And I like to model myself on the great Holmes," he declared, smugness tugging at the corner of his lips. "I take great pride in my detective skills. That's why I am where I am today, sir."

Mike coughed out something under his breath that sounded suspiciously like the word *prat*.

"Dunno what I can tell you, really," Mr Baxter said as he placed his mug down on the draining board. "I've not much recollection of it all, to be honest. Only her saying she could see herself. And me, having a strange feeling like she'd been taken or fetched by something. It was most queer, it really was."

"That's strange, what do you mean?" Kester asked with a frown. *That's an odd choice of words,* he thought. *Why fetched?*

"Excuse me, it's my responsibility to conduct the interview," Higgins interrupted and shot Kester a hostile look. "Shall we commence, Mr Baxter?"

Mr Baxter grimaced. "Very well," he said. "Let's get started. I'd like to get it over with as soon as possible, if you don't mind. I don't really like reliving it, to be honest."

"Understood," Higgins concluded and gestured grandly towards the hallway. "Shall we have our little chat in the living room and leave my colleagues to conduct their investigations?"

As soon as Higgins, Lara, and Mr Baxter had disappeared, Mike pulled out a battered box with some sort of copper funnel on the front from his rucksack. He waved it in the air. "I'll get started then, shall I?"

Miss Wellbeloved looked mildly embarrassed. "Mike, I hate to say it, but in this instance, I do rather agree with Larry. I fail to see what good a thermo-projector is going to do here, given that the murder took place so long ago."

Mike pursed his lips together, beard twitching with irritation. "Well, I've just got to do my best, haven't I?" he muttered. "Given that the bloody frequency projector blew up."

"It looks like a sardine tin," Dimitri observed, narrowing his dark eyes.

"Well, it's not," Mike barked back. "It's a highly sophisticated piece of equipment that I designed myself, thank you very much."

"It is . . . dented."

"No, it's meant to be like that."

Serena sniggered. "Mike, that's a lie. It's because you dropped it on the floor a while back and haven't bothered to hammer it back into shape yet."

"Yeah, well, I didn't think I'd be needing it for a while, did I?"

"No, thinking isn't generally your specialism, is it?"

"Why don't you just do one, you smart-arsed little—"

"Right!" Miss Wellbeloved clapped her hands decisively. "Enough chit-chat. Let's get on with this. Pamela, Dimitri, do you want to carry on? Serena, you're going to work on your own."

"But why?" Serena asked plaintively. "I'd be much better use with you guys, seeing what we can find."

"Absolutely not," Miss Wellbeloved stated and waved a stern finger in the air. "You won't be able to resist making sarcastic comments while Kester is trying to concentrate. And you're definitely not going with Mike."

"Thank the lord for that," Mike added.

"Fine," Serena said defiantly, placing her hands on her hips, black-clad legs wide apart. "I work better alone anyway."

Dimitri smiled. It was the first time Kester had seen him do so, and he couldn't work out whether the gesture made him look debonair or even more sinister than usual. He glided out of the room, following Pamela, gaze still firmly fixed on Serena, who was completely oblivious.

"Shall we?" Miss Wellbeloved suggested and smiled at Kester.

"Lead the way," Kester replied. They clambered up the narrow staircase, avoiding the bannisters, which were mottled with grime. The upstairs was even darker than below, with hardly any natural light entering through the narrow landing window. He peered into the nearest room, which happened to be the bathroom.

"Bit of a pong," he commented, nose wrinkling. The décor was classically 1970s in style, complete with pink toilet rug, plastic panelled bath, and knitted poodle over the toilet roll.

"I don't think we'll find much in there, but we'll check it out later," Miss Wellbeloved replied. Mike whisked past them, thermo-projector suspended in the air.

"Why are you starting in there?" Kester asked curiously. "There's not likely to be any spirit activity to pick up on in the bathroom, is there?" Mike frowned, then waved them urgently out of the room.

"I need the toilet, if you don't mind," he said and closed the door.

Miss Wellbeloved sighed. "I do hope I don't need to remind him to flush," she muttered, massaging her brow.

They went into the next room, which, judging by the

generous dimensions, was clearly the master bedroom. Kester looked around with interest. *So, this is where it happened,* he thought, studying the bed. *This is where Errol Baxter found her in the morning—dead.*

"It doesn't feel right, does it?" Miss Wellbeloved whispered as she looked around. "I mean, I'm not a psychic, but even I can tell that this room doesn't feel nice at all."

"I know what you mean," Kester said with a shiver. The room felt *bad,* like a piece of food with mould growing insidiously around the edges. It had a deep, musty odour of fear—acrid and potent—that seeped out of the plywood fitted wardrobes and bamboo bedside tables. *I can't imagine how Mr Baxter still sleeps in this room,* he thought with a shudder. *It still reeks of death . . . and something worse.*

He walked over to the dressing table, peering out of the net curtains at the small garden below. It was wildly overgrown; a lone, naked fig tree was in one corner, and the flower bed was a mass of waist-high weeds. Kester tugged at the drawer tentatively, and it immediately slid open.

Nothing of much interest, he thought, dimly aware of Miss Wellbeloved rooting around in the wardrobe behind him. He pulled out an old book. *Mills and Boon,* he read. *The Highway Man's Lover.* The cover showed a scantily-clad, heaving-bosomed lady cowering beneath a man in a mask. *Looks raunchy,* he thought and placed it carefully back down. *Not what I would have imagined an old dear to be reading.*

There were a few cosmetics in the drawer, though most looked well past their use-by-date. One lipstick was rusted down the side—orange copper showing through the plastic veneer. *I didn't even know they made metal-cased lipsticks anymore,* Kester mused. *It looks like it should be in a museum.*

"This is interesting," Miss Wellbeloved murmured. Kester quickly looked around.

"What have you found?"

"Look at this for a collection."

Nestled at the bottom of the wardrobe, concealed by a thick winter coat hanging directly above, was a box, now lying open. Kester frowned, peering over his glasses.

"Tarot cards?"

"I know. A strange thing to have hidden in your wardrobe, don't you think?" Miss Wellbeloved commented as she straightened her knees with an audible crack.

"I'll take a photo, shall I?" Kester offered. He whipped his mobile phone out.

"Anything in the dressing table?"

"Not much," he replied with a shrug. "Only a saucy book and some ancient lipsticks."

Miss Wellbeloved smoothed a stray hair from her forehead. "Try the bedside tables."

Kester got to work, but all he could find there was a Crunchie bar wrapper, some angina pills, an old *Woman's Own* magazine, and another steamy novel. He paused, tugging at his collar. The room was stuffy, not to mention unpleasantly smelly, and it was making him light-headed.

"How are you getting on?"

Kester looked up quickly. Pamela and Dimitri stood at the doorway, both wearing matching expressions of concern.

"We've not uncovered very much yet," Miss Wellbeloved said as she dusted her hands off on her trousers. "I take it you've picked up quite a lot?"

Pamela rubbed her eyes, wincing. "We certainly have," she replied heavily. "To be honest, I'm not sure we can keep looking for too much longer. It's a terrible energy, and it's completely draining us both."

"This house has a very bad aura," Dimitri added vehemently. "And I have been in some of the most haunted houses in Russia, so I should know. I am worried."

Miss Wellbeloved looked concerned. "That's not good news,"

she said. "I do hope we're not in over our heads here."

"I am going outside to get some air," Dimitri announced suddenly. Kester was shocked at how white his face was.

"I'm going to join you," Pamela said. "It's this room. This room is the worst."

They lumbered out, and Kester turned to Miss Wellbeloved questioningly. She shrugged. "Let's carry on," she concluded simply.

Kester crouched down by the bed, flinching at the sour smell of the bedsheets. He lifted the flowery divan, spotted the drawer handle, and pulled it open.

Oh boy, he thought with an inward groan as he noticed all the loose papers piled up inside. *There must be hundreds of bits of paperwork in here.* "Fancy lending me a hand?" he called over his shoulder. "Otherwise it'll take me all day to go through this stuff."

"Gosh, that's a big pile, isn't it?" Miss Wellbeloved muttered and crouched beside him. Although she was clearly as unsettled by the smell and the atmosphere as he was, he couldn't help noticing that her grey eyes were sparkling with energy, her posture tense with excitement. *She loves this,* he realised. *This is what she does. It's her life.* Her passion for the job injected him with renewed enthusiasm, and he shuffled over to allow her a better view.

Together, they swiftly skimmed the papers. Most were of little interest: old letters from relatives, various deeds for the house, insurance documents, and old bank statements. Eventually, Kester pulled out a piece of paper that looked more modern than the rest.

"Lyme Regis Ancient History Club," he read aloud. "Lifetime membership. Ancient history, eh? That's my sort of club."

Miss Wellbeloved smiled faintly. "I didn't have Mr Baxter down as a historical man, I must confess."

"It's not his membership. Look, it says here, Mrs Deirdre

Baxter."

"I doubt it has much relevance to this case, to be honest."

"I don't know." Kester frowned, peering hard at the paper. "It might be worth looking into."

"Well, if you think so," Miss Wellbeloved replied. She waved another paper under his nose. "Though this one seems a bit more interesting."

Kester read through quickly. "Subscription to *Ghost-Hunter's Monthly*? Sounds like a good read."

Miss Wellbeloved laughed. "It's absolute bilge. The people who produce it clearly have no experience of the supernatural at all. But this, plus the tarot cards, does give us a bit of insight into Deirdre, doesn't it? I wonder if there's any connection?"

Kester shrugged. They continued to rummage but found nothing else of interest, apart from a large grey spider, who retreated angrily to the corner, coiling its long legs protectively over a cracked biro-lid. After fifteen minutes or so, they moved to the spare room, but there was little to be found other than several moth-eaten clothes in an old wardrobe and a bare mattress with some unnerving stains.

"How are you progressing up there?"

They looked up at the sound of Larry Higgins's voice, echoing flatly up the stairs.

"Come on," Miss Wellbeloved said, standing up and brushing her clothes down. "I don't think we're going to find anything else here. Let's hope Larry's had more luck than we have."

Larry Higgins eyed them as they came down the stairs, bobbing his eyebrows violently at their dishevelled appearance.

"Any luck?" he muttered as Kester passed him.

"Not an awful lot, no."

Mr Baxter leaned against the living room door, his expression unreadable. "You all done then?"

"For now, yes," Larry Higgins replied brusquely and handed

Lara his suitcase in an imperious manner. "Many thanks for your time. We'll be in touch if we require anything more."

"Can I just ask a question?" Kester said suddenly. Higgins's eyebrows bobbed even more energetically.

"Yeah, go on then," Mr Baxter agreed reluctantly.

"I noticed your wife was a member of some Ancient History Club—did she attend the meetings often?"

Mr Baxter scratched his head. "Yes, she went every fortnight. It was her social life really, lots of her friends were members. In fact—"

"It probably has no relevance at all," Higgins interrupted and bustled Kester to one side like a hen shooing a wandering chick. "Many thanks for your time, Mr Baxter. We won't disturb you any longer. Come on, let's go and find Dimitri and Pamela. Where's Mike and Serena?"

"Mike's probably still on the toilet," Kester suggested, gesturing up the stairs.

"He'd better bloody not be," Higgins muttered darkly.

After retrieving Mike from the bathroom and Serena from the garden, they departed the house with significant relief. Dimitri and Pamela were huddled beside the gate, looking wet and depressed. The rain had eased to a misty drizzle but provided welcome coolness to Kester's cheeks. In fact, the sea air made his head feel instantly clearer, ridding it of the stuffiness of the Baxters' home; he felt grateful for the cold, even if the weather was insufferably vile.

"Please tell me you got something good," Higgins barked as they marched along the alleyway.

"Yeah, 'cause we got a big fat nothing from Mr Baxter," Lara chirped, straightening her neck-tie. "He didn't much want to talk, unfortunately. Maybe we were just askin' him the wrong questions."

"That's quite enough, Lara," Higgins snapped testily. "I asked perfectly good questions, thank you very much. It's just the gentleman was being particularly reticent with his answers."

"Maybe because he thought you were a moron," Mike muttered from the back of the group. Higgins's eyes narrowed to dangerous slits, but he wisely chose to ignore the comment.

"Sadly, I'm not sure we found out much either," Miss Well-beloved said as she trotted to keep pace with the others. She smoothed her hair, which had frizzed to a wiry grey halo around her head. "Other than evidence that Mrs Baxter was into the supernatural. But I'm not convinced that's going to provide any clues."

"It was a waste of time, I think." Dimitri concluded.

"No, it absolutely was not!" Larry barked, turning a bright shade of crimson. "Every bit of information gleaned may prove useful. Remember that, please!"

"I certainly didn't find anything useful in the garden shed," Serena volunteered.

"Why were you out there in the first place?" Mike asked loudly as he hoisted his bag over his shoulder. "Looking for haunted trowels? Or maybe a possessed plant pot?"

"I was trying to get away from you actually, Mike. Or more to the point, from the horrible smell you left in the bathroom."

They rounded the corner. Kester could just about make out their van in the distance. For the first time ever, he was actually relieved to see it. He felt as though he'd been standing in a power-shower and was soaked from head to foot.

"Let's reconvene later this week," Larry suggested. He peered into the van with obvious distaste as Kester opened the door. "I suggest we take a bit of time to prepare our next interview in the hope that it's a bit more productive than this one."

Miss Wellbeloved nodded wearily. "I'm sure it will be."

"I'm bloody not," Higgins retorted, then moved aside to let Mike squeeze past. "In fact, I'm becoming very worried about the whole project, quite frankly."

Miss Wellbeloved pressed her lips together. "We'll review

things, then give you a call tomorrow."

Higgins harrumphed like a disgruntled elephant, then stalked off without a parting farewell, leaving Dimitri and Lara looking momentarily confused before scuttling after him like two damp puppies.

Miss Wellbeloved clambered into the back of the van, then promptly rested her head against the seat in front. "Oh goodness," she murmured heavily. "What have we got ourselves into?"

Chapter 8: A Date with Anya

Kester tore down the street, hardly daring to look at his watch. *My first date with Anya,* he thought, *and I'm late. I can't believe it.* He'd started researching doppelgängers online, then before he'd known it, time had slipped away from him, leaving him just ten minutes to race into the centre of town. *And running really isn't my thing,* he realised, panicking about the sweat-patches currently blossoming under his jacket. *Talk about how to make a bad impression.*

The fact was, he couldn't leave the case alone, no matter how much he might want to. There'd been something about Mr Baxter's words the other day that had niggled him, though he couldn't put his finger on what it was exactly. It was driving him mad, like a jigsaw puzzle with missing pieces, and the more time he spent pondering it, the more confusing it became. The others seemed so convinced that the spirit was a doppelgänger, but nothing he'd read online, even on the secret Swww. websites, correlated with the evidence in front of them.

We're missing something, he thought when he finally reached the café. *It's just a question of what. However,* he reminded himself as he took a deep breath and pulled open the door, *now probably isn't the time to carry on torturing myself with it.*

Straightening himself as best as possible, Kester stepped into the warmth of the café, which was filled with people enjoying cooked breakfasts and mugs of pleasingly milky-looking tea. Anya was huddled in one of the booths in the corner. It looked as though she'd already ordered, if the plates of steaming food were anything to go by.

He waved, walked over, then looked down at the plate that was obviously his. Then up again, in confusion. Then down once more.

"So, you literally just ordered me some bacon then?"

Across the table, Anya broke into giggles.

"You told me to get you anything," she said, snorting into her coffee. "And bacon was the only thing that I knew you liked."

Kester grimaced. After texting Anya to let her know he'd be late, he'd happily agreed to let her order for him, presuming she'd get him a nice full English breakfast to tuck into. Eight rashers of bacon, no matter how well cooked they appeared, was a little bit much. He sipped at his coffee, studying his date with curiosity. *She's a bit of a weirdo, isn't she?* he thought with a mixture of alarm and delight. *I suppose that works for me, though. It's not like I'm exactly normal, is it?*

"Can I at least have some of your toast?" he asked eventually.

Her face fell. "Yes, of course," she replied and solemnly handed a few slices from the metal rack. "I am sorry, Kester. I don't know why, but I thought you would find it funny. As last time we met, you kept going on about bacon, you see?"

He smiled and chuckled a little. "Yes, I did a bit, didn't I?" Bravely, he scooped up his knife and fork, and got to work, creating a makeshift, overstuffed bacon sandwich. "Would you be so kind as to pass the ketchup?"

She handed it over obligingly, then shook her head. "You know that stuff is full of sugar?"

"Is it?" He placed it carefully back down. *Is anything not full of sugar?* he wondered, balefully eyeing the ketchup bottle. *This bacon has probably been seasoned with a good sprinkling of it too, knowing my luck.*

"Not that you need to worry about that," Anya clarified swiftly as she wiped her lips with the back of her sleeve. Her tartan shirt, combined with her newly dyed hair, which now had streaks of black in it, made her look rather grungier than before, but infinitely cooler. He felt slightly intimidated.

"Come on, I know I'm a bit tubby," he ventured. "But I'm working on it. I've lost four pounds in total now!"

"I think you look fine as you are," she replied. "Too many people are hung up on their looks anyway."

He nodded. "That's certainly true. My colleague, Serena, is always going on about how fat and greedy I am. The other day, she told me I looked like a prize-winning pig in a farm."

Anya snorted loudly, spraying tea across the table.

"Oh god, please say you don't agree with her."

She laughed and dabbed at her eyes. "No, I honestly don't. It's just a funny thing to say. If it's any comfort, I went out with a boy a while back who said I looked like my ferret."

Kester winced. "Ouch. For what it's worth, you look nothing like a ferret. Anyway, at least he didn't think your ferret was a rat, like I did."

"Hey, I'd forgotten that! We met down by the river, didn't we, when I was taking Thor for a walk? A few months ago?"

Kester spluttered through a mouthful of bacon and bread. "Is that really your ferret's name?"

"Yes. I used to have two, but T-Rex died."

"You had a ferret called T-Rex?"

She nodded. "She was a real sweetheart, but very old. And

Thor kept trying to get . . . frisky with her."

Kester nodded sagely. "Ah. He's one of *those* ferrets, is he?"

She pursed her lips together. "Definitely. He will try it on with anything that moves. Including your leg, if I remember rightly."

"Dear lord, was *that* what he was trying to do to me?" Kester blushed at the memory. "I feel violated."

Anya winked. "It is probably because you had such an attractive leg."

Kester chuckled nervously and nibbled on the rest of his sandwich. *This isn't going as horrendously as I thought it would,* he realised, with considerable shock. *In fact, I'm actually making her laugh, not vomit in revulsion!* He was still concerned about the sweat-patches, though he didn't dare check, in case it drew attention to them.

"So," she continued, jolting him out of his thoughts, "what is it that you do, Kester?"

Hmm, tricky question. Kester didn't have a clue where to start. "I work for an agency," he began slowly as he struggled to find the right words. "It's all a bit hush-hush really. We work with the government."

She nodded approvingly. "I knew it would be something interesting," she said. "Aren't you going to give any more away? Maybe you're a spy, like James Bond."

"Not really," Kester laughed. "He's a bit more debonair than me, I think. Do you still work at the library?" It was probably best to divert the conversation before Anya asked any more questions.

She nodded and finished off her tea with a rather loud slurp. Two suited men at the table next to them looked over with disapproval. "I like working there," she said, "because I love books. And I love working with people. There are so many interesting people in Exeter."

Are there? Kester wondered. Perhaps he needed to get out

more. Still, he supposed that his housemates would be classified as interesting. Or odd, at least.

"But," she continued as she scratched at her chin thoughtfully, "it's not the job I always dreamed of doing, you know what I mean?"

Kester thought of his own job and winced. "Yes," he agreed firmly. "Yes, I most definitely do. What do you want to do, then?"

Anya shrugged, then gazed out the window to the busy road. A double-decker bus passed, shaking the rain-specked window panes. "I guess something that uses my real talents," she said finally. Her eyes unglazed, and she smiled. "I am sure one day, the right job will come along. Are you going to eat the rest of that sandwich?"

Kester looked down at his plate. "It's rather a lot of bacon, to be honest."

With the speed of a pouncing cat, she leant over and grabbed the remainder, before popping it into her mouth in a manner that was reminiscent of a frog snapping up a fly. He gaped.

"We don't want to waste it, do we?" she said by way of explanation.

They lingered for a while longer, waiting for the worst of the rain to pass, then ventured out into the street. The cold hit them immediately, a stark contrast to the snug warmth of the café. Anya shivered and tugged her oversized parka around herself. Kester smiled. She really was very pretty, in an erratic kind of way. He felt a sudden urge to wrap an arm around her, to protect her from the elements, but suspected it would be unwise to do so. *Especially if she recoils in a state of shock and repulsion,* he thought with a grimace.

She caught his eye. "Ah," she declared solemnly, dancing to one side as a passing car whooshed through a particularly deep puddle. "You were checking me out, Kester."

"Gosh, I'm sorry, I honestly wasn't . . ."

She pooched her lip, then smartly stepped out into the road. "Well, why not?"

Kester stuttered. He had no idea how to respond. Nothing in his life thus far had taught him to deal with situations like this. He had a vague notion that this was some form of flirting, but to date, the closest he'd come to flirtation was tickling his pet cat, or blushing whenever he had to talk to the girl in the post office near his childhood home. Thankfully, something else caught his attention instead. Or someone, to be precise—someone tall, dressed in a tassled suede jacket, and striding purposefully towards town.

"Hey, it's Lara!" he announced, pointing to distract from the hot blush in his cheeks. "I wonder what she's doing down here? She works up in Southampton."

Anya peered through the shopping precinct. "Which one is she?"

He pointed. "You can't miss her, she's wearing a cowboy hat."

Lara was scuttling past the shops, head tucked down into her collar. Judging by her pace, she was clearly in a hurry to get somewhere. Kester thought about shouting out to her, but by the time he opened his mouth, she had disappeared into a doorway next to the newsagents.

"How do you know her?" Anya asked.

"She's working with me at the moment . . . on a project," Kester replied cautiously. "She's ever so nice. Texan. Very friendly."

"She looked very striking."

"Yes, she's ever so attractive, in a kind of Wild West, tomboyish way," he replied absent-mindedly. As they approached the door Lara had entered, Kester studied the plaque mounted on the wall. *Tomlins & Wilkins Aesthetic Surgeons.*

"Maybe she isn't as confident about her looks as you think

she is?" Anya commented finally, tapping the sign.

Kester frowned. *That's odd,* he thought. She hadn't struck him as the sort of person to have any insecurity about her appearance. But then, he had only met her twice.

"So, is she someone you are attracted to?" Anya asked suddenly.

He spluttered, then roared with laughter. "No, not at all! I mean, she's a lovely, friendly person, but . . ."

"But what?"

"I don't know. I'm just not. She's not really my type. To be honest, I think she'd eat someone like me for breakfast."

Anya nodded, satisfied. "Like a piece of bacon," she concluded.

Kester thought back to Serena's comment about him looking like a pig and nodded stoically. "Yes, just like a piece of bacon." They caught each other's eye and burst out laughing.

The precinct buzzed with swarms of Saturday shoppers, huddled and tight-lipped from the cold. Kester stuck his hands in his pockets, unsure what to say next.

"What are you doing now?" Anya asked to break the silence.

He looked around. "Well," he began awkwardly, "I haven't got a clue really."

She smiled, then looked at her watch. "I need to head over to work soon," she said. "Why don't you walk over there with me?"

As if I need any excuse to go to the library! he thought with an enthusiastic nod. While he was there, he could log on to the computer and see if he could find out anything more about the Lyme Regis case.

They strolled through the precinct, down past the little historic church—incongruously surrounded by 1960s-built buildings and high street shops—through to the quieter back streets on the other side of the city centre. Kester found himself frequently glancing down at his companion and wondering why she wanted to spend time with him. Although her nose was a little wonky and her eyebrows rather bushy, she was undeniably attractive. And he, as he well knew, resembled a blend of overfed puppy and tortoise that had suffered a particularly nasty shock. What did she see in him?

However, if her behaviour was anything to go by, she certainly seemed to like him. She laughed at all his jokes, even when they were on the feeble side. For the first time in his life, he found himself a little reluctant to arrive at the library, which would bring an end to their date.

They stood awkwardly in the foyer. He smiled, then held out a hand. "It's been very nice talking to you, Anya."

She clasped a hand to her mouth, giggling.

"What? What did I say?"

"Nothing, you are just . . ." she caught his eye, then laughed again. "You are so British!"

Kester raised his eyebrows. "Is that not a good thing?"

Sighing, she leant forward. For a moment, he thought she was going to pat him on the arm, but instead, she clasped it, tilted her head upward, and kissed him on the cheek. He felt blood rush to his face immediately and couldn't stop himself from touching the place where her lips had been.

"Thank you for that," he said, desperately hoping he wasn't blushing too much.

She giggled again. "I've got to get to work. I'm already a little late. But it was nice having brunch with you, Kester."

"Could we do it again sometime?" he asked suddenly, amazed by his own boldness.

She nodded enthusiastically. "That would be nice. I promise I won't make you eat so much bacon next time."

"That's good," he said seriously. "To be honest, I'd started to think you were a bit of a bacon psychopath or something."

"Murdering someone with bacon, now that's an idea!"

"Please don't," Kester shuddered. "It's so salty. Death by

dehydration isn't something I'd relish."

Anya chuckled, then sighed, looking over her shoulder. "I had better get going."

"Yes, I'd better crack on with a bit of research too. For work."

She looked at him quizzically. "Now I am even more curious about what you do."

You really shouldn't be, he thought. He tapped the side of his nose in what he hoped was an alluring manner. "Wouldn't you like to know?"

Watching her disappear to the other end of the library, he let out a deep breath of satisfaction. *That was the first real date I've ever been on,* he thought with a sense of exhilaration, *and I didn't say anything mortifying! I didn't trip over, or get run over by a car, or vomit with fear or anything!* In fact, he thought he'd done rather well, and even better, she'd said that she wanted to see him again. And she'd kissed him! She'd actually leaned up to him and kissed him!

With these cheerful thoughts to buoy him, he headed upstairs to the quiet area and settled himself in front of the nearest free computer. It was difficult to focus on the task. Thoughts of Anya kept floating into his head: her throaty giggle, piercing eyes, and even her crooked nose. Shaking himself, he opened up the internet browser and stared vacantly at the search screen. *Right,* he told himself firmly, *time to concentrate.* The room was completely silent, apart from the steady, comforting hum of the surrounding computers.

Where do I even start with this? he wondered and tapped his fingers gently against the keyboard in contemplation. He typed in "Lyme Regis doppelgänger". Nothing came up, and he wasn't surprised. To be honest, he wasn't even convinced the spirit in question was a doppelgänger. *Perhaps a different approach is needed here,* he mused, staring at the screen. *But what?*

He typed in "Lyme Regis murders". None of the search

results looked relevant, apart from a link to a small article in the local paper. It featured news on the latest death—Meredith Saunders, who had been sixty-seven when she'd been killed—though the article naturally dismissed the incident as an accident.

After wrestling to remove the flashing pop-up ads on the page, he read on. The article didn't tell him anything new, and of course, the paper hadn't mentioned anything supernatural. After all, that was part of Ribero's agency's job, as well as the government's—to ensure the press didn't get even the vaguest whiff of anything ghostly.

"Yes, she slipped in the bath and hit her head on the toilet, I know all this," he muttered to himself as he scrolled down. "What else have we got?"

But a second read-through revealed nothing. Sighing, he returned to the search page and selected the next website on the list. Again, the article was small, though this time it focused on Edna Berry, the second victim, who had died by being asphyxiated by the bell-ringer's ropes. He scrolled through the article earnestly. The victim had been sixty-eight. *Why old people?* he wondered as he tapped the mousepad thoughtfully. *What has this spirit got against the elderly?*

He finished reading, then leant back in his chair, exhaling loudly. Suddenly, his eyes rested on the first paragraph again.

"Mrs Berry, who was an active member of the community and vice-chairman of the Lyme Regis Ancient History Club . . ." He stroked his chin, mulling the sentence over. *Now why does that ring bells?* he wondered, then remembered. *The same club as Deirdre Baxter. That's interesting.*

Quickly, he ran a search for "Lyme Regis Ancient History Club", and clicked through to the website. It was about ten years out of date, with far too much wordy content and some rather odd illustrations. He quickly scanned the home page. For the most part, it was a dense, tedious read— detailing the club's dedication to researching and documenting the ancient heritage of the area.

Kester clicked through to the contact page. *Bingo,* he thought, quickly sifting through his bag for a pen and paper. *Here's the name of the person who runs it. Plus his contact details, which is especially useful.* He jotted down the name—Peter Hopper—then swiftly clicked on the email address link.

Dear Mr Hopper, he typed quickly, *I'm getting in touch with regards to two former members of your club—Deirdre Baxter and Edna Berry—on behalf of a governmental investigation. I'd like to arrange a time we can talk—just to ask a few questions that may be helpful in determining the facts about their deaths. If you'd be so kind as to let me know a time when we can get in touch, that would be most appreciated.*

He signed off, then smiled to himself. It wasn't much of a lead, he knew—but it was worth a shot.

After another half hour of rummaging online, he finally called it a day and logged off. On the way out, he caught sight of Anya, who was helping an old lady to find a book on the shelves. He smiled. It had been an exceptionally good morning—and he hadn't said that in a while.

Perhaps things are looking up, he thought, whistling as he sauntered out into the cold. *Maybe things are going to turn out alright down here in Exeter after all.*

CHAPTER 9: CHATTING WITH THE HIGGINS

At exactly nine o'clock on Monday morning, Dr Ribero strode over to Kester's makeshift desk and slammed the weighty SSFE brochure in front of him, nearly bringing the table down once again.

Kester grabbed at the table legs, glanced down at the brochure, then groaned. "What, you want me to apply for the course now?" he said weakly, then looked up at his father, who towered over him like an Old Testament prophet, glowering in his direction with simmering significance.

"I told you to apply for this last weekend, and then you tell me you have not!" Ribero stormed. "And the weekend before that. You thought you were very clever, leaving the brochure at my house, even when I told you to take it with you. But I am not going to let this drop, my boy!"

"I never said I'd definitely apply for the course," Kester protested as he cowered under the magnitude of his father's righteous indignation.

"It is a good course, a BA no less! What is your problem? I studied at this university. So did Jennifer, and your mother. Serena, Mike, you both studied at the SSFE too, tell this silly boy, please. He won't listen to me."

"It's a good place to study," Mike said automatically, not looking up from the contraption on his desk, which was currently omitting a very ominous, not to mention irritating, hum.

"If you can get in," Serena piped up. "You have to be very good to be accepted."

Mike snorted. "Yeah, right. Like there's thousands of students wanting to study paranormal communications and psychic studies."

"They only take the best," Serena snapped back and flicked her hair irritably.

"If you say so, love."

"Anyway," Ribero interrupted, as he folded his arms in exasperation. "You will have no problem getting on this course. You are a clever boy, with Cambridge University degree. They will snip you up."

"Snap you up," Miss Wellbeloved chimed automatically from her desk.

"Yes, snip or snap, whatever," Ribero barked. He jabbed the brochure aggressively, making the table buckle again. "Now, you are going to apply, or I will have to apply for you, understood?"

"Julio," Miss Wellbeloved said quickly, before he could swoop back into his office. "You have remembered that we've got that teleconference call this morning, haven't you?"

Ribero stiffened, nose pointing in the air like a dog sniffing a fox. "I told you, I would not be joining in this particular telephone call, Jennifer."

Kester looked over at Miss Wellbeloved, who sighed.

"You can't keep avoiding Larry, you know," she said, fighting to keep the irritation from her voice.

"I'm not avoiding him."

"Well, you're not exactly talking to him, are you?" Mike chimed in helpfully. He twisted his screwdriver, and the humming got louder.

"Look, Julio, I understand you don't like him, but you cannot keep hiding away! It's getting ridiculous!"

Ribero's moustache twitched. "I am not hiding away! Do not make me sound like a coward!"

"Well, you are behaving like one, if I'm being perfectly honest . . ."

"So, don't be perfectly honest then!" With a bear-like snort, Ribero stomped back into his office and slammed the door so hard it made the walls shake.

"You do realise, he's going to keep this up for the entire time we're working with Higgins, don't you?" Serena commented, carefully picking at her fingernails.

Miss Wellbeloved sank her head into her hands without replying.

Kester picked up the brochure and held it at arm's length, as though worried it might burst into flames at any moment. He opened it at the marked page—the BA in Spirit Intervention and Business Studies. His father had pressed home the point by circling the title in bold red pen, complete with several large exclamation marks to ensure Kester was left in no doubt about the importance of the issue.

"This course, designed for students with keen interest in the strategic theory behind spirit/human relations . . ." he muttered aloud, scanning the page.

"You should apply," Mike said suddenly with a nod in his direction.

Kester rolled his eyes. "Not you too," he muttered. "I don't see why everyone is so desperate for me to do this course."

"For what it's worth," Serena said pointedly, "I'm not desperate for you to do it at all. In fact, it will probably be a waste of time."

"Why would it be a waste of time?" Kester said, bristling.

"Because you have no natural aptitude for this kind of work."

"I think I've demonstrated a little bit of ability in the field," Kester replied, glaring over his glasses. She raised an eyebrow, smirked, then returned to her computer screen, tapping her high-heeled foot with infuriating buoyancy. He bit his lip and returned to the brochure. *Maybe I will do it, just to prove her completely, utterly wrong,* he thought. *Then she'll have to eat her smug words.*

Flipping up his laptop, he waited for the system to boot up. A soft ping alerted him to a fresh email in his inbox, and he quickly opened it.

"Excellent," he muttered after a quick scan of the contents.

"Is that from your girlfriend?" Mike asked with a leery wink.

"Goodness me, you've got a girlfriend?" Serena asked. "Is she blind? Or just too ugly to be fussy?"

Kester ignored them both. "It's from Peter Hopper," he announced, then leant back and folded his hands behind his head in what he hoped was a suitably nonchalant manner.

The others waited expectantly.

"Care to elaborate?" Mike said finally.

"Peter Hopper," Kester said, "happens to be the president of the Lyme Regis Ancient History Club. Which," he continued, getting into his stride, "I discovered that two of the victims were members of. Deirdre Baxter and Edna Berry, the vicar's wife."

"Edna Berry, is that the one who got hoisted up in the bell-ringing ropes?"

"The one and the same. Anyway, Mr Hopper has agreed to speak to me. It might be a complete waste of time, but then again, it might not."

"Well done, Kester," Miss Wellbeloved said warmly. "You're so very much like your mother at times. That's just the sort of investigative approach she would have used."

"Hmm, I suppose that is quite interesting," Serena admitted before sinking back below her computer screen. "Nice work."

Kester beamed.

At ten o'clock, after Pamela had rolled in late, blaming a combination of a leaky dishwasher and a broken down bus, they gathered around Miss Wellbeloved's desk for the teleconference call with Higgins and his team.

"I am so sorry, I forgot the cakes," Pamela said, still breathing hard as she threw her pashmina across the back of the chair. Collapsing into her chair, she wiped her brow with her handkerchief.

"Oh, I wouldn't worry," Miss Wellbeloved said crisply. "Julio can live without his cream puffs for one day, and besides, he's too busy sulking in his office to come out and eat cake."

Pamela tutted. "He has to speak to Larry soon. We can't keep on saying he's ill."

Well, he is ill, to be fair, Kester thought, feeling suddenly rather defensive over his father. But of course, the others didn't know about Ribero's Parkinson's diagnosis, so he didn't expect them to understand. Plus, they had a point. His father was being rather ridiculous about the whole thing, unwell or not.

"I'm sure he'll come around eventually," he said mildly as he positioned his notepad in front of him. "Just give him time to adjust to the idea."

"Maybe you could have a word with him?" Miss Wellbeloved suggested. "He does seem to listen to you more than the rest of us."

The phone suddenly rang, interrupting them, and she quickly scooped it up.

"Hello, Dr Ribero's Agency," she chorused. She nodded at the others. "Hello there, Larry; hang on, I'll just pop you on loudspeaker."

At once, Higgins's nasal tones boomed around the office.

"Let's keep this short and sweet, we've got work to get on with. Have you gone through your notes yet?"

"Of course," Miss Wellbeloved replied crisply. "Serena has also been looking into doppelgänger behavioural patterns. This seems to be fairly unusual. Doppelgängers occasionally appear to announce a death, but they don't normally cause it."

"That may be so, but it's undeniably a doppelgänger we're dealing with," Higgins retorted. "In nearly all of the murders, the spouse has mentioned the deceased saying something about seeing themselves."

"It does seem the most obvious choice," she replied uncertainly.

Kester frowned. He still wasn't at all happy with the conclusion, but thus far, he couldn't find any evidence to refute it.

"Serena," Miss Wellbeloved continued, "could you quickly fill Larry, Lara, and Dimitri in on what else you've found?"

Serena cleared her throat and edged closer to the phone, rapping her pile of notes on the table. "Well, lots of things don't add up," she began. "For one, there hasn't been a single doppelgänger case in the UK for over 150 years. That's a long period of silence for any kind of spirit. I also looked through the global database; the most recent case I could find was in Beijing, about ninety years ago. They're not a common spirit, they don't tend to come into our world much. They're certainly not normally aggressive."

Dimitri's clipped voice emerged from the phone. "Maybe it is a rogue doppelgänger?"

Serena shook her head slowly. "Let's be honest," she replied, "it's pretty unlikely. Spirits don't tend to go rogue, they normally stick to their true nature."

"Unless they're daemons," Pamela said. "They've been known to misbehave from time to time."

Miss Wellbeloved shook her head crossly. "Hardly ever, Pamela. And most of the time they're model spirits who behave themselves wonderfully. Please remember that."

"I worked on a case in Moscow where a poltergeist went rogue," Dimitri continued as though they hadn't spoken. "You probably heard of it, the Ulitsa Varvarka case?"

"Oh yes, I did hear of that," Serena said, smiling. "Gosh, you were on that case? That's impressive."

Dimitri chuckled down the line. Mike scowled, looking as though he'd happily like to throttle the Russian with his bare hands.

"Kester's got a lead," he growled, still glaring at Serena. "Haven't you, mate?"

Kester nodded and quickly outlined what he'd discovered about Peter Hopper and the Ancient History Club. Larry Higgins grunted, clearly unimpressed.

"Not much to go on, is it?" he muttered with an impatient sigh. "I mean, I bet all the old gits in Lyme Regis are members of that club. Old people love history, don't they?"

"Dunno. You tell us; you'd probably know," Mike retorted, ignoring Miss Wellbeloved's warning nudge.

Higgins spluttered, obviously wanting to make a sharp retort but managing to hold it in. "Myself and Lara," he continued with deliberate coldness, "discovered that Deirdre Baxter also subscribed to *Ghost-Hunter's Monthly*." He paused for dramatic effect. "If you ask me, that's more of a lead."

"Yes, we discovered the subscription paperwork in their bedroom," Miss Wellbeloved added. "But an interest in the supernatural doesn't necessarily link with a vicious spirit murder, as we all know from past experience."

Higgins coughed. "So, how shall we proceed? Interview Frank Saunders, the husband of the latest victim? What was her name again? Millicent? The old biddy who slipped over in the bathroom, anyway."

"Meredith," Miss Wellbeloved corrected. "It's as good a place as any to start, I suppose."

"While you're doing the interview," Kester added, "I'd like to go and talk to Peter Hopper, if you don't mind. I know you think it's nothing, but I reckon it's worth further investigation."

"Bloody hell, he sounded just like Gretchen there, didn't he?" Higgins said with begrudging approval.

"Larry knew your mother too," Miss Wellbeloved explained to Kester. "We were all at university together." She laughed. "Larry, I said that to him myself, literally only about an hour ago. Sometimes they are very alike."

"Hmm, and a talented spirit door-opener too," Higgins said musingly. "Well, well. Anyway, I'll arrange the next interview for sometime this week. I presume you haven't got anything else on, so timing doesn't matter?"

Miss Wellbeloved took a deep breath. "We can be as flexible as you need us to be," she replied politely.

"Yes, thought as much," was the retort.

Kester was briefly tempted to tell Lara that he'd seen her in town on Saturday, then decided against it. *After all,* he reasoned, *she probably wouldn't want everyone to know she'd been visiting the city for cosmetic surgery.* He found himself wondering again why she hadn't just found a clinic in Southampton. It was most odd.

"Lara, would you be able to join me to talk to Mr Hopper?" he said suddenly. "You're good around people, I wonder if you'd get more out of him than me."

Lara laughed. "Yeah, sure, why not? If Mr Higgins is alright with that. I didn't feel like I was a whole lot of use when we were talking to Errol Baxter."

"Yes, I think it's wise if you have additional support from my team," Higgins concluded. "You probably need a bit of help. Right, let's crack on then. Not a moment to lose."

Without any further niceties, Higgins hung up, and they were left with the loud ring of the dial tone echoing around the office. Mike prodded Kester on the arm.

"I like your style!" he said approvingly and gave him a

conspiratorial nod.

"What do you mean?" Kester said, feeling himself redden.

"You've already got one girl on the go, and you're working on the next—you old dog."

He flustered and quickly shut his notepad. "Do you mean Lara?"

"I certainly do mean the lovely Lara."

Oh gosh, if Mike thinks I fancy her, does that mean Lara might think that too? he wondered in a sudden state of panic. He shook his head earnestly. "It really isn't like that at all. I genuinely thought she'd be better at talking to Peter Hopper than me."

Mike gave him a thumbs up. "You've got some smooth moves, Kester. I think I'm going to have to watch and learn."

"For heaven's sake," Serena snapped as she stood up and straightened her skirt. "She's not even that pretty, she looks like a man. Plus, she has the most awful loud Texan accent. Quite brash, if you ask my opinion."

"Ah come on, she looks like Grace Jones crossed with a sexy cowboy," Mike replied. "She's hot, in a kind of androgynous way."

Serena pursed her lips until they had thinned to a dangerous red line. She scowled down at him. "You're just desperate for any sort of female attention, aren't you?" she said sarcastically. "I mean, when did you last have a girlfriend?"

"When did you last have a boyfriend?"

"I'll have you know, I regularly date people. I just don't feel it necessary to discuss my personal life in the office like you do." She tossed her hair as though daring him to continue. Unsurprisingly, Mike rose to the challenge.

"Oh, you regularly date people, do you? You know imaginary boyfriends don't count, right?"

"Well, better imaginary boyfriends than inflatable plastic girlfriends, eh?"

Kester laughed. He couldn't help himself. "You're like an old married couple, you two," he said. Miss Wellbeloved and Pamela nodded in agreement. Mike and Serena looked horrified.

"In his dreams," Serena said snidely.

"In my nightmares, more like."

"Well," Pamela interrupted as she crossed her arms across her enormous bosom. "Wonderful as it would be to watch you two bickering all day, I suppose we'd better get on with some work. Who's for a cup of tea?"

Immediately, all hands shot up—more out of habit than anything else. Dutifully, Pamela bobbed away to the kitchen area. As Kester got up, Miss Wellbeloved tapped him smartly on the arm and nodded towards his father's office door.

"Why don't you have a word now?" she said. "He needs to be kept up to date, it's his agency after all."

"Couldn't you do it?" Kester protested. "He's in a terribly ranty mood today."

"No," Miss Wellbeloved replied. Her jaw tightened, and, for a moment, her steel-grey eyes softened. "I think he needs a gentler approach just now, and you're better at it than I ever was."

Kester sighed. He simply couldn't say no to Miss Wellbeloved when she looked vulnerable, despite his own personal feelings about addressing his father in his present state of mind. Straightening his shirt, he sloped hesitantly over to Ribero's office. His fist hovered over the door. Out of the corner of his eye, he could see Miss Wellbeloved flapping her hands in an encouraging manner. He knocked quietly.

"Dad, alright if I come in?"

Silence greeted him. He pressed his ear against the wood. "Dad? Are you alright?"

He heard a low groan. Alarmed, he shoved the door open. The usual cloud of nicotine-filled smoke billowed out, and he ploughed through it, immediately spotting his father in the armchair, slumped over like a ragdoll.

"Dad, what's happened?"

"Shut the door!" his father hissed, lifting his head. His jaw was taut with pain.

Kester obeyed, then crouched beside Ribero. "What's happened?" he repeated. "Do I need to call for an ambulance?" He noticed the dropped cigarette, singeing a neat black hole into the rug, and quickly scooped it up, squashing it into the ashtray.

"No, no ambulance," his father muttered. "It will pass in a moment."

"What will pass? You look like you're having a heart attack."

His father chuckled, then winced again. "No, it's not the heart attack. Not anything like that." Gradually, he leaned back, pressed his head against the leather, and exhaled deeply.

"What the hell is going on then?" Kester asked.

"Muscle cramp," Ribero replied. "It's part of the Parkinson, right?"

Kester frowned. "That looked like one heck of a painful muscle cramp," he said.

Ribero nodded. He leant across, pulled out another cigarette from the packet, and lit it. Kester noticed that his hands were shaking.

"Dad, I really think you should see a doctor about this."

"Ah." His father waved away the comment, wrapping his lips lovingly around the cigarette and blowing out a perfectly round smoke ring. "I am seeing a doctor, my boy. But there is nothing they can do. This is normal with the Parkinson, you see?"

Kester sat heavily on the swivel chair and rested his elbows on his knees. He watched his father closely; observing the vague tremor in his arms, he wondered how he hadn't noticed it before. Now that he was aware of it, it seemed so obvious.

Ribero stared at the ceiling, chewing his lip. "You know," he said finally, meeting Kester's eye, "it's not something you think will happen, when you are the young man. I remember being your age, coming to England for the first time, all energy and fire, right? I never thought I would get old."

"It happens to everyone, Dad."

Ribero sighed. "I don't expect you to understand. It is only when you get old, you realise that life isn't as long as you thought it was. I still cannot believe Gretchen is dead. So many years have passed, and now I have missed the chance to ever talk to her again."

Kester leaned over and patted his dad's knee. "Dad," he began. "When are you going to tell the others about your illness?"

His father bristled, sitting up straighter. "I do not know," he snapped. "But you will not say a word, okay? I am trusting you with this." He jabbed a finger in Kester's direction to emphasise the point.

"They're going to notice sooner or later," Kester replied.

"You didn't notice, did you?"

Kester shrugged. *That's probably because I'm a bit slow on the uptake,* he thought. They sat in silence, each lost in their thoughts.

"Look, I'll do the BA in Spirit Intervention and Business Studies, okay?" he blurted suddenly. His father looked up, brightening.

"You mean it? You are going to apply?"

"I suppose so, if it would make you happy."

Ribero mumbled something in Spanish and clasped his hands together, a beam of pure white-toothed brilliance spreading under his moustache. "Ah!" he exclaimed, accidentally flicking cigarette ash over the floor. "You have made an old man very happy, Kester! This is good news!"

"Well," Kester began, "I'm glad it makes you happy. I'll put in my application tonight."

"You are a good boy! I am proud of you."

"Perhaps you could do something in return?" Kester ventured. *I may as well seize my opportunity while I can,* he thought, *though I'm pretty sure I know what the answer will be.*

"What is that?"

"Get involved in the Lyme Regis case and talk to Larry Higgins?"

Ribero tutted. His face darkened immediately, like the sun disappearing behind a cloud. He pulled on his moustache, eyes narrowing to slits.

"You know why I cannot work with this man, right?"

"Come on, Dad," Kester pressed. "It's been decades. Isn't it time to just leave the past where it belongs?"

"That man stole my chance in life."

Kester gestured around him at the oversized leather-topped desk, the smart armchair, the faded rug. "You've not done so badly for yourself, have you?" he said. "I mean, you've got your own agency."

"Yes, and so has the Higgins. And even worse, the Higgins set up his agency on his own. I was given my agency by Jennifer's father."

Yes, because he thought you were going to marry his daughter, Kester added silently. He kept his expression neutral. "Well?" he continued. "Do you think there's even the remotest chance you'd give it a go?"

Ribero rubbed at his temples and studied Kester with the intensity of an eagle surveying a vole. "Can I think about it?" he asked finally.

"Tell you what," Kester said, suddenly feeling rather impish. "I'll do to you what you did to me, when I asked if I could think about applying for the BA. I'll harass you about it regularly until you give in. How about that?" He winked at his father.

Ribero glared, then burst out laughing.

"What's so funny?" Kester asked.

Ribero wiped his eyes. "Ah, when you say things like that, I can see clearly that you are my son. Full of nerve, yes?"

Kester grinned. "I surprise myself sometimes."

"Well, it will not be easy," Ribero continued. "Higgins . . . he reminds me of a toad. A big, smug toad, you know what I mean?"

"Oh yes, definitely," Kester agreed. "But I'm sure you'll be able to handle this particular toad perfectly well, Dad. And, if for no other reason, you should watch Mike wind him up. It's great fun."

Ribero's eyes brightened. "Now that would be worth seeing. Tell Mike, if he promises to give the Higgins as hard a time as possible, I will come."

Kester grinned again. "I don't think Mike will have a problem with that." He rose and patted his father on the shoulder. "I'll go and let the others know. They'll be really pleased."

Ribero rolled his eyes and continued to puff away at his cigarette, waving him from the room. Kester turned to leave, keen to let the others know the good news. As he slipped out the door, he turned to say goodbye, and noticed Ribero shuddering with pain. His face fell.

"Are you sure you're okay?" he asked tentatively.

His father looked up and nodded. "Yes, I am fine, now off you go," he declared grandly, and forced a smile.

But Kester could see, as clearly as anything, that he wasn't fine at all.

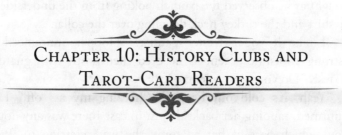

CHAPTER 10: HISTORY CLUBS AND TAROT-CARD READERS

Lyme Regis Town Hall was a rather peculiar building, to say the least. Glowing white in the sharp autumnal sun, its single brick turret jutted into the blue sky, outdone only by its impressive coat-of-arms-clad porch. Beside him, Lara looked up, whistled, then spat reflectively into the road.

"Quite a place to talk about ancient history," she drawled. "You English really have got it going on when it comes to old buildings."

Kester surveyed the town hall sceptically. "Yeah, it is rather flashy, isn't it? And the oversized Union Jack flag probably doesn't help."

"It's definitely overkill," Lara confirmed, then snorted with laughter; a fulsome noise that reminded Kester of a horse whinnying. They'd found the place easily enough—nestled at the far end of the beach—and they'd been enjoying the pleasant weather, even though the sea breeze had been rather bracing. The rest of the team was currently at Meredith Saunders's home, trying to uncover more useful information than they'd found at Deirdre Baxter's.

"Shall we?" Lara leant against the wall, casual as a sheriff in a western movie.

Kester nodded, then rapped smartly. After only a few seconds, the heavy door groaned open, and a balding gentleman peered out at them suspiciously. *Peter Hopper, I presume,* Kester thought as he observed the paunch poking from the underside of the shirt and the turkey neck dangling over the collar.

"I take it you're Kester Lanner?" Hopper announced in a strong Yorkshire accent as he eyed them both with guarded interest. "Do you want to come in?"

"Yeah, it's cold out here. I'm freezing my ass off," Lara confirmed, rapping her backside just in case there was any doubt about which part of her anatomy she was referring to. Peter Hopper's eyes narrowed with disapproval, but he moved to let them through nonetheless.

The inside was much as Kester would have expected: simple, white-washed walls lined with aged wood panels, dark beams and pillars, salt-stained windows. Nothing too pretentious, but nonetheless, a distinct sense of age and tradition. Peter Hopper waited, arms folded across his barrel chest.

"I'd offer you a drink," he began, "but I've got to rush off to a meeting in a few minutes, so we'll have to be quick. I presume this won't take long."

"It shouldn't do," Kester said. He looked around for a chair, saw they were all stacked up against the wall in a distinctly unwelcoming way, and thought he'd better settle for standing instead. "We'd just like to ask you a few questions, to assist our investigations into the recent deaths."

"Yeah, members are dropping like flies, aren't they?" Hopper mumbled. "At this rate, there'll be none of us left."

Kester's eyebrows bobbed upwards with interest. "Were other victims members of the Ancient History Club then? Not just Deirdre Baxter and Edna Berry?"

"All of 'em were members, they were," Hopper confirmed, eyes fixed on the window, which framed the sea beyond like a picture postcard. "Earnest, he was the first to go. Good friend of mine, he was."

Kester reached for his notepad, then rifled through the papers. "That's Earnest Sunningdale, the man who fell on his shears?"

"That's right." Hopper's lips tightened. "Earnest was a lovely chap. Wouldn't hurt a fly. At the time, we all thought it were an accident. But now, we know better."

An interesting comment, Kester thought and mentally filed it for later. *What exactly does this man know, I wonder?* "I presume your second member to be killed was Edna Berry, and the third was the doctor?" he asked, keen to press him further.

"Jürgen Kleinmann," Peter Hopper confirmed. "Fell down the stairs. Or pushed. No one seems to want to tell us exactly what happened, though some of us have our theories. Then the other members, as you already know, were Deirdre Baxter and Meredith. Dear old Meredith. I'd even tried to phone her on the day of her death. But she never got the chance to call back."

Kester glanced at Lara.

"It's a bit weird, ain't it?" she said as she thrust her hands into her wide-legged trousers. "The way you're telling it; it makes me think someone's got it in for your club."

"Perhaps." His expression darkened. "It certainly feels as though something more sinister is afoot, if you take my meaning."

"I do indeed," Kester replied. He started to pace around the room, paying particular attention to the framed photos on the walls. "Is that one of the Ancient History Club?" he asked, striding over to a particularly large black-and-white image, which had been taken against the backdrop of the seafront.

"Yes," Hopper confirmed. "Isn't it sad, thinking that five of 'em aren't with us no more, eh?"

Kester studied the image. There were eight people in total, five now deceased. *Does that mean there's three more victims in this photo?* he wondered. *Or is it just a coincidence?* His instincts were telling him, with a certain level of excitement, that he was on to something. Though what it was exactly, he wasn't sure. *Why would a spirit be targeting a history club, of all things?*

"Do you mind me asking what you do in your meetings?" he asked as he turned to look at Peter Hopper.

The other man sighed, glancing at the clock on the wall. "No, but I haven't got long, as I said. It'll have to be quick."

"Hey, any information you can give us might help us get to the bottom of this thing," Lara added as she perched on top of the closest radiator.

"Well, it's much as you might expect, really," Hopper started. "A lot of time is spent eating homemade cakes and having a chat, to be honest. But we also do a lot of research into the local area. Sometimes, we run presentations and special evenings, telling other folks about Lyme Regis's history."

"I can imagine there's plenty to talk about," Kester said enthusiastically. "Given that this town is the home of the famous Mary Anning."

"The famous Mary who?" Lara echoed, squinting in confusion. Hopper tutted.

"Mary Anning discovered the first ichthyosaurus skeleton," Kester explained quickly.

"An itchy what? Sounds like an STD."

He grinned, then supressed it with a serious shake of the head after catching a glimpse of Hopper's outraged expression. "No, it's a dinosaur. She discovered it in the Victorian era."

"Victorian?" Lara said, looking confused. Then she burst out laughing. "Aw, heck, I'm just ribbing you two. You should see your faces. Don't worry, I know all about your Queen Victoria. Don't get your panties in a bunch."

"Anyway," Peter continued willfully, giving Lara the full benefit of his back, which was now turned coldly in her direction. "Sometimes we investigate fossil discoveries and the like. Other times, we research the people who used to live here. It's fascinating work really, especially if you're retired and haven't got anything better to do."

"I think it sounds like a wonderful way to pass the time," Kester agreed. "So, what were you researching before the murders started?"

Peter Hopper glowered. "I don't see what that would have to do with anything, to be honest," he replied. "Our research would have nothing to do with the deaths of my friends, I can tell you that."

"Perhaps not," Kester said slowly, noticing how prickly his question had made the other man. "But we've got to investigate everything we can, you see."

Hopper nodded. "Well, I'd like you to get to the bottom of it more than anyone else. I've lost some good friends, people that I've known for a long time. I know they were old, but that doesn't make any difference."

"What were you researching then, before they started dying?" Lara persisted.

Peter Hopper scratched awkwardly at his neck. "Nothing much, really," he said with great deliberation. Kester studied him, wondering why the man was being so obviously ambiguous. *What were they up to, and why is he so reluctant to tell us?*

"Can you elaborate?" he probed gently.

"I've got to go in another five minutes or so," Hopper announced suddenly. "You know who you need to talk to? You need to get chatting to Xena Sunningdale, that's who."

Kester reviewed his notes. "Earnest Sunningdale's wife? I've got written here that she's a professional tarot-card reader, somewhere on the seafront?"

"Yeah," Hopper mumbled. His voice had adopted a rather dangerous edge. Kester suddenly appreciated, as he studied the tightened jaw under the slack skin and the low-hanging brow, that Peter Hopper must have been an intimidating man once. Instinctively, he took a step backwards.

"Why should we want to talk to her?" he asked, choosing his words carefully.

"Do you think we should get her to see into the future and solve the case for us?" Lara joked, oblivious to the darkening atmosphere.

"She was the one that put us on to the Celtic site." Hopper placed his hands on his hips and glared at them both. "You ask her about it all. Not that it probably has anything to do with any of this. But she'll tell you all she knows."

The Celtic site? Kester thought, before he began jotting down information in his notepad. *Now that sounds like it might be interesting.*

"What is the Celtic site?" he asked quickly. "It doesn't sound like the sort of thing you'd find in Lyme Regis."

Hopper grunted. "It's brought us nowt but trouble, that's what it's done. And I hold her responsible. That bloody Xena. Her Earnest was always such a down-to-earth chap as well; how he ended up with her, I'll never know."

Kester caught Lara's eye and frowned. She shrugged.

"Where can we find Xena Sunningdale?"

Hopper sighed. "She might be down in her shop, mooching around like she sometimes does. Mind you, the season's nearly over, so she may be back at her house."

"We'll try her shop now, see if we can catch her," Kester said as he folded his notepad away. "Where is it?"

"It's a tiny little hut down by the ice cream parlour on the beach. You can't miss it. There's a big sign outside, what says 'Mistress Xena.' All done in green and pink like a circus sign.

Otherwise, she lives at 74 Turbot Street. You'll know which one it is; the porch is decorated with dreamcatchers and shells and whatnot."

"Thanks," Kester replied. He nodded to Lara, who rose from the radiator. "You've been really helpful, Mr Hopper. We'll be in touch if we need any further information."

Hopper coughed, then gestured to the exit. "Not a problem. I wish you well with the case. It's a nasty thing, a terrible thing. The sooner you catch the evil bastard who's doing it, the better. By the way, you're very young to be a private investigator, if you don't mind me saying. Both of you."

Kester gave Lara a meaningful look. She grinned in response. "Young blood and sharp brains, that's us, sir!" she quipped as she marched towards the door. "Thanks for your time. We'll be heading out into the cold now."

"It's really not that cold," Kester replied, trailing after her.

"I was raised in Texas, out near El Paso. It don't drop below 15°C, even on a cold day. Which makes England like living in a freezer, in my humble opinion."

"Oh, 15°C, that does sound nice," he replied as he mentally steeled himself for the blast of cold sea air. Behind him, Hopper grunted, shaking his head.

"I need to lock up now, so I'll bid you farewell," he said, then pointed down to the seafront. "Keep walking down that way, you'll be at Xena's shop in about five minutes."

Kester glanced down to the grey waves dragging and pulling at the pebbled beach. "Great," he said as he shook Peter Hopper's hand. He smiled at Lara. "Come on, let's go."

They trooped down towards the seafront. Gulls wheeled overhead, their shrill wails muffled by the wind. The beach was almost entirely deserted, apart from a mother and her child eating ice creams and a single old man sitting disconsolately on a bench. In the distance, craggy cliffs loomed over the rocks below, forming a protective barrier that curved out to sea. Lara scanned the breadth of the coastline, then suddenly pointed. "There's a bright-looking shop sign over there. I'll bet that's where we'll find this mysterious Mistress Xena."

"What do you make of this Celtic site then?" Kester asked. "It's a bit of a weird thing to mention, isn't it?"

Lara pursed her lips. "I think a lot of what Mr Hopper had to say didn't make much sense, if you ask me."

"I agree. It didn't quite add up, did it?"

"It couldn't have added more wrongly if he'd have been using a broken calculator," she concluded seriously. "All my senses were telling me something wasn't quite right."

"Well," Kester said, "let's see if we can learn anything more from this mysterious tarot-card reader."

"At least you can get your fortune told while you're there," Lara cackled, keeping her eyes on the row of shops in front of them.

They strode across the beach, trying not to trip over the tumbling stones. Kester found it difficult to keep pace with the Texan, who, he now realised, was quite a bit taller than he was, with considerably longer legs. He glanced across. She was, as Mike had said, very attractive. Probably almost catwalk model attractive, or catalogue model at the very least. However, there was something about her that just wasn't alluring, though he couldn't imagine what it was. She was friendly, funny, and drop-dead gorgeous, but there was something missing. Not that it mattered. Perhaps it was the rather masculine clothes she chose to wear—or maybe that was just the fashion in Texas. He really didn't have a clue.

"You're giving me a hard look there, Kester." Lara caught his eye and gave him a shrewd nod. "Something the matter?"

Kester blushed. "Sorry. I was just admiring your . . . er, your suede jacket. It's just like a cowboy would wear."

She whooped with amusement. "It's my brother's. I stole it before I left for England, along with some of his other clothes. I doubt he was too happy about it."

"Do you make a habit of wearing men's clothing then?"

She bit her lip, then gestured down at her outfit. "Put it like this, I know what suits me, and that's men's clothes. You can ask me about it another time, okay?"

He frowned, perplexed. "Er, okay." *I wonder what that's about,* he thought and scratched his head. *It's a bit of an odd thing to say.*

Finally, they arrived at the shop, which, as Peter Hopper had said, wielded a weathered sign above the windows. Garish gold decoration lined the ledges and doorframe, rusty and splintered due to the relentless attack of the wind and sea water. Big wooden boards covered the front, which Kester took to be a bad sign. He knocked at the door, not expecting a reply.

To his surprise, he heard a crash from within. Lara grinned widely. "Looks like somebody's home," she whispered, leaning against the wall.

A few squeaks, cluttering scrapes, and hushed mutterings later, the door flew open, distributing a floral-dressed old woman between them. A multitude of noisy necklaces bobbed around her neck, and her face was mostly concealed by a vast cloud of grey hairs gathered in a huge, untidy nest.

"I'm not open, dears!" she said breathlessly as she blinked in the sunlight. "If you need a reading, you'll need to book by phone."

"That's okay, Mrs Sunningdale, we don't want a tarot reading," Kester said quickly. "In fact, we just wondered if we could have a chat with you about something rather important?"

Xena Sunningdale paused and looked up at him suspiciously. "It's not the licence again, is it?" she asked, crossing her arms across her voluminous chest. "I told the man from the council only last week, I'm fully paid up, and I'm not operating over the winter anyway—"

"No, it's not that," Kester interrupted with a smile. "I'm

actually from Dr Ribero's Agency, I wonder if maybe one of my colleagues has already been in touch with you?"

Xena stiffened. "You're the supernatural agency," she stated and studied him warily. "I haven't said anything to anyone, you don't need to worry. I know you have to keep it all out of the papers."

Kester smiled as reassuringly as he could. "I know, that's not why we're here. I wonder if we might come in for a few minutes? It's a bit nippy out here."

The elderly woman looked as though she could think of at least fifty things she'd rather be doing instead of inviting them in, but nonetheless, she stood aside, nodding into the small building. In fact, as he entered, Kester realised that it was more of a shack than a proper shop. Ruby-red wallpaper hugged the walls, but the outlines of the wooden slats were clearly visible underneath. Xena Sunningdale pointed to a shapeless velvet sofa by the wall.

"Make yourself at home. Not sure what you expect to find out from me, my dear, but you're welcome to do your best."

Kester glanced at Lara, who had made herself comfortable on the sofa, legs spread so far that they stretched across virtually the whole floor, covering the threadbare Persian rug. "We'll get to the point then," he said, remaining standing. "Can you tell us about the Celtic site?"

The old woman stiffened, looking like a plump hen that had suddenly spotted a fox.

"Who did you hear about that from, my love?" she asked quietly, hand pressed to her chest.

"We've just been talking to Peter Hopper."

She cringed. "That buffoon. I always told dear old Earnest to steer clear of him. Miserable sod." Clutching the side of the doorway, she looked them up and down with sudden severity. "I suppose he told you some awful things about me?"

"Not really," Lara interrupted. "But he said you were the one who put the history club on to the Celtic site. If it's got something to do with the case, we need to know about it."

Xena fiddled with her beaded necklace, twirling it round her finger like a ribbon. "There's not much I can tell you," she said slowly. "But I do want to help you. There's not a day that goes by that I don't miss my husband. He was a silly old goat at times, but he was the kindest man I've ever known."

"We're glad you want to help us," Kester said. "And the only way we're going to stop the murders is if we understand what's going on. Anything you can tell us would be useful."

She massaged her chin thoughtfully before resting her plump bottom on the little polished table opposite the sofa. It squeaked underneath her weight, but, thankfully, held firm.

"As you know, I'm a tarot reader," she began, looking at each of them in turn. "You might think I'm a charlatan, but I've got genuine talent, just like you. I can see into the future, from time to time. And I've always been fascinated by the supernatural."

I've always felt quite the opposite about it, Kester thought as he whipped his notepad out with a wry smile. *Still, no accounting for taste.*

"When I moved to Lyme Regis forty years ago, I made it my business to find out all the local ghost stories. There's a lot of them, you know. The Royal Lion Hotel, now there's a place you should visit. Ghostly footsteps. Ectoplasm on the walls. Fabulous location to pick up on supernatural vibrations."

"I'll take your word for it," Kester replied sceptically.

"Then, a few years back," she continued, "I found a particularly interesting bit of land, out near the outskirts of the town, up on the hill. I'd gone there for a walk one day—before my knee replacement, this was. Beautiful little woods, all covered in bluebells. I walked much further in than I normally would have done, even though it was very overgrown. That's when I found the Celtic stone."

"A what stone?" Lara asked, raising an eyebrow.

"A Celtic stone, love. You know, the Celts? The ancient people who occupied most of Europe before the Romans came along and pushed them out of most of their land."

Kester shook his head slightly at Lara with an expression that he hoped conveyed a silent *I'll explain later.* He didn't want to put the old lady off her stride. "What was the stone?" he asked. "A standing stone?"

Xena shrugged, then eased herself more comfortably on the edge of the table. "I'd say a gravestone. I found more than one of them, you see. Some were just lumps, worn away by the rain and the wind. But others, once I'd cleared the grass away, still had the ancient carvings on them."

"You think it was an ancient burial ground, then?"

"That's exactly what I think."

"Why do you call it the Celtic site?"

She massaged her temples, breathing deeply. "I started to look into the ancient history of Lyme Regis. Further back than most textbooks go. I found that thousands of years ago, Celts attacked this region, likely trying to push the Romans back out, but they were captured instead. I'm presuming the stones mark their graves."

"I'm sorry to interrupt your flow," Lara said as she shifted in her seat. "But what has all this got to do with the murders?"

"I don't know," Xena replied. Her face crumpled into a folded cushion of concern. "I wish I did know. But all I can tell you is that the killing started after Earnest shared my news with the history club. They all got quite obsessed with it. It was all just a bit of a laugh to begin with, but then things went too far. I told them as much. Deirdre and Peter, they wouldn't let it drop."

Kester scribbled down notes as fast as possible. *I'm not sure what any of this means,* he thought, chewing on his pen and gazing down at his notes, *but it surely must mean something. But what connection could an ancient Celtic burial ground possibly have with a murderous spirit that mimics its victims?*

"Mrs Sunningdale," Kester said seriously as he closed his notepad with a business-like snap. "You're obviously familiar with the supernatural. What do *you* think is going on here?"

Xena glanced down at her patent-shoed toes, which poked out from beneath her large skirts like two shiny beetles. She seemed lost for words.

"When my dear Earnest died," she began at last, "I heard him cry out from the garden shed that he could see himself. That his twin had come to *fetch* him." She paused. It was clear that the memory was painful.

"Yes, I know," Kester said gently. "We read the notes on the case."

She looked up. "He also cried out something about wanting to go home. Or his twin wanting to go home. I don't know which. I knew, even then, that it hadn't been an accident. It wasn't just that he'd said he'd seen his own double; it was the terror in his voice. Earnest was never frightened of anything, you see. And the atmosphere in the shed, when I . . . when I . . ."

Lara cleared her throat and shot Kester a warning look. He nodded, whipping out a packet of tissues from his pocket.

"Here," he muttered. "I'm sorry to bring it all up again. I can only imagine how painful it was for you. But we need to get to the bottom of this."

She nodded, then blew her nose energetically. "At first," she went on, "I didn't connect it to the Celtic site. None of us did. But after Dr Kleinmann's wife told us that he'd seen his double too? Well, then I just *knew.*"

"Knew what?"

"That we'd disturbed something. Something that should have been left well alone." She sniffed and dragged a sleeve across her eyes. "I sometimes wonder when it will come for me."

"It seems to be working on finishing off the Ancient History Club first," Lara said, brushing down her jeans. "I guess you're safe for a while, as you're not a member."

"There's not many more members left." Xena rose. She looked more haggard than she had a few minutes previously—as though the conversation had aged her by years, not minutes. "Peter Hopper's obviously one. Grace McCready and Denzil Powers are the only others."

Kester hastily wrote their names down. *The government needs to know who these people are,* he thought, nervously biting his lip. *Given that it looks like they might be next on the list.*

"And what do you think the Ancient History Club did to disturb the graves?" he continued, pen poised.

The old lady winced and shook her head. "I'm sorry, young man," she replied. "If you want to arrange a proper time to talk, that's fine. But I'm not feeling very well today. It's my migraines you see. They've been terrible since Earnest passed away—I think it's the stress." Without pausing for a response, she opened the door and waited patiently beside it, gazing out at the rolling sea.

Kester nodded and tucked his pen back into his breast pocket. Lara joined him, towering beside him and reminding him once more of his own distinctly average height.

"You've been most kind, Mrs Sunningdale," he concluded. "And you've given us plenty of food for thought."

Xena smiled faintly. "Just remember," she said as she led them out into the cold again, "whatever Peter Hopper says, I'm not the villain here." She sighed heavily, fingers restlessly plucking at her necklace.

A few grey clouds had started to roll in from the sea, threatening rain on the otherwise flawless blue sky. Kester glanced at the old woman and noticed the sadness in her expression, mingled with a tinge of anger and regret.

Xena turned back to Kester and pressed a finger against his arm, so firmly that it startled him.

"It might have been me that discovered whatever it is that's plaguing us," she continued as she wrapped herself in her woollen cardigan. "But let me tell you one thing."

"Go on," Kester said gently, studying her intently.

Xena removed her hand and shivered. "I wasn't the one who woke it up."

CHAPTER 11: DOWN THE PUB

The week that followed the visit to Lyme Regis felt particularly long and exhausting. Kester spent the majority of the time online, trying to discover more about the mysterious Celtic burial ground in Lyme Regis, but, so far, all his searches had come up with nothing. He still felt that he was missing something—a vital piece of information, dangling right in front of him, just waiting to be grasped. There was more to these murders than met the eye, but he couldn't figure out exactly what.

It was frustrating, not least because Larry Higgins phoned every morning to check their progress and gloated with obvious delight at the delay. In fact, the only thing that they'd really achieved was to make sure the remaining members of the Lyme Regis Ancient History Club—Denzil Powers, Peter Hopper, and Grace McCready—were protected. Now, inconspicuous government officials had been hired to regularly check up on all of them.

Kester's head ached. It was a particularly gloomy, windswept Friday night, and he was fighting hard against the urge to order a takeaway pizza and officially postpone the diet for a month or so.

Sitting in his tiny bedroom, he shivered. A stiff breeze was currently wafting his curtains around like a pair of billowing spectres, presumably because the windows hadn't been replaced since the house had been built over a hundred years ago. His laptop glowed unnaturally in the dimness, casting a milky light over the School of Supernatural Further Education brochure, which seemed to be goading him with its very presence, refusing to let him ignore it. Opening it up with a sigh, Kester typed in the Swww. web address printed on the first page and logged in.

Here goes nothing, he thought, waiting for the site to load. It looked much like any other academic website, with a traditional logo at the top and plenty of photos of pupils looking rather pleased with themselves. The lack of sinister images comforted him somewhat, even though he still felt unsettled at the prospect of enrolling in a supernatural course. Clicking through to the menu, he scrolled through the list, until he found the BA in Spirit Intervention and Business Studies.

Oh boy, Kester thought, scanning the details. *Do I really want to do this?*

His mouse cursor hovered over the "enrol now" button, white arrow icon blinking in a manner that was almost teasing. *Just get on with it,* he told himself sternly, and clicked through to the application page.

Just as he'd completed entering his details and hit the "submit" button, a series of rhythmic knocks on the door startled him. Before he could call out, the door flew open, revealing a flushed-looking Daisy, wrapped in a stripy apron, covered in flour, and wielding a plate of rather ostentatiously iced cakes. Kester shut the site down as discreetly as possible, then turned to face her.

"Want one?" she chimed as she sauntered in and dangled the plate liberally under his nose. He inhaled deeply, then grimaced.

"What are they?"

"They're beetroot and courgette muffins with carob icing. Danielo, my yoga instructor, said that courgettes are excellent for unlocking your fourth chakra."

He gently pushed the plate aside. "I think my fourth chakra's just fine, thanks anyway."

Daisy sniffed. "Suit yourself. Me and Pineapple are going out later, down the Three Tuns. Did you want to come? You could ask that nice friend of yours?"

Kester closed his laptop, swivelling round to face her. "Which nice friend is that? Do you mean Anya, my girlfriend?" He still felt silly calling her that, especially considering they'd only had one date, but the opportunity to claim that a female actually liked him was too good to pass up.

"No, not her. The guy you work with. Mike, I think he's called?"

Oh god, please don't tell me she fancies him, he thought, taking in the sight of her two pigtails, which were currently tied up with flowery scrunchies. Not to mention the vast array of plastic rings on her fingers—at least two of which portrayed popular 1980s cartoon characters. *She couldn't be less Mike's type if she tried,* he thought, not knowing whether to laugh or feel sorry for her.

"Er, Mike might want to come out, I suppose," he said as he rubbed his hands together, trying to warm them up. Then he remembered what Mike had said about Pineapple when he'd last met him, and regretted his statement immediately. He couldn't remember the exact phrase Mike had used, but he was sure it had included the words "intolerable" and "moron."

Daisy beamed, jiggling the plate of cakes until they teetered wildly, threatening to tumble to the threadbare carpet. "Yes, do ask him. I thought he was so nice. He had such a positive energy, you know? It really flowed through him."

"Well, more to the point, he likes beer flowing through him, so I'm sure he'll be up for it," Kester replied. "I'll ask Anya too."

"Yeah, whatever," Daisy said as she dusted some flour off her nose. "We'll be heading out around nine o'clock. Just don't ask that mean girl you work with. What was her name? Selina?"

"Serena," he corrected. Last time Serena had joined them all down the pub, she had spent the entire time sulking in the corner, glaring dangerously at anyone who dared to come within three metres of her. "Don't worry, she won't want to come. That I can guarantee you."

"Ugh, yes. *That* girl. She had some seriously blocked energy. Standing too close to her was like receiving a punch to my spiritual core."

I'm fairly sure she would have liked to give your physical core a good kicking too, Kester thought, grinning. He straightened, then reached for his phone. "Count me in," he said. "I'll see if Anya can come."

"And Mike?"

He sighed. "Yes, and Mike." *Though don't blame me if he spends all evening avoiding you,* he finished silently.

After a deeply unpleasant lukewarm shower and a change of clothes, Kester was ready to go. To his delight, Anya had responded to his text immediately and agreed to see him there. With less pleasure, he noted that Mike had also replied with an agreement to meet—but judging by the spelling errors and general misuse of the English language, Kester presumed he was already quite a few beers into his evening.

He headed out into the windy night, maintaining a respectable distance from his housemates, in case anyone thought that he was associated with them. They were looking particularly mortifying tonight. Pineapple was clad in a day-glo waistcoat and faux-leather harem pants—giving him the general appearance of a drug-addled New Romantic mixed with a hyperactive toddler. Daisy wasn't much better, with a pair of revolting purple dungarees and crop top, which showed far too much flesh for such a chilly evening.

Thankfully, the pub was only a short walk from their house. Tugging the door open with a sense of relief, he stepped out of the icy breeze and into the welcoming warmth of the fire-toasted bar area. He spotted Anya immediately, propped against the fireside and chatting to a bearded man who looked slightly bemused by her attention. Spotting him, she gave a cheerful wave and trotted over, exuberant and bouncy as a Labrador out for a run.

"Hello!" she sang, then leaned over and kissed him on the cheek. "I am so glad you invited me out! I was feeling bored at home with only Thor to keep me company, and then you texted."

"I aim to please," he replied, aware that his wide smile was perhaps veering towards the imbecilic. "I'm very glad you wanted to come."

She chuckled, then glanced at his companions, who'd headed straight to the bar. "I didn't know you liked to hang around with your housemates," she said, watching Pineapple hopping energetically from foot to foot, finger hovering in mid-air as he tried to decide whether to have peanuts or a packet of ready salted crisps.

Kester winced. "I don't," he replied, "but it was either agree to come out or be forced to eat one of Daisy's awful courgette cupcakes."

"A wise decision, then. Plus, it means you get to meet up with me, which is always fun!"

He grinned. "Yes, it certainly is."

Spying a vacant table, they quickly wove a path through the crowd, avoiding the sticky puddle on the floorboards that might have been beer or something more unpleasant. To Kester's annoyance, Pineapple and Daisy joined them, squeezing in tightly on the narrow bench and slopping wine over his sleeve in the process.

"Well, this is nice!" Daisy gushed as she wrapped an arm around Anya, who looked distinctly uncomfortable. "I am so pleased to meet you, Anna."

"Anya."

"Same thing, right?"

"Not really."

Daisy patted her hand in a manner that was reminiscent of an elderly woman indulging a child. "Understood, my love. Now, shall we gossip about something? Girlie stuff, yeah?"

Anya released a strangled choking noise, which was thankfully muffled out by the sudden familiar bellow of Mike, who had just staggered through the door. Kester glanced up, then groaned. *Christ, how many has he had?* he wondered. Mike wiggled his hips provocatively, nearly knocking over a group of chatting females in the process.

"Hello there, you lovely people!"

"Hi Mike," Kester replied, instantly regretting his decision to invite him. Mike spotted Anya, pointed at her in a distinctly leery manner, then winked. Anya raised an eyebrow. She took his offered hand reluctantly and shook it, even though he didn't seem to notice, as he was too busy eyeing up the bar.

"Right, who's up for a drinky-poo?" he greeted without preamble.

"Oh, I certainly am!" Daisy chimed and turned her face upwards like a flower reaching for the sun.

"Fabulous." He crashed down on the end of the bench, then slammed a hand on to the table. "Make mine a pint of local ale, love."

Daisy looked baffled. Kester shrugged and resisted the urge to laugh. *Perhaps I should have warned her,* he thought.

"Hey, dudes, I am totally without funds at the moment," Pineapple drawled. "Daisy, can you get me a drink too?"

"You told me you just got paid on Monday!"

"Yeah, but you know. Bills. Electricity bills. Water bills. They totally drain you."

"We haven't had any bills yet this month."

Pineapple nodded sagely, topknot wobbling dangerously to one side. "But those bills will get me in the end, right? Like, you know what I'm saying?"

"I personally haven't got a flaming clue what you're saying," Mike slurred, rolling backwards and leaning uncomfortably against Kester's shoulder. "In fact, I'm not sure you're even talking English half the time."

"I'm on a higher plane, man."

"You're plain bonkers, more like."

Pineapple nodded appreciatively, clearly agreeing with the sentiment. Daisy gave Kester a pleading stare before giving up and slinking to the bar.

"So," Anya began as she eased herself into a more comfortable position in Daisy's absence. "I take it that you've had a hard week, Mike?"

Mike groaned, then rolled his head into his hands. "When is a week not hard?"

"What is it that you actually do? Kester won't tell me."

"Aha." He nudged the side of his nose and nodded at Kester. "Wouldn't you like to know?"

She grinned. "I guess, given all the secrecy, you either do something really exciting or something so boring that you don't want to admit it."

Actually, try "so weird that no one would believe you," Kester thought, twiddling his fingers anxiously. He knew that, at some point, he was going to have to give Anya some idea what his job was, but he didn't have a clue where to even start. *What if she thinks I'm completely crazy? After all, that's what I would have thought if someone had told me they worked in a supernatural agency. I don't want her to think I'm a certified lunatic, not when things are going so well.*

"Mike works in IT," he offered, then flinched under the sudden force of Mike's drunken glare.

"I create highly sophisticated electrical equipment," he bellowed, leaning haphazardly against Anya and waggling a finger in her face.

"But you also maintain our website. That's an IT thing."

Mike rolled his eyes, then lurched towards Kester with the unrestrained strength of a wrecking ball. "Yes, but I'm not 'the IT guy,' okay? I didn't do three years at university to be called an IT nerd. Speaking of which, have you signed up for that course yet?" He punctuated his sentence with a hiccup, closely followed by a beery belch.

"What course is this?" Anya asked as she leaned around Mike's swaying body.

"Um, it's a business studies degree," he replied. The statement was partly true at least.

Anya frowned. "You two are very mysterious people. But I'll get to the bottom of it one day, let me tell you." She winked. "I have my ways."

Kester gulped, then jumped as Daisy plunked the drinks in front of him, slopping wine and beer over the table.

"That cost over twenty pounds," she exclaimed, pressing against Kester until he moved over. "I'll be destitute if I carry on spending money like that."

"That's what a bloody round costs, isn't it, love?" Mike slurred, then raised his glass and poured it cheerfully down his throat. "Real world, and all that. Taxes. Bills. Booze."

"Wise words, man," Pineapple added, nodding vigorously. Mike wiped his lips then examined Pineapple's drink.

"Are you seriously drinking pineapple juice?"

"Yeah, why?"

"When you call yourself Pineapple?"

"It's my vibe, innit? And it cleanses the body and soul. It's a healing fruit."

Mike cackled, launching himself over to Pineapple, who was starting to look distinctly worried. "It's not a bloody healing fruit, and you're not a fruit either. What's your real name?"

"I go by the name of Pineapple, man. Be cool." He flapped his hands placatingly whilst sending wide-eyed pleas of help across the table to his housemates. Kester sipped his beer and shrugged. There was no point trying to stop Mike once he'd got stuck onto something. He knew better than to get involved.

"Your parents did not call you Pineapple. What's your real name?"

"I was born free of a name, like all humans, right? You feel me?"

"Nope, not in the slightest. What name's on your birth certificate?"

Daisy leaned over and placed a hand on Mike's arm. "Mike, he's Pineapple. We're all okay with that. Let's leave it."

He grunted, then flicked her hand like a horse's tail batting off a fly. "You're not much better," he growled. "Honestly, Kester, how did you end up living with a flower and a fruit?"

Kester grinned. "My name's not much better."

"So, go on," Mike persisted. "What's your real name, Pine-apple? Tell me now, or I'll slowly pour your pineapple drink down the back of that lovely neon top." He raised the glass, tilting it precariously in the air over Pineapple's jiggling topknot.

"Dude, this isn't cool. It's creating bad vibes when we should be having good times, right?"

A splash of juice descended. Pineapple yelped.

"Not cool! Not cool! Kester, tell him to stop!"

Kester sighed. "Mike, pack it in."

Mike grinned, then sent another dribble of sticky juice directly into Pineapple's hair. "Come on."

Pineapple shrieked, then he muttered something under his breath.

"What was that? Speak up!" Another splash. Pineapple

writhed like a day-glo jellyfish.

"I said, it's Percy!"

Mike's roar managed to momentarily silence the throngs of people around them. "Percy? You're actually called Percy?"

Pineapple nodded miserably, straightening his hair, which was now sagging soggily to one side.

"Like, short for Percival?"

"It is, actually, yeah. Happy now?"

Mike roared again and slammed his fist on the table. "Massively so! I didn't even know people were called Percival any more. That's amazing, that is." He draped an arm over Pineapple's slumped shoulders and pulled him closer. "I like you a whole lot more now, Percy."

Anya shook her head in disbelief. "Is he always like this?"

Kester nodded. "When beer is involved, yes. That's when it helps to have Serena around—to keep him in check."

"Hey," Mike reeled around and batted Kester's shoulder in protest. "I do not need that woman to keep me in check, thank you very much."

"Serena, that's your girlfriend, right?" Pineapple asked, face still pressed tight against Mike's rather sweaty checked shirt.

"She's not his girlfriend!" Daisy squeaked.

"Too bloody right she's not," Mike said. He shook his head vigorously. "That woman is a perpetual thorn up my backside, I can tell you."

"He really likes her," Kester whispered to Anya, who giggled.

"I assure you that I do not," Mike barked, poking Kester in the centre of his chest. "If Serena were to leave the company tomorrow, it wouldn't bother me one bit."

"It sounds like the gentleman doth protest too much." Anya grinned, then ducked out of the way as Mike reeled across in her direction.

"There's no dothing or protesting or anything like what you just said." Mike slumped in his seat like a petulant toddler.

"Serena is a right pain in the bum, and that's the end of it. She's like Satan himself, sent to fetch me down to hell, every working day of my life."

Kester started to laugh, then suddenly gasped. He sat up straight, mouth open. "Say that again, Mike."

Mike winced, then burped. "Which bit?"

"The last bit."

"What, that she's Satan, sent to fetch me—"

"That's it!" Kester thrust his drink down onto the table, eyes shining. "That's the connection! *Fetch!* Mike, you're a genius!"

Mike pulled a face and shrugged at the others. "I have literally no idea what you're talking about, mate. I mean, I am a genius, that's true, but—"

"That's what the link between the killings in Lyme Regis is! The word *fetch!*" Kester exclaimed. "Xena Sunningdale said that her husband said something about being *fetched* before he died. Mr Baxter said it too, about his wife. That must mean—" He paused suddenly, remembering where he was and who he was with. His mouth clamped shut as abruptly as it had opened. The others looked at him in amazement.

"Excuse me?" Anya said with a quizzical look.

"Um." Kester looked desperately around for inspiration. "Er, yes. That must mean . . ." *Come on, brain, think!* he commanded himself. *You've been told countless times not to blow your cover about the supernatural!* Finally, he came up with something passable. "That means it's an interesting theory for those deaths in Lyme Regis, that we read about in the paper. Right, Mike?"

Mike looked confused, looked around at the others, then winked. "Ah yes. Yes, that story we read in the newspaper the other day. Don't know why you'd choose to bring that up now." He gave Kester a meaningful nod. "It's not like it's any relevance to us, is it?"

Kester shook his head. He was buzzing with excitement but also horribly aware he'd said far too much in front of the others, who were all looking at him as though he'd gone completely insane.

"How about another drink?" Mike suggested, nodding several times at Daisy, who pretended not to notice.

"You finished the last one in under a minute!" Anya said. She looked down at her own glass, which was still full.

"That's why I always line them up, you see," Mike explained with a devoted rub of the stomach. "You can't just buy one drink at a time. That's a schoolboy error, that is."

Kester's pocket started vibrating, and he patted down his phone, nearly managing to throw it into his drink in the process. He was glad of the diversion and hoped he hadn't revealed too much in front of his housemates and Anya.

"It's Miss Wellbeloved," he said, showing the screen to Mike. "What the hell do you think she wants?"

"Probably a wild night out with all of us," Mike drawled, completely ignoring Daisy, who kept sidling closer to him with alarming desperation.

Or maybe something's wrong with Dad, Kester thought as he clambered to his feet. He clicked the screen, pressing the phone to his ear.

"Hello?"

A tinny mutter was all he could make out above the noise. He flapped at the others, then started to weave through the crowds to the front door. "Hang on, I can't hear you," he shouted, narrowly avoiding being elbowed by a couple of students playing pool. Leaping outside, he pushed the door firmly shut and braced himself against the cold evening air. "Right, we can talk now. What's up? Is Dad okay?"

"Yes, of course your father's fine." Miss Wellbeloved's familiar clipped tones rattled down the line. "However, the agency isn't."

Kester sighed and leaned against the brick wall. "What's the problem?" *This had better be good, given you're calling me on a Friday evening,* he silently added. He wondered if now would be a good time to tell her about his realisation about the word "fetch," but suspected it might not be, judging by the tone of her voice.

"There's been another murder."

"What, in Lyme Regis?"

"Yes, of course in Lyme Regis, Kester! Where did you think? It was Denzil Powers this time."

Kester looked longingly through the window. Through the crowds, he could just make out Mike, cuddling against Anya in a rather over-friendly way. *He's just drunk,* he told himself. *Don't start getting silly about it.*

"Well?" The single word cut into his ear like a knife through butter.

"Well what?" Kester stuttered.

"Did you just hear what I said?"

"Which bit?"

There was an explosive noise on the other end of the phone, which Kester presumed was Miss Wellbeloved practically combusting in frustration.

"Please listen to me, Kester. Larry Higgins has just been on the phone, in an absolute state, because Curtis Philpot has threatened to pull us off the case. You remember Mr Philpot? The government official who we met at Larry's office? As in the *very important* Mr Philpot?"

Kester massaged his forehead. He remembered the spindly-limbed man well, with his PowerPoint presentations and huge case files. Across the road, a group of teens bellowed uproariously, nudging each other playfully as they headed into town. He envied their carefree attitude. *Why can't I ever just enjoy a night out with mates?* he wondered, then realised it was because, until recently, he hadn't had any mates.

"I don't really see what I can do about it," he said slowly, easing out each word like a dog-owner pacifying a particularly unpredictable Rottweiler.

"Larry has insisted we meet this weekend, to come up with an emergency plan."

"Why can't you and Dad go?" Kester asked as he thrust his hands into his pockets, the phone pinned between his ear and shoulder. "It's his agency after all."

There was a brief silence.

"Come on, Kester. I think we both know that you need to take a more active part in things from now on."

Why does this feel like it's suddenly my responsibility? he thought, feeling rather like a deer about to get hit by a lorry. *I only found out about the agency a few months ago, and now they're ready to palm all the pressure directly on my shoulders!*

"Kester, are you able to come along tomorrow?"

"I don't know!" he shouted. An old man leaning against the wall next to him jumped and nearly dropped his cigarette. Kester pressed his lips together. "Sorry. I didn't mean to sound annoyed. It's just, this is a Friday night, and I already spend enough time worrying about this Lyme Regis case as it is without it eating into my weekend too."

Miss Wellbeloved paused.

"I do understand," she said finally. "But you had the choice, Kester. You chose to become a part of the team. And you surely know by now, this isn't like other jobs. This isn't a nine-to-five that you can just walk away from."

He sighed. "Yeah, I realised that. Fine, okay. I'll make sure I come tomorrow. Do you want me to tell Mike?"

"Why, is he with you?"

Kester looked through the window. Mike was easy to spot this time, given that he was standing on the table and appeared to be singing. He winced.

"Yep, he's with me. What state he'll be in tomorrow, I have no idea."

"Well, he needs to be there, stinking hangover or no stinking hangover."

"I'll let him know."

"Thank you, Kester. I'll let you get back to your evening."

He nodded. "Miss Wellbeloved?"

"Yes?"

"Don't worry. It'll be okay. I think I might have had a bit of a breakthrough, but I'll tell you about it some other time."

He thought he detected a sniff from Miss Wellbeloved..

"I'm glad one of us has some optimism left. Goodbye, Kester."

He pocketed his phone, then glanced up at the full moon, which looked unnaturally bright against the black sky. *So much for the nice lie-in tomorrow,* he thought glumly. *Now I'd better go and rescue my girlfriend from Mike.*

CHAPTER 12: THE EMERGENCY MEETING

The following morning, they gathered in the office car park, their huddled bodies casting long shadows in the wintry sunlight. No one looked particularly pleased to be there, especially Mike.

"Why sodding Lyme Regis again?" he moaned as he rubbed the sleep from his eyes. Although the morning breeze was pleasantly fresh, he looked rather green, and the pong of stale alcohol billowed from his shirt. Kester guessed that he'd probably only stopped drinking about four hours ago, if not less. He certainly hadn't bothered to get changed.

"We needed somewhere to meet up quickly," Miss Wellbeloved replied, nostrils flaring in horror at the sight of him. "And it was the only place Larry could find on short notice."

"Plus, it's a lot less far to travel than Southampton, so it's not all bad," Serena added as she tapped her nails against the van door. "Shall we get going?"

"No Ribero as per usual then?" Mike asked, clambering into

the driving seat. Miss Wellbeloved extended a finger, curled it over his shirt collar, then hoisted him firmly out again.

"No, Dr Ribero won't be joining us," she muttered. "And there's absolutely no chance that you're driving the van in this state."

Serena nudged Mike out of the way, then slid into the driver's seat. They set off along the silent road, each lost in their own private thoughts for most of the journey. Kester stared out of the window, musing on the latest murder. It was deeply frustrating, not to mention worrying. *We warned the government,* he thought, tracing a finger through the condensation on the glass. *They were meant to be protecting Denzil Powers. It was them who let him down, not us.* He personally felt that they'd done quite well with the case so far, and uncovered a lot of useful information. *So why does the government seem intent on blaming us for everything that goes wrong?*

"You've got a dark face on you this morning, my lovely," Pamela chirruped as she leant over from the backseat. "Whatever's the matter?"

"Didn't sleep well." Kester craned round, neck cracking uncomfortably as he did so. "And I'm not really in the mood for a meet-up with Higgins, to be honest."

Pamela rolled down the window, leaning out like a dog enjoying the wind. "Ah, but it's a nice fresh day," she chuckled. "Get a bit of air, that'll wake you up."

"Kester?" Miss Wellbeloved wound down her own window, making the temperature in the van even more glacial. "You said you had a breakthrough last night. What was it? Lord knows we could do with some good news."

Kester brightened. "Yes, I did, but I haven't had a chance to look into it yet. It was something Mike said in the pub, actually."

"What did I say?" groaned Mike, who was holding his head in his hands and looking distinctly queasy.

"You made some comment about Serena being like Satan,

fetching you down to hell—"

"Oh, thank you very much!" Serena snapped and thrust the van angrily into a lower gear as they lurched up the hill. "Nice to know you were saying lovely things behind my back."

"Go on, Kester," Miss Wellbeloved pressed.

"Well," he continued, "it was that word, you see. *Fetch*. Mr Baxter, Deirdre's husband, said something about his wife being fetched, do you remember? Xena Sunningdale, the tarot-card reader—she made a similar comment about Earnest. Mike's comment just reminded me of it."

"A fetch!" Pamela exclaimed loudly, prodding Miss Wellbeloved on the back. "Gosh, why didn't that occur to us before?"

Miss Wellbeloved nodded. "Exactly what I was thinking. My goodness. It could be. It's a possibility, I suppose."

"A what?" Kester looked from face to face, bemused.

"A fetch is similar to a doppelgänger," Miss Wellbeloved explained. "But far rarer. And we never get them down here. Ever."

Kester felt baffled. "What's the difference between a doppelgänger and a fetch then?"

"Fetches thrive on fetching humans to their death." Pamela beamed, giving him a wink. "They appear as a human double, just like a doppelgänger. Not much is known about them, actually. Some are perfectly innocent and focus on fetching people who were due to die anyway. Others have more malevolent intentions."

"I've got to say, it does add up nicely," Miss Wellbeloved said slowly, thinking it over. "Good detective work, Kester."

"Yes, but the problem is," Serena interrupted, "fetches only live in Ireland, don't they? There's no chance one would end up down here."

Miss Wellbeloved scratched her head. "That is true. Ireland mostly, but occasionally Scotland too. And they're formidable spirits. Very intelligent shapeshifters. It's highly unlikely that one would have accidentally got lost and ended up here. They're extremely attached to their homelands."

"But it's certainly worth keeping in mind, eh?" Pamela said brightly. "After all, if it's a fetch, we've got a clear motivation here, haven't we? It's doing what it does best—fetching people to their deaths."

"Oh, can you stop talking about death?" Mike moaned, curling up into a ball. "I feel like I could die at any moment."

"Ten beers and six vodka shots will do that," Kester commented. Mike's face went a worrying shade of grey, and he clamped both hands over his mouth.

They rolled into the hotel car park in Lyme Regis about an hour later. It was a dour, gravelly car park with a distinct aura of neglect, which happened to match the accompanying building perfectly. Kester glanced up, and any residual optimism that he might have felt swiftly faded.

"They call this a hotel?" he said, raising an eyebrow. *It's not even a nice hotel,* he thought. *In fact, it's about as ugly a hotel as you can get. Are they sure it's not actually a prison?*

"As I said, it was the only location Larry could book on short notice," Miss Wellbeloved explained as she scooped up her handbag. "So we'd best make the most of it. Come on."

Serena gingerly stepped out of the van, studying the building with deep distaste. "Not exactly the Ritz, is it?"

Kester grimaced. The plastic sign over the entrance was hanging off its hinges, and the mottled curtains clung stickily to the windows. It might once have been nice forty or fifty years ago, but Kester was willing to bet the exterior hadn't been cleaned since. They reluctantly tugged open the front door and were instantly hit with the scent of damp carpets and mould.

"Can I help you?"

The man behind the reception desk looked not a day under eighty-five, with crepe-paper wrinkles that cascaded down his face before arriving at a flabby stop at his shirt collar. Looking up, his rheumy eyes studied each of them in turn, then returned slowly to his newspaper.

Miss Wellbeloved stepped forward. "Hello there, Mr—?"

"My name's right here." He flapped his cardigan, revealing a battered-looking name tag.

"Hello, Mr O'Nions, we're—"

The old man roared with laughter. "O'Nions? O'Nions? Do I look like an Irishman? It's Onions. Mr Onions."

Kester bit his lip. *Don't laugh,* he thought. *That man doesn't look like he appreciates guests at the best of times.*

"Well, Mr Onions, I believe my colleague, Mr Higgins, booked your meeting room for us today?"

The man wheezed before erupting into a succession of hacking coughs. "What meeting room, dearie? Do we look like we're running some fancy conference centre or something?"

She grimaced. "Well then, I presume Mr Higgins has made a reservation of some sort?"

Mr Onions trailed a bony finger down the book in front of him, then tapped it. "Biggins, you say?"

"No, Higgins."

"Ah. I see. Mr Higgins. In the Corfe Suite. Down the hall, second door on your left. Teas and coffees at eleven. We don't do lunch though."

"No lunch?" Pamela squawked as she peered over Miss Wellbeloved's shoulder.

"There's a café just down the road. Does a lovely fry-up, it does. Good local grub, nice and greasy."

To Kester's amusement, Mike paled and clutched at his stomach. "Please," he muttered. "Don't."

"Not in the mood for a nice bit of meaty sausage and gooey fried eggs?" Serena said, smiling innocently.

Mike gagged. "Shut it."

They pressed down the narrow corridor, desperately trying to avoid touching anything. Everything about the décor looked dated, from the stained carpet to the hideous flock wallpaper, not to mention the peculiar wall lights that were obviously designed to resemble flickering candles. It reminded Kester of being in a cross between an old person's residential home and a Hieronymus Bosch painting.

In the Corfe Suite, things got even worse. *To call this a suite,* Kester thought, *is rather over-stating it.* Wallpaper was peeling so badly around the window frame, it seemed to be taking a gentle walk to the floor. Patches of damp spotted the ceiling. The sum total of furniture in the desolate space was a single round table, a cluster of stacked plastic chairs, and an ample layer of dust over everything. Plus, it smelt as though something had died in there. The vague reek of decay was enough to make Kester feel ill, and he hadn't even drunk much the night before.

"Christ, someone get that window open," Mike muttered and pulled his shirt collar over his nose.

"Is this really the best that Larry could get?" Serena ran a finger across the window's ledge, then groaned. "It smells like Mike's underwear in here."

"I'd love to ask how you know what Mike's underwear smells like," Pamela began with a chortle before catching Serena's eye, which silenced her in an instant.

After five minutes or so, the door flew open and Larry Higgins burst through. Lara and Dimitri scuttled behind, looking distinctly nervous.

"This is an absolute, grade-A catastrophe! Look at this!" Without pausing for breath, Higgins slammed a newspaper on the table. The noise echoed flatly off the nicotine-stained walls. Miss Wellbeloved scooped the paper up, scanned the headline story, then clasped a hand over her mouth. She swore. Kester gasped. He'd never heard her utter a single swear word before. It was worse than hearing his own late mother doing it.

"Yes," Higgins agreed before pulling a plastic chair off the pile and thrusting it under himself. "Bad, isn't it? Absolutely hideously nightmarishly *bad*."

Miss Wellbeloved placed the newspaper back on the table. Kester huddled across and jostled next to Serena, who was trying to grab at the paper first.

"*Are Lyme Regis's murders linked to the supernatural?*" he read aloud. "Blimey, that's a bit of a headline, isn't it?"

Higgins snarled. "It's not just a 'bit of a headline', Kester," he snapped. "It's a complete disaster. Once the press gets hold of the fact that there's spirits involved, it causes serious problems for us. No wonder the government was so furious."

Kester scratched his head. "But no one will believe it, will they?" he said, looking from face to face. "I mean, I wouldn't believe it, if I read it."

Higgins went purple, then made a noise that sounded remarkably like a duck being strangled. Miss Wellbeloved nervously tucked her hair behind her ear before grabbing a chair. She settled next to Larry, clearing her throat. "Kester," she began. "You're still relatively new to all this, which goes some way to explain—"

"—why you'd ask such a bloody stupid question," Higgins concluded, eyes narrowing to furious slits. He waited until the others had collected chairs for themselves, then continued. "The fact is, people *do* believe what they read in the press. All the time, in fact. And that's our sodding job, isn't it? To make sure that the world runs smoothly and people don't get wind of any supernatural goings on."

Miss Wellbeloved nodded. "Essentially," she carried on, "once people start to read about spirits—"

"—especially bloody murderous ones!"

"Yes, thank you, Larry—especially murderous ones. Once people start to think that there's even a remote possibility that spirits could exist, it rocks their foundations. They start to question what else could be out there. Fear starts to creep into their lives. Then, before you know it, you've got widespread panic. Do you see?"

"I think so," Kester said as he pondered over her comments. "But surely one little local newspaper isn't going to have much impact, is it?" He gestured at it. "I mean, I wouldn't take it too seriously, if it was me."

Higgins laughed: a sour, humourless bark that made Kester shrink against the back of his seat. "Oh, it gets worse. Much worse. Dimitri, do you want to tell them what Curtis Philpot also shouted at us down the phone yesterday?"

Dimitri sighed. "It is not just the local papers. *The Serial Suspector* has been in contact with your government. Saying that they know there is a story. Threatening to expose us all. Bribery."

Serena groaned. "Oh god, it couldn't get any worse!"

"Hang on, you mean that really rubbish paper that no one reads?" Kester interrupted.

"That 'really rubbish paper' gets 152,000 readers worldwide every month," Dimitri muttered, his brow furrowing to Neanderthal proportions. "No supernatural agency wants a story to be leaked in *The Serial Suspector*. It is not good."

Kester chuckled in disbelief, then hastily turned it into a cough under the force of everyone else's glare. "But everyone knows that their stories are just made up," he said, raising his hands soothingly. "They just write about vampire attacks and alien autopsies and fake stuff, don't they?"

Pamela sat back, lacing her fingers across her cardigan-clad stomach. "Most of the time, yes. But the thing is, Kester, people still believe it. *The Serial Suspector's* readers think that every word of the paper is gospel truth. Last thing we need is Lyme Regis becoming some hotspot for dreadful ghost-hunters and supernatural tourists."

"Why not? It might bring some money into the area." Kester suggested. The collective frustration radiating out of his colleagues made him swiftly close his mouth again.

"The journalists that work for *The Serial Suspector* are *slime-*

balls," Dimitri continued, pronouncing the word with deliberate disgust. "When they find out about a supernatural case, they call the government and bribe them for as much money as possible, saying if they are paid, they will keep quiet."

"Couldn't the government just pay it?" Kester said.

Higgins slammed his fists on the table. "Goodness me, does this boy not listen to the news?" he cried. "Aren't you aware there's a recession going on? Cuts are being made everywhere! The government simply does not have the money to pay reporters off every time a supernatural agency messes it up!"

"Hang on," Kester replied, his cheeks reddening. "I think that's unfair. How have any of us messed up?"

"How have we messed up?" Higgins squawked incredulously, nearly toppling off his chair. "How have we messed up? Kester, we've been working on this case for nearly three weeks now, and so far, we've not managed to get anywhere with it! This case was of utmost importance, and the government wanted us to get it sorted as soon as possible!"

"We've made progress!" Kester retorted, leaning across the table. "We've found out valuable evidence!"

Higgins erupted into cynical laughter, then slapped his hands across his belly. "Don't make me laugh!" he spat, face suddenly turning thunderous. "All you lot have been doing is poking around in old ladies' drawers, interviewing people with no connection to the case whatsoever, and having a right old laugh at the government's expense!"

"We think we've discovered that the spirit is a fetch!" Kester snapped back.

The impact of fist on table made everyone jump. "Are you being serious?" Higgins exploded. "Fetches don't exist in this part of the world. It's common knowledge! How would it get here? Do any of you ever do anything of any use, apart from researching fanciful ideas and wasting time?"

"Larry!" Miss Wellbeloved shouted, rearing up in her seat

like an aggrieved cobra. "How dare you say that? What have you been doing, I'd like to ask?"

"I've been co-ordinating it all!"

"Then I would suggest the blame lies firmly on your shoulders, not ours!"

"How very dare you, Jennifer! If we didn't go way back, I'd have serious words to say to you right now, you and your joke of an agency!"

"My joke of an agency? Are you aware what people say about you behind your back, you pompous prat?"

Mike sniggered, then quickly converted the noise into a sneeze.

"What the hell is going on here?" Lara suddenly shouted. Miss Wellbeloved and Larry fell silent, both breathing heavily and shooting vengeful glances at one another.

Lara shook her head, looking at each of them in turn. "I think, with the greatest of respect, Mr Higgins, Kester has done some mighty fine work so far. More than any of the rest of us has done. And Miss Wellbeloved, with respect to you too, I don't find it professional that you called my employer a prat."

"She was only speaking the truth," Mike muttered, giving Kester a wink.

"Now see here, I didn't want to come today." Lara adjusted her collar and took a deep breath. "I doubt any of you fine people wanted to be here either. But we're here, and we've got a job to do. So let's just get to work and stop this fighting, which ain't getting us nowhere."

"Never a truer word said," Mike agreed energetically. Kester noticed that he suddenly looked much perkier.

Miss Wellbeloved sighed, then adjusted her hair. "Very well." She looked over at Larry, who looked as deflated as a helium balloon with a puncture. "You're right, of course. Larry, you have my apology for calling you a prat."

"Notice that she didn't apologise for calling him pompous

though," Mike whispered.

"I can actually hear what you're saying, you know," Higgins said, delivering him a glower of pure, portentous dislike, which would have withered even the world's thickest-skinned person. Mike shrugged, then gave him a grin. Larry's lips pursed tightly before he turned deliberately to Miss Wellbeloved.

"My apologies, madam," he said stiffly. "As I'm sure you appreciate, being shouted at by one of the government's highest officials wasn't terribly pleasant. Not to mention the rest of it, which I haven't told you yet."

"Oh gosh, you mean there's more?" Pamela stuttered.

"Oh yes." Higgins massaged his brow, as though the memory alone was enough to spark off a migraine. "The government wanted to pull us off the case, as you know. Dimitri and I had to think fast. So we requested that we have one more week to work on this, and if we don't deliver any results—"

"Please don't say what I think you're about to say," Miss Wellbeloved said flatly.

"—we don't receive any payment."

"Oh god." She pressed her head downwards, disappearing into the narrow crook of her folded arms. Kester couldn't be absolutely certain, but judging by the vague bobbing of her head, she seemed to be head-butting the table over and over again.

"So we have a week to solve this case," Dimitri added, ignoring the anguished scene playing out only half a metre from him. "Or we do not get paid."

"Yes, we figured that much out," Mike said as he rubbed his beard. He'd started to look vaguely pale again. "That's not *great*, is it?"

"As I said before," Higgins continued. "It's a catastrophe. I don't even know where to start."

"Why don't we just quit now?" Serena said, chewing her nails. "At least that way we get a week off for no pay, rather than slogging our guts out and wasting more time for nothing."

"No!" Miss Wellbeloved's finger shot up first, closely followed by the rest of her. A tell-tale red splotch on her forehead confirmed Kester's suspicions about the head-butting. "No, we're not giving up. This is *not over*."

Higgins winced. "What do you propose we do? How the heck are we going to solve this case with hardly anything to go on?"

Miss Wellbeloved's eyes glowed with desperate, feverish energy. "Firstly," she began slowly, "we move up to Lyme Regis for the week. All this driving backwards and forwards is a waste of time. We need to be here 24/7."

The others groaned.

"Secondly," she continued as she pointed around the table at each of them, "we work our backsides off, every day. We interview everyone we can. We visit every crime scene; we search for every clue. We get researching. We don't sleep or eat unless we're sure we've done as much as we can."

Mike nudged Kester in the ribs. "Sounds like a fun week."

"You're expecting us to spend out more money to stay in Lyme Regis for a week?" Higgins said, rolling his eyes. "It's one of Dorset's most famous seaside towns, it'll cost an arm and a leg!"

"So we cut corners where possible!" Miss Wellbeloved retorted. "We share rooms. We stay in the most unpleasant, cheap motel we can find. It doesn't matter, as long as we get the job done. Right?"

Lara raised her hands and started to clap. "Right on," she agreed. "You nailed it, Miss W. If you don't care about what you do, if you don't want to make a difference, what's the point anyway?"

Miss Wellbeloved beamed at her. Even Serena looked fairly impressed.

Larry Higgins stuck his hand in the air, a sarcastic smile

pasted on his large face. "Excuse me? Hate to break up the love-in here, but where exactly do you propose we're going to find accommodation for all eight of us at such short notice? This is Lyme Regis you know, not Chernobyl. Hotels are always in high demand around here."

Kester looked around them. "Except this one, perhaps?"

Mike clapped his hands over his face.

Serena groaned. "No," she stated firmly. "Just *no*. Not a chance."

"Yes, the bedrooms will be filthy," Dimitri added with a shudder.

"Well, it looks pretty empty," Kester continued. He pressed a finger on the table to emphasise the point, felt the years of sticky grime, and wished he hadn't. "I reckon we'd easily be able to book rooms for us all."

Miss Wellbeloved observed the browning walls and the balding carpet and grimaced. "Hmm. Perhaps we should try other places first?"

"Agreed," Higgins added. "There's absolutely no bloody way I'm staying in this appalling dung-pile of a hotel. I've got standards, you know."

"Well, how about you go and find a nice £100 a night hotel by the seafront and the rest of us stay here?" Kester snapped.

Higgins raised an eyebrow. "You're a cheeky young whipper-snapper, aren't you?"

"He does have a point," Miss Wellbeloved conceded. "It's probably very cheap."

"No." Mike said. He leaned back on his chair until the two back legs wobbled alarmingly. "Please. Don't make me do it. Things have *died* here. I can smell it. It's a horrible place and I think it would actually kill me if I stayed here."

"Don't be such a whining baby," Serena said as she prodded him in the stomach. Unfortunately, it was a poke too far. The chair toppled like a trapeze in motion, and the back legs bowed uncontrollably outwards, releasing their burden with sudden energy. All Kester saw was Mike's terrified expression whizzing through the air before disappearing under the table, immediately followed by a deafening crash and a howl of rage.

"Oops," Serena said. "Sorry." Her amused expression indicated the contrary.

Mike released a tornado of wild expletives, closely followed by a bellow of pain.

"I've done my back in!"

"Of course you have, you ridiculous man," Miss Wellbeloved snapped. She hauled him up like a fisherman pulling an ungainly fish from the water. "Honestly, Mike, it's like having a toddler on the team sometimes."

He whimpered, clutching his back, and pointed at Serena. "She bloody started it, pushing me off my chair like that!"

Serena held her hands up in defence. "Hey, I wasn't the one leaning back on my chair. Don't pin this one on me."

The door to the suite opened abruptly and brought with it a gust of cold air. Mr Onions peered at them all in amazement, shaking his ancient head.

"You lot are making a right old noise in here, and no mistake," he announced, then folded his arms and leant against the doorframe. "I did say on the telephone, Mr Biggins, that the room weren't suitable for lively activities. We've got some cracks in the walls, you see. Loud noises makes 'em worse."

"It's Higgins, not Biggins," Larry growled, straightening in his seat. "And the only activity going on was one of us falling off your substandard seating here."

"However," Miss Wellbeloved interrupted quickly as she brushed down her skirt. "We'd like to apologise for the noise and also ask you whether you've got any rooms available for the next week."

"No, we sodding well wouldn't!" Larry hissed. Miss Wellbeloved ignored him and gave the hotel proprietor her most winning smile.

"What, you lot want to stay here?" the man said, looking incredulous. He scratched inside his ear with the precise expertise of an archaeologist. Whatever he discovered in there was apparently something of a delicacy, judging by his enjoyment when he shoved it into his mouth. "You actually want to stay in our rooms?"

"Yes," Miss Wellbeloved answered slowly. "Do you have any rooms?"

"Course we do, we're a hotel, aren't we? It's just that we normally just have builders and the like staying here. Not people such as yourselves."

"Go on then, break it to us," Higgins said, breathing heavily. "How much will it cost us to stay here for a week?"

"Did you all want your own room?"

"No."

The man grinned. "That's lucky. Two of my bedrooms have got issues with the beds."

"What issues?" Mike asked, still rubbing his spine.

"They haven't got beds. That's the issue. I usually keep my dogs in there."

"We'd like as few rooms as possible," Miss Wellbeloved continued, "and we'd like to keep costs down any way we can. We're on a strict budget."

The man coughed, a rheumatic, phlegmy noise that began somewhere in his chest and finished up as a wet snort in his nostrils. "Well. If you men are happy to go in my bunk room, and you ladies can share twin rooms, you can have them for £150 for the week."

"Make it £100 and you've got a deal," Miss Wellbeloved answered, pacing over to the door. The man coughed again, rubbed his brow, then nodded. They shook hands.

"A bunk room?" Higgins exclaimed, reddening. "I'm not bunking down with your merry band of morons here. Not a chance."

"Doesn't look like you've got a choice," Mike said with a sadistic smile.

Higgins rose, solid and aggressive as a rhino about to charge. He raised a finger and pointed it directly at Miss Wellbeloved, leaving it to hover mid-air like a furious arrow.

"Fine." His jaw was so tight and face so red that Kester was concerned the older man might go into cardiac arrest. They waited. Higgins repeated himself, sounding, if anything, even angrier than before. "*Fine*. You win. We'll do this your way and I'll bunk up with the kindergarten crew for the week. But if this doesn't work . . ."

"Yes?" Miss Wellbeloved drawled as she picked up her handbag from the floor and threw it over her arm.

"I'll be holding you personally responsible. Understood?" The finger jabbed the air one final time, then rested, quivering, by Larry's ample thigh.

She nodded. "Very well. Whatever you say. Shall we go and look at our rooms?"

"I was planning to at least return home and get some fresh underpants!"

Miss Wellbeloved glanced at her watch. "That'll be an hour's drive home, then an hour back, not to mention petrol costs. It's probably cheaper buying a few pairs of pants in town."

"What about fresh clothes?"

Mike sniffed his armpit and winced. "Yeah, I could do with at least one change of outfit."

"Buy some cheap clothes in town, and the rest of the time, we'll use the laundrette. Come on, there's not a moment to lose."

They watched, mouths agape, as she marched out of the room. Lara chuckled, then followed.

"The woman's demented," Higgins mumbled, eyes crinkling. Kester couldn't tell if the comment was meant scathingly or admiringly.

He wrinkled his nose, stacked his chair back on the pile, then trotted after Miss Wellbeloved.

I pray the bedrooms aren't as disgusting as the rest of this place, Kester thought, nearly tripping over a rip in the hallway carpet. However, as he watched the proprietor hand over three keys to Miss Wellbeloved, each complete with grimy plastic keyring and blackened with age, he suspected his prayers had already been ignored.

Welcome to hell, he thought, gaze drifting to the top of the staircase, which looked thoroughly uninviting, not to mention almost completely pitch-black. *This is going to be a week to remember.*

CHAPTER 13: AN ANCIENT FIND

"What do you mean, you've got to stay there all week? Surely you knew about this beforehand, didn't you?" Anya's disapproval was palpable, even over the phone—the coldness of her tone matched the chill air in the surrounding wood. Kester was reminded uncomfortably of his mother on the rare occasions he'd disappointed her.

He swallowed hard, horribly aware of the collective eyes of his colleagues boring into his back, and moved behind the nearest tree, keeping his voice as low as possible.

"I honestly had no idea I'd have to come away," he said as he leant back against the bark and studied the naked branches above, probing at the death-white sky. From his elevated position on the cliff, he could see the famous Lyme Regis Cobb, a rough stone wall snaking into the sea mist. He could even see a few people walking their dogs along it, which made him feel more isolated still.

At the other end of the line, Anya sighed. Then paused. The

silence stretched uncomfortably. Kester wondered whether he should say something, then chose not to. *Knowing me, whatever I say will just make it worse.*

"It would help if you'd just tell me where you are and what you're doing," she said finally. "I know we've only just started dating, but already this secrecy is becoming a problem."

"I know." He closed his eyes. He hadn't slept well the night before. Not least because he was stuck in an unbearably whiffy room with three men who snored in a variety of irritating pitches and tones. He'd also managed to end up with one of the top bunks, which had at least four springs protruding painfully through the mattress. "I really am sorry. I wouldn't have suggested meeting this week if I'd known this was going to happen."

"Oi! Hurry up, mate, I'm freezing up here!"

Kester glanced over to see Mike stamping from foot to foot, rubbing at his arms. He hadn't brought a coat, and so far, they'd had no chance to go into town and buy a change of clothes.

"I've got to go," Kester said. "Can we rearrange for next week instead? I really would like to see you again."

Anya paused. "I suppose so," she said finally with a wry chuckle. "But on one condition."

"What's that?"

"You tell me *everything*. I get to ask you at least five questions and you have to answer all of them. Deal?"

Christ, I very much doubt Dad would be happy about that, Kester thought as he adjusted his glasses. "Sure," he agreed eventually. *I'll figure out how to handle this nearer the time.*

Pocketing his phone, he skipped over the dead branches and stones to his colleagues.

"Had enough smoochy-time with the girlfriend?" Serena kicked a rock with her shoe, grinning.

"Yes, thank you," he replied tartly. "Have you finished booting the ground yet? How are you finding those stilettoes in this mud, by the way?"

She grimaced. "If I'd have known we'd be trekking into the woods, I wouldn't have worn them."

"It must be really annoying, having the heels sinking into the ground with every step," Mike added and gave Kester a wink.

"It is, but I'm sure I'll feel less annoyed if I sink them into your backside instead."

"Now, now, you lot." Pamela hurried over like a spinning top, whirling to an energetic halt beside them. She looked around, took in the spectral trees and wintry clouds, then exhaled noisily. "This woodland is interesting. I'm not picking up much yet, but it's got atmosphere, I'll give it that. What about you, Dimitri?"

He shuffled forward, hands thrust into his leather pockets. "Nothing yet," he declared as he coughed and spat on the ground. "Are you sure this is the right place, Kester?"

"Xena Sunningdale, the tarot-card woman, told us that the Celtic graveyard was in this wood. Didn't she, Lara?"

Lara nodded. "She said it was up on the headland. This is the only damn headland I can see."

"Well," Miss Wellbeloved said, rubbing her hands together and peering through the thick trees behind them. "Shall we get on with it? We've got a lot to get done today."

"Goodness me, woman, it's a Sunday!"

She raised an eyebrow in the direction of the complaint. "Ah, Larry. I see you've finally woken up."

Kester smothered a laugh. Since being rudely awoken by Dimitri at seven this morning, Larry had hardly said a word, except to order a fried egg sandwich at the café down the road and to berate Lara for taking the last sachet of tomato ketchup. Even by Larry's usual irate standards, he looked furious.

"Let's just crack on," he muttered, glaring at them all. "I don't appreciate spending my precious weekends mucking around in woods."

"What are you talking about?" Lara exclaimed and gestured around her. "Seriously, you guys take all this greenery for granted. Come to El Paso. Ain't nothing but dry old desert for miles."

Higgins grunted. "I'd rather not, thank you all the same."

They trudged through the woods. If anything, it got colder the further in they went. Mike looked as though he might be slowly dying of hypothermia, if the rate of his shivering was anything to go by. They passed through copse after copse, wrestling through thick tangles of briars and mountainous piles of fading leaves. After a while, Larry held up a hand, imperious as an emperor.

"Stop!"

Obediently, they halted.

Higgins surveyed the woodland, wiping a hand across his forehead. "This is getting ridiculous. Do we have any idea where we're going here?"

"Absolutely none whatsoever," Lara confirmed cheerfully.

"I hadn't realised the woods were quite so big," Kester said, taking the opportunity to catch his breath.

"What did you think they'd be? The size of a children's playground?"

Serena perched on a nearby rock, then folded one leg neatly over the other. "Well, thanks to you lot, my leather trousers are now ruined. Look at the mud on them."

"Ever heard of a washing machine?" Mike said.

She grimaced. "You obviously have no idea how to care for leather, do you?"

Miss Wellbeloved scratched her head. Her hair sprung from behind her ear like a steel spring. "I must admit," she said as she looked around, "this doesn't feel terribly productive."

Kester ran his hands over his face, massaging the tension out of his temples. Stubble was already forming in grainy patches on his cheeks, and goodness knows when he would be able to get into town to buy a razor. "I know what you mean," he said. He felt suddenly very tired, not to mention utterly unenthusiastic about the task at hand. "Perhaps we should turn back?"

"Too right we should turn back," Larry retorted. "This whole thing has been a waste of time. Let's go and get on with some real work instead."

Serena rose from her rock, flexing her calf muscles with a wince. As she stood, Pamela suddenly let out a squeal and gesticulated wildly in Serena's direction. The others watched her in consternation. She began to bounce on the spot and kept stabbing her finger in the direction of Serena's legs.

"She's flipped," Higgins concluded finally. "Gone stark-raving mad. Shall we just leave her here, and see if she can find her own way back?"

"Pamela, why the hell are you pointing at me?" Serena asked. She looked down at herself in confusion. "I know my trousers are muddy, but they're not that bad, are they?"

"The stone! The stone! Look!"

"Oh my giddy aunt. What is she wittering on about?" Higgins leaned against the nearest tree and shook his head. "Does she often have these sorts of seizures?"

Pamela wheezed in exasperation, then slapped him on the arm. "Look at the stone that Serena was sitting on!" she said, ignoring Larry's fury at being man-handled.

"Yes, it's a stone. Just like any other bloody stone. What's your point, woman?"

"It's not just any old stone, Larry! Look at it!"

Kester moved closer to get a better look, then beamed with delight. "Pamela, you're a genius," he said slowly, casting his eye over the weathered stone surface.

Serena peered behind herself, then started to laugh. "Oh, you've got to be kidding me."

"Well," Miss Wellbeloved said as she strode to the stone and stroked its surface. "It appears you found our first Celtic stone, Pamela."

"I found it first," Serena corrected.

"Sitting on it doesn't count," Mike said. "Unless you normally identify objects using your bum-cheeks." He marched over to join Miss Wellbeloved and examined the stone in more detail. In the autumnal morning light, the vague markings were easy to miss, the carved lines brimming with moss and weathered with age. But they were there nonetheless—a soft, barely visible geometric pattern decorating the top right-hand corner like a spider's web.

Lara and Dimitri quickly scouted the rest of the clearing. A minute later Lara hollered, cutting through the quiet. "Here's another one!"

Kester raced over to join her. They tugged the loose weeds gripping the surface. Sure enough, vague linear patterns traced the edge of the rock, just like the previous one. Dimitri discovered another only a moment later.

"I knew we'd find it in the end!" Kester declared as he wiped the dirt from his hands. They stood in the centre of the clearing, huddled together, studying the surrounding stones in wonder. The sea wind blew around them, its icy bite whistling through the trees.

"Now what?" Serena said after a while.

Kester shrugged. "I rather thought this would be the point that Pamela and Dimitri took over. Can either of you pick anything up?"

Pamela frowned, body tense as a hunting dog trying to pick up a scent. Likewise, Dimitri froze, his expression showing his concentration. The others waited patiently.

Finally, she shook her head. "Nothing."

"What do you mean, nothing?" Larry sputtered. "Come on, try again. There must be something here."

Dimitri pulled his leather coat more tightly across his chest, frowning. "She is right," he confirmed. "There is nothing here. It is *flat*. No energy at all."

"Seriously?" Serena said with a bleak look at the nearest Celtic stone. "You can't even detect any residual energy?"

"That's the strangest thing," Pamela replied as she raked a hand through her hair. "I'd have expected to pick up at least a trace of whatever this thing is. But there's literally nothing. If a spirit was ever here, it hasn't been here for a while."

Miss Wellbeloved circled the stone. "That's problematic," she said thoughtfully. "A fetch is one of those spirits that roots itself to a particular place, Kester. I would have thought it would have been here, if your suggestion was correct."

"Really?" Kester looked around and felt suddenly rather gloomy again. *Why do we keep running up against dead ends?* he wondered as he kicked at the dirt. *When are we going to get a lucky break?*

"Yes, fetches usually attach themselves to places or people," Pamela added, interrupting his thoughts. "And there aren't any people here for a fetch to attach itself to—unless anyone's been here who's from the right area in Ireland or Scotland. So it looks like your idea might not be quite right after all. It was a good suggestion, though."

"Oh great. Just great." Larry's expression turned even more murderous. "Yet more time wasted."

"Not necessarily," Miss Wellbeloved said quickly. "Kester told us that the members of the Lyme Regis Ancient History Club, or whatever they're called, started dying after they'd visited this place. Right?"

They nodded.

"And we've come up here today, expecting to find what they found. We expected to find the spirit here, because we thought this was where it lived? Yes?"

"Do get on with it, Jennifer."

She waved a hand. "Bear with me. What if we're looking at

this wrongly? Let's forget about the suggestion of the fetch for now, as it may just be a red herring. What if, rather than simply disturbing this spirit, causing it to get angry, the Lyme Regis History Club actually ended up taking it away with them?"

"A take-away spirit?" Kester repeated, blinking.

"Not like a Chinese take-away, don't worry, mate." Mike patted him on the back.

"Sometimes," Miss Wellbeloved continued, "as Pamela said a few minutes ago, a spirit chooses to latch onto a person. So it follows them around everywhere. In fact, lots of spirits exhibit this behaviour, as we all know. I wonder if that's what's happened here?"

"Nope. Doesn't add up." Higgins shook his head vehemently to emphasise the point.

"Why ever not?"

"If it had attached itself to one person, why would it bother murdering all the rest of them? That's not common spirit behaviour. Doppelgängers especially. They do attach themselves to one person, I'll grant you that. But they don't then go around killing loads of other people."

No one replied. Kester could feel the optimism draining out of his colleagues, a darkening in the atmosphere as each of them dwelled on the complexity of the case. He was finding it difficult to remain positive himself. Every lead they uncovered seemed to point to nothing. The different elements jostled in his mind, clamouring for attention. *The Ancient History Club. Peter Hopper. Xena Sunningdale. A Celtic graveyard. Tarot cards. Murders, made to look like accidents.* He needed time to sit and think about it all properly, but time was exactly what they didn't have. The puzzle was becoming more complex, not less so—and his frustration was growing.

"Let's head back," Miss Wellbeloved said. She glared at the Celtic stones, as though berating them for not giving up their secrets. "There's nothing more we can do here, that's for sure."

"We could try digging up the graves," Mike suggested, tugging at his shirt sleeves.

"What, with our bare hands?" Higgins scoffed. "Have you felt how cold it is? The ground will be hard as anything."

"Also, what do you think you'll find?" Serena said. "At best, you'll just find a knackered old skeleton or two."

Kester pushed his glasses further up his nose. "That's not such a bad idea," he said slowly, as he surveyed the surrounding area. "I mean, what have we got to lose? Plus," he added, kicking at the ground, "it's not so hard. Remember, the soil is sandy here. We're by the sea."

"You are kidding, surely?" Dimitri said. "We cannot just dig up ancient graves. That is not right! Such a thing would horrify my mother." He crossed himself diligently and cast his eyes to the skies.

"Oh, poor dear mummy," Mike muttered.

"And I'm certainly not dressed for it," Serena said, emphatically pointing at her shoes. "I'm going back. You can have a go at digging up graves in the freezing cold if you want, but you can leave me right out of it."

"Me too," Dimitri said. "I think it is more sensible for me and Pamela to go to each of the murder locations and check the residual energy."

"Yes, good idea," Higgins said, brightening. "I can try phoning the victims' partners, see if they'll let us into the house. You never know, we might be able to get them to agree."

Mike and Kester looked at one another and shrugged.

"I'm game for a bit of grave-digging if you are, mate," Mike said.

"Hey, I'll help too," Lara offered and flexed her biceps in their direction. "I'm built for the job."

"No offence love, but this is man's work." As soon as Mike finished his sentence and saw Lara's furious expression, he realised his mistake.

"I'm as strong as any guy, you sexist moron. Now cut the BS and let's get to work."

Kester laughed. "Quite right," he replied. Lara grinned at him and started looking around for a suitable stone or branch to use as a makeshift shovel. Watching her roving around the clearing like a big cat prowling for prey, he could fully see why she was well equipped for the task. *She's very muscly,* he thought, looking down at his own paltry arms with a grimace. *Perhaps I should join a gym when we get back. Or at least do some sort of exercise.*

"We'll leave you to it then and carry on with investigations in town," Miss Wellbeloved said. She observed them in turn, concern wrinkling her brow. "Don't push yourselves too hard, we don't want you burning out before we've even got started."

"Yes, especially as you're probably wasting your time," Serena added, delicately picking a bit of leaf off her shin.

Kester nodded. "We'll just dig for a couple of hours. If we don't find anything, we'll head back."

"Let's arrange to meet back at the hotel at one o'clock then. Good luck."

Kester watched them head off into the dense thicket of brambles until they were completely out of sight. A lone pigeon cooed mournfully in a neighbouring tree before flapping off in a clatter of feathers. He shivered.

"Are you joining us, or just watching while we do all the heavy work?" Mike brandished a large branch in his direction.

Spotting a particularly large, pointy-looking stone by the root of a tree, Kester scooped it up and held it aloft, mirroring Mike's movements. "I'm with you. Let's get going."

As the others had predicted, the ground was fairly hard. However, once they'd broken through the top layers, the soil soon lost its firmness, becoming far looser and sandier. Worms and bugs writhed in the dirt, aggravated by the sudden exposure to light, and pale pebbles gleamed like tiny eggs against the darkness.

"We need to have a system here, guys," Lara said finally. She wiped her forehead and observed their shallow hole with concern.

"Ah, sod systems, let's just dig!" Mike said, accidentally flicking soil into Kester's face.

"Nah, we need to be more organised, because as soon as I'm digging stuff up, you're chucking more stuff back down," Lara said firmly. "Trust me. Me and my brother, we used to dig holes all the time, out in the desert."

Kester stood up and stretched his back. "That sounds a bit ominous."

"It was a good way to catch lizards."

"Not very fair on the lizards."

She grinned, rolling up her sleeves. "Yup. I suppose that's true. But we didn't care much about that back then."

"Does your brother still live in El Paso?" Kester asked, getting back to work. His shoulders were already starting to ache, and they'd only been doing it twenty minutes or so.

Lara shrugged. "Darned if I know. He ain't spoken to me for years."

Kester glanced at Mike, who shook his head slightly.

"Families, eh?" he said finally, not knowing what else to say. As an only child, he had no idea what having siblings was like, though he imagined having the company must be nice. His own childhood had been quiet, to say the least.

Lara nodded, tugged a flat rock from the soil, and tossed it to one side. "Yeah, *families*. You got that right."

"My brother's a complete moron," Mike said conversationally.

Kester looked up. "You don't really talk about him much, do you?"

"For good reason. He's completely mental."

"Where does he live?" Lara asked.

"London. He's . . ." Mike paused for dramatic effect, "an *investment banker.*"

"Ouch." Lara started to laugh. "I bet he's a laugh-a-minute."

"He's an absolute prat of the highest order. My parents *love* him. They're always saying 'ooh Mike, I wish you'd be more like Crispian.' It drives me mad."

"With a name like Crispian, he was destined to go into banking though, really, wasn't he?" Kester said. His finger slipped off the rock, and he scraped his nail against a shard of stone. "Ouch! This is lethal work."

"Yeah, I bashed my fingers too," Lara said, rubbing her shorn head and glaring at the hole with dislike. "But we gotta get on with it. I doubt we're gonna find much, but we have to give it our best shot, right?"

"S'pose," Mike said reluctantly.

"You're the one who suggested doing this in the first place!" Kester pointed out, nudging him.

Mike scratched his head thoughtfully. "Yeah, I didn't think you'd actually take me up on the idea though, did I? Mind you, the soil's looser than I thought it would be."

"Yeah, I know what you mean," Kester agreed. It reminded him of freshly ploughed soil in the farmer's field near his old house in Cambridge, which was strange, given how long the ground must have remained undisturbed for. *I wonder if someone's tried to dig it up before?* he thought, then remembered how old the Ancient History Club members were and changed his mind. *Surely nobody would bother doing this unless they had to.*

They continued in silence. After a while, the sun rose higher in the sky, warming the air just a little. The wind also began to dip, and the dead leaves hung eerily still on the branches in its absence. It was an unusually quiet spot. Aside from the occasional bird, it was completely silent. No other people passed them, which was fortunate, given that they were effectively digging up someone's grave. *It probably wasn't a popular place to walk,* Kester thought. *Because it's so overgrown. Obviously, they all stick to the beach instead. Or perhaps they're sensibly staying indoors in the warm, rather than freezing to death like us.*

After an hour, they stopped digging simultaneously: an unspoken, unanimous agreement. The hole was now about three-feet deep, but still looked frustratingly shallow. Kester surveyed his watch with dismay. It was already past eleven, and they only had an hour at most to continue with the task.

"Whadd'ya think, guys?" Lara scuffed her boot across the top of the pile of soil, studying the hole with disappointment.

"I personally think we're wasting our time," Mike said with a contemplative rub at his beard. "Look at it. We're never going to get down deep enough. We need proper shovels."

"So what do you propose we do?" Kester asked, a note of testiness creeping into his voice. His arms ached, his back hurt, and he felt unbearably frustrated with it all. He also suspected they weren't going to achieve anything, but the last thing he wanted to do was admit it. "Do you think we should give up?"

Mike raised his hands. "Hey, it's your call, mate."

Kester looked at Lara. "What're your thoughts on the matter?"

Lara swilled her mouth thoughtfully before spitting on the ground. "I say we give it a bit longer. Truth is, I don't much like the idea of telling Larry that we came up with diddly-squat."

"You and me both," Kester agreed. He crouched down and peered intently into the gloom of the hole. "Mike, are you in for another hour's digging or so?"

"Or are you getting a bit too old for this sort of thing?" Lara said, slapping him on the back.

"Less of that, thank you," Mike grumbled as he massaged his shoulders. With a sigh, he scooped up his branch again. "Go on then. You talked me into it. Let's get it over with."

Lara chuckled. "Let's rock and roll, folks."

They dug in grim silence. The blisters on Kester's hands

started to burn, but he steeled himself against the pain, dragging his jacket sleeves further over his palms to provide some protection. As he dug, he started to chant a mantra in his head. *This is ridiculous. This is ridiculous. This is ridiculous.* A glance at Mike's face indicated that he was feeling exactly the same.

Why did I even think this would be a good idea? He ploughed the rock deeper into the soil and flicked it behind him with irate abandon. *Now I'm going to have to return and admit to Larry that yet again, we've come up with nothing. It isn't fair!*

Grunting with exertion, his mother's face swam before his eyes—how she'd looked when he'd been a boy, with brown curls and rosy cheeks, before the cancer took hold. Clapping fervently as he came last in the 100 metre race. Hugging him when he'd got his GCSE results. Consoling him when his pet hamster had died. She'd always been there, every time he felt like giving up. Every time he thought he wouldn't make it. Although she'd been dead for close to five months now, he felt like she was suddenly there with him, if only in his head.

Perhaps it's all this hard labour, he thought, muscles burning with exertion. *It's making me go delirious.* His rock slammed into something hard, and he yelped.

"You alright there, partner?" Lara looked over, pausing her digging.

Kester wiped his nose. "Yes. I just hit another stone I think." He massaged his wrists, which were starting to swell up with the effort of digging for so long. Deep in the hole, there was something jutting out of the soil, which didn't look like it should be there at all. Kester looked away and rubbed his eyes. Then looked back again. His mouth dropped open. "Hang on a minute."

Leaning over, he reached into the hole, nearly pitching forward into it as he did so. A gleam of metal poked out, a smooth, perfectly round edge of dull silver. *It's probably the top of a tin can or something,* he thought and issued himself a stern order not to get excited. *Surely it can't be anything useful. Can it?*

Gently, he dug around the sides of the metal object until he could wriggle it free. Then he gasped.

"Look!"

Mike raised his eyebrows, then let out a laugh. "Well, well, well. Is that what I think it is?"

Kester looked again at the object in his hands. Although age and dirt had mottled and warped it, it was undoubtedly some form of ancient brooch or necklace—complete with an intricate Celtic pattern. He delicately dusted it down, pushing the dirt from the metalwork, then held it up to the light.

Lara squealed. "Aw man, I don't believe it! Do you think it's genuine?"

Kester shrugged, studying it intently. The circular side was crusty and dented, though the dimpled metal still gleamed in the weak daylight. "Who knows? But it's certainly worth getting someone to check it."

Mike roared and waved his arms towards the sky. "Come on then!" he said. "Keep digging!"

"Really?"

"Yes, if we've found an ancient brooch, I guess there's every chance there's an equally ancient skeleton not too far away!"

Kester's eyes widened. "Gosh. You could be right."

Breathlessly, they tore into the soil, energy renewed by the discovery. For fifteen minutes, they dug in silence, a trio of ceaseless grave-robbers, with eyes focused firmly on the soil in front of them. Then, after another five minutes, Lara gasped.

"I definitely hit something," she said and clambered into the hole to gain better access. Mike and Kester stood back, giving her room. After a while, she threw her branch out and got to work with her bare hands.

"Well?" Mike asked finally, unable to contain himself. "Found anything?"

"Jeez, Mike, give me a minute, would you?"

They waited impatiently, hopping from foot to foot, trying to see better over Lara's shoulder. Finally she straightened and grinned back up at them.

"Bingo."

Kester and Mike looked at one another with widening eyes. They helped Lara clamber out, then crouched by the hole, scanning the disrupted soil. There, poking out like a piece of dead wood, was a yellowed piece of bone.

Kester steadied himself. He felt rather faint. *I don't believe it. I don't believe we've actually found it.*

With a thump, Mike leapt into the grave and began digging at the sides of the bone.

"Be careful!" Kester croaked. "If this skeleton is as old as we suspect it might be, it's probably very fragile."

Mike dug in silence. They waited, hardly able to contain their excitement, before Mike finally turned around and gave them a thumbs-up. He clicked his fingers to Kester and Lara, who pulled him out of the hole. "Check that out," he said, pointing behind him.

Now that Mike's shadow wasn't obscuring the view, Kester strained to get a better look. His glasses were filthy, which wasn't helping. However, after he gave them a quick rub on his shirt, he could clearly see the bones on display, in all their ancient, mossy glory. A ribcage. Broken and pock-marked, filthy with centuries of underground imprisonment, but a ribcage nonetheless. And protruding from the centre, about where the heart must have once been, a rusted knife.

Now we're on to something, Kester realised, heart beating faster. *Now we're finally on the right track.*

Chapter 14: The House at Smuggler's Path

After locating the skeleton, they'd replaced the soil, even though it was frustrating after their hours of hard work. However, as Lara rationally pointed out, the last thing they needed was an innocent passer-by falling into the grave and injuring themselves on the skeleton's ribcage. *Now, that would give the government something to complain about,* Kester realised with a dry chuckle. *A lawsuit in addition to the rest of our problems.*

Once the hole was properly covered up, they trudged back down the headland, muscles aching from the exertion, and found the others at the hotel, who had been ecstatic at their news. Larry had immediately got in contact with Curtis Philpot, who had given him the number of a local archaeologist who had been involved in a few projects in the past. With astonishing speed, the archaeologist had arrived—with an associate to help him dig—only a couple of hours later.

That night, Kester slept incredibly well, especially considering that another spring had gone in his mattress and was now poking directly into his already sore back. The labours of the day had completely exhausted him, and within a few minutes, he was fast asleep.

Despite getting eight hours' solid sleep, he still found it difficult to climb out of bed the following morning. His clothes were starting to look distinctly rumpled and dirty, and the stubble on his chin was threatening to burgeon into a bristly beard. Kester had never missed a day of shaving since he'd first started growing facial hair, and it felt distinctly alien under his fingers. *Almost like I'm turning into a different person,* he thought, hoping he'd be able to buy a razor soon.

Whilst the others were getting dressed, he flicked his laptop on. Amazingly, there was Wi-Fi in the hotel, which meant Kester didn't have to rely on his faulty dongle to pick up a signal. Opening his inbox, he surveyed the contents. An email from Anya. That was good. *Well, hopefully.* An email from Ribero. Potentially not so good. And last, an email from the SSFE. *The School of Supernatural Education. Yikes,* he thought, eyeing the screen with trepidation. *Now's the time to find out whether they've thrown out my application form in disgust.*

He opened Anya's first. It was a strange, rambling tome, telling him about the latest story in the *Exeter Herald*, about an eagle owl on the loose, and that she'd found a book on secret agents in the library, and would he like to read it. He didn't think so, somehow. *She's a bit barmy,* he thought, but vowed to reply to her later, when he'd had a chance to wake up properly. After all, she might be slightly mad, but she was equally lovely, not to mention the prettiest girl who'd ever shown any interest in him whatsoever. *Actually,* he thought stoically, *she's the only girl who's ever shown me any interest. So I'd better not mess it up.*

Ribero's email was typically curt, asking for updates on the case. It featured several expletives and exclamation marks. He shut it down. He simply didn't have the energy to go through it all just yet. It was far too early in the morning to try to write an email about their progress so far, especially without mentioning Larry Higgins, which he knew would only set his father off again.

Kester lingered a little longer over the final email from the SSFE. Finger hovering on the mouse, it took a while before he finally clicked with weary resignation. *Let's get this over with,* he thought, not even quite sure what outcome he was hoping for. He was desperately hoping that his application had been rejected but felt nettled at the prospect of not being considered good enough for the course. It was a strange mix of emotions.

Just get on with it, he ordered himself and began to read.

Dear Kester,

Many thanks for your recent application to study a Bachelor of Arts in Spirit Intervention and Business Studies. Upon reviewing your application, we'd like to invite you to a Skype interview on Tuesday the 13th of December, at 10 a.m., with Dr Barqa-Abu, who is principal lecturer on this course.

Please let us know if this time is not convenient for you.

Yours sincerely,
Miranda Trollope
Secretary to the Headmaster, SSFE

Kester leaned back with a low whistle. *Oh boy,* he thought. *Dr Barqu-Abu. That's the genie woman that Dad told me about. Am I seriously going to have an interview with a genie? Tomorrow?*

His bunk shuddered with a seismic rattle, nearly knocking the laptop off his knees. Dimitri appeared soon after, hand clasped over his forehead. He muttered something in Russian, then glared darkly at Kester as though it was somehow his fault.

"These stupid English beds," he concluded. "They are so low down that I bang my head every time I stand up."

"Try looking where you put that big old head of yours then, mate," Mike suggested, yawning, stretching, and taking up most of the available space in the room in the process.

"My head is not so big." Dimitri glowered, then patted himself as though to verify the fact. "Why do you call it big?"

"It's a fairly sizeable cranium. Come on, you must have noticed." Mike's expression lit up.

Here he goes again, Kester thought.

Dimitri bristled and tugged his jumper over his head. "No, I have not noticed. I think my head is the right size for my body. And I think you are trying to pull my leg."

"Your head is a perfectly adequate size. Do stop fussing about it," Larry barked as he squeezed himself into his jacket. "Now, are we going to get some breakfast or not? I'm absolutely starving."

"We have to buy some toiletries too," Kester said, shutting his laptop. "If I don't clean my teeth soon, I think I might pass out with nausea at my own horrible breath."

"It is pretty bad," Mike agreed whilst smoothing down his duvet.

"Trust me," Kester retorted, "yours is hardly fragrant."

"Yes, well the simple fact is that all of us utterly stink," Higgins snapped. "But there's not much we can do about it now, so let's go. I have an urgent physical requirement for fried breakfast goods. Right now."

"Any word from the archaeologist about the grave?" Kester asked. He leapt nimbly from the bunk, then wished he hadn't. His muscles ached from the previous day, and his neck felt horribly stiff, like someone had used it as a punch-bag while he'd been sleeping.

"Good god, boy, give the man a chance!" Higgins huffed past him, tugged the door open, and let in an unpleasantly damp, malodourous draft from the corridor outside. "He hasn't even had twenty-four hours yet."

"I think the point Kester's being too polite to mention is that we've only got until the end of the week," Mike said, striding out of the door. "If we don't nail this case by Friday, we're all officially skint."

"Yes, no results, no pay. We must not forget this," Dimitri added as he wrapped himself in his jacket.

Higgins grunted, ushering them out of the room. A quick round of knocks on the neighbouring bedrooms summoned the ladies from their rooms, though no one looked very happy about the prospect of the forthcoming day.

After a mirthless trudge to the café, followed by a quiet breakfast of bacon, parched baked beans, and some hideously slimy mushrooms, they commenced planning.

"I'd like to make some suggestions," Miss Wellbeloved began. She tugged her tiny notepad out of her handbag and dislodged a sea of tissues in the process. "If that's acceptable, Larry?"

He grunted, sipping his tea. "Be my guest."

"I think we need to divide into teams." She looked around expectantly and nodded at each of them in turn. "One team should head to the library, see if they can find anything out about this Celtic graveyard, or, indeed, anything to do with the case. I'm sure Lyme Regis's library is small, but hopefully they'll have some good books on local history and a computer at least."

"I wouldn't be so sure," Serena said, mopping up the last of the baked bean sauce with a piece of cold toast.

"Well, we must try our best. I finally got through to Dr Jürgen Kleinmann's widow, so I propose some of us head over there. Obviously we'll need one of the psychics to assist—that means Pamela or Dimitri."

Kester raised his hand. "Can I suggest something?"

"What's that?"

Kester delved into his pocket and pulled out the ancient Celtic brooch that they'd found yesterday. "This might not come to anything," he began, "but I think it's worth trying to find out if this can give us any clues. I'd like to get in contact with Peter Hopper again, see if he can shed any light on it. Presumably, as a local historian, he might have some insight."

Miss Wellbeloved nodded. "I don't see why not. It can't hurt to try."

"I'll go to the library," Serena offered. "I've got a stinking headache, and I could do with a bit of peace and quiet."

"Excellent," Miss Wellbeloved said. "How about Mike and Dimitri join you?"

"Oh goodie, books," Mike said sarcastically.

"Don't worry, I'll let you play on the computer," Serena said with a consoling pat on his shoulder.

Larry rapped his fist on the table for attention. "Right. Jennifer, how about you and I tackle Dr Kleinmann's wife and take Pamela with us?"

"Does that mean I'm teamed up with Kester again?" Lara slapped him enthusiastically on the back, nearly making him spit out his tea.

"No," Higgins retorted, finishing off his food in a flourish of toast crumbs. "Someone needs to trot to the woods and see how our archaeologist friend is doing. His phone's gone dead, I can only presume he's struggling to get a signal. Lara, you're best qualified for the job because you're the only one of us that can run up a flight of stairs without getting out of breath."

"Aw, nuts." Lara looked out the window and directed her attention to the sky, which was filled with portentous clouds. "Well, you're the boss, I guess."

"You guess correctly." He nodded pompously. "Kester, I suppose you know what you're doing? Actually, I don't know why I just made that statement. You've never shown me any evidence to prove it."

"I'll be perfectly fine, thank you," Kester muttered. "Leave it with me."

After scraping together enough money to pay, they trooped out into the cold, oozing a general demeanour of exhaustion and gloom. A lone gull shrieked from a neighbouring chimney-pot, then circled twice into the sky before wheeling out towards the seafront.

"Shall we meet up in three hours?" Miss Wellbeloved suggested as she peered at her watch. "Will that give everyone enough time?"

"Enough time to nod off in the library, I should think," Mike said, rolling his sleeves down and stamping from foot to foot.

"Don't even think about it." Flinging her handbag over her shoulder, Miss Wellbeloved nodded to Larry and Pamela. "Shall we?"

Kester waved the rest of the group off. He wished that he was heading to the library, rather than getting stuck out in the cold. *Well, best get on with it,* he thought, then pulled out his phone and dialled Peter Hopper's number.

To his surprise, the phone was answered after only a couple of rings. A familiar northern voice issued a brisk, wary, "Hello?"

"Hello Peter, apologies for bothering you, it's Kester Lanner again." He waited for a response. Nothing was forthcoming, so he continued. "Do you remember we spoke the other day?"

Peter Hopper didn't even bother to conceal his sigh. "Yep."

Oh boy, he sounds cheerful, Kester thought. *This should be fun.* "I hope you don't mind," he pressed on, "but I wanted to ask you about something I found the other day. I believe it may relate to the case."

"Oh aye? What's that then?"

"We visited the Celtic site the other day. The ancient graves, up in the woods."

Peter Hopper was silent. *What is his problem?* Kester wondered, waiting for a response. *Why does he freeze up whenever we discuss that place?*

"And?" The voice was distinctly hostile.

Kester cleared his throat. "We found what appears to be an ancient Celtic brooch in the ground. As you're the local history expert, I wondered if you might have a look at it for us. See if you can shed any light on how old it is, or where it originally came from."

"I'm not the right person to ask."

"I thought your history club studied the Celtic burial ground quite extensively?"

The other man cleared his throat. It sounded unnervingly like a growl. "We did. But I know nothing about these sorts of things. You should ask Grace McCready."

A spot of rain landed on Kester's cheek, closely followed by another. He quickly darted to the grocer's shop across the road, phone still pressed against his ear, and sheltered under the bright red canopy—the only splash of colour in the granite-grey street. "Why Grace McCready?" he asked.

"Celtic history's her thing. She moved here from Scotland," Peter Hopper replied. "Better hurry, though."

"Why?"

"Well, the rate we're dropping, she'll be murdered too by the time the month's out."

Kester winced. "My condolences about Denzil Powers."

"Yeah," the other man grunted. "It wasn't a shock. Not really. We're all on the list, aren't we? Just catch whoever's doing it, so the rest of us can sleep easy at night."

"I'm working on it. Where can I find Mrs McCready?"

"Miss. She never married." Hopper cleared his throat awkwardly. "She and her daughter live up on Smuggler's Path, on the outskirts of town. Go past the Cobb and head up the main road from there. It's right at the top of the hill, on your left."

"What's the house number?"

Peter Hopper chuckled humourlessly. "It hasn't got a number, it's the only bloody house up there."

"Right, okay. Do you have her phone number, so I can let her know I'm coming?"

"Goodbye, Kester."

The line went dead before he could reply. He looked blankly at the screen before stuffing it into his pocket. *Weird old man,* he thought as he stepped back out into the road. *I don't see why he needs to be quite so rude. After all, we're trying to help him.* He was getting the distinct impression that Peter Hopper was hiding something, though exactly what, he couldn't imagine.

A fine mist of rain, blown in from the sea, glued itself to his face. It was eerily quiet for a Monday morning. *Does nobody work in Lyme Regis?* he wondered as he strode towards the seafront. *Or are they all retired?* If so, he envied them, still being tucked up in bed on a day like this. He'd have given anything to be snuggled under his duvet back in Exeter, even if it was in the same house as Pineapple and Daisy.

Once he'd reached the beach, he turned left, paced down the promenade, and headed towards the Cobb. On a sunny day, he could imagine the ancient stone walls lined with people eating ice creams or strolling along with dogs straining at their leads. However, on this wintry morning, it was devoid of life. The stones looked forbiddingly black, and the shack at the end, which he'd been told was an aquarium, was ominously boarded up.

Trust us to end up having to come out of season, he thought, hands stuffed even further into his coat pockets. *Just to make everything even more unpleasant than it needs to be.*

The road that led up the hill was far steeper than he'd imagined, not to mention rather precarious, given the speed at which the cars seemed to zip around the corner. Even pressing himself into the ferns and nettles of the rocky verge didn't seem to do much good, and twice his foot nearly got squashed under the wheels of a passing vehicle.

He was thoroughly damp and depressed when he finally reached the road at the top. The aged street sign with "Smuggler's Path" written upon it was only just visible, poking out of the dense hedgerow. Even the impressive view of the cove below couldn't cheer him up. Instead, he pointedly turned away from it and focused his attention on his destination, keen to get the whole thing over and done with, so he could return to the café for another cup of tea.

There was only one house on the narrow road, just as Peter Hopper had said. It was one of the most ramshackle buildings he'd ever laid eyes on: a craggy, whitewashed box that squatted below ground-level, shrinking into the grey rocks behind. Indeed, it looked as though it had glued itself onto the landscape, like a limpet clinging to a cliff face.

Approaching it cautiously, he noted the outhouse with the fallen-in roof, the weed-riddled garden, and the filthy windowpanes. None of the details filled him with great enthusiasm for meeting the residents inside. *Who the hell lives like this?* he wondered as he pushed open the garden gate, which was hanging off its hinges. It squealed loudly, breaking the silence.

Skipping around the sodden bin bag outside the door, he knocked against the peeling wood. He wasn't sure which would be worse—nobody being in, or somebody being in. The idea of simply turning around and heading back down the hill was getting more tempting by the second, especially as he realised that nobody knew where he was. *This old woman could bump me off and dump my body in the woods,* he thought with a nervous laugh, *and no one would be any the wiser. Except Peter Hopper, but I bet he'd be in no rush to help out.*

The door creaked open. He jumped, just managing to

supress a squeal of surprise.

"Hello?" A woman peered out of the gloom with a look of confusion. He wondered if he'd just woken her up.

She can't be Grace, Kester realised immediately. This person was only about thirty-five at the most, though her unkempt appearance made her look more world-weary than her age implied.

"Hi," he replied and twiddled his hands together self-consciously. "I'm looking for Grace McCready?"

The woman nodded and thrust her straggly hair over her shoulder. "My mother," she said slowly as she eyed him with suspicion. "What do you want with her?"

"I'm from Dr Ribero's Agency in Exeter. I need to speak to her about the deaths of her friends."

The daughter studied him for an uncomfortably long time, looking from head to feet as though surveying a piece of meat in a butcher's shop. "She wondered when you'd show up," she said inexplicably and opened the door with a dismissive gesture inside.

"Oh, did she? Excellent," Kester replied and shuffled past her. He looked around for a doormat to wipe his feet. There was none, only a balding red carpet stretching down the dark corridor. "Shall I take off my shoes?" he offered, pointing downwards.

The woman produced a sound that could have been a laugh or a derisive grunt then walked away. Feeling rather unnerved, Kester followed. As he passed, he took in the crooked watercolour paintings and the low ceilings, not to mention the general atmosphere of neglect. He couldn't imagine a place like this ever feeling like a home.

They entered a cramped lounge, overstuffed with ornaments, knitted cushions, and old armchairs. It was uncomfortably warm and silent, aside from a mantelpiece clock ticking quietly on the tiled fireplace. A bundle of old blankets twitched on the furthest chair, and Kester realised that it had a living creature underneath it.

"Miss McCready?" he guessed.

"Mum, it's a man from an agency, wants a word with you." Without waiting for an answer, the daughter stalked back out of the room.

The mass of material sat up straighter. A thin head jutted out, with wild white hair and black eyes.

"I wondered when you'd finally get around to me," Grace McCready said, smiling. It wasn't a joyful expression, but rather one of resignation. Although she looked old and tired, her eyes were bright and watchful as a rodent. They fixed upon him, and he shifted under her gaze.

I don't like you, Grace McCready, he thought irrationally, then chastised himself for thinking it. After all, she was only an old woman, and a frail, helpless one at that. He forced himself to smile. "Did Peter Hopper tell you that we were investigating the case?" he asked as he looked for somewhere to sit. It was clear that nobody was going to invite him to do so, and he was fairly certain he wasn't going to get offered something to drink either.

The woman shook her head and let out a dry laugh. "That idiot hasn't been in contact for weeks. Word gets around, Mr . . . ?"

"Kester, just call me Kester," he said, as he eased himself onto a chair. A sudden yowl alerted him to the fact that he'd just sat on a cat, and he hastily got back up again, nimbly shifting to one side as a set of claws flicked out to give him a warning scratch.

"Aloysius, get out!" Grace McCready hissed and waved frantically at the cat, who slunk out of the room, glaring at Kester as he went.

"Sorry about that," Kester said, trying to hide his embarrassment.

"Don't be. Useless fat moggy. We're just waiting for him to die."

He settled back down again. The room smelt vaguely of cooked fish. Dust blanketed the windowpanes, limiting light in the room. Yet it wasn't just the smell or unpleasant surroundings that unsettled him. There was an atmosphere in the home, a sense of watchfulness that made him eager to get out of there as soon as possible. *It's probably the residents,* he thought, looking at Grace McCready, who wasn't as old as he'd initially thought, just emaciated and pale. *They're not exactly the most welcoming hosts.*

"Do you mind if I ask you some questions?" he began, folding his hands across his lap.

Grace sank back into the faded velvet folds of the chair and eyed him keenly. "I do not," she said finally. He noticed that she seldom blinked. It unnerved him, and he looked away, focusing on the dreary landscape painting above her head. It was a particularly grimy oil painting, darkened and tinted with age. The wild crags and heather-clad ground made him wonder if it was a picture of the Highlands.

"Is that where you came from?" he asked, pointing at it. "It's lovely scenery. Is it Scotland or somewhere like that?"

"It's a painting of a place near where I was born," she answered curtly. "Shall we begin?"

Kester coughed. *I see,* he thought, feeling more uncomfortable by the second. *That's how she wants to be. Fair enough. Let's get down to business.*

"Firstly," he began as he rummaged in his pocket, "I wondered if you might take a look at something for me. Peter Hopper said you were an expert in Celtic history."

Grace stiffened, then licked her lips. "Did he, now?"

"Is it true? Can you help us?"

She grimaced. "I've got some knowledge. I specialised in Celtic history at Dundee University. I've lived in Lyme Regis for over forty years now, though."

He finally located the Celtic brooch and leant over to show her. Taking a deep breath, she craned forward and studied it intently.

"Where did you find this?"

He was surprised by the intensity of the question and felt suddenly guilty, like a schoolboy caught stealing sweets. "Um," he began, shifting uncomfortably, "we found it up in the woods. Peter Hopper and Xena Sunningdale had both told us about the Celtic burial site . . ."

"Oh, I bet they did," Grace spat with a venomous glance at the brooch. She extended a hand, then clicked her fingers at him. "Give it to me. I want to see it better."

He handed it across, and she pulled it in, fingering the surface with a caress. He waited with nothing but the sound of the ticking clock to interrupt the silence. Finally, she looked up.

"What is it you want from me, Kester?" Her eyes dug needles into his own.

"We need to stop whatever's causing the deaths of your friends." He resisted looking away, regardless of his deep desire to do so. There was something horrible about her expression, her eyes in particular, that made him feel frightened, though he didn't know exactly why. "We think you might be able to help us, Grace."

"But they're nearly all gone anyway," she replied as she leaned back against the chair. "Why bother now?"

Kester frowned. "What do you mean by that?"

"What do you think I mean? Isn't it obvious?" Her fingers curled around the armrests, digging into the fabric.

"Miss McCready, if there's any chance that we can save you and Peter Hopper, then—"

The old woman shook herself, then sat up straight. "Helen! Helen, I need my inhaler!"

A few seconds later, her daughter reappeared, a blue inhaler clutched tightly in her fist. Glaring at Kester, she positioned it between her mother's lips and pressed the cylinder.

"Mum, you know you shouldn't get excited," she muttered

with a brief squeeze of her mother's shoulder. "If you need some quiet time, I'm sure this man here will understand."

Grace shrugged. "It seems we're surrounded by quiet time these days, doesn't it? Too much quiet."

"Until the baby arrives, yes. Then there'll be plenty of noise to deal with."

"Are you having a baby?" Kester asked, gaze instinctively flitting to the woman's stomach. She was wearing a shapeless knitted jumper, but underneath, he could detect the distinctive swell of her stomach. Helen observed him coolly, then placed a protective hand across herself.

"I am, yes. Not that anyone cares, apart from Mum."

"What about the father?" Kester asked, then bit his lip. "Sorry, that was a nosey question."

Helen tensed. "The father didn't want to know." She glanced at her mother. "Like history repeating itself, eh?"

Grace nodded. "We don't seem to have very good taste in men in this family."

"It's like we're cursed or something, eh, mum?"

A look passed between them. Kester couldn't decipher it, but there was something desperate in their eyes that made him shiver. The clock suddenly chimed, making him jump. He looked across the room at the noisy timepiece. 10:30 a.m. *Gosh, is that all?* he thought incredulously. *I feel like I've been here forever.* There was something still, hot, and stifling about the room that made it seem as though time had simply given up and moved out, leaving them all in a vacuum.

"What can you tell me about the brooch?" he asked in an attempt to bring the woman back to the case.

She passed it back to him, giving it one last contemplative squeeze. "It's old, if that's what you want to know."

"How old? Are we talking a few hundred years, or a few thousand?"

She shook her head faintly. "It looks similar to pieces I've seen in the past that date back to the Roman era."

His eyes widened. "So we're talking two thousand years old? Are you serious?"

Grace shrugged. "Could be. I can't say for sure." Again, she glanced at her daughter, who stared impassively at the fireplace. "If it is genuine, I'd say you've discovered something worth possibly tens of thousands of pounds, Kester."

Gosh, that'd sort out the cash-flow problem for the agency, Kester thought and pocketed the Celtic brooch rather more respectfully than before.

"Not that you could sell it," she continued, guessing his thoughts. "The decent thing would be to donate it to a museum. Was that all you wanted to know?" She wrapped herself more tightly in her blankets. "My chest is rather tight today, I'm not sure I'm in the right mood for long chats."

"Just a few more questions, if you'd be so kind," Kester pressed. "This Celtic site . . ."

Her eyes narrowed. "Yes?"

Kester pressed his glasses up his nose. "What exactly happened up there?"

She stiffened. Her daughter shut her eyes, stroking her belly. The wind whistled through the windowpanes, causing the trees outside to scrape restlessly against the glass.

"What makes you think anything happened up there?"

He scratched his forehead, then paused. "I don't know," he said eventually. "Perhaps I'm being silly. But a few people have suggested that the deaths started happening after you all visited that place."

Grace's jaw tightened. In the gloomy light, she looked uncannily like an animated skull. The thought alone was enough to make him shudder. "You seem to be suggesting that it's something supernatural," she said, choosing her words carefully, fingers clawing ceaselessly at the armrest. Kester wished she would stop. There was something about the action that made the old woman seem predatory, like an animal about to pounce.

"Miss McCready, I'm from a supernatural agency," he said finally, deciding to take the risk and be honest. "That's precisely what I'm suggesting." He leant back, waiting for her to absorb the full impact of his revelation. "I've confided that in you, and I'd ask you to not repeat it to anyone. But yes, we do believe there's a spirit behind the killings, and we think it's connected to that Celtic burial ground."

"It's a horrible place," Helen blurted out.

Her mother glared. "Don't be fanciful, Helen."

"Why do you think it's horrible?" Kester studied the younger woman, but her expression had closed again. She glanced at her mother, then shook her head faintly.

"It's just a bit quiet up there." She nodded, eyes fixed to the floor. "A bit spooky. Nothing much."

Grace grasped the armrests and hoisted herself free of the blankets. As she stood, Kester could see that the rest of her body was just as scrawny—loose congregation of twig-like limbs and oversized, billowing clothes.

"We don't believe in all that nonsense," she said, folding her arms. "If I'd have known you were from a ridiculous agency like that, I never would have agreed to talk to you. I thought you were conducting a criminal investigation."

Kester stood. "Miss McCready," he began, "that's exactly what I am doing. And if you don't mind me saying so, I think you're concealing something."

The old lady scoffed, then gestured to her daughter. "Helen, will you show him out? I've not got the time for this."

Helen nodded. She jerked her head in the direction of the door. "Come on," she said, gesturing. "I think you'd better leave."

He sighed and ran a hand through his hair. "Very well," he agreed and gave the old lady a nod. "The last thing I'd want is to pester you. However, if you do change your mind, get in touch with Peter Hopper. He has my number; he'll pass the message on to me."

"I doubt that will be necessary," she said. She turned and stared obstinately out the window.

Kester followed Helen down the hallway. He could see the slight waddle to her walk—the wider gait that demonstrated clearly that she was pregnant—and wondered how he hadn't noticed it before. *Probably because I'm not very observant when it comes to the important things in life,* he thought ruefully. His mother always used to tell him to stop focusing on the small details and take a more active role in the world around him. *Too wrapped up in books,* she used to say. *Too intent on the small stuff to notice the bigger picture.*

"Thank you for your time," he said as the door opened. "I do apologise if I've upset your mother."

Helen sighed. "She's always upset," she said with a shrug.

He paused. "Is there anything *you* want to tell me?"

The woman opened her mouth, then closed it again. "No. No, there's not." She looked out the door. "You're going to get wet. It's pouring out. Haven't you got an umbrella?"

Kester shook his head. "I didn't come very well prepared."

A ghost of a smile played at her lips. "You're young, aren't you?"

"I suppose so."

"Do you want to borrow an umbrella? Just leave it with Mr Mason in The Anchor pub on the seafront, I'll pick it up when I'm next there."

Kester smiled at the unexpected kindness. Given how hostile they'd both been to him only moments before, it was rather a surprise. "Well, if you don't mind, that'd be appreciated."

A round of aggressive coughs echoed from the lounge. Helen's brow furrowed. "You'd better go."

He took the umbrella. It had bright green frogs printed all over it, but the rain was pelting down so hard, he really didn't mind.

"Thank you," he said. "It was nice meeting you."

A smile flitted to her face, then was gone. The door slammed behind him.

As soon as he'd rounded the corner and got back on the main road, he pulled his phone out of his pocket.

"Miss Wellbeloved?" he said as soon as she answered. He had to shout to make himself heard over the rain, which was now pounding on the umbrella like a ceaseless drumroll.

"Hello Kester, is everything okay? We're still at the Kleinmann house, where are you?"

"I've just been to see Grace McCready," he said, wheezing as he strode down the hill.

"Have you now? I won't ask why; you can tell me later. What happened?"

He pursed his lips together, as he took in the landscape in front of him. The thunderous sea slapping waves against the harbour walls. The rolling clouds clinging to the horizon. And to his left, the dark woods, hiding the Celtic burial ground in its depths.

"We need to get Pamela or Dimitri up to Grace McCready's house as soon as possible," he continued.

"Why, what did you pick up?"

"I'm not sure. But one thing I can definitely confirm . . ."

"Yes?"

"There's something badly wrong in that house. And—"

"Yes?" Miss Wellbeloved's excitement was palpable, even via a crackly phone connection.

Kester took a deep breath. "I think it's where the spirit is next likely to strike. In fact, I wonder if it might be there already."

CHAPTER 15: THE PASSING OF PETER

The town hall door squealed as Peter Hopper opened it, casting a long shadow across the stone steps. The moon hung pale and fat above the sea, its reflection splintered by the waves. However, he hardly noticed the dark landscape beside him. Instead, he slunk into the building, then closed the door quietly behind him.

It had been a bad day. A bad few months, if he was being completely honest. When he'd first moved down to Dorset as a young man, he'd thought that he'd found his spiritual home. A place where he finally felt wanted and where he liked the people around him. But not anymore. He hadn't felt like that about Lyme Regis for a long time.

Flicking on the light, he checked his phone, half-expecting to see another call from the young chap from the agency. However, the screen remained resolutely dark, no matter how hard he jabbed at the home button. *Damned thing's run out of batteries,* he realised, and resisted the urge to throw it on the floor. *Useless piece of junk.*

His eyes travelled instinctively to Denzil's photo on the wall. It must have been taken over twenty years ago, but Denzil hadn't aged that much. *Lucky bastard,* he thought, then checked himself. Actually, it was fair to say that Denzil's luck had rather run out. It pained him to think of his friend's last hours. It frightened him to think of the terror he'd experienced before dying.

But not me, he thought, drinking in the sight of the familiar hall. *I won't be hanging around to be the next victim. No chance.* He'd wanted to come back here one last time, to stand by the old podium, to remember the talks they'd given in here, the hundreds of cosy meetings, the parties—back in happier days, before things went badly wrong. If he closed his eyes, he could almost imagine them all here again: sat on their plastic chairs, hobnobbing about the town gossip, laughing, getting worked up over silly little historical details.

It's not that I blame any of you, he thought as he gazed at each of the photos in turn. Deirdre Baxter, trophy clutched firmly in hand, at the local fossil festival back in 1995. Edna Berry, arms linked with Meredith Saunders, striding along the beach with their dresses blowing in the breeze. *God, that one must have been back in the eighties,* he realised, astonished at how slim the ladies had both looked back then. Before age got a grip on them all, fattened them up and wrinkled them in on themselves, stealing the youth from under their noses.

Here was another photo, of himself and Jürgen leading the local history event just a couple of years back. Earnest and his wife. Grace McCready, standing close to the back, always with that strange, mournful expression on her face. He'd believed he'd had feelings for her, once upon a time. He could even remember when she'd first moved into the town, fresh from Scotland, full of wariness for the southern locals. They'd bonded as fellow northerners, always feeling slightly out of place amongst the

Dorset residents. *But those days are long gone now,* he thought. The narrow-faced, big-eyed beauty had long since disappeared, leaving a white-haired wisp of a woman in her place.

"I did you wrong though, girl," he said aloud and touched the photo briefly with his finger. "Not that it matters much now."

The fluorescent lights hummed, flickering slightly, casting an epileptic glow in the room. Outside, the sea-salt stained windows revealed an empty road. Another quiet night in Lyme Regis, as always. The town rested as silent as a graveyard out of the summer season.

He took a breath and walked over to the desk in the corner. Fingered the wrought-iron handle of the drawer. It was locked, of course. He made sure it stayed locked at all times, and he was the only one with the key, which happened to be on a piece of string around his neck.

Peter removed it, then paused. The key hovered, uncertain, squeezed between his finger and thumb. He thought about his house. The fire still glowing in the lounge. Martha, his faithful old Labrador, curled up in her wicker basket. His favourite cushion plumped on the sofa. He could just return home. Go back, carry on like usual. Pretend nothing was happening.

Until it actually happens, he told himself sternly. *No, Peter, the time for pretending is long gone. You'd best take action before the action finds you.*

The key made contact with the lock. The drawer slid open. He rifled through the old papers, pushing them out of the way, until he located the slender piece of ribbon, only just visible, poking right at the back of the drawer. One tug and it lifted, revealing the secret compartment underneath.

There you are, my beauty.

He pulled the gun free and examined it more closely. He hadn't had it out in years. It showed no signs of age, despite having belonged to his father during the war. The barrel gleamed in the light, feeling satisfyingly weighty in his hand.

"I think it's time we end all this nonsense once and for all, don't you?" he said aloud, then glanced around the hall, up into the empty rafters. *We've all been through hell and back,* he added silently. *And there's only one way to stop the hell now, isn't there? There's only one way out.*

His hand shook, just by the tiniest amount, as he flicked the light off again and left the hall in milky-moon darkness. The door clanked shut behind him. He didn't bother locking it.

Peter stood by the water's edge, letting the waves drift around his boots. It was a cold night. His breath puffed in front of him before vaporising into the misty black. Behind him, the twinkling lights of the promenade dangled and bobbed in the breeze, like rows of dancing fireflies.

A solitary light shone dimly from the top of the hillside, near the woods. He wondered if it was coming from Grace's house. *Maybe she's looking down here now,* he thought as he flicked a pebble into the sea with his toe. *Wondering what I'm doing. Wondering if I'll be next.*

Except I'm not going to wait around to be picked off like a pheasant in shooting season.

He raised the gun, placed it between his lips, then fixed his eyes at the moon.

Chapter 16: The Police

Kester awoke to pandemonium. A pair of hands shook at his arm, and he rolled around, meeting Larry Higgins's fleshy, pale face, which was alarmingly close to his own.

"Get up! Get up now!"

"But it's still dark!" Kester looked over at the window, then blinked furiously.

"I don't give a toss if it's still dark, get your backside out of bed now! Emergency situation!" Larry hauled Kester's duvet off, leaving him shivering like a damp dog.

He sat up and hastily wiped his chin, which was embarrassingly wet with dribble. "What emergency situation?" The bunkbed squeaked as he flipped his legs over the side, narrowly missing Dimitri's head in the process. Dimitri groaned, then stretched his arms into the air with a yawn.

"Peter Hopper." Larry barked, hands on hips. "Dead."

Mike nodded, flinging Kester's shirt across to him. "Come on. We've got to get there before the press do, otherwise there'll be hell to pay."

"Hang on, hang on." Kester held up a hand, massaging his forehead. His head felt as though it had been stuffed with shaving foam. "Just a second. I don't understand. What time is it?"

Larry Higgins emitted a noise that sounded like an engine bursting. "Good god, just get up and get out! We'll fill you in on the details as we go along!"

Kester's shoulders slumped. "Righty-ho." He jumped from the bunk and nearly twisted his ankle as he landed. He really wasn't in any fit state to start work, especially as he felt like he'd only been asleep for ten minutes.

Someone rapped at the door, which creaked open only a second later.

"Are you ready in here?" Pamela asked as she observed the whirlwind of clothes, bags, and belongings scattered around the room. "Jennifer says we need to leave now, the paramedics are already on their way, and we need to see the body first."

"Hang on a moment, did you just say 'see the body'?" Kester said, feeling a bit weak. "I'm not really too down with the whole 'see a body' thing, to be perfectly honest."

"Oh, do stop being a snivelling baby," Higgins barked, then leant over and hauled Kester's trousers up like a parent hurrying a toddler. "Get on with it, you're holding us all up."

"So, Peter Hopper is dead?"

"Yes!"

"Right. Right." Kester struggled to process the information. "Okay." He paused, then scratched his head. "Gosh. That's *awful*. How?"

Mike tugged him by the arm. "Come on, I'll explain as we're walking. It's just before five in the morning, as you asked what time it was."

"Five o'clock? No wonder I'm feeling like someone's used my head as a toilet."

They crept down the stairs as quietly as possible, to avoid waking the proprietor of the hotel, who, they were fairly sure, was the only other person in the building. Miss Wellbeloved managed to locate the front door key in the office, which let them out on to the silent street.

"Better lock up after ourselves, we don't want the hotel getting burgled," Pamela suggested, bracing herself against the cold.

Lara looked up at the cracked hotel sign above the door. "I don't think that's gonna happen. It's not exactly the sort of place that screams affluence, is it?"

"Come on, we really haven't got time to waste," Miss Wellbeloved said, then gestured down the street. "Curtis Philpot told me that they found Peter Hopper down by the seashore."

"Wait a second, I'm a bit confused," Kester said, trotting to keep up. The street was eerily still, with only the moonlight to guide them, which cast wobbly shadows across the cobblestones. "How did Curtis Philpot know about Peter Hopper?"

"Use your brain, boy!" Higgins snapped as he marched out in front. "Philpot sent government men over to provide protection for the remaining Ancient History Club members, didn't he? One of them noticed that Hopper didn't return home and found him on the beach. Dead."

Kester swallowed hard. He hadn't warmed to the dour northerner. In fact, he'd actually found the man rather unpleasant. However, it was still horrible to hear that he'd died. "Was it the spirit again?" he asked, thinking of his over-confident assertion yesterday that the spirit was definitely going to strike in Grace McCready's house. *Shows what I know,* he thought, looking out to the sea glittering at the end of the road. The steady whoosh of the waves was hypnotic and made him wish desperately he was back in bed again and didn't have to deal with this level of stress.

"We're not sure," Miss Wellbeloved replied as she zipped

her coat up. "Details are hazy at this point. That's why we're trying to get down there before the paramedics start moving him around. The police are already there."

"And the press?"

She shuddered. "Let's hope not. For the sake of all our future careers, let's hope and pray not."

They clambered onto the beach, all of them struggling to keep balance in the darkness. Lyme Regis's beach was mostly made up of large pebbles, which shifted and rolled under every step. Judging by the level of swearing, Serena was finding it most difficult to stay upright, which was hardly surprising, given she was still tottering around in stilettoes.

A glint of red and blue light towards the other end alerted them to the presence of the police car. Kester squinted. It all felt surreal, as though he'd suddenly been plunged into a gritty crime series. Wordlessly, they all headed towards the flashing lights, drawn to the centre of the activity. Silhouettes of people milled around, and the occasional burst of bright light indicated that somebody was taking photographs.

As they approached, Higgins stepped forwards, flashing a card in his wallet at the nearest police officer. "Hello there, my name is Larry Higgins . . ."

"Yep, don't bother speaking to me." The man rubbed his stubble irritably. "Talk to Chief Inspector Wilmott. She's the one in charge." He thumbed in the direction of a towering female, who was currently deep in conversation with a man in a weighty anorak.

Kester glanced down as they passed through the centre of the congregation. Even though every part of him wanted to avoid it, he couldn't *not* look. His eyes were magnetised to the body, which had yet to be covered. Kester shuddered. It wasn't the blood pooling at the man's lips that bothered him most, nor the splayed hand, stretched out over the pebbles. It was the expansive whites of his eyes, rolled out towards the sea, seeking something beyond the horizon.

My god, I was only talking to him on the phone yesterday, Kester thought, hypnotised by the sight. *Is that how it happens? One minute alive, the next, not?* It reminded him horribly of his mother dying. The way she'd slipped from animation to complete stillness, as though someone had simply flicked a switch, then left the building. He shivered.

Pamela slipped a hand around his shoulders, guessing his thoughts. "Come on, dearie," she whispered, giving him a comforting squeeze. "Let's get on with our work, shall we? Best not to dwell on the dead."

They strode over to the Chief Inspector, who seemed determined to ignore their arrival. Indeed, aside from a brisk irritated glance, she deliberately repositioned herself, offering them the perfect view of her broad back.

"Chief Inspector Wilmott?" Higgins interrupted, positioning himself firmly in her view. He flashed his card again. "I'm Larry Higgins. We've got permission to examine the body."

Crikey, she must be at least six-foot, if not more, Kester thought, looking up. Even Mike and Lara, who were both pretty tall themselves, were awed by her statuesque presence.

The woman tutted, folded her arms, and looked down at them with disapproval. "I'd heard you were coming. Took your time, didn't you? The government official said you'd be here twenty minutes ago."

Larry shot the others a mutinous look. "Yes, some of us took longer to get ready than others."

The Chief Inspector exhaled noisily, reminding Kester of an impatient horse. "You'd better hurry up. Our forensics team has done all the preliminaries, and the paramedics are coming in soon to collect the body."

"Any sign of the press yet?" Miss Wellbeloved asked, wrestling her fingers together in an anxious knot. She glanced back to the road, as though expecting to see hordes of journalists running towards her at any moment.

Wilmott shook her head. "No sign yet, thank goodness. But let's not tempt fate, eh? Get cracking."

Dimitri moved towards Peter Hopper's body and knelt awkwardly by his outstretched arm. He closed his eyes, frowning.

"What's he doing?" Wilmott asked, trying not to look too interested.

"Seeing if he can pick up any residual energies," Pamela said as she walked over to join him.

Wilmott grimaced. "It's a funny old business, isn't it? I remember when I first joined the police force. Nothing prepared me for you lot. That's something they don't mention on the application form, I can tell you."

"We're not so different to you," Miss Wellbeloved replied sharply.

"Oh, but you are. What you guys do and what we do, it's very different. *Very different indeed.*"

There was a definite edge to the Chief Inspector's voice. Kester noticed Miss Wellbeloved stiffen, then move closer to the others. Serena was talking earnestly to the man with the anorak, who Kester presumed was part of the forensics team. He turned his attention to Pamela and Dimitri, who were both now kneeling with their eyes closed tightly. It never ceased to fascinate him, watching them at work. He wondered what they were picking up.

"Doesn't look like the work of a spirit to me," Mike announced as he squatted by Peter Hopper's head. "Looks like he got busy with the gun all by himself."

"Funnily enough, we'd already established that." Wilmott narrowed her eyes and examined him in detail. "Anything else of value you can add?"

Mike stood, slapping his hands against his thighs. "Nope. That's your lot for today from me."

"Just be thankful for small mercies," Higgins muttered. "Trust me, he's come out with worse in the past."

Pamela opened her eyes, then shook her head. "Nope," she said, accepting Mike's arm as she stood. "Absolutely nothing supernatural going on here. I'm not even picking up much residual emotion. I don't think he was feeling much of anything when he shot himself."

"I don't see how you can possibly tell that, just from being near him," Wilmott said with a glance at her colleagues.

Pamela patted her as she walked past. "I just can, love. I don't need to justify myself." Lara chuckled, then edged away as she caught sight of the Chief Inspector's expression.

A whirl of flashing lights brought their attention to the main road. The ambulance had arrived and was parking next to the town hall; its siren switched off to ensure as much privacy as possible. Two paramedics climbed out.

Chief Inspector Wilmott stepped forward. "Forensics, how are you getting along? Steve?"

The man in the anorak nodded. "We'll need a while longer, but we're going as quickly as possible. We know it's important to keep this as low-profile as possible."

Wilmott nodded at Larry. "Is there any reason why you lot need to be here now?"

Larry looked at the others. Dimitri paused, then shook his head slightly.

"No," Larry replied. He thrust his hands into his pockets and looked vaguely disgusted, then turned to Dimitri. "Are you absolutely certain this wasn't caused by the spirit?"

Dimitri nodded. "Absolutely. As Pamela said, this man shot himself. There was no supernatural influence."

Mike whistled and glanced at his watch. "Time for my beddie-byes then, I believe. Shall we?"

"What a waste of time," Serena cursed, glaring at Peter Hopper's corpse as though it was personally to blame.

"Yeah, leave the professionals to finish up," one of the other policemen muttered. He caught their eye, then turned away with a sneer.

Kester looked at Miss Wellbeloved, who grimaced. Without another word, she started pacing back across the beach. "We get that a lot from the police," she whispered. "Don't worry too much about it, we've got every bit as much right to be here as they have."

A clank of stones told them that the others were right behind them, hurrying to catch up. Somewhere over the horizon, the sun was starting to creep upwards, as Kester could now just about make out their pale and sallow features in the oncoming light.

"It may not have been a supernatural killing," Pamela wheezed as she slowed to a stroll. "But I picked up a lot of strange emotion. Didn't you, Dimitri?"

The Russian prowled alongside them with the precision of a stalking panther. "Certainly. Regret. The Hopper man regretted something as he died. Guilt. Perhaps even love."

Pamela nodded. "Yes, exactly. But no fear. That man met his death without a shred of fear, I can tell you that for sure."

Miss Wellbeloved sighed. She looked over at Larry. "What do you make of all this?"

"The old codger was clearly worried that the spirit was going to pick him off next, wasn't he?"

Dimitri frowned. "I do not think he was worried. I think he was accepting of his death and met it bravely."

"Is brave the right word for putting a bullet in your brain?" Mike said, breaking into a run and jumping over the wall onto the promenade.

"Ah, you clearly do not understand the moment of death. Particularly if it is caused by your own hand," Dimitri answered as he extended a leg and climbed over the wall with deliberate care. He held out a hand to Serena, who took it with a giggle.

Mike scowled. "Sorry, Dimitri, I'd forgotten that you'd committed suicide so many times that you were an expert on it."

The Russian rose to his full height, eyeing Mike with irritation. "You have no soul," he concluded.

"You mean I don't talk a load of old nonsense," Mike muttered as he stalked ahead.

Serena tutted, delivered a megawatt smile to Dimitri, and fell into step next to him. "Just ignore him," she advised. "The rest of us do."

"Well, time to head back to bed," Higgins snapped. "A few hours' sleep should sort us all out."

"Are you joking?" Miss Wellbeloved said as they rounded the corner. "We should use every second we have. Remember, we've only got four more days. That's not long at all."

"Yes, yes, I didn't need reminding," he retorted. "But we do need to perform basic bodily functions during that time, Jennifer."

"His basic bodily functions are absolutely awful," Mike whispered to Kester. "I couldn't actually enter the toilet yesterday after he'd finished in there. It was like a nuclear wasteland."

"I meant sleep!" Higgins yelped furiously.

Mike grinned.

"Well," Miss Wellbeloved interrupted quickly. "Perhaps all bodily functions can be marked as low priority during this week, eh?" She pulled the hotel keys from her pocket and jangled them before her like a miniature bell. "Let's take an hour to freshen up, then meet downstairs in the Corfe Suite."

"At least we're able to brush our teeth now," Serena said as she entered the hotel. "I don't think I could have stood all your nasty breath for much longer."

"I still need to buy a razor," Kester added with a thoughtful stroke of his cheeks. He'd never had a beard before. It was horribly itchy, and from what he could tell in the speckled mirror above the sink in the toilet, it looked utterly ridiculous on him.

Mike slapped him on the back. "Embrace the beard, Kester. Just go with it. It suits you. Makes you look dashing."

"He looks like an upside-down toilet brush," Serena said, laughing. Kester glared before following her reluctantly up the creaking stairs. Worst of all, he suspected she was right.

After a depressingly lukewarm shower, Kester yanked his clothes back on, though they were now starting to smell more than a bit stale, and stomped morosely back downstairs. It had only just gone seven o' clock, and he felt utterly wretched, not to mention starving hungry. Worse still, the café didn't open until eight, and all he had upstairs were two pieces of chewing gum.

He peeped around the door of the Corfe Suite to see Miss Wellbeloved sat neatly on a chair, staring out the window at the bleary dawn. She turned as he entered, giving him a faint smile as he sat down next to her.

"You do remember I've got my interview with the Supernatural School of Further Education today, don't you?" He rolled his neck in an attempt to ease out the stiff muscles. *God knows how I'm going to manage impressing anyone in an interview in this state,* he thought, *much less a genie.*

Miss Wellbeloved nodded. "I hadn't forgotten. I had a chat with your father about it last night, actually. He said to wish you good luck."

"I think I'll need it." Kester leaned back, then followed Miss Wellbeloved's gaze to the window. A single beam of sun pierced the thick clouds for a brief moment before retreating once more behind the grey. "What else did he say?"

"Nothing much. He wanted to know how we were getting on. I think he rather misses us all, actually." She shifted her chair and placed her hands on the table. "Kester, you are aware that I know about his illness, aren't you?"

He swallowed awkwardly, unsure how to reply. "Are you?"

"Yes. I guessed, actually. My cousin had Parkinson's. I

recognised the signs."

Kester pressed his chin into his hands and took a deep breath. "It sucks, doesn't it?" he said simply.

She squeezed his arm. "Yes, it does. But it's not a death sentence, you know. He'll be okay, as long as he doesn't push himself. That's why I insisted he stayed at home this week. He was going to join us, you know."

"What, even with Larry here?"

"Even with Larry here."

Kester whistled. "Gosh. That's progress, isn't it? Who knows, maybe one day they'll even be friends."

She chuckled. "I very much doubt it. They never really got on, not even at university. Some people just rub one another up the wrong way, don't they?"

"What did my mum think of Larry?" he asked suddenly. He knew that his mother had gone to university with them all and had even shared a room with Miss Wellbeloved, back when they'd been good friends and not rivals for Ribero's attentions.

Miss Wellbeloved's jaw tightened, then she forced out a weak laugh. "Gretchen thought Larry was every bit as self-important as the rest of us did." She wrung her hands together, eyes glazing as she revisited the memories. "However, she was nicer to him than your father was, as I'm sure you can imagine. Julio was always in fierce competition with Larry, always striving to be the best. Your mother and I found it hilarious."

The door swung open with a loud bang, and Mike entered shortly after, waving his hand in mock-salute. "Hello, you lovely people." Without another word, he plummeted into the nearest chair with a disbelieving glance at his watch.

Serena, Lara, Pamela, and Dimitri followed close behind, all looking similarly hollow-eyed and exhausted. They waited a few minutes for the rest of the group to join them. Larry was last in, hulking through the door with an expression that suggested he'd rather murder all of them than sit down and have a civilised meeting.

"Alright there, Larry?" Pamela asked with a wink at the others.

"No, I'm bloody not." He fixed her with a baleful glare. "Somebody used up all the hot water in the shower."

"Ah well," Miss Wellbeloved commented with a philosophical nod. "That's why it pays to get in there quick, rather than trying to sneak in a quick nap while everyone else has a wash. Anyway," she continued hastily as she noticed the furious twitch of his nostrils, "I think we all know what the plan is for today, don't we?"

"Get over to Grace McCready's house as soon as possible," Serena said as she licked her finger and polished the mud off her shoes.

"We need to phone the archaeologist too," Lara added, rubbing her eyes. "He reckoned he'd be just about finished by today. Then we can find out how old that skeleton is, not to mention the knife sticking out of its chest."

"I've got my SSFE interview at ten," Kester reminded them all.

Higgins snorted. "Hardly a convenient time to have it, is it? Can't you postpone it?"

"No, he cannot," Miss Wellbeloved said firmly. "It's important that he gets on this course, and you know as well as I do that you don't just cancel meetings with Dr Barqa-Abu."

He sniffed, then folded his arms across his chest. "Yes, I suppose you do have a point there. She's terrifying."

"Thanks for telling me that," Kester said, now regretting his decision to apply even more than previously. *God, if Larry Higgins thinks she's frightening,* he realised, *she must be even worse than I imagined.*

"I think we should try to get into Town Hall too, see if there's anything in there that can provide more clues," Larry suggested.

A flurry of impatient knocking pulled all eyes towards the door. Moments later, Mr Onions poked his ancient head around the doorframe, flinching in the light. They waited patiently until the rest of his person had scuffled into the room, decked out in a rather mildewy-looking green dressing gown. He coughed, a series of barks that sounded alarmingly like an attack of tuberculosis, then patted his chest for added effect.

"Now, see here." He paused, arthritic finger suspended dramatically in the air. "I don't get nosey with my guests, but when they're coming and going in the night, I need to know why, okay?"

"Of course, of course." Miss Wellbeloved stood in a flourish of scraping chair legs, quickly smoothing her clothes down. "And we're more than happy to explain."

"And another thing," the man stormed on, oblivious to her comment. He'd obviously been working himself up to the moment and didn't want to lose momentum. "I'm presuming you must 'ave taken my set of door keys with you. Which I'm not happy about at all. What would have happened if there'd been a fire, eh? How would I have got out?"

She blushed. "I do apologise, I had presumed you'd have a spare set of keys."

"I do! I do have a spare set. But you didn't know that for sure, and you had no right snooping in my office, did you?"

Larry rose, knocking the plastic chair over in the process. "I'd hardly call it snooping, sir. We were merely trying to exit your hotel, which we needed to do in a hurry."

"No, Larry, he's absolutely right; we should have asked him."

"At five in the morning?" Higgins was starting to go red in the face, which Kester knew was never a good sign. "I very much doubt he would have liked being woken up at that time!"

"Excuse me," the hotel owner interrupted, showering spittle over the carpet in the process. "I'll be the judge of that, thank you. More to the point, what were you all doing, sneaking out in the middle of the night? Sounds shady, if you ask me."

Higgins's chest puffed out even further. "I'll have you know that there was absolutely nothing shady about it, my good man. We were engaged in perfectly respectable business."

The old man looked incredulous. "I can think of no decent profession that needs to creep off in the night."

"What are you trying to suggest?"

"That you lot were up to no good." He narrowed his eyes, then jabbed a knobbly finger at them all. "I had my reservations about you lot when you arrived, to be honest."

"How dare you!"

Miss Wellbeloved threw the others a worried glance. "Now then, Larry," she muttered. "Let's just keep our calm, I'm sure this can be easily sorted out."

"I'm not going to let some old fool tell me I'm shady!"

Mr Onions gasped before erupting into another indignant coughing fit. "Old fool? Who are you calling an old fool?"

"He's not calling anyone an old fool, honestly." Miss Wellbeloved positioned herself between the two of them, arms extended appeasingly. "Please, do accept our apologies."

The old man stamped a foot, then pointed at them. "I want you out. *All of you.*"

The room fell silent.

"Hang on a minute, mate," Mike said, clambering to his feet. "We're paid up until Friday."

"Fine, you can have your money back. But I don't want you here no more. I won't be called a fool, and that's final."

Lara let out a humourless laugh. "I don't believe this."

Miss Wellbeloved's face creased. "Please, don't listen to my colleague here. We're terribly sorry about taking the keys in the night. If we'd have known that we were putting you in any danger, of course we wouldn't have done it."

The old man shook his head, impassive as an ancient basset hound. "Too late, I'm afraid. I won't be called a fool by anyone.

You can stay tonight, but then you're out tomorrow morning. Understood?"

Serena groaned and buried her face in her hands. Miss Wellbeloved's jaw tightened. "Very well," she said stiffly, and gave Higgins a glare that would have frozen a hot-water bottle. "I understand. We'll make sure we're out by tomorrow."

The old man's face twitched, then hardened again. "Yep. I'll return the money that you're owed. Let's agree to stay out of one another's way until then."

With a final, judgemental nod, he swooped from the room, dressing gown billowing behind him. The others stared at one another, mouths open. Kester felt as though his tired brain simply couldn't cope with much more drama.

"It's a bit of a pigsty anyway, isn't it?" Mike said finally. "I bet we can find somewhere else to stay. It's not like it's the holiday season, is it?"

"But they'll all be too expensive," Miss Wellbeloved replied. She slung her chair back into the corner with a fury that was quite out of character. "We're not going to be able to find anywhere else that'll put all seven of us up for under twenty pounds a night, are we?"

Larry threw his chair on top of Miss Wellbeloved's. "If you ask me, we're well shot of this place. In fact, I think we should move out today, after what that idiot just said to us."

"You're the idiot, Larry!" Miss Wellbeloved quivered and pointed a finger in his face. "You're an absolute bloody moron!"

Mike let out a low whistle and was silenced by a prod in the ribs from Serena.

Higgins gawped for a moment like a fish pulled from a river. "Excuse me?"

"We've endured your arrogance and negativity for long enough!" Her lips started to shake. Kester wondered if he should intervene. He felt sure she was about to cry.

The room felt suddenly rather colder. Everyone squirmed

awkwardly in their seats.

"Working with your lot hasn't exactly been easy," Larry muttered. For the first time, he seemed slightly unsure of himself.

"Well, working with you has been completely impossible," Miss Wellbeloved spat. "From the first day, you've been putting us down, criticising our techniques, and making obstacles wherever you can. If anyone has caused the failure of this project, it's you."

Higgins opened his mouth, then closed it. Then opened it again, looking hurt. "I think your comments are most unfair," he said finally, scratching his bald spot. "Don't you agree, Lara? Dimitri?"

Lara and Dimitri glanced at one another, then shrugged. Higgins's shoulders slumped.

"So that's how it is, is it?" He looked from face to face. Everyone looked away. He sighed. For the briefest moment, Kester even felt a bit sorry for him. He looked like a bully at school who'd just found out that nobody in the class liked him.

"I'll be in the room, if anyone needs me," he said finally. "Though by the sounds of it, that seems unlikely."

"Larry, hang on a moment, mate," Mike said, reaching across. However, the older man turned with surprising speed and stormed from the room.

Kester twiddled his fingers. He felt as though he should say something. He wanted to say something. But his head felt as though it had been filled with ten bags of cotton wool, and the power of speech seemed to have completely deserted him. Instead, he looked at the floor and kept his eyes fixed on a particularly bald patch of carpet by the leg of the table.

"Where do we go from here, Miss W?" Mike said eventually, resting a hand on her arm. "Carry on as planned?"

Her eyes started to shine over, a tear threatening to spill over her lower lid. "I'm not sure, to be honest. I think . . . the stress of the last few days . . ."

Lara stood up immediately and pulled her into a hug. "It's been incredibly stressful, ain't it?" Miss Wellbeloved let out a sob, then nodded into the warm suede of Lara's shirt collar.

"Lara, you're very good at saying the right thing at the right time," Mike said admiringly.

Serena tutted. "Will you stop fawning over her, Mike? It's making me queasy."

Mike bristled. "Speak for yourself, Miss 'I've got a thing for Russians'."

She blushed, then glanced at Dimitri, who pretended to be incredibly interested in the opposite wall. "Mike, why don't you just shut up?"

"You bloody started it, as per usual."

Pamela groaned and leaned on Kester's shoulder. "Please, can we stop fighting? Things are fraught enough as it is."

Serena snorted. "I was merely pointing out that Mike seems particularly impressed by every single thing Lara does."

"Hey, what's not to be impressed by?" Lara held her arms aloft and beamed at them all.

"He's like a sad little puppy, sniffing around your ankles!"

"Are you kidding? With a beard like that? He looks like a St Bernard, not a pup," Kester quipped in an attempt to lighten the atmosphere, which had become horribly intense. *Does anyone actually like anyone else in this room right now?* he wondered, toying with the idea of simply walking out and retreating to the safety of his bed. Then he remembered that Larry was also up there, which put him off somewhat.

"Grow up, Serena," Mike growled. "You can be such a cow at times."

"I'm a cow? You're the one who's constantly making fun of me!"

He sniggered. "Stop giving me so much material to work with, then."

Serena hoisted herself up and placed her hands on her hips. Despite the fact that she was nearly a foot shorter than Mike, not to mention about five stone lighter, Kester would have still put money on her in a fight. "Also," she said with cold deliberation, "haven't you noticed that your *girlfriend* here has the start of a moustache?"

Ouch, Kester thought, immediately looking at Lara, who still seemed unconcerned. It was true though, he'd noticed it the other day. Not much of a moustache, to be fair. Certainly not anything that detracted from her overall good looks. But a definite shadow, nonetheless, with just a couple of whiskers protruding next to the nostrils.

"That's so bloody unkind of you," Mike flared. "What do you get out of being so horrible to everyone, eh?"

Lara reached out and patted Mike on the shoulder. "Hey, don't let it bother you," she said, giving them both a big smile. "She's right. I do have the start of a moustache. Big deal."

Serena looked slightly nettled. "Yeah, you do," she continued, folding her arms defensively. "Have you considered waxing?"

"Serena!" Pamela, Miss Wellbeloved, and Mike chorused in unison.

Lara started to laugh. "No. I'm growing it." She looked at their faces and laughed harder. "Gee, I don't even know where to start. Dimitri, give me a hand here."

Dimitri sighed and swept around with a theatrical flourish. "You English are very slow. You need to open your eyes a little. See things for how they really are."

"I don't follow," Mike said, looking with confusion at them all.

"Lara is transgender, yes? She is changing to a man. Okay? It's no big deal. Let's move on."

"Oh. *Oh.*" Mike nodded. He pondered, then looked at the ceiling. Then he looked back at Lara and rubbed his chin.

"Well," he concluded, with a grin. "That explains it, then."

"You don't have to treat me different, you know," Lara said. "I'm exactly the same person I ever was, okay?"

Serena looked shell-shocked and more than a little bit guilty. Kester eyed her with satisfaction. *That'll teach you for being such an inutterable git,* he thought, enjoying her discomfort.

"Gosh, that's a bit of a bombshell," Miss Wellbeloved said. "But of course," she added quickly, "we fully support your decision."

Lara batted the comment away. "Honestly, it's no big deal. I always thought of myself as a boy anyway, so getting the operations done is the logical step."

"Is that why your brother doesn't speak to you anymore?" Kester asked.

Lara sighed. "Yup." She looked out of the window. "It was pretty hurtful, if I'm honest. We always got along so well. Maybe he'll come around one day."

"Ah, brothers can be such a pain," Mike said sympathetically.

"Could you let us know what you'd prefer us to call you?" Miss Wellbeloved added. "We don't want to make you feel uncomfortable by referring to you by the wrong name."

Lara laughed. "Well, it's up to you. I know some people are still trying to get used to it. If you want to call me by the name I feel comfortable with, it's Luke."

"Okay," Miss Wellbeloved said. "From hereon in, it's Luke, then."

They all nodded. Pamela smiled. "I do like the name Luke. I once had the most enormous crush on an old dentist of mine who was called Luke. He had the loveliest smile."

"As you might imagine, if he was a bloody dentist," Mike remarked dryly.

Kester suddenly remembered. "Was that why you were going into that cosmetic surgeon in Exeter then, Lara? I mean Luke. Sorry about that. It might take me a while to adjust."

Luke looked surprised. "You saw me? Why didn't you say hello?"

"I thought you were having some work done and might not want people to know."

"Aw, that's kind of you to think about my feelings. So you didn't tell anyone?"

Kester shook his head.

"Yeah," Luke continued, looking out of the window. "It's been a real long process. I can't have the main operation until another year and a half because the doctors have to make sure you're committed to it. But I'll get there in the end."

Serena swallowed. "Lara. Sorry, Luke, I mean. I'd like to apologise. I didn't mean to be rude. I was angry at Mike, not you."

Luke shrugged. "It doesn't matter. It's no biggie. I suppose it feels really strange that people are starting to notice now, though."

Mike patted his own beard proudly. "You've got a way to go until you reach the bushiness of this little beauty though."

"As if anyone would want a beard that looked like their grandmother's knitted beret," Serena scowled.

"I'd recommend a beard for you, Serena," he replied. "Then you could grow it over your mouth and shut yourself up."

Miss Wellbeloved wiped her eyes and gathered the folds of her cardigan about herself. "Well, enough of all this chat. Though thank you very much for telling us, Luke." She smiled. "The name suits you very well, I think. Right, it's nearly seven, and I could do with a walk along the seafront to clear my head a little. Does anyone want to join me?"

Everyone nodded except Kester, who shook his head. "I'm going to stay here, if that's alright," he said. "I want to see if I can find anything out about the Celtic brooch, and I need to prepare for my interview."

"Of course." Miss Wellbeloved clicked her fingers at the

others. "No time like the present. Let's see what's happening with the police too. I presume they will have cordoned off the area. It's probably a good idea to buy a newspaper too, see what story the journalists have run with on Peter Hopper's death."

"I'll meet you all for breakfast in an hour," Kester called after them as they trooped towards the front door. "Don't order without me, I'm already starving." He waited until they'd left, then retreated up the stairs. The hotel seemed unnervingly silent, apart from the sound of a dog barking somewhere nearby. He hoped Mr Onions wasn't lurking somewhere in the shadows, waiting to berate him again.

Fortunately, the landing was empty. Kester knocked timidly on the bedroom door. "Everything alright in there?" He peered in.

Larry sat on his usual bottom bunk. He looked impossibly large in the cramped space, like a sizeable toad squeezed into a tiny box. "Everything is perfectly fine, I assure you."

His face suggested the contrary. In fact, Kester noticed his eyes were red. *Surely he hasn't been crying?* he thought and hastily looked away with embarrassment. "Um, don't mind me," he continued as he shuffled up the rickety ladder to his bed atop the other bunk. "I'm just going to do a bit of research on the Celtic brooch, see if I can find anything out."

Higgins grunted, shifting his weight on the bed. "Is there any point?"

"What do you mean?"

"I mean exactly what I say. We've failed, Kester. Failed miserably. And now Jennifer hates me."

Kester raised an eyebrow. *Why's he so bothered about what Miss Wellbeloved thinks of him? I always thought he disliked her as much as he dislikes the rest of us.*

"I don't think she hates you," he said as he reached for his laptop. "She's just passionate about what she does, and she wants us to succeed."

"Hmm. Fat chance."

Kester bit his lip. "Please don't take this the wrong way, but don't you think that kind of negativity is what's causing the problem?"

Higgins rolled onto his back, stomach rising upwards like an ancient hill. The mattress wheezed under his weight, along with the flimsy metal bedframe. "I'm only being realistic," he muttered, staring at the bunk above. "Someone has to be."

The laptop whirred into action with a low, soothing hum. Kester lowered himself onto his stomach, preparing himself to settle in for an hour or so. "The thing is," he continued, casually glancing across, "it rubs off on everyone else. If you keep telling us that we won't succeed, then it's more likely to be true, isn't it?"

"I don't see any logic whatsoever in that argument."

"I mean," Kester pressed on, "if you tell yourself you'll never succeed, then you've failed before you've even got started, haven't you?"

"No. That's a complete fallacy."

"Miss Wellbeloved likes you, you know. She just wishes you'd be more positive and work with her to make this operation a success. That's all."

Higgins sighed like a whale surfacing for air, then rolled pointedly onto his side, facing the wall. His buttock-crack poked unappealingly over the top of his slacks, with a few sprouting grey hairs popping out for good measure. Kester rolled his eyes. *Silly old sod,* he thought as he opened the internet browser. *You can't say I didn't try.*

He saw some fresh emails in his inbox from Anya and his dad, but chose to ignore them. He had precious little time as it was without having to update his father on events and think of something witty to say to Anya. *I don't even think I could come up with a decent knock-knock joke at the moment,* he thought, massaging his eyelids. *God, I wish I could just go back to sleep.*

An online search for "Celtic brooches" brought up page

after page of images. Nothing even vaguely matched the brooch they'd found up in the woods. They were all much more complex patterns. The brooch they'd found was very simple—just a basic cross formation with a hollow in the middle, where he guessed a precious stone must have once sat. The edges featured knotted detailing between the four arms of the cross, but other than that, it was relatively plain.

Still, he thought, as he frowned at the screen. *One of the brooches online must look something like this one. I can't believe we've found a one-of-a-kind piece.*

However, page after page revealed nothing that even remotely resembled it. He tried typing in "ancient Celtic brooches" instead. A low grunt from the bunk opposite informed him that Larry had nodded off. Sure enough, when he glanced over, he could see the rhythmic rise and fall of his hip, like a mountain range about to experience an earthquake.

Again, page after page returned nothing similar. He yawned. It was tempting to just give up, roll over, and enjoy a nap. *It would be so nice,* he thought, *to just forget about all of this, if only just for an hour or two.* But then Miss Wellbeloved's face flashed before him, along with Mike's, Serena's, Pamela's, Lara's. *Luke's,* he corrected himself sternly, hoping he'd remember in future. *It's going to take a bit of getting used to.* Even Dimitri's sour expression came to mind, though for what reason, he wasn't quite sure. *I can't let them all down,* he realised. *I just can't.*

He tried a few more searches. Again, nothing came up that even remotely resembled it. The laptop screen seemed unbearably vibrant, somehow mocking him with its perky backlight. An urge came over him to slam his fist on the keyboard and lob the entire thing onto the floor.

One last page, he thought, looking at his watch. It was nearly breakfast time, and there was no way he was missing the opportunity to tuck into a sausage sandwich, even if the sausages did taste disturbingly like they'd been made several years ago and half-stuffed with sawdust.

Then he saw it. Halfway down the page. The exact same pattern. He yelped and sprang up on the bed. Higgins grunted, tremored slightly, then rolled over onto his back, his mouth gaping bowl-like towards the ceiling. Kester compared the brooch with the image, hand shaking. It was definitely the same. Not just slightly similar. *Identical.* He clicked through to the website, quietly praying that it wasn't an outdated link. However, the screen loaded up—a page from Cambridge University's Archaeology department.

"Yes, yes, yes!" he squeaked with a triumphant punch in the air. "Larry! Wake up!"

Larry snorted, choking on his own saliva. "What? What's happening?" He wiped his mouth, then fixed an accusing eye on Kester's bunk. "What did you wake me up for, halfwit?"

"I woke you up for a bloody good reason! Come and look at this!"

The older man got out of bed with all the energy and grace of a slug rolling off a flowerpot. "This had better be good."

Kester grinned. "It is. Look at this."

Larry examined the screen, wincing at its brightness, then stared at the brooch in Kester's palm. His eyes widened. "Well I'll be blowed," he murmured as he stroked his moustache. "It's exactly the same." With his usual lack of manners, he seized the laptop and started reading.

"Says it dates back to 50 CE to 100 CE," he read, as he patted his shirt pocket for his glasses. "That it was believed to be Celtic, from Scotland." He looked up, all hints of sleep erased. "So, it's definitely a Scottish brooch. That's interesting. But the big question is, what the devil were the Scots doing down here?"

Kester scratched his head. "Grace McCready dated it to the Roman era, and Xena Sunningdale told us that some Celtic warriors attacked this region, but were captured by the Romans. That would explain it, wouldn't it?"

"It certainly would. The age of the brooch is right too, the Romans were in England around 50 CE." Higgins passed the laptop back, then pressed his finger against his lips. "This is interesting. Most interesting. How does this link to our problematic spirit, though? If indeed it does at all."

Kester looked up, eyes shining. "Wouldn't this make sense if the spirit was a fetch? Didn't Miss Wellbeloved say that they were from Ireland or Scotland, and that they latched themselves on to people sometimes? What if the fetch travelled down from Scotland with the Celtic warrior that we dug up in the woods?"

Larry shook his head. "No. Nice theory, but there would be nothing keeping the spirit here after the Celtic chap had died. There's absolutely no reason why it would hide in the ground for centuries, no motivation at all. Fetches don't do that."

Kester sighed then looked at his watch. "I need to think some more about it. There are some clues here, I'm sure; it's just a matter of working out what they are." *I'm sure Grace McCready has something to do with all of this too,* he thought, remembering her horrible cottage, the dark, depressive atmosphere of her living room. *She's from Scotland, maybe she's more involved in all of this than she's admitting.*

"Well," Higgins concluded, "you'll need to work it out quickly, for all our sakes. Otherwise, this case is doomed."

Kester grinned. *Negative yet again,* he thought, wondering if Larry Higgins was capable of being optimistic, or whether it was a physical impossibility. "A steaming pile of hot sausages and buttery toast should help," he suggested. "Are you coming?"

Higgins's face darkened. "I'd better not. I'll get something later." Kester leapt down from the bunk.

"Look," he said and fixed the older man with his most earnest, forceful expression. "Miss Wellbeloved would be horrified if she thought she'd upset you. If you come with me now, she'll be really pleased, because then she'll know that you do care about the job after all."

"Of course I bloody care about it!"

"Well then. Are you joining me?"

He sighed. "Oh, alright. Just to stop you going on at me." He pulled open the door, letting in an immediate draught. "And by the way . . ."

Kester turned. "Yes?"

To his surprise, Larry patted him on the shoulder. Awkwardly, as one might pat an alarming Rottweiler, but it was a pat nonetheless. "You've done a good job," he muttered, then looked away, concealing his expression. "Well done. You have your mother's determination."

"Thanks very much." Kester waited for him to depart, then smiled at his broad, overbearing back as it disappeared down the gloomy landing. *Goodness me,* he thought, closing the door behind him. *Did I just get a compliment from Larry Higgins? Perhaps the old boy isn't as bad as I thought he was.*

I just wish I could work out what's niggling me about this case, he thought as they went downstairs and out into the open. If only he wasn't so tired, then his brain could process it properly. *What am I missing? And more importantly,* he concluded with a frown, *will I have enough time to figure it out?*

CHAPTER 17: TALKING TO A DJINN

Kester sat down at the café table, then immediately ducked as Luke thrust a mobile phone dangerously close to his head.

"Guess who we just heard from?" He rubbed his buzz-cut with excitement and pressed the phone even closer towards Kester's face.

"I have no idea," Kester mumbled, shielding himself. He peered at the screen. "Who's that? It's not a number I recognise."

"It's the archaeologist, dummy," Serena chimed. Kester was irritated to see that she'd already ordered and was currently sipping a mug of tea, which smelt tantalisingly pleasant.

He blinked, then moved aside as Larry squeezed himself down on the chair beside him. "The archaeologist? Gosh, he's up early, isn't he?"

Luke laughed and tweaked his shirt-collar. "He is now."

Mike leant across, pulling the sugar pot to his end of the table. "I don't think he was best pleased to get woken up. Apparently he'd been up all last night examining the skeleton and all the other things they found down in the grave."

"Lara, could you pass me the sugar?" Pamela said, then slapped her forehead. "Oh sod it. Sorry, love. Luke. I will get it in the end."

Mike chuckled. "You know," he said slowly, "the closest equivalent male name to Lara is Larry. You could have called yourself Larry Junior instead."

"That wasn't an option, thank you very much!" Larry barked as he gestured to the waitress with a curled finger. "There is only room for one Larry in this agency. And it's not as though Lara here will be my son."

"Don't you mean Luke?" Serena said snippily.

Larry scratched his head. "Yes, I suppose if the rest of you are going to start calling her that—"

"You mean him," Miss Wellbeloved corrected. "If Luke has felt like a male all his life, then he'd probably prefer to be called by the correct pronoun, don't you think?"

"Look," Larry said. "I don't have a problem with it at all. Don't make out like I'm being a backward idiot over this. I've been very supportive, haven't I, Lara?"

Luke waved a hand in his direction. "Hey, it's fine, I understand. It takes some adjustment. I'm kind of getting used to it all myself, really. I never thought I'd get to the stage where I'd finally be accepted for the surgery. You know, it feels great, but overwhelming at the same time."

"Would you rather we stopped going on about it?" Serena asked. "It's probably even more overwhelming having us constantly firing questions at you." She smiled winningly, leaning her chin on her hands.

Kester couldn't help noticing how much nicer Serena was being towards Luke since she'd heard the news. *Perhaps it's taught her a lesson,* he thought, *about not being so mean to everyone all the time.*

Luke shrugged. "It's okay," he said. "I don't mind if you

want to ask questions. I'd rather people were just open about it rather than being scared to talk about it with me, to be honest. But at the moment, we'd better just focus on this case, hadn't we? Especially now we've been kicked out of the hotel. That's added a bit more pressure."

Larry looked abashed. "Yes, well, that's probably my fault," he muttered. Everyone waited. "Erm, I probably shouldn't have flown off the handle like that." Miss Wellbeloved's jaw flew open. She looked at Kester, who grinned. *Looks like the old boy's keen to make amends,* he thought, liking him a tiny fraction more.

"Anyway, do you all want to hear what the archaeologist had to say?" Luke interrupted.

"Absolutely. Out with it." Higgins rested his elbows on the table, happy to divert the attention from himself.

"Those bones we dug up on the headland? They're about *2,000 years old.* The archaeologist reckons the guy was buried there in the Roman times."

Kester grinned. "That's exactly what we thought." He quickly filled the others in on what he'd found out online about the brooch.

"Yeah, but it gets more interesting than that," Luke continued, practically vibrating in the seat with excitement. "He couldn't tell much else from the skeleton itself, apart from that it was a male, well-built and very tall, over six foot—which in those days was more unusual. However," he added, leaning forward. "The interesting thing was the knife in his chest."

"Go on." Higgins nodded, disregarding his tea when it arrived, despite the inviting puffs of steam it was sending into the air.

"Turns out it's a sacrificial dagger. But the archaeologist said the man wasn't murdered. The position of the knife suggested that he'd fallen deliberately on his weapon."

"So, he killed himself?" Kester said, eyes widening.

"Yep." Luke beamed. "But there's more."

Kester wriggled in his seat, feeling as excited as a child at a birthday party. He slurped at his tea without even being aware he was doing so. "Go on, tell us!"

"The pattern on the hilt is apparently an ancient Celtic pattern, and the archaeologist said it was from a particular part of Scotland, near the Angus region? I don't even know where that is."

"Angus is between Perthshire and Aberdeenshire," Miss Wellbeloved said. She gave the waitress a grateful smile as she deposited a fried egg sandwich in front of her. "I went there on holiday once, a long time ago. Beautiful scenery, very dramatic."

Kester frowned. *Why does that feel like it should be significant?* he wondered. Perhaps it was just tiredness, making even minor details suddenly seem important. He took another gulp of tea, hoping that it would wake him up a bit.

"But guess what?" Luke piped up with an impatient rap of his fist on the tabletop. "There's more. Brace yourselves."

"This had better be good," Larry muttered. "We need something solid to go on."

"This is good," Dimitri confirmed, rubbing his hands together. "Really good. Just wait and see."

Kester leaned forward, feeling more excited by the moment. *Finally, a breakthrough. After so many dead ends, it's about time we got lucky.*

"The archaeologist found a few other things in the grave," Luke continued. "A rotted piece of cloth. Part of an old scabbard. And, a weird clay figure that had broken in two. Most of the markings on it had been rubbed away over time, but the guy said he thought it was some kind of poppet."

"What the heck is a poppet?" Kester asked. He'd always thought it was a brand of chocolate, but he was guessing that in this instance, it wasn't. *Unless the warrior asked to be buried with some snacks,* he thought and bit back a giggle.

Luke looked at Dimitri, who nodded, happy to take centre stage. "A poppet is a little figure," he explained, "used in magic rituals. That is the right word, ritual?"

"Yes, absolutely," Pamela confirmed, nodding enthusiastically. "I took a course in magic ritual a few years back. Pagans used special figures, called poppets, in their spells. They sometimes represented gods or even people that they didn't like and wanted to hurt."

"Like voodoo dolls?" Kester asked. He'd watched a horror film about voodoo doctors as a child and hadn't been able to sleep for about a week afterwards.

"Yes, similar to voodoo dolls," Pamela said with a smile. "Sometimes, Pagans even used these figures to trap spirits. A bit like how we trap spirits in water bottles, I suppose."

"Only their method was rather classier," Larry added with a sanctimonious nod.

"What does this poppet look like, then?" Kester watched the others receive their breakfasts, inhaled the wonderful aroma of grease, fat, and meat, and felt incredibly jealous. He looked longingly at Mike's fry-up, wondering if Mike would mind if he stole a slice of toast.

"According to the archaeologist, it's real simple-looking," Luke said, oblivious to Kester's yearning gaze at his food as he bit into his beans on toast. "Made of limestone. Looks like two identical human-shaped figures that were once stuck together, but have now snapped in two, holding their hands over their hearts."

"Two figures?" Kester looked up. "Two identical figures?"

"Aha, now he gets it!" Dimitri said with a sarcastic smile. "Go on, Kester. You are the detective, you have worked it out, I can tell."

"This must relate to our spirit," Kester breathed. "Two identical figures. *Twins. Doppelgängers.* And Pamela, you just said these poppets were used to trap spirits. That sounds like one hell of a coincidence to me."

Miss Wellbeloved beamed. "We were thinking exactly the same, Kester. We wondered if the spirit had been trapped in this limestone figurine, and, when it broke, it was suddenly released."

"So, the poor fetch has been trapped in a poppet for a couple of thousand years," Mike said, scratching his chin thoughtfully. "That'd be enough to make any spirit furious, wouldn't it?"

Kester thought hard. It all made a lot of sense. "What caused the poppet to break, I wonder?" he asked.

Dimitri shrugged. "It could happen over time, the land shifting, you know."

"Yes, the coastline around here erodes frequently," Pamela added. "Or it could have just happened through impact. Or," she said significantly, "if someone was nosing around up there, digging up graves like we were."

"Someone like the Lyme Regis Ancient History Club, you mean?" Kester suggested.

"Hey, we all thought the soil felt weirdly loose when we were digging up the skeleton, didn't we?" Mike said suddenly, looking excited.

"So perhaps someone had dug it up already, then replaced the soil," Miss Wellbeloved said breathlessly.

They all nodded. Kester whistled and leaned back in his chair. "Wow. That's intense. But why would they cover the grave back over, then? Wouldn't they want to tell the whole town what they'd discovered?"

"It depends who discovered it, I suppose," Pamela said. "And whether they realised that they'd disturbed a spirit or not."

Kester swallowed. The new information answered a lot of questions but left still more unanswered. They now knew the spirit was old, angry, and murderous, and targeting a particular group of people. But where was it hiding? And what kind of spirit was it?

"So," he began as he tried to make sense of it all. "Surely it must be a fetch then? Miss Wellbeloved, you said that fetches linked themselves to Ireland or Scotland—"

"It's rarer to find them in Scotland," she interrupted.

"Yeah, but still. This ancient Celtic warrior comes from Scotland. Isn't it safe to presume that the fetch came from Scotland with the warrior, then was imprisoned here for centuries? And now he's roaming around Lyme Regis, furious with humans for trapping it for so long?"

Miss Wellbeloved took a deep breath. "The thing is," she said slowly, "a fetch is a very particular type of spirit. It's deeply wedded to a particular location. If it can't be in that location, it weds itself to a person."

"Like the Celtic warrior?" Kester suggested.

Miss Wellbeloved nodded, then shook her head. "Well, yes," she admitted, "it's entirely possible that the fetch could have been trapped down there all this time. But when it escaped, it would have either needed to return to Scotland, which it would have struggled to do, or find another person from Scotland to latch on to."

Kester frowned. "What about Grace McCready? She's from Scotland."

Pamela leant across, and squeezed his arm. "Yes, but she would need to be from the exact same place the fetch came from originally."

"Which, in this case, is this Angus region, right?" Luke asked. "If the archaeologist's findings can be trusted."

Kester shook his head. He could tell that the others were sceptical, but they hadn't been the ones in Grace McCready's house, with its eerie silence and sense of watchfulness. *Maybe they're right,* he thought, taking a deep breath. He knew how easy it was to get excited about a possible lead, only to find out that it was a red herring. But still, it niggled away at him, the nagging feeling that Grace McCready was the key to all of this.

"The main thing," Larry said as he dabbed the corner of his mouth with a napkin, "is that this spirit is incredibly old, extremely powerful, and very angry. Which puts us all in a worrying position, doesn't it?"

"Yep!" Mike agreed. He swallowed his last mouthful, gave his stomach a contemplative pat, then belched.

"Well, let's focus on the positive," Miss Wellbeloved said, looking deliberately in Larry's direction. "I feel like we're making some progress, which is good."

Kester gulped. He thought back to his last experience with an old, angry spirit, back in Exeter. That particular event had ended up with Serena nearly being killed, Pamela and Miss Wellbeloved being lobbed around a room like rag dolls, and Mike accidentally burning someone's house down. He dreaded to think what would happen this time.

Resting his chin on his fingers, he studied the quiet street outside. As usual, it was deserted. The thin hand of the waitress emerged in front of his line of vision, complete with a plate full of sausage sandwiches, which instantly made him feel much better. He made room for the plate, choosing to ignore his feelings of disquiet and focus on the important task of eating instead.

The others joined him, steadily munching their breakfasts until they were all finished.

"Anything else to report?" Kester asked as he ate the last bite of sandwich. Now that he'd eaten the sandwich, he rather wished he hadn't. It sat heavily in his stomach, like a bowling ball.

"Yes actually, there's more good news," Miss Wellbeloved replied. She whipped out a pocket mirror and started checking her teeth. "The newspapers made no mention of anything supernatural in this morning's edition. They simply focused on it being a suicide, as a result of Peter Hopper being in mourning for his friends."

"That's great," Kester said. "Does that mean the government

will back off a bit now?"

"Let's hope so. However, even better—Philpot hired some undercover men to log on to the local newspaper website and leave comments, declaring how ridiculous the whole supernatural angle was."

Kester laughed. "What, the government was actually trolling the local paper? What about *The Serial Suspector*?"

"No point trolling *The Serial Suspector*," Mike said. "Everyone who reads it is probably a trolling lunatic anyway."

"But the best part about trolling the local paper," Miss Wellbeloved continued, "is that lots of the local people started joining in, criticising the press for running such a silly story. So that's great news."

Larry gave a significant cough. "Looks like things might be finally improving for us all, eh?" The forced brightness of his tone made Kester smile. *He's having a go at being optimistic for a change,* he thought. *Who would have thought that he'd actually listen to what somebody told him?*

Miss Wellbeloved narrowed her eyes, then delivered a wisp of a smile. "Yes. I think you could say that."

"One might almost think we stand a chance of solving the case."

She stared at him, scrutinising his expression, then burst into laughter. "You might be right, Larry. And why the sudden change of heart? You were all doom and gloom before."

He cleared his throat again, tugged at his shirt collar, then muttered something inaudible.

"Pardon?"

"I said, I'd like to formally apologise for my behaviour earlier."

A gasp erupted around the table. Higgins reddened. "Alright, alright, you don't have to make such a big thing about it," he grumbled, picking at a crumb on the table. "I have been a bit negative, and I admit that it hasn't helped. So you have my apology, Jennifer, if you'll accept it."

"Of course I will." She reached over and clasped him on the hand. "Thank you. Let's move forward as a team, shall we?"

He looked at her hand and simpered.

Kester cringed. The sight of a sickly-sweet Higgins was even worse than a grumpy one. "I'm going to head back, to get prepared for my interview," he announced as he pushed his chair back with a metallic shriek.

Miss Wellbeloved nodded approvingly. "Absolutely. Good luck, Kester. This means a lot to your father."

Who might have at least rung me to wish me good luck, he thought. *Goodness knows I could do with it.* The prospect of talking to an actual, real genie was making him break out in a nervous sweat.

"Don't let her scare you," Higgins said with a jovial little wave. "Because my word, she really is terrifying. An excellent teacher, of course, but enough to give anyone nightmares."

"Thanks for that," Kester mumbled, yanking the door open. "I'll see you all later. I presume you're going to go and visit Grace McCready after you've finished here?"

"That's right," Miss Wellbeloved said. "I think she needs further investigation, especially after what you said about her house, Kester. We'll meet you back at the hotel. Then I suppose we need to think about where we're going to stay for the next few nights."

"I spotted a few nice comfortable benches down by the promenade," Mike added.

Kester grimaced, then stepped out into the cold. *No, thank you very much,* he thought. Staying in their current hotel had been quite bad enough. Looking down the street, he could see a small crowd gathered in a huddle on the pavement and wondered if it was to do with Peter Hopper. *Surely people in Lyme Regis are starting to get rattled now,* he thought, marching back up to the hotel. *If I lived here and was over the age of sixty,*

I'd definitely be concerned.

The hotel was unsettlingly silent when he entered. The familiar odour of mould and burnt toast immediately hit him, but there was no sign of the proprietor. *Presumably, he's somewhere out back, skulking around,* Kester thought as he twisted his head around the dark corridor. The whole place was deserted. It was slightly creepy, but then, everything seemed a little bit sinister at the moment, especially when feeling utterly exhausted and rather over-sensitive.

Maybe Mr Onions is the murderer, Kester thought, tiptoeing up the stairs. *Wouldn't that be a great horror story, that we've been living in the same hotel as the murderer all along and chasing after doppelgänger spirits that didn't really exist?* Though somehow, he couldn't quite envisage it. Even though the old man had been rather odd, he moved with roughly the same speed as a three-toed sloth, which would presumably be a hindrance to any self-respecting killer.

Plus, you're not going to be able to get away from the fact that there's something supernatural at work in Lyme Regis, he chastised himself as he entered the bedroom. *You've had months to get used to this whole ghost thing now, so you may as well start accepting it.* He looked across at his laptop, still perched on the pillow of his bunk, and swallowed. *Especially as you've got to talk to a three-thousand-year-old spirit in about half an hour's time.*

To take his mind off things, he opened Anya's email, scanning the contents for evidence that she might still be annoyed at him. Thankfully, her tone still seemed fairly upbeat, though she said she wouldn't be able to see him next Wednesday, as she had a book club event to go to. *She's always at that bloody book club,* he thought with a wry smile. *That's probably why I like her so much. I've finally found someone whose love of books equals my own.*

For the remaining few minutes, he readied himself for the interview and ran through a few responses in his head. His heart was starting to hammer hard against his ribcage, despite his best attempts to calm himself.

"It'd help if I had any idea what to expect," he whispered, staring at the laptop screen and biting his lip. As if in response, a familiar beeping tune alerted him to the fact that there was an incoming Skype call. Gulping, he quickly answered it and braced himself for the worst.

"Er . . . hello?" He stared at the screen in confusion. Whatever he'd been expecting, it certainly wasn't this. All he could see was an office, an impressive bookshelf stuffed with ancient texts lined up in neat rows, but no actual person or spirit to talk to. The screen flickered, momentarily freezing. *Bloody reception,* Kester thought, feeling more anxious than ever. *What should I do, hang up and try again later?*

"Good morning, Kester. I trust you are well?"

The voice sounded like a flood of ball bearings rolling across sand—smooth yet metallic. It most definitely didn't sound human. Kester squinted, then gasped. His heart plummeted. *My god, what the hell is that thing?* he thought desperately, eyes widening with disbelief and fright.

Say something! You have to say something! he reminded himself, aware that the silence had dragged on for far too long already. "Oh, er . . . hello there, Doctor . . . Doctor . . ." *Oh Christ, I've forgotten her name!* It was hardly surprising, but nonetheless absolutely mortifying. Now that he could see the genie, he'd lost his ability to speak or even think properly. *What sort of spirit is this?* he thought, scarcely able to comprehend the sight in front of him. *And how do I even begin to start talking to it?*

A shifting mist rolled impatiently in front of the screen, glimmering icy-blue every so often before fading to nothing. When it paused, Kester could make out the vague shape of a head, complete with two terrifyingly black eyes, which bored through the screen like lasers.

"Dr Barqa-Abu," the genie reminded him as she roved

and shifted with cobra-like precision. He got the uncomfortable feeling that she wasn't terribly impressed with him, which didn't help to steady his nerves at all. "Kester," she continued, "I presume this is the first time you've spoken to a Jiniri?"

"A what? Sorry, I . . ."

"A Jiniri? One of the Djinn? I would have presumed, being Julio Ribero's son, that you would be more than familiar with us."

Gosh, I'm messing this interview up even more badly than I thought I would, he realised and tugged at his shirt. A moment ago, the room had seemed chilly, but now he thought he might melt in the heat.

"I'm very sorry, Dr Barqa-Abu," he said, hoping he'd pronounced it right. "You're right, I've never met a Djinn before. I'm probably coming across as a bit of an idiot."

The shape stopped moving, which enabled him to see her face more clearly. Upon reflection, he wished she'd return to moving around instead. When she was still, he could grasp the outline of her features: sharp, bone-like, and severe. *And those eyes!* he thought with rising horror. They were just pits of darkness in the misty face: empty, endless, terrible holes. *I know I shouldn't be prejudiced,* he thought, *but she really is like something out of a nightmare.*

"You are not an idiot," she concluded finally, roving restlessly once more. "It is common to be uncomfortable around a Djinn to begin with. Shall we begin talking about your application?"

"Yes, please, by all means," he bumbled. His voice emerged uncomfortably high-pitched, like a terrified mouse. *I must sound like an absolute pillock,* he realised with a sinking heart. *I might as well hang up now and save myself the pain of messing it up any more.*

Dr Barqa-Abu moved closer to the screen. He wished she hadn't, and instinctively shrank back, worried she might somehow slip through the monitor and out into his room.

"I am intrigued by your role in your father's agency," she began. "Could you tell me more about that?"

Kester coughed and loosened his collar. "Um, well, I've only been working with my father for four months. To be honest, I didn't even know I had a father until then. I just lived with my mum in Cambridge."

"Yes, the great Gretchen Lanner, is that correct?"

He nodded. The mention of his mother's name helped to calm him down a fraction.

"I was sorry to hear of her death. Your mother was a formidable student."

Blimey, is there anyone who this genie hasn't taught? he wondered. "Thank you," he replied, fighting to regain control of his voice. "She was pretty amazing."

"You indicated on your application form that you are a spirit door-opener, like your late mother?"

Kester took a deep breath. "Well, that's what Dad says, anyway," he replied, choosing his words carefully. "I think so. I've managed to properly open the spirit door once before, but to be honest, I'm not sure I've got much control over it."

The Djinn paused. "Interesting. And you worked on the Bloody Mary case in Exeter? The spirit hidden in Robert Ransome's oil painting? Your father's agency received a lot of publicity for it."

He nodded. "Yes, I helped get rid of that spirit."

Dr Barqa-Abu stiffened, spinning back to the screen with horrifying speed. Her pointed features once again came into sharp focus. "We do not use terminology like that. Spirits are not lesser creatures, to be simply got rid of. We are not inferior beings. Do you understand?"

Kester's eyes widened. "Yes, of course. I'm sorry, I didn't mean it like that."

She retreated, hulking to the back of the room, her black, empty eyes scorching right through the screen into his own.

"Very well. Do not make the same mistake again. I do not tolerate spiritist comments." She paused, still glaring. "Let us continue. I would like you to tell me why you're interested in the business studies aspect of this course."

He swallowed, fighting to compose himself. "My father wants me to take over the family business one day."

"The family business?" Again, the Djinn shot forward, and Kester backed away, starting to wish he'd never answered the call. This was going about as badly as he could have imagined, and he'd already been prepared for it to go appallingly. "Surely you mean Jennifer Wellbeloved's family business? After all, it was her family who built it up all those years ago. Your father merely stole it, like a magpie."

"Technically, he was given it by Miss Wellbeloved's father," Kester mentioned, then shut his mouth when he saw the hostility in the Djinn's eyes.

"Humans," she muttered. "A thoroughly patriarchal species. It is a shame. I always felt Jennifer would make an exceptional agency owner. Your father, on the other hand—"

"Hey, my father's okay," Kester said, bristling instinctively. "He is a bit of a hothead at times, but his heart's in the right place."

Dr Barqa-Abu let out a brittle whistle of noise, which might have been a laugh. "Remember, I taught your father," she replied. "I know what he is like. I remember him well." She straightened, then fixed Kester in her gaze once more. "So, you want to learn business studies in order to take over a business that is not yours to take, is that correct?"

Kester hung his head. "Well, I think so. But I don't feel comfortable with the idea that we stole it off Miss Wellbeloved. She's so nice."

The Djinn paused, as though mulling over his answer. "You are interesting," she said finally, shifting at such a rate that she was almost invisible. "Certainly your previous qualifications are impressive, if not rather unusual in our industry. A degree from Cambridge University is a significant achievement."

Kester watched as the mist sloped around before solidifying once more into a vaguely human shape.

"However, I am concerned at your lack of experience," she concluded and leaned in to study him better. "Most of my students have been immersed in the supernatural for years. They have grown up among spirits. They understand this world. I sense no such understanding in you."

Kester nodded. "That's probably true. But I'm a fast learner." *Why am I fighting my corner here?* he wondered, bemused at his own words. *I'm not even sure I want to do this course!*

Dr Barqa-Abu tapped what may or may not have been her chin, thoughtfully looking into the distance. "Very well," she said finally. "One final question. Why do you *really* want to study this course, Kester?"

He took a deep breath. *That's a very good question.*

"I want to make my mother proud," he blurted. Dr Barqa-Abu went still, her features now clearer than ever before, listening intently to his reply. "I want to make my father proud too. And I want to do the right thing. I think this is the right thing."

"Do you?" She paused and studied him with fierce intensity.

"Yes." Once he'd said it, he realised that it was the truth. Only, he hadn't really appreciated it until now. "Yes, I want to do something that makes a difference in the world. And I think this does."

The genie reclined and folded a pair of tiny skeletal hands over what might have been her stomach. Then, she started to shift again, and the hands vanished into the smoky vapours of her body.

"Thank you, Kester." Her voice was impassive, revealing nothing. "I will review your application and this interview. Then I will let you know my decision. It has been most interesting talking to you."

"You too," Kester said as he pushed up his glasses. "Thank you for your time."

The mist softened a little around the edges before swirling into invisibility. "Thank you. Goodbye, Kester."

The screen went dead immediately. Kester let out a low whistle. He felt as though he'd just been involved in a fight with a heavyweight boxer and had somehow managed to avoid being knocked out. *Well, that went horribly,* he thought and flung himself against the pillow. *I could be wrong here, but I'm fairly sure I won't be offered a place on the course.* He bit his lip, surveying the dirty ceiling above his head, not quite sure how to feel. In the end, he decided to not feel anything about it at all. It was the simpler option. There were far too many things for him to worry about as it was.

His phone vibrated against the bedpost, startling him. He reached over, hoping it was someone he could moan at. He fancied a big moan about things. *I hope it's Anya, perhaps she'll cheer me up,* he thought, then glanced at the screen. Unfortunately, it wasn't.

Miss Wellbeloved. Hmm. What's gone wrong now? He sat up. "Hello?"

"Kester, have you had your interview?" She sounded worried.

"Yes, I've actually just finished."

"Great. Strange things are afoot. We need you up here."

He flicked his legs over the edge of the bed and let them dangle in the air. "Where? Grace McCready's house?"

"Yes. We're here at the moment."

"Is she giving you all a hard time?"

Miss Wellbeloved sighed. Kester could imagine her right now, running her hands over her hair, as she always did when she was anxious.

"No, Kester. She's not giving us a hard time. Because she's

not here."

Kester frowned. "How are you in the house then? Did her daughter let you in?"

"No. There's no one here at all."

"Hang on, you've lost me." He cleared his throat. "What's going on?"

There was a scuffling noise, then a gruff snort echoed down the line. "Kester, get over here now," Larry ordered, sounding breathless. "The house is completely empty; it looks like the place has been ransacked or something. The door was wide open. We need all hands on deck, so stop sodding around."

Crikey, Kester thought. *Does that mean our spirit has struck again?*

"Okay, I'm on my way," he replied, then jumped off the bunk bed and grabbed his jacket. His mind was racing. *What could it mean? If the spirit was going to kill her, why not just do it in her house? Unless this is just another false start and doesn't mean anything at all.*

The hotel hallway was silent, apart from the dim, faraway tick of an unseen clock. Kester paused. He couldn't shake off the feeling of disquiet—a sense that something bad was going to happen, and soon. Suddenly, his skin prickled, and he had the uncomfortable sensation of being watched.

Don't be silly, he told himself, clutching the bannister. It was horribly sticky under his fingers, so he swiftly let it go again. *You're not missing anything, and nobody is watching you. You're just feeling jittery because it's already been a long day and it's not even lunchtime yet.*

A low creak made him look up. The front door was opening. *Have the others come back to hurry me up?* he wondered, then realised that was impossible. There was no way they could have made it back down the hill and along the promenade in such a short space of time. He waited at the top of the stairs, feeling oddly apprehensive. After all, who was likely to come to this hotel? He knew there were no other guests but them.

It's probably the owner, he thought, then immediately hoped not.

The door shuddered on its hinges before flying open and smashing into the umbrella stand. Kester's mouth fell open.

Surely not, he thought with disbelief. He rubbed his eyes, then looked again.

"What a ridiculous door, eh? How is anyone meant to get in with such a foolish door?" The owner of the familiar voice stalked into the reception area, then caught Kester's eye.

Kester gawped.

His father beamed, swung his fedora off his head, and placed it on the reception desk with elegant precision. It rested on the side like a small mountain, resolute and wonderfully symbolic of the man who owned it.

"Hello there, Kester." He gestured, and Kester obediently descended, still unable to find quite the right words to express his surprise.

"What are you—?"

Dr Ribero silenced him with a shush of the lips and a knowing look. "I know, I know. I have been absent for much of this project. But," he continued as he wrapped an arm around Kester's shoulders and pulled him tight, "now I am here. And now it is time for us to wrap this case up, right?"

Kester stared at him, then slowly started to grin.

"It definitely is." He returned the embrace, patting his father gently on the back, surprised at just how glad he was to see him. "I was on my way out to do just that."

Ribero nodded, then extended a hand in front of them to lead the way. "Let's get to work then."

"Are you . . ." Kester paused, not quite knowing what the right choice of words was. "Are you sure you're okay? I mean, that you're well enough to—"

"Ah, I am fine," Ribero interrupted grandly. "And now I am

here to solve the case for you all, yes?" Without waiting for a response, he guided Kester towards the door. "Now, shall we?"

Kester gestured politely, mimicking Ribero's suave movement. "After you," he replied, and delivered what he hoped was his most dashing wink. "I insist."

Ribero chuckled. "See? You grow more like me every day."

Let's hope that's not too true, Kester thought with a wry smile. *I think there's only so much Argentinian fire I can safely handle.*

CHAPTER 18: SCOTTISH CONNECTIONS

After an energetic pant up the hill and a quick-fire recap of all the recent developments of the case, Kester led his father down the narrow road that led to Grace McCready's house. Ribero surveyed the property with distaste, observing the tumbledown brickwork, mossy roof, and bin bags spewing out over the garden, and shook his head in disbelief.

"I don't understand this," he concluded as he strode down the path, stepping over a rotten pile of potato peelings. "The English, they say this is quaint and charming, right? When, actually, it is just smelly and unpleasant."

"I don't think many people would call this house quaint and charming," Kester said, eyeing a nearby gull, which was studying the rubbish at their feet with interest. "It may well have been nice a few decades ago, but Grace and her daughter clearly haven't looked after it."

"It's probably difficult without a man in the house," Ribero declared with a note of smugness. "The ladies struggle with even simple DIY tasks, right?"

I wouldn't try saying that to any of the ladies you work with, Kester thought. He could imagine the fury on Miss Wellbeloved's, Pamela's, and Serena's faces at the mere suggestion that men were superior in any way. *Perhaps one day Dad will embrace gender equality,* he thought with a wry snigger. *But then again, perhaps not.*

The front door was wide open. It looked horribly like an open mouth, agape at their arrival. They stepped inside and peered into the gloom.

"Anyone home?" Kester called. He craned his neck up the staircase. Mike's head immediately popped over the top bannister.

"Glad you could make it, mate," he began, then faltered to a halt as he spotted Dr Ribero. "Crikey!" he exclaimed with an expression that was half-shocked, half-delighted. "Haven't seen you in a while."

"Yes, yes, I have been unwell," Ribero retorted as he strode up the stairs. "Let us not make a great big thing of it, okay?"

Mike saluted, and stood to one side. "Right you are, sir. The others will be happy to see you here."

"Well, most of the others," Kester muttered. He wasn't looking forward to the inevitable meeting between his father and Larry Higgins.

Serena, Dimitri, and Luke emerged from one of the bedrooms, closely followed by Pamela, who looked worried. They stopped at the sight of Dr Ribero, mouths open in collective speechlessness.

"Hello Julio," Pamela said, recovering first. "We weren't expecting you. Not that it isn't lovely to see you, of course."

Ribero rapped the bannister impatiently, then gestured at the other two. "Who are these people?"

"That's Luke and Dimitri," Kester said, quickly trotting up the stairs. "They work for Larry Higgins."

His father stiffened. "I see." He studied Luke with confusion. "Luke? Are you a man, then?"

Kester nudged him in the ribs. "He will be soon."

Ribero frowned. "But hang on a minute, that is an impossibility, yes? That does not make any sense. Why would you—"

Luke stepped forward and pumped Ribero's hand energetically. "I have heard so much about you!" he exclaimed, eyes shining. "It's awesome to finally meet you. The great Ribero!"

Ribero looked mollified, though still rather confused. "Well, yes, I am the great—"

A low murmur of conversation from along the corridor interrupted them. Miss Wellbeloved emerged from another room. Larry followed behind, hand clasped on her shoulder. *They seem cosy all of a sudden,* Kester thought and watched his father's reaction. *This should be interesting.*

Miss Wellbeloved looked up, spotted Ribero, then blinked, looking like an owl that had been pushed off its perch. "Goodness me," she murmured and pressed her hand to her chest. "I didn't know you were joining us, Julio. You might have warned us."

Ribero's jaw tightened. He smoothed his moustache between his fingers, then glared at Higgins down the fairly sizeable length of his nose. "Yes, it is clear you were not expecting me," he muttered, shooting poisonous looks in their direction.

"Good god, the prodigal Argentinian returns," Higgins blustered, recovering his composure. "I thought you were still cowering back in your little office in Exeter."

Mike let out a low whistle. Kester shook his head at the others in silent apology. *I should have known this would happen,* he thought, wondering if it would be possible for the rest of them to sneak downstairs and simply let Ribero and Higgins have a brawl up here by themselves.

"I see that you and Jennifer are getting along like a house on fire, yes?" Ribero seized the bannister, then drew himself up to his full height, eyes brimming with righteous indignation.

"I'd hardly go that far," Miss Wellbeloved said quietly. She stepped forward and gave Ribero a quick hug. "Calm down, Julio. You've only been here a minute and you look as though you're about to combust."

Higgins and Ribero glowered at each other. The hostility was so palpable that Kester felt almost suffocated by it. It hung in the air, as dense as the smoke emerging from one of Ribero's cigarettes. The others shifted uncomfortably.

"Shall we go back downstairs?" Serena said, her voice cutting through the quiet. "I don't know about you, but I'm not entirely happy roaming around a complete stranger's home."

"Yes, I agree," Miss Wellbeloved said, casting a worried look at Ribero and Higgins, who were stood like two gunslingers at dawn, attempting to glare the other into submission. "And I'm deeply concerned about the state of the property. We should consider calling the police."

Kester glanced into the bedroom closest to him. It looked alright to him, apart from the damp wallpaper and the cupboard door hanging off one hinge. "What's the problem with the house?" he asked. "This room looks alright."

"It's only the lounge, really," Miss Wellbeloved said as she shepherded them down. She concluded by giving Ribero a prod in the ribs, which startled him out of his venomous glare. "Come on you two. You can continue this fight when we find the next available children's playground to drop you off in."

"It's also the atmosphere," Pamela whispered, following them down the stairs. "There's some dreadful residual energy. There isn't any spirit activity here now, but I guarantee you there has been in the recent past."

Dimitri sniffed, then whirled around like a crow in flight. "The air stinks of it. It is very worrying."

"There's only one reek in here," Dr Ribero muttered and flicked a thumb back in Higgins's direction.

"Excuse me, I will not tolerate you calling me a 'reek', thank you very much." Higgins drew himself up to his full height, chest heaving like a bullfrog. "You've absolutely no right to come storming in here and start throwing insults around—"

"But there is so much of you to insult, Higgins! You provide such a huge target for my insults, it is difficult to resist. Look at you, you elephant of a man. You have grown so fat!"

"Your comments seem rather rich coming from the man with the world's most ridiculous moustache. Honestly, aren't you aware that look died out with the 1920s?"

Miss Wellbeloved wheeled on her heels and stepped firmly in between the two of them. "Pack it in this instant!"

The two men looked mutinous. "He started it," Higgins pointed out, throwing a furious glance at Ribero over the top of Miss Wellbeloved's shoulder.

"Well, now it's time to stop it." She looked at each of them in turn. "You both know how much this case means to us all. If we fail, I don't want it to be because you two were too busy throwing your toys out of your collective prams." She breathed in, then patted down her cardigan. "Kester, allow me to quickly show you the lounge. Then you can tell us how it looks compared to yesterday."

Kester scurried down the dark hallway, which still smelt unpleasantly of fish. *Is that all they eat?* he wondered, peering into the kitchen on the way past. It was so dingy in there that couldn't see much, only an oven, which had been left open, a tiny fold-down kitchen table, and an old tea towel draped over the unit.

He looked into the lounge, then looked back at Miss Wellbeloved. "Okay," he said as he surveyed the scene in front of him. "I now see what you mean."

Grace McCready's armchair had been flung over so that it rested on one side, legs pointing crazily at the window. The cushions and throws were strewn across the floor, and every picture had been thrown down, spreading smashed glass across the threadbare carpet. Even more disturbingly, the sofa looked as though it had been attacked with a knife. Large slashes spewed stuffing onto the seat. *I hope the cat's okay,* Kester thought irrationally and instinctively surveyed the corners to see if he could spot it.

"What do you make of it?" Miss Wellbeloved looked over his shoulder and squinted with concern.

"It's been totally trashed," Kester said, staring round the room. He sighed. "It also feels very *hostile* in here, doesn't it?" he said. Reluctantly, he stepped into the room. "I felt it yesterday, but it's much more noticeable now. It feels horrible." He didn't like to admit it, but the room was making him feel a bit sick. The floral wallpaper started to twist before his eyes, and it made his head hurt.

Pamela joined him, placing her hands on her ample hips. "It's exactly the same atmosphere that Dimitri and I picked up at Deirdre Baxter's house. Not to mention Jürgen Kleinmann's. It's the same spirit, I can tell." She looked at him with interest. "Though it's interesting that you're so good at picking up atmospheres, Kester. Maybe you've got a touch of the gift too."

Kester shrugged, looking back round at the others. "The big question is . . . where's Grace?"

Mike shrugged. "Perhaps she ran away? Pretty shrewd move, if you ask me."

Kester shook his head and moved aside to let the others squeeze into the room. "No, that doesn't make sense. None of the others had any chance to run away. This spirit seems far too clever to let a victim escape."

"Unless it lured her somewhere else," Serena said, crossing her arms and giving Kester a baleful look, as though he was somehow responsible.

Miss Wellbeloved tutted. "Serena, don't start being prejudiced again."

"What do you mean?"

"I can hear it in the tone of your voice. Remember, this spirit may well have motivation to behave like this. We know it was locked up in the ground for centuries, after all."

"Or perhaps it's just a nasty sod," Higgins suggested. He stepped over the cushion and hoisted the chair back into place. "Jennifer, you must cease this naivety when it comes to spirits. Some are just downright evil. Accept it."

Ribero swept over to Miss Wellbeloved, then placed a proprietous hand on her shoulder. "Jennifer," he began, casting a smug look at Larry, "I defend your right to defend the spirits. Your compassion is to be commended."

"Oh shut up, you blistering old git," Higgins spat. "I'm just telling it like it is. I don't hold with all this airy-fairy nonsense about spirits being like us. They're damned troublesome, and they need sorting out, which is where we come in. Now, let's get back on track here."

Miss Wellbeloved shook her head. "I can't believe I'm hearing this."

"Let's just focus on the task at hand," Kester whispered and gave her arm a squeeze. "For what it's worth, I'm sure you're right. You usually are. But having another argument isn't going to achieve anything."

She nodded and returned his squeeze with a grateful clasp of her own. "What should we do then? Shall I call the police?"

"I think you're going to have to," Higgins said as he surveyed the mess. "After all, a woman's life could be in danger here."

Serena picked up a cushion. She placed it gingerly on the sofa, as though afraid it might rear up and bite her hand. "Everything is filthy in here. Do you think that's a clue to what happened?"

Kester shook his head. "No. It was already pretty dirty yesterday. I don't think they do much cleaning."

"It stinks as well," Mike said, wrinkling his nose. "I thought it was you to begin with, Serena, but even you're not quite that foul."

"Shut up, Mike," Serena said smoothly and lobbed a cushion at his head. "Especially given that you look like a caveman at the moment. I notice that you seem to be enjoying the fact that you haven't been able to change your clothes since we've been away."

"Well, this is my favourite shirt."

"It'll be crawling off you and walking down the corridor soon, judging by the number of bacteria living in it now."

"Let's move on from Mike's bacteria, lovely though it may be," Pamela suggested with a wave of the hand, as though fending off the smell. "Should we wait outside until the police arrive?"

"Technically, we have as much right to investigate this house as they do," Miss Wellbeloved said pertly. "Just because they wear shiny metal badges, doesn't mean they have any more authority than us."

Kester scooped up the painting that had been hanging above Grace's armchair. He remembered it now, the dreary Highland scene. The glass had shattered across the centre, and as he picked it up, sections fell out, tinkling quietly to the floor. The image bothered him, but he couldn't work out why. *It is a particularly gloomy picture,* he thought as he studied the thick oil brush-strokes, glinting in the weak daylight.

"That's a bloody awful painting, isn't it?" Larry said, peering over his shoulder. "Christ knows why anyone would want to hang that monstrosity up in their living room."

"It is a stinker," Kester agreed as he turned the frame over in his hands. The label on the back told him the artist's name—*F Livingstone,* whoever he or she might have been. Painted in 1962. The title of the painting was simple and to the point—*Visions of Dundee.*

"Which part of Scotland is Dundee in?" he asked casually, wondering if there was a connection. He remembered that Grace

McCready had said something about the landscape being close to where she'd lived when she'd been younger.

Miss Wellbeloved ran her hand over the writing on the canvas. "It's on the east coast. Why?"

"Is it near where the Celtic brooch came from? The Angus region, or whatever you said it was?"

She nodded slowly, then looked back down at the painting, eyes widening. "It is. Are you thinking what I'm thinking?"

"What *are* you bloody thinking?" Larry Higgins said, grabbing the painting from Kester's hand and studying it furiously.

"The archaeologist told us that the knife embedded in the Celtic warrior was from the Angus region," Kester explained, looking at the others with growing excitement. "Which suggests that the Celtic warrior himself was from the region. Not to mention the fetch that came down to Lyme Regis with him."

Serena broke into a rare smile. "And of course, a fetch will only want to be in its homeland or with people from the area . . ."

". . . and Grace McCready was from the same place!" Pamela concluded triumphantly. "My god, Kester, so you were right. It *is* a fetch. And it's latched on to Grace. *Wow.*"

"That's a bit of a coincidence, isn't it?" Higgins scoffed, passing the painting back to Miss Wellbeloved. "What are the odds, eh?"

"It's not that surprising that someone from the region should turn up sooner or later," Miss Wellbeloved replied, rubbing at the canvas thoughtfully.

Mike nodded. "Especially down here. It's a popular place with tourists and old people, isn't it? Living the good life and all that."

"So, hang on," Larry said as he paced around the room. "Let's say I'm prepared to go along with the fact that she's from the same place as this murderous fetch. I simply don't swallow the notion that she coincidentally managed to stumble upon the spirit's resting place and free it. That's preposterous."

"Unless the fetch called to her," Miss Wellbeloved interrupted, eyes glowing.

"That would make it absurdly powerful."

"Given that it's over 2,000 years old, that's not impossible, is it?" Pamela added. "You know that they get stronger over time. Particularly if they're angry about something."

"So she's freed the spirit, and now it's doing what it does best," Serena concluded, eyes sparkling. "It's *fetching* people."

"More pressing at the moment," Kester interrupted, "is the fact that wherever Grace, is the fetch is too. Which means either she's in danger or someone else is."

The others all gasped.

"But who else is there left to kill?" Pamela said as she looked at the others with confusion. "It's polished off all the members of the Ancient History Club now."

Miss Wellbeloved shook her head. She looked suddenly sick. "You know as well as I do, Pamela. A malevolent fetch won't stop, not until it's back where it belongs. It'll simply move on to fresh victims—unless it finds a way to get home again."

"Then we need to get to her quickly," Serena suggested, already moving towards the door. "There's no time to lose."

"And when we find her, we can get that spirit stuffed into a water bottle before it can say 'och aye'?" Mike said as he punched Kester on the arm.

"Fantastic, casual Scottish racism as well as spiritism now," Miss Wellbeloved groaned, slapping a hand across her forehead in protest. However, in spite of her comment, she looked more excited than Kester had seen her all week.

"Now," Ribero continued, taking to the centre of the floor and gesturing at them all in a manner rather like a ringmaster at a circus. "Where do we find this woman?"

Kester pondered. He looked around the room for inspiration. The others waited expectantly.

"Well," he started, his brain whirring at greater speeds than it had been for at least a fortnight. "Let's think about this rationally. If the spirit has latched itself onto Grace McCready, she either knows it's there or she doesn't."

"Let's assume she doesn't." Miss Wellbeloved nodded. "What would that mean, then?"

He thought again. "If she didn't know the spirit was following her, then she'd naturally be scared that she'd be next on the list to get murdered. After all, she's the only one left. So, she'd presumably try to head somewhere that she thought the spirit couldn't get to."

"A church, perhaps?" Higgins offered.

Ribero scoffed. "Edna Berry was killed in a church, you silly man. She got tangled in the bell-ropes, don't you remember?"

"Excuse me, don't you dare tell me what I do and do not remember, given that you only bothered to join us on this job about ten minutes ago!"

Miss Wellbeloved shot them both a disapproving look. "How about we presume Grace McCready does know the spirit's with her? What are the implications then?"

The implications aren't pretty at all, Kester thought. *The implications are: if Grace knows that the spirit is with her, then she had to know it was killing her friends. Which makes her complicit in the murders.* He caught Miss Wellbeloved's eye and could tell she was thinking the same thing.

"I think we can safely conclude that she won't have headed to the church," he said, choosing his words carefully. "As you so rightly point out, Dad, the church is where one of her friends got killed." He glanced out the window. Dark clouds loomed over the woodlands on the distant headland. *It's looking cold out there,* he thought. *I wouldn't much fancy going up to the Celtic graves now, it's about to pour down.*

"Hang on," he said, holding his finger in the air. "The Celtic burial site." He looked out the window again. "Could she have gone there?"

Higgins rolled his eyes. "You're just making this up, aren't you? It all sounds like one big, silly stab in the dark to me."

"Of course I'm making it up!" Kester shouted, exasperation finally getting the better of him. "What else can we do? We've got hardly any time to get this case solved, and we *have* to make silly stabs in the dark if we're going to get anywhere! Now will you please stop being so obstructive!"

"Hmm, just ignore me then," Higgins muttered. He folded his arms and glared mutinously out of the window.

"Why don't we split up?" Pamela suggested. "Some of us can head up to the graves, some of us down to the seafront, the rest of us into town?"

"Unless she's got a car and driven off somewhere," Larry said. "Which is entirely possible."

Miss Wellbeloved pulled out her phone. "I've got to call the police," she said, walking towards the hallway. "Pamela, I think your idea is probably our best option at the moment. We need to try to find Grace. If she has driven away . . . well, there's not much we can do about it, is there?"

"Sounds like yet another wild-goose chase to me," Larry concluded, glaring at them all. "However, as that seems to be the way you lot do things, I'll go along with it for now."

"Because you have no better ideas in that big thick head of yours," Ribero added with a tweak of his jacket collar. "Isn't that right?"

Higgins scowled and stalked down the hallway after Miss Wellbeloved. "Whatever you do, don't pair me up with that moron," he grumbled, his voice echoing back to the lounge. The rest of them followed, returning with relief to the fresh air outside. The same seagull sat perched by the wall, beady eyes fixed on their movements with an impassive lack of interest.

They quickly assigned themselves to teams, deliberately ensuring that Ribero and Higgins wouldn't be within a mile radius of one another. Kester volunteered to head to the Celtic site, even though he knew it was likely to be the most sinister location of them all. He glanced up at the distant woods with a sense of foreboding. The trees sprouted from the headland, dark and ceaselessly shifting in the strong westerly wind. He could even hear the breeze passing through the branches if he listened carefully. Ribero offered to come with him, along with Serena— as they needed an extinguisher—Pamela, and, for some reason best known to himself, Mike.

The others agreed to head into town, then on to the seafront to see if they could catch sight of a deranged-looking woman with white hair, plus a heavily pregnant daughter.

"You'll probably need longer than us," Miss Wellbeloved said after she had got off the phone, scouring the woods with a squint. "So we'll head up there to join you once we've checked the town. We'll be as quick as we can. Make sure you keep your mobiles switched on."

"No point, is there?" Mike said. He waved his mobile in her face. "No signal. Don't you remember? We couldn't call the archaeologist the other day because his phone didn't work up in the headlands."

She rubbed her mouth thoughtfully. "Yes, that's true. Well, stick together and be careful. If you do find Grace, you may well find the spirit too, and we know that it's a tricky customer."

"You mean absolute bloody maniac out of our worst nightmares," Higgins chimed.

"No, I didn't mean that at all. Stop trying to bait me," Miss Wellbeloved said, raising a warning eyebrow in his direction. She gestured down the silent road, then nodded. "Shall we?"

"If we must," Pamela said with a cheerful nod. She linked arms with Ribero and Kester, and yanked them close against her squidgy hips, which gave gently against their weight like a well-sprung mattress. "Come on you two, let's get going. I don't know about the rest of you, but I'm keen to wrap this case up and get back home."

"Don't let the Higgins take control," Ribero growled to Miss Wellbeloved as they paced down the road. "The man is a halfwit. He could not organise a siesta in Spain."

Higgins snorted like a bull about to charge. "Honestly, what is it with you lot? Do you really think I can't hear you? You whisper about as loudly as a stampeding herd of buffalo!"

"Maybe we just want you to hear us," Mike said, nudging Higgins in the ribs as he went past. "It's more fun that way. I like seeing your face go all puffy and red. It's like watching someone slowly over-inflate a balloon."

They parted company a little further down the main road; Miss Wellbeloved's group headed straight down the steep hill, and Ribero's team clambered over the stile and onto the winding grass path that led up to the woods. Judging by the profusion of nettles and brambles, it didn't get used very often. Kester climbed through the tangled undergrowth, trying not to fret too much about the holes the thorns were making as they ripped at his trousers. *I suppose I needed a new pair anyway,* he thought. To his delight, his clothes were becoming a bit looser, which he hoped might be to do with his weight loss. *Certainly this week's stress must have helped burn off the pounds.*

He heard his father wheezing behind him and waited for him to catch up.

"Are you okay there?"

His father waved an impatient hand in his face. "Ah, just because I am old, you think I am not fit." He leant across and poked Kester's stomach. "I can out-walk you any day of the month, yes?"

Kester sighed. *Obviously I haven't lost as much weight as I'd hoped,* he thought and cast a dark look at his belly.

"It's a steep old climb, isn't it?" Pamela shouted from the back. Her face was sweaty and purple, despite the cold. She craned her neck, examined the steep rock-face, then patted it contemplatively. "If I have a heart attack, will someone scoop me off the ground and run me to the nearest hospital?"

"You're not the one wearing stilettoes," Serena said, tottering along the muddy path like a new-born foal. She pointed at her feet and groaned. "Seriously, I'm never wearing heels again. My feet look like someone's attacked them with a cheese grater."

"Do you want a piggy-back?" Mike offered, who was annoyingly unfazed by the climb. He strode ahead, arms swinging in a jovial rhythm.

"Not from you, I bloody don't."

"Ooh look, we can see the others from up here," Pamela said and cupped her hands to her mouth. "Coo-ee! Jennifer! Luke! Dimitri! Up here!"

"Pamela, you do realise that's probably the most deafening noise Lyme Regis has experienced all season?" Mike said. He reached behind and yanked her unceremoniously onwards. "This is retirement central. Don't go waking all the pensioners."

Finally, they made it to the top. Kester bent over, clutching his knees and struggling to get his breath back. *This had better be worth it,* he thought, a stitch burning in his belly. Distant waves tumbled around the harbour walls, grey and forbidding in the wintery light, and the wind whipped furiously around their heads.

"So this is where you found the grave of that Scottish warrior guy, yes?" Ribero stood beside Kester, and they both gazed out across the ocean below.

Kester shook his head. "No, we've got a bit of a walk ahead of us, I'm afraid." He studied his father, who looked worryingly pallid. Ribero noticed Kester's scrutinising expression and frowned, lifting his chin towards the wind like a lion surveying the savannah.

"I am perfectly capable of walking, and don't forget it, Kester. I am not dead yet."

Kester patted him on the back. "I know, I know. Let's get

moving then. If Grace is up here, we need to get to her as soon as possible."

A shrill noise startled them both. Kester quickly looked to his right, trying to identify the source. As far as he could see, the area was deserted.

"What the hell was that?" Serena strode over to them, eyes flicking across the landscape.

"I don't know." Kester scratched his head. "I thought it was a person crying, but perhaps it was just a bird or something."

"Yeah, it's just another gull," Mike said. He was struggling to support Pamela, who was leaning heavily against him, still trying to get her breath back. "Shall we go?"

The noise came again. A cry. Kester was sure of it. He looked at the others, eyes widening.

"Did you hear that?" Serena whispered. Kester hushed her and gestured to the distance.

"Shh, listen," he hissed, pushing his glasses up his nose. There was a quieter noise. It was difficult to tell what it was. The wind tugged at the sound, distorting and muffling it, but Kester could have sworn it was a sob.

"That's no seagull," Ribero muttered.

"Shall we go and look?" Mike suggested.

"I'm worried if we all march over, it'll scare off whoever's there," Kester said, still scanning the direction of the noise in an attempt to catch a glimpse of its source. It sounded as though it was coming from further along the headland, somewhere past the scattering of trees that clung close to the edge of the cliff.

Ribero rubbed his hands together anxiously. "What if there is someone needing our help, eh?"

"Let me scout over there, see what I can see, then I'll shout back to you," Kester suggested.

"You?" Serena shook her head and summoned up the most incredulous look she could muster. "Since when have you been some sort of superhero?"

Kester sighed. "Okay, let's save the usual insults for later, shall we? I suggested myself because I'm quiet. Unlike you. The last thing we need is your stilettoes accidentally tripping you right off the cliff."

Without another word, he started to walk towards the source of the sound, which had now gone eerily silent. The closer he got to the cliff, the more the wind whipped around him, whisking his jacket around and flinging his fringe into his eyes. He looked over the edge, then wished he hadn't. It was a long way down, and rocks poked out of the sea foam like talons.

As he slipped through the trees, he thought he heard another noise, quieter this time, but more unmistakably like a sob. It was difficult to tell exactly where it was coming from, but it sounded as though it was more to his left than his right, which meant it was nearer the cliff than the wood. He looked back. The others were now out of sight, concealed by the foliage and the natural rise of the headland. A lone crow cawed on a branch above and fixed a beady eye in his direction. He felt uncomfortably alone.

He crept out of the trees, into the open. The vast expanse of the Dorset coast lay before him, rust-red cliffs piled haphazardly on endless lengths of mud-brown beaches. It was spectacular, yet haunting: a wild, untamed panorama that clearly hadn't changed much in thousands of years. *Our friend the Celtic warrior probably looked out over this,* he realised with a shiver. *I wonder if he felt as scared as I do now.*

There was a dark shape on the cliff edge in front of him, which he swiftly noted, with growing horror, was a person. It was difficult to make out the details from this distance, but the long wind-tossed hair and small, hunched shoulders suggested it was female. Not Grace though, he realised. The hair was the wrong colour. This person looked younger.

He approached with caution, again glancing back, hopeful that the others might have decided to follow him. They hadn't. He was most definitely on his own here, and he wasn't sure what to do.

"Hello?" he called out. His voice sounded reedy and uncertain and was lost quickly in the low moan of the breeze. The woman didn't turn. He swallowed hard, edging closer.

Is she even awake? he wondered. He studied her more intently. The woman's head was slumped against her left shoulder, pitching her forward, dangerously close to the edge of the cliff. He saw, with shock, that her legs were hanging over the edge.

"Excuse me? Are you okay?" *What a stupid question,* he reprimanded himself. *Of course she's not!*

To his relief, the woman raised her head slowly, as though moving her neck caused her pain. He waited behind her, not daring to come any closer. Her hands were wrapped protectively over her stomach, which made him suddenly realise who she was. *Grace's daughter.*

"Helen?" he whispered, remembering, with horribly inappropriate sense of timing, that he hadn't yet returned her umbrella.

She turned. Her eyes were raw and her cheeks streaked with dirt and tears. "Don't come any closer," she whispered and pressed a hand in his direction, as though warding off a demon.

"Why not?" Kester replied, though he already knew what her answer would be.

"I'll jump."

CHAPTER 19: CLIFFSIDE ENCOUNTERS

I wonder if now is a good time to call the others? Kester watched the pregnant woman, terrified that she would jump at any moment and smash herself on the rocks below.

"Please," he began and edged closer, hands held out to calm her.

She hissed, turning away. "Don't. If you take another step forward, I swear I'll throw myself off this cliff."

Kester took a deep breath, then gently kneeled to a crouch. "Okay," he said slowly. "I won't come any closer. I promise. Is it okay if I just sit here?"

Helen didn't answer. She turned her attention back to the endless grey of the ocean, resuming her protective hold over her belly. Time lengthened and silence took over. Kester took her lack of response as an affirmative and eased himself into a cross-legged position.

"Can I ask you why you're sitting on the cliff?"

"No."

He looked out over the coastline. The sea rolled restlessly below them, dark and forbidding, and his eyes watered from the cold. "Can I guess?"

She laughed, a bitter chuckle laced with desolation. "I very much doubt it."

Okay, here goes, he thought. He leaned forward to ensure she could hear him clearly. "Is it to do with your mother?" he ventured. "And the spirit that's been following her around?"

Helen's reaction was immediate. She swung around, right thigh hanging precariously over the edge. "How did you know about it?"

Kester winced. "Helen, be careful." He wondered if he could pull her back to safety, but didn't think he could; she was hanging too far over. "You're too close," he continued, starting to feel desperate. "You're going to fall."

She laughed again, then sniffed, wiping her nose against her sleeve. "How did you know about the spirit?" she asked again, ignoring his concern.

Kester took a deep breath. "I told you both the other day. I work with a supernatural agency. We've been investigating the case for a while now. It was only a matter of time before we linked the spirit to your mother."

Helen gasped—a wrenching noise somewhere between a laugh and a sob. "You're too late," she muttered. "If you'd have come sooner, perhaps you could have helped. But there's nothing you can do now."

"I know. We can't save all her friends, but we can stop this spirit from—"

"Don't be so *stupid*. I'm not talking about the fools from the Ancient History Club. It was them that got us into this mess in the first place, they had it coming to them!"

Whoa, Kester thought, instinctively retreating from the woman's fury. *I wasn't expecting that.* He looked over his shoulder and wondered again if it was the right time to call for the others.

The unhinged look in her eye was making him very nervous, but he was terrified that calling for help would cause her to jump.

"Okay," he said gently. Taking a chance, he shifted towards her. "Helen, do you think you could move away from the cliff, so we can talk properly?"

She shook her head, squeezing her eyes shut. A tear rolled down her cheek. "You don't know what it's been like," she whispered, vulnerable as a little child. "It's been a living hell."

"Can you tell me about it?" he asked, creeping tentatively forward again. He was now uncomfortably close to the cliff's edge himself, but he sensed he wasn't going to be able to persuade her to move back. *At least if I'm close to her,* he thought, *I can try to grab her if she jumps. But please, please don't let it come to that. I'm not sure I'm strong enough to hold the weight of a pregnant woman.*

"I don't know what you know already," she said and rubbed her eyes.

"Presume not much," he replied with a wry nod. *Which is probably true,* he added silently.

"You know about the Celtic graves, though?"

He nodded, then, with a deep breath, eased his own legs over the edge of the cliff. *What am I doing?* he thought, scarcely daring to take his eyes off the horizon. His feet dangled into nothingness, and the ground was disconcertingly spongy beneath his backside, not solid like he'd hoped. *God, this cliff could crumble at any moment,* he realised, fighting hard to maintain his composure. *This is insanity.*

"Why are you sitting next to me?" She glanced at him, then at his legs, which were currently stuck out rigidly in mid-air, mainly through sheer terror.

He smiled, trying to hide his fear. "Thought you looked like you could do with the company. Do you come here often?"

She chuckled briefly, a dry, humourless noise, then her expression hardened.

"It was Deirdre Baxter who wouldn't let it drop," she said quietly. "Her and Xena Sunningdale."

"What, the tarot-card lady?"

Helen nodded, grimacing. "They were always obsessed with the occult. It used to drive Mum mad. Every project the history group worked on, those two had to start making it about the supernatural." She sighed and looked down, past her protruding bump, over the edge. Kester felt sick watching her.

"Peter Hopper said it was Xena Sunningdale that found the site?"

"Yeah, that's right." Helen looked at him, her expression full of torment. "Xena said that she'd made contact with a spirit when she was doing a reading, who'd told her about the graves. She got her husband to get the Ancient History Club involved."

He raised an eyebrow. "Did they believe her?"

She shrugged. "Most of them didn't. Deirdre did, though. Like I said, those two were thick as thieves in the beginning, laughing and having fun like it was all one big joke. You know what people are like about supernatural stuff."

"I suppose so." Kester himself had never been one for ghosts and things; in fact, prior to joining the agency, he would have rather walked around naked all day long than meet a spirit. However, he realised that some people were excited by the supernatural, for reasons best known to themselves. "So what happened when they got up there?" he continued.

"Nothing at first." Helen plucked at a blade of grass and wound it around her finger until it dug into her flesh, turning it white. "They found the Celtic stones, got excited about it, dug up the grave, discovered a skeleton and a load of other stuff, freaked out, and buried it all again. Xena started telling everyone they'd disturbed a spirit; she got Deirdre in a right state. Mum was sceptical, of course. But then she started behaving strangely." She gulped and closed her eyes again.

Kester thought back to his meeting with Grace McCready.

She'd struck him as the sort of person who'd probably been strange for quite a few years, but perhaps her daughter simply meant she'd got worse.

"Strange? In what way?"

Helen bit her lip. "Nightmares. She started screaming in the night, waking me up at all hours. Using weird words, not English ones. And her *eyes*. It was like she was awake but somewhere else, if you know what I mean?"

He nodded. "I think so."

"I heard her say other things too," Helen continued. "Muttering to herself that she was being *called,* that she had to go. Then, when I pressed her to tell me what was going on, she'd just go silent. It was like she wasn't even my mother anymore."

Kester rested his hand on her arm. "It must have been terrible," he said gently.

The woman let out a low whimper. "I told her not to keep going back up there. It was a bad place; you could feel it. I even forcibly held her back one day; I locked the door so she couldn't get out. But she told me she couldn't help it. She was pulled back up there by something she couldn't see or understand."

Kester looked over his shoulder. He'd thought he'd heard a noise, somewhere in the direction he'd come from, but the wind muted it to an echoing moan. *I wish one of the others would hurry up and come over here,* he thought, anxiously looking over at Helen again. She was tugging at the tufts of grass by the edge, and he worried that she'd pull out a root that was holding the crumbling cliff-top in place, sending them tumbling to the sharp rocks below.

"Go on," he said and slid his bottom as far back from the edge as he could without pulling his legs back onto solid land. "I'm listening."

"One day, I came in from work, and she wasn't home. I knew where she'd gone, I could just feel it. I waited for her to come back down, which was a terrible mistake. I should have gone to find her as soon as I could." She took a deep breath, as though steeling herself. "When it got dark, I headed out with a torch. As I was going up, Deirdre and Peter ran into me. They were running, I tell you. Running faster than I'd ever seen them move before."

"Running from what?"

"They wouldn't stop to talk to me. Peter just shouted over his shoulder that my mum was up there, but they didn't dare stay." She stopped, massaging her head as though the memory hurt her.

"Did you carry on?"

"Of course I did! I had to, my mum was there, all alone in the dark."

"What did you find?"

Helen raised her head to the sky, then shook it slowly. She clasped herself more closely, enclosing her stomach in shell-like safety. "Mum," she replied heavily. "Deep in the grave. They'd dug it up again, you see. She was shouting in the weird language I'd heard her use before." Helen cringed at the memory and gazed out once again to the sea.

"Go on," Kester pressed.

"She looked at me, and it was like she'd never seen me before in her life. Then she started laughing. She . . ." Helen faltered and another tear rolled down her cheek. "She laughed so hard that she choked, then she looked up again, and I could see that she was crying. Like her heart would break. And she told me to *run*."

Kester shivered. As she spoke, he could imagine the scene only too well. "And did you?"

Helen groaned, then threw her head into her hands. He had to reach out to steady her, his heart hammering in his chest. *Don't you dare lean forward on this cliff,* he thought, desperately trying to ease her back. *I'm not sure I can catch you if you lose your balance.*

"I'm ashamed to say that I did run," she said, meeting his eyes. "Not because of Mum, though that was horrible enough. But because of what was coming out of the soil behind her."

He studied her intently. "What was it?"

She looked at him with an expression that was alive with fear. "It was the most awful thing I've ever seen. It was transparent but solid at the same time. And its eyes . . . its eyes were burning. It leaned over Mum, and she leaned back towards it, then it started to . . ."

Kester waited. "Yes?" he said gently.

Helen started to cry in earnest, sobbing so hard that her back shook with the effort. "It *went into her*," she whispered. "Actually inside her, like water going into a sponge. And she looked at me and said one thing."

"What?"

The woman covered her mouth, horrified by the memory. Her eyes widened. "She said '*I'm free at last.*' But it wasn't her voice. Do you see? *It wasn't her saying it.*"

Kester reached over and placed a tentative hand across the woman's shoulders. She wept even harder, folding herself over her belly, hair hanging over her face.

"We need to get you away from this cliff," he said as firmly as he could and gave her arm a reassuring squeeze. "It's not safe."

"I don't want to move." Her voice was muffled, like someone talking from deep within a well.

He dared to drop his gaze. It was a horribly long way down. The waves threw themselves against the rocks as though punishing them. He could only imagine what they'd do to his and Helen's bodies. "You must," he said with a bit more force. "If not for you, then for your baby. You don't want to put its life in danger, do you?"

Helen's head jerked up, nearly knocking him off balance. To his horror, she started to laugh—a high-pitched chuckle with more than a hint of hysteria to it. "Don't you get it?" she asked, bloodshot eyes gleaming. "Don't you see?"

Kester looked over his shoulder again. "See what? What should I be seeing?" *Because at the moment,* he added silently, *all I can see is a terrifyingly long drop down and an almost certain death.*

"It won't stop with Mum," she said, then to his surprise, reached over and grabbed his chin, forcing him to look at her. With the other hand, she took his hand and placed it over her stomach, pressing his fingers against the taut, full flesh of her bump. "And it won't stop with *me,* either."

Kester pulled his hand away, instinctively flicking his legs up onto the cliff-top. *Enough is enough,* he thought. *I've got to take control of the situation.* "Come away from the cliff now, Helen." He stood up, breathing hard. "Nothing is as bad as it seems. I know you've had a horrible time of it, but we can help. But I need you to stand up slowly and move away from the—"

Another noise caught his attention. He whipped his head back in the direction of the others. *That was a scream,* he realised, his heart racing. *Oh no.*

"Did you hear that?" He looked back at Helen, scanning her face for answers.

She nodded, then looked back over the headland. "Who else is up here with you?"

"Some of my colleagues."

She leant back, licking her lips, considering the options. Then she nodded. "You need to get back to them. Quickly."

He studied her for a moment, then understood. *Grace is with them,* he realised, panic pressing into him like a ten-tonne weight. *And that means so is the spirit.*

"Will you come with me?" he said, scrambling to his feet. "I might need your help."

Helen shrugged, then resumed staring out to sea.

I can't wait for her to make up her mind, Kester thought. "Please, don't jump!" he said as he started to run. "Whatever you do, just don't do it, okay? We can sort this out!"

Without waiting for an answer, Kester pounded back towards the trees. Dashing alongside the cliffs, he pushed past stray branches and jumped over jutting rocks, his breath pluming out in front of him in misty bursts—lungs struggling for air as they battled against the icy breeze.

Please don't let anything bad have happened, please don't let anything bad have happened, he thought over and over, then finally emerged into the open. In the distance, he could see the others, gathered in a group. He squinted. It was difficult to focus whilst running, especially as his glasses had started to fog up in the cold.

"Are you okay?" he shouted as loudly as he could, but breathlessness had stripped his voice of most of its power. "Hey! Are you alright there?"

Why aren't they answering? He was still too far away to see what was going on, but could just about make out Mike's broad back. He looked like he was clutching someone. *Is that Serena? Surely not, Serena wouldn't let Mike touch her, much less hold her tightly,* he thought, confused. To his horror, he realised that Grace was standing with them, her white hair strewn behind her like a decaying veil. Pamela was there too, beside Mike. *Where's Dad?* he wondered, straining his eyes to see better. *Why can't I see him?*

As he ran closer, he noticed a shape on the ground. At first he thought, inexplicably, that it was a pile of clothes with a pair of shoes at the bottom. Then he realised that he wasn't looking at a heap of clothes at all, but a body. His father's body, to be precise—limbs outstretched as though he'd been thrown down, head twisted against the earth. Kester groaned and pulled to a halt, staring with horror at the scene before him.

"What have you done?" His accusation tore above the wind as he sunk to his knees beside his father's unconscious body. "Grace, what have you done to him?"

The old woman laughed. Although she was small, she seemed far taller—a prophetess from a bygone era—hair whipping out towards the sea and blouse billowing like a cape. Her veiny hands clasped at her throat, scraping the skin. Kester stared at her in horror, and her face fell. Without warning, she dropped to her knees.

"I'm truly sorry," she whispered, still holding onto her throat. Kester could see that her nails had gouged the thin skin, leaving livid red marks. "It's not my fault, you have to understand that."

"Kester, be careful," Mike warned. He was still clutching hold of Serena, arm wrapped around her like a padlock. "She just came out of nowhere, and then the spirit leapt out of her and attacked your dad."

"Where's the spirit now?" Kester pressed a finger against his father's neck. He felt a pulse and could see his chest rising and falling in shallow, halting movements. *Thank god,* he thought as he pushed his fringe from his eyes. *For a moment, I thought I'd lost him.*

"It's gone back inside her," Pamela said, scrutinising Grace warily. "I can feel it there, deep within her body." She sighed, then extended a hand in the woman's direction. "What a burden to bear, I can't imagine how you've managed to stand it for this long."

Grace let out a sob. It echoed in the cold air, feral and completely devoid of hope. "You have no idea," she croaked.

"Why did the spirit attack my father?" Kester asked, still studying Ribero's unconscious face. Minus his usual bluster, he looked suddenly much younger, like a child about to wake up from a bad dream. Gravity eased out his lines, and Kester could see the man that he'd once been: high-cheekboned, chiselled, and handsome.

"We have no idea," Mike said, eyes still glued to the old woman. "Serena immediately got to work trying to extinguish it, but we couldn't get the water bottle out in time. By then, the spirit was trying to attack her, but Pamela stepped in, so it disappeared back into Grace."

Kester breathed deeply. He looked at Grace, then edged closer to her. "You've got the spirit inside you right now, and we need to get it out," he said gently and reached out to touch her arm. She flinched.

"You won't be able to," she said heavily. "It's waited too long to find someone else to carry it. Do you know what it is?"

Kester looked up at the others. "We believe it's a fetch," he said. "We think it came from the Angus region in Scotland, and that's why it's latched on to you, because you're from the same place."

The old woman looked amazed. "How did you find out? None of the others knew, they couldn't have told you."

"Your oil painting gave it away," Kester said. "Do you remember, you told me it was where you originally came from?"

Pamela nodded. "Solving mysteries like this is our job, Grace. Though you would have made our lives a lot easier if you'd have told us sooner."

Grace shook her head. Her hair fell about her face, witch-like, concealing all but one clear blue eye. "I couldn't tell anyone. Surely you can understand why?"

"Not really, no," Serena said flatly. "You could have stopped a lot of people from being killed. Instead, you allowed this spirit to do horrendous things."

"Why don't we let Grace tell us what happened?" Kester suggested. He looked back over the headland and hoped that Helen hadn't done anything silly. He knew he'd never forgive himself if anything happened.

Grace placed a hand on the ground to steady herself, then laughed again before wincing in pain.

"Yes, it's a fetch," she confirmed, grimacing at the word. "And it wanted revenge. It had laid in that grave for hundreds of years, just waiting for the right person to carry it. And that's where I came in handy." She laughed bitterly. "Because the fetch and I share a home, back in Scotland."

"Why did it kill the people from the Ancient History Club?" Kester asked.

Grace flinched, as though she'd been slapped. "I had to offer it someone, don't you see? I *had no choice.*"

"What sort of person sacrifices their friends?" Serena spat, eyes flashing. Kester shot her a warning look. Grace said nothing, only fixed her gaze on the ground.

"Do you know why the fetch was trapped in the first place?" Kester pressed, tiptoeing closer to the old woman. *We have to try to understand its motivation,* he realised, *if we're going to stand any chance of stopping it. Plus, if I keep her distracted, we might buy ourselves some more time.*

Grace bent over, wrapping an arm around her stomach. "I know some of it, from the garbled messages it spits in my head. It travelled down here with the Celtic army thousands of years ago. They welcomed its presence and lured it away from the land it loved, promising it the lives of countless Roman soldiers to fetch to their deaths."

"Sounds bloodthirsty," Mike commented.

"But then the Celts were captured," Grace continued, as though Mike hadn't spoken. "The warriors refused to give it any more lives. They were imprisoned—broken and damaged—and they were done with revenge." She looked up, meeting Kester's eye. "And if they were anything like me, they were probably terrified when they realised what it was capable of."

"So the Celtic warrior trapped it in the poppet?" Kester studied the woman intently. She'd started to scrape at the ground with her nails, and the desperate rhythm of her scratching unsettled him deeply. *It's like an animal, pacing in a small cage,* he realised. *I have to remember, she might look like a frail old lady, but she's got a murderous spirit within her.*

She laughed at the word, not taking her eyes off the ground. "A vessel designed to trap it, yes. Anything will do, if you know how to do it. You know that already, given that you tried to capture it with a water bottle."

"Yeah, we're on a budget," Mike muttered.

"And then the warrior killed himself," Kester said, remembering the knife through the skeleton's chest. "Perhaps he couldn't live with the knowledge of what he'd done."

"I know the feeling," Grace said heavily.

"Why murder your friends, though?" Serena asked, expression filled with distaste. "What had they done to deserve it?"

Grace's scratching became more earnest. The sound of brittle nails against hard soil set Kester's teeth on edge.

"The fetch needed victims. It demanded them. I couldn't stop it. You can't imagine what it's like, living with that voice in your head, day and night." She looked up, her expression filled with hostility. "And it was those idiots who found the fetch in the first place. They were the ones who dug it up because they couldn't stop themselves from prying into matters that should never have been explored. Who else should I have chosen, eh?"

"Why didn't you just take it back to Scotland, where it wants to be?" Kester asked. "Surely that's a logical solution?"

Grace gave a mirthless chuckle. "It wouldn't have stopped fetching, believe me. Especially as it had been trapped in the ground for so long, it was out for revenge. It just would have been different people, that's all. Even if I'd have let it fetch me, it wouldn't have stopped."

"But I presume I'm right in thinking," Kester said slowly, trying to figure out a way to calm Grace, who was becoming more agitated by the second, "that you want to get rid of this fetch?" He glanced at the others, trying to communicate silently to them to run at the first sign of the spirit emerging, which he had no doubt would happen sooner or later. The cliff-side was uncomfortably close, and he especially didn't like Serena and

Mike's proximity to it. *One slip of the foot,* he thought, looking at Serena's mud-stained stilettoes, *and she could be over the edge before any of us could get to her.* He gestured to her to move away from the edge, but she just frowned, not understanding.

Grace chuckled. It sounded more like a snarl. "What do you think? Can you imagine living like this, with a spirit in your head twenty-four hours a day?"

"Why didn't you just *tell* someone?" Serena muttered. "That's what our job is, to help people like you."

Grace's back rose and fell like an earthquake, thrusting her spine into the air. Kester couldn't tell whether she was laughing, crying, or having an asthma attack. He looked at the others, who looked as worried as he was.

"I couldn't," the old woman wheezed as she leaned closer to the ground. "Don't you see?"

Kester studied her anxiously, then remembered something else Grace's daughter had said. He gasped. "It won't stop with you," he said, eyes widening. "That's what Helen meant earlier. If the fetch kills you, it'll come for your daughter next! You didn't want to get help because you were worried that it would harm your family. That's right, isn't it?"

Grace clutched her face and fell to the ground. "Yes," she groaned. "And the next generation. And the next. It won't stop. It'll stay with our family forever." She started to cry, wrenching sobs that made her thin body convulse. Then she shuddered, looking up at them all pleadingly. "You need to go," she whispered. Her eyes rolled back in her head until only the whites remained, staring at them sightlessly.

Before Kester could react, the old woman's mouth opened. He thought she was going to be sick and moved backward instinctively. Beside him, Ribero groaned, as though aware, on some subconscious level, that something terrible was about to happen.

"Serena, get the water bottle," Pamela said in a low voice,

gaze fixed intently on the old woman. Serena nodded, scrabbling in Mike's oversized shoulder bag with increasing urgency. Kester watched with shock as a curling, foamy mist started to seep from Grace's mouth. It stank of mildew, rot, and cloying, revolting sweetness.

"Oh god, here we go again," Mike groaned. He chucked his bag down and stood firm. "You know the drill everyone. Be ready. We'll only get one shot at this."

"What if I can't get it into the bottle?" Serena whispered, her eyes travelling up to the floating form, which was now towering ten feet above their heads.

"Now isn't the time for self-doubt!" Mike retorted. He surveyed the pinnacle of the towering mist, then gulped. "Come on, where's the usual arrogant Serena when we need her, eh? You can do this. I know you can."

Serena's expression softened. "Haven't you got any inventions in your bag to help me?"

Mike grimaced. "Yeah, I meant to say something about that. I didn't really bring anything suitable with me. Didn't know we'd be staying in Lyme Regis, did I?"

Serena groaned and shut her eyes. "You idiot."

Kester's mouth hung open. He stared upwards with horrified fascination. A pair of eyes had appeared in the midst of the spectral mist: two balls of furious fire which were now aimed entirely in his direction. A ragged, gaping hole appeared below—a black mouth, stretched wide with menace. The stench thickened, turning his stomach, and he watched, helpless, as Grace fell to the ground, tiny as a mouse underneath the looming mass of the fetch.

Serena moved forward, bottle held aloft before her. Kester noticed her hands were shaking.

"Serena, be careful," he said and wished he'd asked her to remove her shoes. He was terrified that she'd lose her balance, and a glance backwards told him Mike was thinking exactly the same thing.

"I'm not sure I can do this on my own," Serena whispered. "Where's the others when you need them, eh?"

Kester stood as slowly as possible, not taking his eyes off the fetch, which was now swirling from side to side, hissing with rage. "Yes, another extinguisher would have been very useful right now," he said, thinking of Luke—completely oblivious to their situation, probably still strolling along the promenade below.

The fetch suddenly reared into the air and threw itself forward with terrifying speed. Kester flew backwards, eyes stinging from the heat of the spirit's breath.

It started to chant words that Kester didn't recognise in a guttural, throbbing voice that boomed deep within his ears, making his internal organs ache. Serena stepped forward and started to mutter words of her own, focusing all her energy on driving the spirit into the bottle.

The fetch began to shimmer. Parts of its body gleamed like minerals in a rock-face. *She's got it!* Kester thought, daring to hope. *I think she's extinguishing it!* He watched, hypnotised, as the spirit started to vibrate. It shifted, growing smaller, and he nodded at the others, who looked as excited as him. *Gosh,* he thought, *this is much easier than we thought! Imagine what Larry will say when he realises we've done it?*

He looked at Serena. She was biting her lip and stepping away. *Why is she looking so frightened?* he wondered. *She should be looking pleased!*

"It's turning into me," she whispered and edged backwards. Her heel snagged on a rock and she tripped, with a sickening lurch towards the cliff's edge.

For a moment, Kester didn't understand. Then, with horrible clarity, he realised what she meant. He peered, disbelievingly, into the mist and saw what Serena had spotted first: her own face, peering out like a perfect reflection.

"It's going to hurt her!" Mike shouted. He reached out and yanked her behind him, then faced the spirit, glaring with a fury that Kester had never seen before. "Not on my watch, pal! You back off right now!"

Kester looked around desperately. The fetch opened its mouth and roared, instantly submerging Mike in a stagnant mist. *Think!* Kester told himself, looking desperately from Grace to his father, then to Pamela. *Come on, think! What can I do?*

In the distance, he saw a group of people walking towards them. He realised, with a relief that was almost painful, that it was the others. He waved, leaping on the spot to catch their attention.

"Get over here now!" he screamed, not caring how shrill or how scared his voice sounded. "We need your help!"

To his relief, the group broke into a run. He turned, ready to tell the others what had happened, but the words froze on his lips. News forgotten, he watched, helpless, as Mike buckled to his knees, then fell like a chopped tree in front of the vibrating mist.

CHAPTER 20: PROMISES TO THE FETCH

"Luke, help us, quickly!" Kester waved as frantically as he could, blocking Serena from the spirit whilst trying not to think too hard about what had happened to Mike. He knew if he dwelt on it for too long, he'd lose his nerve, and that was the last thing anyone needed right now. *Two of our team down,* he thought as he looked at the newcomers, who wore identical expressions of horror. *How many more before this day is through?*

Luke broke first from his trance and stepped forward. "Jeez," he muttered, looking upwards. "I ain't never seen anything like this before . . ."

"Enough about that," Kester shouted. "Help us get rid of it! You're the extinguisher!" The spirit weaved in front of him, hot, stinking wind pouring from its mouth. Kester retched, struggling to keep down the contents of his stomach. Now was not the time to cover everyone in vomit.

Recovering himself, Luke tugged his rucksack open and pulled out a rectangular, metal device, which looked unnervingly like a miniature coffin. He thrust it directly at the spirit's shuddering form, and started to mutter strange words. Serena pushed Kester aside and started to chant too.

"Be careful!" Miss Wellbeloved shouted. She stared at Ribero's unconscious body with horror. "Let me try to reason with it first!"

"Oh for goodness' sake, woman!" Larry bellowed, holding her back. "We're a long way past reasoning, aren't we? It's attacked two of your team!"

"I am a conversant, and it is my job to negotiate with spirits!" Miss Wellbeloved screamed and pushed past him. "It's what my father would have done!"

"Balls to what your father would have done; I'm not letting you do something so spectacularly stupid!"

Luke squeezed his eyes shut. "Guys, please shut up, I'm losing focus." The spirit howled, then grew in size again, looming above them like a black, shifting umbrella.

Staring from face to face, Kester tried to think rationally. *What would Dad do?* he wondered, looking at Ribero lying helpless on the ground. *And more to the point, why can't I see the spirit door? Why does it only appear at certain times and not when I bloody need it most?* Out of the corner of his eye, he could see Miss Wellbeloved gazing at him hopefully and probably wondering the same thing. Feeling terrible, he shook his head in silent apology.

The fetch roared, then lurched down with astonishing speed, like a cobra striking. Luke stumbled, then bumped into Serena, who fell to the ground. At any other time, it would have been funny, but this close to the cliff, with a murderous spirit dancing about above their heads, it was terrifying.

"It's not working!" Luke shouted as he staggered backwards. "I can't get a grip on it, it's way too strong!"

Ribero groaned again. He lifted his head and surveyed them all with confusion. "What is going on here?"

Great timing, Dad! Kester thought, shaking his head in disbelief. Without any further ado, he grasped his father under his armpits and dragged him away from the spirit. "No time to explain," he hissed, keeping his eyes fixed on the fetch, who was beginning to shift and weave again, changing its form. Ribero moaned with pain, then saw the fetch and moaned even louder.

"Oh boy, you haven't extinguished it yet," he muttered and rubbed his head.

"That's absolutely correct," Kester confirmed with a glance up at the fetch, scarcely daring to look directly at it. *Don't let it be myself that I see next,* he wished fervently. He was aware that it was a petty, selfish thought, but he was petrified at the prospect of being the next victim.

Ribero looked across at Grace, then grimaced. "Not going well, then?" he shouted back at the others.

"That's a pretty accurate summary of the situation," Serena said as she rose to her feet. She winced with pain, lifting her foot up quickly. "Damn it, I've twisted my ankle."

"Oh no," Luke breathed and took another step backwards. "Look at the fetch now. Can you see it, guys?"

Kester nodded. The spirit had shifted again, and at its centre was a perfect replica of Luke leaning out of the thrumming mist. Luke pulled his extinguishing device up again and pushed it into the spirit as hard as he could.

"Stop," Miss Wellbeloved said as she grabbed his arm. "Luke, it's doing more harm than good—"

"What do ya mean, stop?" Luke shook his head, trembling. "This fetch wants a victim, and I'm next on the menu by the looks of it. Ain't no way I'm going to stop."

"Please. Let me try."

Without warning, the older woman shunted Luke to one side and faced the fetch squarely, without fear. It was a formidable sight: a giant twisting spirit writhing like a nest of eels in front of the bony figure of Miss Wellbeloved, standing with her hands on her hips like a warrior.

"Listen to me, fetch!" Her scream travelled across the cliff before losing itself to the whistle of the wind. "You don't have to continue doing this! There is another way!"

"I don't believe this," Larry shouted. He lurched forward, hands extended. "Jennifer, stop it, this is dangerous—"

Ribero reached over and grasped one of Larry's ankles. "Let her try," he wheezed.

"Don't be preposterous, she could get hurt—"

"Let her try."

"You're killing and killing because you've been imprisoned for so long, and you're angry," Miss Wellbeloved continued, chin upturned, meeting the fetch's black gaze without flinching. "All you've ever known is how to fetch, but these are not your people down here! And they weren't ready to die! Remember, spirit, you belong to Scotland. It's a Scottish person you should be fetching, if anyone at all."

Grace looked up. "Don't you dare offer me as a sacrifice," she snarled as she pulled herself to her feet. "I'd rather jump off this cliff now than volunteer myself as this fetch's victim."

What is it with her and her daughter wanting to leap off cliffs all the time? Kester wondered. A hysterical giggle bubbled up into his throat. *It's lucky no one's out walking their dog this morning,* he thought as he looked around in bewilderment. *They'd get a rather nasty shock, to say the least.*

"There doesn't need to be a victim!" Miss Wellbeloved called out. The fetch froze and fixed her with a bleak, malevolent stare. "It's true," she continued. "There's another way. You leave this world, and you return to the spirit world. I know you've been gone for thousands of years and it's hard to readjust. But at least you'll know peace in the spirit world. You won't be tormented by the need to fetch humans to their deaths anymore."

The spirit curled backwards, then arched over like a question mark. Without warning, it opened its mouth and roared, spewing hot, foul air over them all. Serena winced, leaning protectively over Mike's unconscious body.

"It's not working!" Larry shouted as he yanked free of Ribero's grip. "Jennifer, I insist that you come back here, look at what this *thing* has already done to Mike!"

"Larry, be quiet!" Miss Wellbeloved snapped. "At university, you were just the same! You and Julio! Always telling me what I could and couldn't do. I ask you to put some trust in me, just this once!" She turned once again to the fetch. "Listen to me. We'll try to find a way to get you back to the spirit world."

The spirit rolled through the air, then descended towards Grace, who screamed. "It's saying that you're a liar," she called out and clutched her head in her hands. "It needs to fetch people to know peace. There is no way back to the spirit world unless it keeps on killing."

"Tell the fetch that I understand," Miss Wellbeloved said as she sank to the ground in front of the other woman. "I know it's endured terrible torment, being imprisoned for so long. I know it's in pain, and the only way to make the pain stop is to kill. But there is a way to get it back to its own kind. There's another agency in London called Infinite Enterprises. They've got the facilities to transfer spirits back to their own world."

The fetch howled again and flung itself over Grace in a shower of hot sparks and smoke. She screamed again. "No! It said not London! Not anywhere else! It's sick of being in places where it doesn't belong!"

Miss Wellbeloved looked around at the others and held her hands up in defeat. "I don't know what to suggest, then," she said with a helpless shrug.

Kester stepped forward without even realising what he was doing. "What if I can open the spirit door back in Scotland, where the fetch feels at home? Would that help?"

Grace shuddered. "He says he doesn't believe you. Humans are all liars, they've just tricked him time and time again."

Probably an improvement on murdering them, Kester thought, but chose to remain silent. He'd been working with the agency long enough to understand that spirits didn't think in quite the same way as humans—that rational logic didn't have much impact.

"I think I can do it," he said. Actually, he was fairly positive that he couldn't, but he felt that now wasn't the time to voice that opinion. "Tell the fetch I'm a spirit door-opener like my mother before me. And if the fetch will enter our water bottle—"

"Storage device," Ribero corrected automatically.

"Our water bottle," Kester persisted, ignoring him, "then we'll escort him back to Scotland, out in the land he loves, and open a spirit door to set him free. He'll finally be with his own kind again, and he won't need to fetch anyone anymore."

There was a silence. Even the wind seemed to pause for a moment, hovering in stasis while the fetch pondered its decision. Kester waited and cast a quick glance at Mike, who was still out cold. His face was horribly pale and had a pinched, sickly look that worried Kester deeply.

Grace buckled to her knees, startling them all. *Oh god, I take it that's a no then,* Kester thought with a sinking heart. He wondered what on earth to do next. They'd tried everything; what else was there that they could do?

"He agrees," Grace mumbled and stared at the ground in disbelief.

"Excuse me?" Kester blinked. He tilted his head in a rather stupid manner, scarcely able to register her words.

The old woman raised her head. Her hair streamed out behind her like spectral ribbons. "The fetch agrees," she repeated. "It has no other choice. It hates this place and says it can sense truth in you. But you mustn't betray it! Do you understand? You *mustn't let it down.* Otherwise the consequences will be *terrible.*"

Everyone gasped.

"Are you serious?" Kester spluttered. "It'll actually co-operate?"

"Of course it's serious!" Miss Wellbeloved snapped, and pushed Kester to one side. She looked elated. "Come on, Serena, Luke! Get on with it! We haven't a moment to lose!"

Before it changes its mind, Kester added silently, mouth hanging open. He still couldn't quite believe it. *But what happens when you can't open the spirit door when you get to Scotland?* a nagging voice persisted deep inside. *What happens when you have to tell the fetch that you've messed things up? Grace said the consequences would be terrible, which doesn't sound good at all.*

Serena and Luke clambered to their feet, clutching one another like two lost kittens.

"Are you ready?" Serena asked in a low voice.

"Come on then, get on with it!" Larry shouted.

"We don't need telling twice," Luke growled as he scooped up his extinguisher device. "Serena, are you okay using my equipment rather than your device?"

"It's very nice of you to even pretend ours is a device and not a plastic bottle," Serena replied. "Yes, of course. Let's get on with it."

They began to mutter under their breaths, both clutching the metal contraption and pointing it directly at the fetch. The air thrummed with their combined incantations, and, for a moment, the pair of them looked like ancient pagans presiding over a ritual. Kester had seen Serena at work before, but watching the two of them together was doubly impressive— Serena's pale, tiny hand pressed next to Luke's long, dark fingers. To Kester's amazement, the fetch rose into the air, then slid into the contraption without a hint of resistance, shrinking to a tiny wisp and popping itself inside.

Luke slammed it shut, then closed his eyes. "Wow."

"I know," Serena agreed as she wiped her brow. "I've had some tricky jobs before, but I never experienced one like that."

She glanced down before crouching next to Mike and checking his throat for a pulse.

"Is he okay?" Kester knelt beside her. He'd never seen Mike looking so vulnerable. The blood had drained from his face, and his breathing was shallow.

Behind them, Dr Ribero sat up, clutching his forehead. "I have got a headache," he declared to nobody in particular. No one responded. "Er, hello? Excuse me? I am damaged too, yes?"

"You're fine for the moment," Miss Wellbeloved snapped. She looked over Serena's shoulder, her expression full of concern. "Is Mike breathing?"

Serena nodded. "Yes, but he doesn't look healthy. Look at him."

Grace got up and took a deep breath. "You really managed to get rid of it," she said with a shake of her head. She looked at them in wonder. "I don't believe it."

"Yes, well. Next time, perhaps tell us that you're harbouring a murderous spirit rather than making us go through the ordeal of trying to locate it," Larry snapped as he thumped his hands on his hips and glowered in her direction.

The old woman slumped. "You don't know what it was like," she whispered.

Miss Wellbeloved nodded, glaring at Larry. "No, we understand," she said. "It must have been terrifying. The whole situation has been dreadful, but it's over now."

"Well, not quite over," Kester piped up. He looked at Luke's extinguishing device with great reluctance, knowing full well what was nestled inside, waiting for him to make good on his promise.

Serena followed his eye and winced, guessing his thoughts. "Yes, you've got yourself in a bit of bother here, haven't you? Given that you've not been able to open the spirit door since the Bloody Mary job four months ago."

"Thanks for reminding me," he retorted, biting his lip

nervously.

"Perhaps we can worry about this later?" Dimitri stepped forward and gestured at Mike and Ribero. "We have other things to focus on."

"Yes, I'm sure we'll figure something out," Larry barked. He studied Ribero on the ground as though he was a nasty stain on a carpet. "If the worst comes to the worst, we can simply drive over to Infinite Enterprises and get rid of the damned spirit there, can't we?"

"No, we cannot!" Miss Wellbeloved blazed. "How disrespectful!"

Higgins puffed up like a bullfrog. "Jennifer, this nonsense needs to stop. The spirit killed five people and just tried to knock off a couple of your team for good measure!"

Serena nodded. "I know you're all for good spirit relations, but this is ridiculous. I say don't bother going up to Scotland, where Kester's only going to fail anyway. Just dump the spirit with Infinite Enterprises. Job done."

"And then what do you suppose happens next?" Miss Wellbeloved said, fighting to stay calm. "The spirit returns to its own world, finds out we've deceived it, and gets into a fury. Then it returns to Scotland at the first available opportunity, except this time, it will be doubly furious at humans—and probably go on an even bigger murderous rampage than before." She sighed, then ran her hands through her hair. "Why can't you see the bigger picture?"

"Hey, let's discuss this later," Ribero said as he stumbled to his feet, still clutching his head. "Grace, you must go home now. Be aware, the police will want to have words with you."

"Hang on," Kester interrupted. "You can't go home yet."

"Why not?" Grace muttered. "I need to sleep. I just want to sleep for days and days."

"Because your daughter is sitting on a cliff-top, just past those trees. She was threatening to jump."

Grace's eyes widened. "Oh no," she breathed, craning her neck to stare past Kester and into the distance. "It's because of the fetch. She was frightened, and we had a fight. I thought she'd stormed off home."

"Actually," Dimitri said, pointing towards the woods. "Maybe that is her over there? There is a lady watching us, you see?"

They all looked instinctively in the direction of Dimitri's finger. Sure enough, a messy-haired, pregnant figure was standing by the trees, watching them intently. *Helen,* Kester realised, and puffed his cheeks out with relief. *Thank goodness. She came to help after all.* He held up a hand, and she started to head over, jogging awkwardly and supporting her bump.

"I saw everything," Helen said after she'd caught her breath. She moved over to her mother and draped an arm around her shoulders, pulling her close. "Mum, thank god you're okay."

The older woman started to cry and buried her head against her daughter's top. "They've got rid of the fetch," she whispered. "It's over, Helen. We've got our lives back. Can you believe it?"

"Well, you'll still have to answer some fairly difficult questions when the police come," Larry corrected with a sanctimonious nod. "They still need an official answer about why so many pensioners snuffed it in Lyme Regis, and we'll all need to work together to come up with something convincing for the official records."

"It's not as though they'll throw mum in prison though, is it?" Helen said with a nervous laugh.

"I wouldn't be so sure," Higgins muttered, folding his arms. "They'll throw anything in prison these days."

A groan interrupted them, and they all turned towards the direction of the noise.

"Mike!" Serena beamed, then hastily rearranged her features into the usual scowl. "You had us all terrified there. What were you thinking of, fronting up to the fetch like that?"

Mike shuddered. With difficulty, he hoisted himself up onto his knees. "Ugh," he muttered, closing his eyes as he sat upright. "Nice to see you too, love."

She softened and touched his shoulder, just once. "You scared me, you really did."

He looked over, grinned, then burped. "I aim to please." He looked horribly pale still, and his throat was bobbing in a most unusual manner. Without warning, he opened his mouth. Instantly, a jet of vomit fired out like water from a fire extinguisher, covering Serena's lap and dripping onto the ground. She looked down at the revolting mess, her mouth in a perfect circle of horror.

"Oh dearie me," Pamela muttered with an expression that suggested she might be trying not to laugh. "I bet you feel much better after that, don't you, Mike?"

"Sorry about that," Mike mumbled. He leant over, dry-heaved a few more times, then wiped his mouth.

"You . . . you puked all over my clothes!" Serena's expression curdled as she flapped like a flustered chicken. "Ugh! It . . . it *stinks!*"

Mike belched again, then studied her—much as an artist would look at a completed canvas. "Ah, I always said black wasn't your colour anyway," he said with a grin.

"You . . . disgusting *pig!*"

"Time to go back to the hotel?" Miss Wellbeloved suggested, grimacing.

"Definitely time to go back to the bloody hotel," Higgins agreed. "Then time to go home."

CHAPTER 21: HEADING TO SCOTLAND

After a final celebratory lunch in the pub on the seafront, not to mention a cheerful conversation with Curtis Philpot, telling him the good news about the case, Larry Higgins and his team prepared to depart. They gathered in the car park under the glare of the hotel owner, who was watching them through the net curtains, presumably to check they were definitely leaving the premises and not planning to sneak back in when he wasn't looking.

"Well, I'd like to say it's been a pleasure," Higgins began as he rummaged in his coat pocket for his car keys. "But it hasn't. So I shan't."

Luke hoisted his rucksack onto his shoulder and held his arms out. "C'mere, you guys." He hugged each of them in turn. "It's been a blast. What a week, eh?"

"You can certainly say that again," Miss Wellbeloved said, returning Luke's squeeze with enthusiasm. "You've been a joy to work with, I shall quite miss you." She stood back, then added,

"You too, Dimitri, of course."

Dimitri gave a small bow, then, to everyone's surprise, pulled Pamela into a bear hug. "It has been an honour working with you," he declared as he pulled out a tissue and patted his eyes.

Pamela giggled. "Oh my goodness me, young man. What a nice thing to say!"

"You are a highly respected psychic," he continued earnestly. "I have enjoyed seeing you at work. It was . . . educational."

"Which is another way of saying it's an experience he won't forget in a hurry," Larry growled as he yanked open the car door. "Come on, you two, enough with the fond farewells."

"Goodbye Larry," Miss Wellbeloved said. She trotted around to the driver's side and held out her hand. He eyed it for a moment, then took it, as though handling a rare, dangerous animal.

"It's been good to see you again, Jennifer."

"You too. Have a safe journey back."

"Yes, make sure you don't crash the car or anything," Ribero muttered as he leant against Mike's van. "A world without the Higgins would be a terrible thing, yes?"

"Shut up, Ribero."

"You first."

Miss Wellbeloved rolled her eyes. "We'll be in touch soon," she said as Larry hoisted his bulk into the driver's seat. "To sort out the final reports and everything. After we've got back from Scotland, obviously."

"I still can't believe you're making us *all* go up there," Serena whined, watching the others get into the car. "How come they get to go home and we don't?"

"Because Kester suggested that we go to Scotland," Ribero snapped above the noise of the gravel as the car pulled out of the drive. "So it is our responsibility, right?"

"Send Kester up on his own. It was his dumb idea."

"So much for solidarity!" Kester squeaked, feeling rather

put out. "If it hadn't been for my suggestion, the fetch never would have got in the extinguisher device in the first place!" He waved at Luke and Dimitri, who were grinning through the car window.

"See ya later, guys!"

He grinned. Luke's enthusiasm was infectious. Kester suspected he was going to miss him. Dimitri less so, though he had his moments. And Higgins? Not at all, really, though Kester was starting to get used to his smug comments and irritable outbursts.

The car rolled out onto the main road, leaving them in silence. They watched it drive down the road and out of sight, then all sighed in unison. Kester could tell from their expressions that nobody was particularly enthused about the task ahead of them.

Ribero clapped his hands, snapping them out of their thoughts, and gestured to his saloon car. "Right. Who is coming with me, and who is travelling in the van?"

Unsurprisingly, everyone apart from Mike wanted to go in the car. Mike took this as a personal insult and patted the side of the van like a protective parent whose child had just been bullied.

"You know, this van hasn't broken down in three months now," he muttered, lips pursed together in protestation.

"Apart from the journey back from Larry's offices a few weeks ago," Kester piped up.

Mike glowered mutinously.

"This is a ten-hour drive," Pamela stated. "No offence, my love, but there's no way I'm sitting in that death trap when Julio's got his nice leather-seated car on offer."

"I'll come with you," Kester volunteered. He felt sorry for Mike but promptly regretted his decision as soon as he turned to look at the van, which, thanks to its broken suspension, was leaning at a worryingly drunken angle. *I'm sure we won't break down again,* he told himself, surveying the rusty wheel rims and flat tyres with considerable trepidation. *Well, hopefully it won't.*

"I've phoned ahead," Miss Wellbeloved said as she strode over to Ribero's car. "I've managed to book us into a bed and breakfast on the outskirts of Dundee. If the traffic isn't too bad, we should be there around midnight."

"Fabulous," Mike muttered, yawning. "Another fun day. Tell you what, I can't wait to be shot of this spirit. It's been a real pain in the arse."

"Agreed," Kester said. He was looking forward to heading back and catching up with Anya and didn't want her to think that he'd lost interest. *It would be absolutely typical,* he thought as he climbed into the van, feeling the suspension protest as he placed his weight on the seat, *if I managed to make a mess of the one and only relationship I've ever managed to have before it even got started.*

After a few false starts, the van finally roared to life, spitting black smoke into the car park behind them. They rolled out onto the street, past the fishermen's cottages and quaint Victorian townhouses. Kester watched out of his window and felt strangely sad to be leaving. It had been the most stressful week of his life, but he'd almost become used to Lyme Regis and its windswept, sea-soaked charm. It was as though someone had pressed pause on the town at some point in the nineteenth century, and it had remained the same ever since. He rather liked that. Things always seemed much simpler when modern life didn't take over so much. *In fact,* he thought with a wry smile, *without the murderous spirit, it would have been positively idyllic.*

As they groaned up the hill, he surveyed the distant woodland, then Grace McCready's house as they passed it. *I hope she and her daughter will be alright,* he thought, thinking back to the cliff-top—the terror he'd experienced, the horror of believing Helen was going to jump. He wondered if Grace would struggle to live with the guilt of what she'd done, even though she hadn't had much choice in the matter.

At least their part in this is over now, he thought ruefully. *That's certainly not the case for us.* He glanced over his shoulder at Luke's extinguisher box, sitting innocently in the back of the van, and shuddered.

They travelled along the entire length of the country as the landscape changed from the rolling hills of Dorset to the industrial landscapes of the Midlands and the North. Kester relaxed in the seat, peering out of the window with fascination. Apart from travelling down to Exeter to find his father, he'd hardly ever been anywhere, and he was entranced by the scenery. *It's all so diverse,* he thought. *This country is like a huge patchwork quilt, and each section is completely different from the last.* It made him realise what a sheltered life he'd had in the past and how little he understood his own homeland.

The van finally bounced over the border into Scotland at around nine o'clock in the evening. It was pitch-black, which meant Kester could get no sense of what it was actually like. He glanced over to Mike, who was hanging over the steering wheel, eyelids drooping alarmingly.

"You need to hurry up and learn to drive," Mike mumbled and opened the window to let some fresh air in. "Ten hours behind the wheel isn't good for anyone."

"Especially after you've just been savaged by a spirit," Kester added.

"Yes, exactly. I'm *knackered.*"

"And you managed to puke all over Serena."

Mike grinned. "That was pretty awful, wasn't it? I doubt she'll ever speak to me again."

"I don't know," Kester mused as he fiddled with the heating. He was fairly sure it had stopped working about three hours ago, but he thought it was worth a try anyway. "She was pretty upset when you got knocked out by the fetch."

"Was she?" Mike looked over. "Not that it matters, of course. It just surprises me. I'd have thought she'd have been dancing with delight to see me unconscious."

Kester shook his head. "No, quite the opposite. She was actually stroking your hair at one point."

Mike smiled, then coughed. "That doesn't sound like our Serena at all, does it?"

"And you were very gallant, jumping in front of the fetch to protect her."

"Yeah, alright mate." Mike held up a hand. "I can see what you're trying to do here, and you can pack it in right now."

"I have no idea what you mean," Kester replied with the most innocent smile he could muster.

Mike sniffed, then shifted gears. "You know exactly what I mean."

Two hours later, they finally pulled into their bed and breakfast—a tall Georgian townhouse on the outskirts of a village just outside Dundee. Managing to find the place, using just Miss Wellbeloved's terse instructions on the phone and a battered old map of the UK, was a miracle. Nonetheless, they had arrived, and Kester was relieved to see it was a much nicer establishment than the one they'd left behind in Lyme Regis. Mike pulled the van to a halt next to Ribero's sleek saloon car and leant over the wheel with relief.

"See, we didn't break down," he muttered and closed his eyes. "I told you. Never doubt the power of the van, alright?"

Kester climbed out and stretched his limbs. His neck ached. In fact, every part of him was feeling decidedly delicate. He needed to sleep, preferably in a place that wasn't either an uncomfortable bunk bed or an even more uncomfortable van. He looked at his watch. *11:25 p.m.* "You must be shattered," he called to Mike. Mike grunted in response.

The elegant front door opened smoothly, as though welcoming their presence. It was a good sign, Kester thought with approval. At once, he spotted an envelope on the reception desk with their names on it. He pulled out a note and a set of keys.

"Hello Mike and Kester," he read aloud. "Hopefully you won't arrive too much later than we did. We've already checked in and gone to bed. I took the liberty of checking you in too, as the owner of the bed and breakfast wanted to go to sleep. You're in room five, next to Julio. Make sure you lock the front door before you come up. We'll meet tomorrow at breakfast, around 8:30 a.m. See you tomorrow, Jennifer."

Without a word, Mike scooped the keys up and headed to the staircase, clutching the bannister for support.

"I dunno about you," he muttered, keeping his feet to the outside of the stairs to avoid creaking, "but I am getting heartily sick of wearing the same clothes now. This isn't my favourite shirt anymore, I can tell you. In fact, I can't bear the sight of it now."

I'm a little bit sick of the smell of it, too, Kester thought after locking the front door behind them. He was walking downwind of Mike, which didn't help. *Mind you, my own clothes are no better.* His beard was growing at a rapid rate. He couldn't quite decide whether it suited him or not. *I'll have to ask Anya when I get back,* he thought. He suspected she was the type to like rugged men.

The door to their bedroom was just along the corridor; to Kester, it was the most welcome sight in the world, save for his own bedroom back home. Stepping inside, they collapsed simultaneously on the twin beds. The room was small and spartan, but it was comfortable, which was all Kester wanted. He whipped his phone out and sent Anya a text to let her know where he was and that he planned to be home tomorrow.

Hopefully she might want to meet up this weekend, he thought with a yawn. He looked over. Mike was already snoring, laid out on top of the frilly duvet cover like a ragdoll. Kester chuckled.

Poor Mike, he must be absolutely out of his mind with tiredness to fall asleep that quickly.

Folding his clothes on the chair, Kester clambered into bed. Within about five minutes, he'd fallen asleep too.

The next morning, he opened a bleary eye. Initially he was confused about where he was. Sunlight streamed in through netted curtains, and the room glowed like the inside of a seashell, light tickling the pink sheets and frilly eiderdowns. He looked over to see Mike, still in exactly the same position he'd fallen asleep in the night before, snoring like a bear in hibernation.

Kester glanced at his phone. No reply from Anya yet. *Maybe she hasn't looked at her phone since last night,* he thought, then noticed the time.

"It's quarter to nine!" he squawked to nobody in particular. "How did we manage to sleep that long?"

Mike stirred, opened an eye, then closed it again, muttering.

"Mike, we've got to get up." Kester attempted to sit up and nearly fell off the bed. "Miss Wellbeloved said we had to meet them for breakfast at 8:30, which was fifteen minutes ago."

The only response was a non-decipherable grumble and possibly a muttered expletive.

"Mike?"

"I said no."

Kester sighed, stood up, and grabbed his shirt. "Seriously, we need to get downstairs," he persisted. "Let's get on with this job, then we can go home, right?"

Mike groaned and rolled to face the other wall. "Then I have to drive all the way back again. That's a horrible thought."

"Ask one of the others to drive?"

"Nah, they don't know the van like I do. They'll only make her break down." With a moan, Mike sat up, then grabbed his neck. "Christ, I feel like an elephant has stamped on me."

Kester grabbed him under the armpit and tugged him up.

"Come on, or else I'm going to leave you here."

"Suits me fine."

"Then you won't get any of the nice full Scottish breakfast that's currently cooking downstairs."

Mike paused, then swung himself out of bed. "Fair point."

Downstairs, the others were already in the dining room, sat around an elegant round table which looked like it had escaped directly from the nearest period drama. Lace doilies covered the surface, and frilly napkins were laid beside each placemat.

"You seem to have rather a loose interpretation of half-past eight," Miss Wellbeloved remarked, lip curled at the sight of them both. "Mike, did you sleep in your clothes last night?"

"You try driving for a whole day," Mike retorted as he slumped into the empty seat next to Pamela.

Kester squeezed next to Ribero. "I'm sorry we overslept," he explained, muffling a yawn behind his hand. "I completely forgot to set my alarm. I don't think I've ever been so tired in my life."

"I already ordered your breakfast," his father said. For someone who had recently been attacked by a fetch then driven from one end of the country to the other, he looked remarkably chipper.

"Please say it has plenty of bacon and eggs on it," Mike said, reaching for the orange juice.

"I ordered the full breakfast for you, Mike; for Kester, just some baked beans on toast."

"Why?" Kester squeaked, feeling put out.

"Because you told me you were on the diet, yes? I do not want to stop you losing this belly of yours."

Kester sighed. It was probably too late now to change the order. *Baked beans it is then,* he thought. *Great. The day's already off to a flying start.*

"Can we start making plans, then?" Serena poured herself another glass of water and wiped her eyes. She'd clearly slept in her make-up, if the dark rings around her eyes were anything to go by.

"Yes," Miss Wellbeloved said, resting her elbows on the table. "Julio and I have already discussed it. We're going to head out to the countryside, then Kester's going to do his thing."

"And that's it?" Serena trilled, nearly spilling her drink. She gestured at Kester with all the horror of a schoolgirl pointing out a particularly hairy spider. "Are you serious?"

"What else did you have in mind?" Ribero asked, eyes narrowing.

She pondered. "I don't know. But something a bit more solid than that, ideally. What happens if he can't see the spirit door? Which is, let's face it, highly likely?"

Miss Wellbeloved grimaced. "That would be a bit of a problem, wouldn't it?"

"I don't fancy your chances of getting it back into Lara's extinguisher box once you've let it out," Mike added, fixing his eyes on the door that led to the kitchen.

"Luke," Pamela corrected automatically. "Come on, Mike. If I can remember his new name, I'm sure you can. I'm twenty years older than you and far more forgetful."

"Yeah, you didn't spend all day yesterday driving, though," he muttered. "Where is our breakfast? I'm starving."

Everyone ignored him. "Kester?" Miss Wellbeloved continued. "Do you think you'll be able to do it?"

The table fell silent.

Kester swallowed. His throat felt suddenly uncomfortably dry. "I've been asking myself that question since yesterday," he said. "The truth is, I haven't been able to see it again since that time in Coleton Crescent with the Bloody Mary spirit. I don't know why, but that's the truth."

"Which spells disaster for the rest of us," Serena added. "Nice one, Kester. Once again, you've landed us in a right mess."

"It isn't a mess yet," Miss Wellbeloved snapped. "We'll give it a go. After all, what choice do we have?"

"We could have just driven down to Infinite Enterprises and given them the spirit to dispose of," Mike suggested, patting his stomach reflectively.

"Let's not start this again. We made a promise to the spirit, so we're duty-bound to honour it."

"And what happens if it escapes and goes charging over the Scottish hillsides on a murderous rampage?" Serena asked.

"She's got a point," Pamela said, polishing off her orange juice with a slurp.

"We have to try," Miss Wellbeloved said. "Lying to the spirit could cause a lot more problems. Remember, the fetch could return to our world again. If the fetch had felt angry that we'd tricked him, he might come back and take revenge."

"Or he might not," Ribero added.

Miss Wellbeloved flashed him a look that made him wilt in his seat. Thankfully, the food arrived, providing a welcome distraction.

After they'd had breakfast and freshened up, they met outside in the car park. Kester tucked his phone away, perturbed that he'd still heard nothing from Anya. *I hope she's not annoyed,* he thought as he clambered into the back seat of the van. *Maybe she's got sick of all the secrecy and has given up on me.* He vaguely remembered her mentioning something about going to her book club; maybe she'd gone last night, had a late one, then left her phone at home by accident when she went to work. *Yes,* he thought, satisfied. *That sounds entirely plausible. She'll reply when she gets back this evening.*

"Right, everyone," Miss Wellbeloved said as she fastened her seatbelt. "Are we all ready?"

"Ready for certain doom, yes," Serena moaned. She stared out the window, glowering as though the landscape itself was offending her.

"Ready to fall asleep again," Mike added, yawning. "I'm sick of the sight of this steering wheel, I can tell you."

They sped out of the village, past granite cottage after granite cottage, out into the lush green countryside. Although it was cold, a strong winter sun shone, casting a deceptively warm glow over the ploughed fields and bushy fir trees. They rolled past racing streams and heather-carpeted glens until they were out in the middle of nowhere, bouncing along a narrow farm track.

"Do you have any idea where we're going?" Mike asked as he fought to avoid the deep ditch beside them.

"Kind of," Miss Wellbeloved said with a nervous nibble of her lip. "As long as we get the general area right, I think it should be fine. It's not an exact science."

"Why is it so attached to here, anyway?" Kester asked.

Miss Wellbeloved turned around. "It's how most spirits operate," she explained. "No one's quite sure why. When they visit our world, they invariably link with a particular place, and it upsets them very much if they're displaced."

"Yeah, don't you remember the little Japanese spirit? Out in the woods?" Mike reminded him.

Kester nodded. He could remember it well. It had been his first job with the team, and he'd been utterly terrified. He recollected being told that the Japanese spirit had got lost in England, which was why it was causing such problems for the unfortunate MP it had chosen to set up home with.

"So the fetch will be pleased to be back home, then?" he said a little too hopefully. *Maybe it'll be so pleased, it will forget all about the promise I made to get him back to the spirit world,* he thought, without much conviction.

Miss Wellbeloved blew out her cheeks and sighed. "Let's hope so." She pointed at a grass verge. "Why don't you park here, Mike? I saw a footpath back there; I think that should lead us into the fields. It'll be nice and quiet there, and we won't be disturbed."

"Please don't tell me I've got to do yet another hike in the mud with high-heels on," Serena moaned as she staggered out the van. "My feet can't take much more. Even my blisters have blisters."

"Perhaps you should invest in some sensible shoes then," Miss Wellbeloved tutted. She surveyed the road, then pointed. "There we go, there's the footpath. You can just see the sign from here."

"There's nothing wrong with my shoes," Serena muttered, following them. "They're just not designed for crazy marches across the countryside."

"For what it's worth," Mike said over his shoulder, "I think you should carry on wearing them."

Serena raised an eyebrow. "Really?"

"Yeah. I mean, without them, you'd only be about four foot ten, wouldn't you? You're child-sized." He yelped as Serena kicked him firmly up the backside, like a horse being whipped on a racecourse.

They waded through the thick mud until they reached the path, which, to everyone's dismay, was even muddier than the road. It winded for an indeterminable length into the distance with no signs of ending. Dense brambles knotted and twined at either side.

"Obviously been raining here," Pamela commented as she weaved a path around the puddles.

"That is all it does in this country, yes?" Ribero added as he slid into a particularly gloopy pile of mud. He cursed in Spanish, then gestured at the ground as though berating it personally. "Rain, rain, and more rain!" he concluded with a flourish to the sky. "How I miss Argentina."

"Shall we just get on with this and stop whining about it?" Miss Wellbeloved plucked a bramble from her cardigan. "Then we can return home and forget all about this."

They trudged along, single file, until finally they emerged into an open field. The area was completely deserted, save for a silhouette rooted behind a stone wall in the distance—a solid mass of dark, unmoving flesh, hulking on four solid legs. Kester pointed. "Is that a bull?"

Ribero squinted. "No, that is a cow. I am sure of it."

"Are you? It's got big horns."

"Er . . . yes. Yes, I think it is a cow. They don't have bulls in Scotland, do they?"

Kester coughed. "Yes. They definitely do have bulls, Dad. And that gate's not closed either, so there's nothing to stop it coming into this field."

"Let's just ignore it for now," Miss Wellbeloved suggested and fished Luke's spirit extinguishing device from her bag. "It's miles away, anyway. We need to get on with this."

Mike surveyed the animal with narrowed eyes. "What, ignore it until it starts stampeding us, you mean?"

"Yes, that's exactly what I mean. I'm sure we'll be fine."

Kester studied the beast. Especially the horns. They were pretty huge. *Oh boy,* he thought, looking to the sky. *It's never easy, is it?* "Are you sure this is a good place to do it?" he asked.

"Hey, I'm not wading through any more mud," Serena snapped.

Kester sighed. *Well, it's now or never.* He bit his lip. *Please let this go well,* he thought without any real hope. *Let's face it,* he thought, *this is going to be a complete unmitigated disaster.*

"Go on then," he muttered. "Let's get it over with."

"The voice of optimism has spoken," Mike snorted. He planted his hands on his hips. "Kester, try to sound a bit more positive. You're not filling us with confidence here."

"That's because I'm not filled with confidence myself!" Kester gulped. *Perhaps it'll be fine,* he thought, desperately trying to give himself some reassurance, a small glimmer of hope to cling onto. *Maybe the spirit door will reveal itself, and it'll all be okay.* A low, ominous rumble echoed in the distance from somewhere across the other end of the field. He prayed it wasn't the bull.

"Shall we get on with it?" Miss Wellbeloved held up the extinguisher device, finger poised on the button.

"Um, perhaps?"

"I'll take that as a yes." Without any further preamble, Miss Wellbeloved pressed down. For a second or two, nothing happened. Then a thick mist started to ooze into the open, coiling around itself like an awakening snake. Kester briefly toyed with the idea of running away but suspected the others wouldn't be too impressed. He desperately scanned the landscape, silently begging for the air to start opening up. But, as he'd predicted, nothing happened. The Scottish scenery remained resolutely the same, though the bull looked suspiciously like it had edged a bit closer.

A low hissing began, which slowly got louder as the fetch swelled to greater proportions. It weaved above them, hovering over their heads like the world's strangest parasol and filling the air with a foetid, sulphurous stink. Miss Wellbeloved nodded urgently at Kester, who pretended not to notice.

I don't believe it, he thought, his heart racing. *I always knew this plan wouldn't work. But I didn't actually really think it wouldn't work! This is a disaster!*

"Spirit!" he quavered, scarcely daring to look up. He didn't want to encounter the raging, fiery eyes again or the mouth that seemed to stretch to horrific proportions at a moment's notice. The hissing stopped, as though the fetch was listening.

"Spirit," he repeated again with less confidence. "Uh, we're experiencing some delays here, but . . ."

"This isn't a bloody train announcement!" Mike whispered. "Get on with it, mate; otherwise we're all screwed!"

"If you'll just bear with me a bit," Kester continued, squeezing his eyes shut, "we hope to get the spirit door open for you soon. Okay?"

The spirit was silent a moment, before it unleashed a roar.

316 of Dr Ribero's Agency of the Supernatural

Hot air gusted over Kester's head, which burned through to his scalp. He resisted the urge to burst into tears. "It's not happy, is it?" he whispered.

"I should say not," Mike retorted. "Shall we make a run for it?"

Ribero squinted into the mist. "He is angry, yes," he began, scratching his head. "But the spirit is also scared. And disappointed."

"How can you tell?" Kester asked. He lurched back as another scorching burst of air erupted around his ears. "It just seems plain furious to me."

"I can see spirit intentions, can't I, stupid boy? You need to reassure him. Get on with it, Kester."

"Easier said than done!"

"Er, I hate to interrupt this wildly successful event," Serena said as she poked Kester urgently on the shoulder, "but could you hurry up a bit?"

"What do you think I'm trying to do?" Kester squeaked. He gestured to the spirit, who was rearing back, ready to spew another gust of boiling air at them all.

"When I say hurry up a bit, I mean hurry up a lot," Serena continued. She sounded oddly nervous and even more twitchy than usual.

"Can you get off my case? I really don't need additional aggravation at the moment when—"

Serena grabbed his arm, swivelled him around, then pointed. "You need to hurry up," she repeated, "because the bull is now charging at us."

Kester looked up. Sure enough, the bull was galloping across the field, head down, horns locked firmly in their direction. He swore and felt his stomach turn.

"Oh bugger," he said, heart sinking. He wasn't sure what was worse: being murdered by a furious spirit or being gored to death by a charging bull.

"Yes, that's a fair summary of the situation," Pamela agreed faintly. "I suppose he must have noticed the spirit and come over to see what's going on."

"Right, dunno about the rest of you, but I'm off to the nearest tree to get out of its way," Mike announced. In a series of surprisingly nimble leaps, he bounded off into the distance. Serena followed him, running as quickly as her towering heels allowed her, with Pamela wobbling close behind.

"Thanks very much, guys!" Kester shouted. Above his head, the spirit wheeled with a yowl and pressed down into his face. He hissed a series of words that Kester didn't understand—ancient, guttural words that chilled him to the core.

"I'm trying to help you!" he bellowed above the noise; he didn't know whether to focus his attention on the angry spirit or the crazily stampeding animal, which was now almost halfway across the field. "Don't you see? But now we've got a bloody great bull about to attack us!"

"Kester, we need to get away!" Miss Wellbeloved shouted, tugging his arm. "That bull is getting horribly close!"

"Yes, it is definitely a bull," Ribero announced with a ponderous stroke of his chin. "I can see I made a mistake earlier. That is a shame. A cow would have been much easier to deal with."

"You two go," Kester shouted as the spirit took another swoop above his head, raining down red-hot sparks. "I've got to keep trying!" He scanned the landscape again, praying for even the tiniest hint that the spirit door might be opening.

"No, my boy! You come away now!" His father surveyed the approaching bull, shaking his head. "That is a big animal, and you are a small, plump boy. It would make a mess of you. Come on!"

"Yes, hurry up!" Miss Wellbeloved grabbed Ribero's arms and started pulling him towards the hedgerow. He yanked himself free, shaking his head.

Kester closed his eyes. The situation was hopeless. He'd failed, yet again. *I'm such a let-down,* he thought. He felt bitter rage at himself and his own incompetence.

Suddenly, an image of his mother filled his mind. Smiling, waving him gently on. He had no idea why he should think of her now, in this moment of utter madness, but he was grateful nonetheless. The thought of her settled him, made him calmer in spite of everything. *I wish you were here,* he thought, remembering her endless encouragement, her unshakeable belief in him. He looked upwards, and took a deep breath.

Mother, what would you do? How can I make this right? It was a desperate situation, and he simply didn't have any ideas left. He imagined her again, as clear as a photograph: smiling, firm-backed, and strong-chinned—not as she was after the cancer took hold. *I can imagine how good you were at this job,* he thought and remembered her resolve, her quiet determination. *You wouldn't have messed up like this.*

"Kester, if you are going to do it, do it now."

He glanced over to see his father waiting—gazing at him with steadfast faith. *He's still here,* he realised and felt suddenly much more clear-headed. *He could have run away, but he stayed. Him and Miss Wellbeloved, they're both here, despite being scared.*

Suddenly, it happened. The air rippled, and, without warning, it fractured like a balloon bursting in slow motion. Kester watched with fascinated detachment as a rip formed, then splintered down through the air like a tongue of lightning.

"There it is," he whispered. The spirit stopped hissing and froze.

"Kester, you've done it," his father said, gawping, the bull momentarily forgotten.

Kester felt his focus weaken and deliberately concentrated on his mother, holding onto the feeling he'd had earlier when he'd remembered her strength. The rip remained, widening until it had formed a shimmering, quivering door.

"Go on," he said. The spirit wavered, hovering before the entrance. "Go on!" Kester shouted again with greater urgency. "Now is your chance! I'm not sure how long I can hold it open for!"

The spirit paused before floating through. Kester couldn't be sure, but he thought he saw the spirit raise a hand in farewell as it passed. He sighed as the fetch disappeared, then slumped down to his knees, exhausted. *I did it!* he realised, pride rising within him. *I managed to do something right for once!*

"Ah, I know you are tired, my boy," Ribero muttered with a rough tug on his arm, "but this is not the time to be having a rest, right?"

Kester looked up to see the bull bearing down towards them. *Christ, those horns are deadly,* he thought, falling back to sharp reality. In a daze, he allowed himself to be pulled away. They raced across the thick grass, the feet of the bull storming only metres away from them. His father threw him through the bramble bushes before diving in after him in a flurry of rustling leaves and panting. The animal's hot snorts pulsed through the foliage behind them.

"Get in deeper, get in deeper!"

They crawled in a confusion of mud, snagging thorns, and prickly leaves until finally collapsing in a heap, directly in a muddy puddle. Kester closed his eyes, his shoulders dropping.

"You did it," his father whispered. "You actually did it."

Kester looked around for the bull, which seemed to have given up the chase. He could just about make out its hulking form through the tangled briars and hear the wet snorts emanating from its nostrils. But the main thing was, they were safe, against all the odds. It felt like a miracle.

"I know," he acknowledged with a faint smile, picking bits of bramble out of his hair. "I actually did."

CHAPTER 22: MISSING

The next day, they prepared for the long drive back to Exeter. Kester still felt exhausted, despite having had almost fourteen hours sleep the previous night. It all still seemed unreal to him. He'd prepared himself so well for failure that the fact he'd succeeded hadn't fully registered in his mind yet.

Mike climbed into the driving seat with great reluctance. This time, Serena had chosen to come with them to "avoid being subjected to Pamela's continual singing." She launched herself onto the back seat, kicked off her shoes, and started massaging her feet, which looked horrendously sore.

They waved at the others before finally rolling out onto the road. Kester leaned back against the seat and sighed.

"You can't still be tired, mate," Mike said as he indicated left. "You slept for ages."

"I know, I know." Kester rubbed his eyes, then yawned. "I think it's all just caught up with me."

Serena wound down the window, letting in a sharp gust

of winter air. "That's classic stress, isn't it? You keep yourself going for ages, then, once the stress is removed, you collapse. It happens all the time."

"If you say so," Kester replied, too tired to enter into a conversation about it.

They rumbled back through granite villages and craggy landscapes, each largely silent, lost in their private thoughts. Kester still couldn't believe that he'd managed it. He recollected the tiny wave that the spirit had given him as it had passed through the door. In a strange way, it had been almost endearing, despite the fact that it had been trying to kill him only a few moments before. It was almost as if the fetch had been saying thank you and apologising for giving him such a hard time. *I think Miss Wellbeloved might be right after all,* he thought. *These spirits are more like us than we realise.*

He switched on his phone. Anya still hadn't replied, despite the fact that he'd sent her another message last night. *I suppose I just have to accept she's angry at me,* he thought, tapping his knuckles on the side of the window. *Hopefully when she hears my explanation, she'll understand. Except, what am I going to say to her, exactly? It's not like I can tell her what's been happening.*

He checked his emails. There were the usual junk ones, promising him fifty-pound gift vouchers and free insurance. Then he spotted one from the School of Supernatural Further Education. *Oh boy,* he thought, his stomach sinking. *Here it is. The letter of rejection.* There was no way he'd been accepted on the course, not after his abysmal performance at interview. He couldn't be entirely sure, but he was fairly convinced Dr Barqa-Abu had loathed him on sight and would probably rather offer a cockroach a place on the course than him.

"I've got an email from the SSFE," he muttered.

Mike turned off the radio, grinning. "Well, open it then!"

"I know what it's going to say."

"You don't know what it's going to say," Serena said and

leant over the seat. "Don't be so negative."

"I majorly messed up the interview."

"We all mess up at interview," Serena snapped. "I told them I hated spirits. Imagine how well that went down!"

"I turned up drunk and told them I'd got into spirits because I liked Halloween," Mike added. "Don't worry, mate, they expect you to perform badly at interview. It's all part of it."

Kester grimaced. "Shall I open it then?"

"Yes!"

He clicked on the email, then scanned the contents.

"Well?" Mike leaned over to see the screen, veering into the oncoming traffic in the process.

Kester exhaled heavily. "Well, I never," he murmured as he stroked the beginnings of his beard.

"Let me guess," Serena drawled, leaning back. "You got in."

Kester grinned. "I did! Isn't that odd?"

"I personally wouldn't teach you," Serena retorted. "But it's their funeral." But nonetheless, she reached across and patted him on the back, giving him a tiny smile.

What a peculiar few days it has been, he thought, leaning against the threadbare headrest and looking out the window. *In under a week, I've encountered a murderous spirit, a possessed woman, and been accepted to a supernatural school. It doesn't get odder than that.* He grinned again. *Why am I even pleased about it? What's happening to me?*

"Congratulations," Mike said. "That's great news. It's hard work, mind. You'll be knackered, let me tell you. I studied online too. It's difficult when you have to do the dissertations in the evenings."

"I don't mind," Kester said. "I like dissertations."

"That's just weird. Don't tell your girlfriend that—you'll put her right off."

Kester grimaced. "I think she might have been put off already."

"Don't tell me," Serena said, groaning. "You've messed things up already? What was that, two weeks?"

"You're not exactly known for your successful relationships, you old cow-bag," Mike interrupted.

Kester sighed. "You're absolutely right," he said. "I'm useless. It's not even as if I can explain things when I get back, can I?"

"It's the curse of our job," Mike agreed. "All this hush-hush. Drives women mad, it does."

"Why don't you treat her to something special?" Serena suggested.

"Like what?" Kester replied. "It's not like I'm rolling in money, is it?"

Mike stuck his finger in the air and grinned. "How about tickets to the Billy Dagger gig? He's performing in Bristol this weekend."

"Oh, tell me you're not serious," Serena groaned, wincing. "Billy Dagger is about eighty, isn't he?"

"He's late sixties, and he's an absolute legend," Mike barked, glaring at her in the rear-view mirror. "I won't hear a word said against Dagger in this car, thank you very much."

"There's no way I can afford tickets to a Dagger gig," Kester said. "Anyway, they'll all be sold out."

Mike's eyes twinkled. "Not if a good friend of yours happens to have some going spare, eh?"

"How the hell do you have spare tickets?" Serena squawked, edging forward.

"I bought as many as I was allowed to when the phone lines opened," he explained. "Most of my mates snapped them up, but I've still got a few left over. Kester, they're yours if you want them."

Kester smiled. "That's nice of you, but I still can't afford them."

"On the house. Seriously. Without your help on this case, none of us would be getting paid, so it's the least I can do."

"I can't accept that!" Kester was touched. After all, he'd only known Mike a few months. Once again, he found himself appreciating how nice the team had been to him, how they'd welcomed him in as one of the family. Even Serena seemed to be finally thawing towards him.

"You can, and you shall," Mike persisted. "And I bet your girlfriend will be delighted and forgive you on the spot. Now, say thank you to your Uncle Mike."

"Thanks, Uncle Mike."

"I might have wanted to go too, you know," Serena interrupted, with a mutinous look.

"You just said you thought Billy Dagger was past it!"

"I didn't say that, I just commented on his age." She folded her arms. "I never passed judgement on his talent."

Mike winked. "Are you trying to get a free ticket too, Serena?"

She drummed her fingers on the edge of the seat. "Of course not. Why, have you got another spare one?" She caught sight of Mike's face and added, "Not that I'd want it, of course."

"Yeah right," Mike retorted. "I do have one more spare, actually, as old Johnno pulled out. But if you don't want it—"

"I didn't say I didn't want it."

"That's exactly what you said, actually," Kester interrupted. "Your precise words, in fact."

"Shut up, Kester."

"I'll take it that you do want to come then," Mike said with a gleam in his eye. "You'll have to pay me back though. I'm not giving you a freebie. You don't deserve it."

The rest of the journey passed uneventfully, apart from a minor incident at the service station involving an irate BMW driver and a malfunctioning petrol pump. Fortunately, Mike managed to accelerate out of the station before the petrol-drenched man had a chance to catch up with them, which, given the van's past performance, was something of a miracle.

They finally reached the outskirts of Exeter as the sun was starting to set. Kester stared up at the now familiar blue bridge that spanned the motorway, heralding their arrival back into the city. The surrounding fields were bathed in a soft orange glow, which looked almost impossibly idyllic.

"It's good to be back," he said and checked his phone for the hundredth time. The screen was frustratingly devoid of message notifications, despite the fact that he'd now texted Anya four times.

His phone suddenly vibrated in his hand, startling him.

"Oh, is it your lover-girl?" Serena crooned, waking up.

"Yes, it is," Kester said with a deep sense of relief. "It's her home number. Maybe she's lost her mobile."

"See, lover's tiffs are soon sorted out," Mike added with a yawn. "Best answer it, mate."

Kester pressed the phone to his ear. "Hello Anya!"

"This isn't Anya." The voice on the other end of the line was unfamiliar. *What's going on?* Kester wondered.

"Er, who is it then?"

"It's Wendy, Anya's housemate. I hope you don't mind me calling, I found your number on a post-it note in Anya's bedroom."

Kester frowned. *Weird,* he thought. *Why's she calling me? I've never even met her.* "Hi," he said. "How can I help you, Wendy? Is Anya okay?"

Wendy gulped. "I don't know."

Kester froze. "Why, what's wrong?" Mike looked over, concerned.

"We don't know where Anya is," Wendy continued. "Have you heard from her?"

"No," Kester stuttered. "I mean . . . Why, what's going on? When did you last see her?"

Wendy sighed. "She went to her book club two nights ago. We haven't seen her since. I've called her parents in Denmark, but there wasn't much point; they don't speak much English. I don't know anybody at her book group, so I couldn't call anyone there."

Kester took a deep breath and closed his eyes. *Think,* he commanded himself. *What rational explanation could there be?* "Could she have gone to a friend's house?" he asked.

"We wondered if she was with you to begin with," Wendy said. "She hasn't got many other friends in Exeter, apart from this mysterious book club of hers."

"She's not been with me," Kester said, suddenly feeling rather sick. "I've been away." *Oh my god, that's why she's not been answering her text messages,* he realised, eyes widening. *Something's happened to her.*

"Do you think I should call the police?"

"Yes, call them," he said, massaging his head and trying not to get in a panic. "And keep thinking of anyone else who might know where she is. What was her book club called?"

"I have no idea. She's never told us anything about it."

"I'll try to find out some more information," Kester said.

He hung up, then looked over at Mike.

"What's going on?" Mike asked, stopping the van at the traffic lights.

"Anya's gone missing."

Mike whistled. "Since when?"

"Since two nights ago."

"Has she gone back to her parents?" Serena asked, now wide awake.

Kester shook his head. "Her housemate doesn't think so. It's rather worrying."

"Yes, it is a bit," Mike said as he revved the engine and nearly drove into the car in front. "Still, there's usually a rational explanation for this sort of thing, isn't there?"

Kester swallowed hard. "I hope so."

Serena leant over and patted him on the shoulder. "Hey,

don't worry. People don't just go missing in Exeter, it's not that kind of place."

He nodded, then reached for his phone again. Anya, he typed, fingers whizzing across the screen.

Wendy just called and said you were missing. Pls let me know you're alright. Am worried. Kester.

Finally, the van pulled onto Kester's road. Mike switched off the ignition and turned to look at him.

"You sure you're alright?" he asked, looking concerned.

Kester shrugged. "Not really. I don't know what to do. I'm really worried."

"She'll turn up," Mike said. "She's probably having a strop about something and has stormed off for a bit. You know what women are like."

"Excuse me?" Serena snorted. "Less of the appalling gender stereotypes, please."

Kester attempted a watery smile and climbed out the van. "I'm sure it'll be fine," he said, not feeling convinced. He surveyed his front door warily. *God, the last thing I need at the moment is Pineapple and Daisy,* he thought with a sinking heart. *Any talk of chakras, yoga, or spiritual cleansing might just send me over the edge.*

After waving goodbye to the others, Kester trudged inside. It felt strange to be back. The house seemed smaller and dirtier than when he'd left it, and, as usual, it was freezing. *The landlord obviously hasn't sorted the boiler out,* he thought, unable to stop himself from glancing at his phone again. *Not that the heating really matters at the moment.*

Pineapple appeared at the top of the stairs like a rabbit in a magic trick. "Yo, Kester! My main man!" he shouted with a disturbing wiggle of the hips. "Long time no see, yeah? Where you been?"

"You actually noticed I wasn't here, then?" Kester observed as he headed towards his bedroom.

"Yeah, right on, course I did." Pineapple reached across and tugged at Kester's chin. "Digging this facial growth, dude. That's like super-tight, innit? Real manly, like."

"I'm going to shave it off," Kester announced as he extracted Pineapple from his path. "Did you know you've spilt something down your t-shirt by the way?"

Pineapple looked down. "Nah, that's the look. Bought it online. Some artist in Camden, he throws food on tops, right, but he does it in a real sharp, artistic way, yeah? You feel me?"

"Not really," Kester admitted and escaped to his room before Pineapple could say anything more. It had been a long day. A long week, in fact. He was in no mood to talk about food-stained tops with a man named after a fruit.

He slumped on his bed and stared at the stained ceiling. *It was meant to feel good to be back,* he thought with a sigh. *But now I'm even more worried than I was about the fetch!*

Suddenly, his phone beeped. He grabbed it, hoisting himself into a sitting position.

"Yes!" he shouted and pumped a fist into the air. It was a text message from Anya. *Finally,* he thought, opening it up. *God, you had us all terrified there. Where the hell are you?* He wondered.

He read the message. His mouth fell open.

"Need help," he read aloud. His mouth went dry. "Can't talk. I'm with the Thelemites. I've made a big mistake." There was nothing else, only that.

What the hell does that mean? Kester wondered, reading it through again. He felt even more afraid than before, though he didn't entirely understand her message. *Who are the Thelemites? And what mistake has she made, exactly?*

Some instinct, deep inside him, told him who might know who the mysterious Thelemites were. He scrolled through his contacts and dialled his father's number.

About the Author

Lucy Banks grew up in provincial Hertfordshire, before fleeing to the wilds of Devon, where she now lives with her husband and two boys. As a child, she spent a disproportionate amount of time lurking in libraries, and prowling car-boot sales to feed both her hunger for books and her book collection. It's fair to say that she's bypassed being a bookworm, and become a book-python instead. Today, most of the available space in her house is stuffed to the brim with literature, which is just the way she likes it.

After teaching English Literature to teens, Lucy set up her own copywriting company and turned her love of the written word into a full-time career. However, the desire to create never went away, so Lucy turned her insomnia into a useful tool—penning her novels in the wee small hours of the night and the stolen moments of the day.

Lucy has enjoyed inhabiting worlds of her own creation from a young age. While her initial creations were somewhat dubious, thankfully, her writing grew as she did. She takes particular delight in creating worlds that closely overlap reality . . . with strange, supernatural differences.

The Case of the Deadly Doppelgänger is Lucy's second published novel, and the second in the series, *Dr Ribero's Agency of the Supernatural*. The series unites the realm of the strange with the everyday world. It's a place where chaotic spirits rub shoulders with businessmen, and nothing is quite as it seems.